A WOMAN

LIKE YOU

A WOMAN LIKE YOU

NOW & THEN SERIES

KATE RYAN

LAST PAGE PUBLISHING

A Woman Like You
Kate Ryan
Copyright © 2017 Kate Ryan

Cover by Jacqueline Sweet

Dedication

To a woman like you—
one who looks back
on her twenties, blushes
AND cringes, before smiling...
We made it!

Acknowledgments

First or firstly, thank you to Mr. Ryan for his love, support, and belief in me. I've spent countless hours sequestered in our bedroom ignoring my family and spilling deep thoughts onto the computer screen. Seriously, days went by before we had actual conversations. I know that I tested his patience—mostly because he told me. I love you, Mr. Ryan.

Second or secondly, every woman needs a *Village*. I am blessed beyond measure with mine. To Adriane and Barbara and the rest of the "inner circle" bound by the sisterhood and the motherhood, including but not limited to: Amber, Angie, Bonnie, Danielle, Dawn, Genie, Hayley, Heather, Holly, Ilma, Jen, Jennifer, Karen, Kristi, Lisa, Michelle, Patti, Robyn, Ronda, Rose, Sherry, and Sunny. Timing brought us together so many years ago, but trust and love are binding.

Third or thirdly, enormous props and appreciation for the people who make publishing way less complicated. (Mostly because I don't have to do it myself!) There's the amazing combo of M & M at Last Page Publishing who make all things possible, and I dig our *stimulating* Skype sessions. Plus, red shoes are an actual *thing* now! Thank you to the copy editor, proofreader, and the talented Kate Stone who designed my cover. A special thank you to author Alathia Morgan who graciously provided a fresh set of eyes on the manuscript because mine were exhausted. Last or lastly, thank you to the Readers of this series. If you grow to care about Amanda even half as much as I do—imperfections, neuroses, and all—I will be thrilled. Please laugh, cry, and cringe throughout the twists and turns during her journey through life. I endeavor to keep you guessing before leaving you satisfied with Amanda's *happily ever Now & Then*.

CONTENTS

CHAPTER 1

SUMMER CAMP

Sunday, July 15, 2012

Day Eight

I HAVEN'T SLEPT THROUGH THE night since last Saturday. Queasy from exhaustion and raw emotions breaking through my formerly numbed defenses, I'd kill for a joint. Okay, maybe not kill, but I'd definitely maim.

Eight days ago, my husband left me here at this upscale rehabilitation center specializing in the treatment of co-occurring disorders to face my shame and the consequences of my decisions. My stay in rehab or, as I like to call it, Summer Camp, will last at least twenty-eight days. Yes, it was voluntary and completely my idea. And, no, that doesn't make being here any easier.

There's nowhere to hide in this place. We have to leave our cabins by 8 a.m. each morning. The doors to our living quarters are locked until 12:15 p.m. After that, they remain locked again from 12:45 p.m. to 4:30 p.m. I can't even try to sneak in a catnap, which is probably their point. I have a daily schedule that includes two hours a day with my Primary Group and some choices to make about which workshops or meetings I want to attend. Twice a day we have Community.

The Sonoran Desert surrounding Tucson is hot in July, obviously, and the sun beats down from every direction. Even grabbing a cigarette is inconvenient. (Don't judge me for smoking—it's my only remaining vice.) The women can only smoke on one part of the property. There's nowhere to sit—just a bunch of gravel and scrub brush, and it's almost too scary to smoke at night. This place is alive with wildlife and assorted creepy crawlies.

My least favorite are the gigantic tarantulas that come out after the sun goes down and meander down the walking paths like they own the place. I'm not fond of frogs either. They squawk and cry all night looking for another frog to love. They are also known to jump out from nowhere which might induce a heart attack in my heightened state of anxiety.

I'm getting to know my fellow Summer Campers during workshops, Community, and over meals. Community takes place at 11:30 a.m. and 9 p.m. Every Camper is expected to attend because we're all part of this highly dysfunctional Community. We sit in a huge circle and go around the room—first name, malfunction(s), and one word that best describes your Core Feeling at the moment.

In case you can't think of a Core Feeling, there's a handy chart on the wall with round yellow faces whose expressions match the word next to it: happy, lonely, sad, grateful, proud, afraid, loved, hopeful, hurt, peaceful, guilty, ashamed, relieved, angry. If a Camper is feeling creative, he or she can use a combination of Core Feelings.

What the fuck am I doing here is not a Core Feeling.

The Patient Advocates use the time to update the Campers on Summer Camp News, and there are a lot of reminders about following the rules because there are a lot of Campers breaking the rules. Campers have to volunteer for chores that help the Community, and I'll pick a new assignment tomorrow.

Then things get interesting. Campers get to give *constructive feedback* to other Campers with any issues they might have with a fellow Camper, but it has to follow a very specific formula: [NAME], when you [BEHAVIOR], I feel [CORE FEELING(S)].

There's always drama at Summer Camp—especially with the younger ones. I steer clear, but admittedly I enjoy the show because it's the main source of entertainment. Too bad John Hughes is dead; he could produce and direct *The Rehab Club*, which would be way more interesting than *The Breakfast Club*.

While the Campers are varying degrees of messed up, most fall into distinct categories. We have the Alcoholics, with a division between the Hardcore and the Chardonistas. Addicts are mostly Hardcore—heroine, meth, crack, cocaine, and a bunch of stuff from the list that nineteen-year-old kid Jacob rattled off to me on my first night here.

Pill poppers and/or pot smokers are not Hardcore. It's difficult for the Addicts to take a pot smoking Klonopin-popper seriously. I know this because they laugh at me when they find out why I'm here. It's not mean-spirited laughter. They simply can't understand, because to them—even though most of them are practically still children themselves—marijuana is child's play.

Oh, there was a Gambler here, but she went through Family Week and walked around in tears when she was outside of sessions. She went home with her husband today.

* * *

Meals are a whole other adventure and exercise in social hierarchies. Our cafeteria is gourmet, staffed with professional chefs who prepare delicious organic meals and present them with flourish. By day two, every chef memorized my name. There's no sugar in the place—I'm not kidding. Choking down coffee is a challenge, so I switch back to Diet Pepsi.

Meal time is kind of like eating in prison except the food is appetizing and we don't segregate by race. We predominantly segregate by age with sub-segregation of Alcoholics and Addicts. Jacob, the nineteen-year-old heroin addict I met on my first night, was right—there aren't many people here my age. We have a well-represented under twenty-five crowd, one woman in her early thirties, me on the brink of my fortieth birthday, and the over fifty set. Since I'm a wife and a mom and a person with actual life responsibilities, I mostly hang with the over fifty.

Sometimes the Adult Camper tables are full, so I have to slide in with the Child Campers. Initially a hush falls over the table when I crash the under twenty-five set. An Adult Camper can kill a Child

Camper conversation in less than two seconds flat, but I quickly learn that I can start a conversation by asking a question or introducing a new topic.

I also pick up bits of Child Camper gossip over mealtime—that new guy/girl is totally hot, So and So had sex in the shower when the rooms were open before Group yesterday, Haley got caught smoking the crack she smuggled onto the grounds inside of a pen, and now a PA has to follow her around 24/7 for the next two weeks. Yes, *The Breakfast Club* would have nothing on *The Rehab Club*.

* * *

Seeing so much of my younger self in these Child Campers, I spend a lot of time cringing and biting my tongue. Like me, most of them had everything handed to them on a silver platter. Like me, they took what was handed to them before bashing their parents over the head with the silver platter. Selfish. Ungrateful. Entitled. *My parents are stupid. My parents don't get it. My life is so hard.* Unlike me—because I see it now—it doesn't matter that I might have some *Wisdom* to share. They already know everything.

I'm sure most of them have no idea how expensive it is to attend Summer Camp. They probably have no idea that their horrible parents are most likely broken-hearted and desperate to get them healthy and on the path to becoming productive members of society. Rooming with two child Campers—Amber and Melanie from my Group—I'm a Resident Advisor of sorts.

Amber and I are building a decent relationship, although every time I say her name out loud, I remember another *Amber* from the night before I married my husband. I have a hard time not telling her about that whole *situation*. I'd love for her to see me as a cautionary tale, but she isn't there yet.

Also from a life of opportunity, she's an only child forced here by her parents to help with her pending legal charges for underage consumption and possession of marijuana. Amber claims that she's not an Alcoholic or Addict; she's no different than other college students except she was unlucky and got caught—three times. If she can get out of her legal *situation* without serious repercussions, there's no doubt in my mind that she'll continue on her current path, which means she has a good chance of winding up like me one day. She doesn't understand that her behavior can spiral out of control and suck her into a dark vortex.

Melanie... ah, Melanie. I can't stand her. I'm not sure if she's an Addict or an Alcoholic or some combination thereof. I am sure that she's coddled, entitled, and has no direction in her twenty-four-year-old life. She's a filthy roommate with zero organizational skills and no respect for keeping her things confined to her personal space. Her crap spills into the walkways and is scattered all over the bathroom we share. She keeps using my towel even though I've told her that this hook is mine. Sure, she reminds me a little of myself with her upbringing and the way she treats her parents—who should cut her off already—but I had my act back together by her age. She needs to lay off the liquor and the bad boys and grow the fuck up.

* * *

I called home on Wednesday. The phones are in a public area and it was noisy—not conducive to deep or private conversations. Besides, at that point, I wasn't ready to share much with my husband. I'm very much a work in progress so I've been avoiding him, but I assured him that I'm sticking to the game plan. We talked about bills and my mother. She's preparing to move out of my childhood home in Pine Ridge, Arizona, to be closer to our family and Dad. Looking at three houses this week, he promised me that he'll help her make a good decision.

When he passed the phone to Nicki, our seven-year-old daughter, the sound of her sweet voice brought tears to my eyes. Every sentence started with *Mommy* while she chattered on and on about nail polish and ice cream and swim parties. I listened with a small smile on my face as tears spilled silently down my skin.

No longer numbed from the inside out by copious amounts of marijuana and excessive doses of Klonopin, the thoughts in my head never quiet. I'm trying to let them out. We're supposed to tell our story at least fifty times while we're at Summer Camp. My primary therapist Jeff claims that it normalizes the *situation* and is a huge part of learning to live in truth instead of covering it up with drugs and lies. But that's twice a day of regurgitating the shit storm of my life that led to me walking through these doors.

I've shared my story in Group, and, when appropriate, I gather my courage and talk during a session or workshop. Baring my soul to these Campers—practically strangers—in such an ugly way is embarrassing. I always break down in gut-wrenching, body-wracking sobs. After I locate Kleenex and finish talking, the small group is generally silent because no one has heard a story like mine. Hallmark has yet to design a greeting card that covers this occasion in a person's life. And, hell yes, I'm sure there are degrees of judgment about my unwavering loyalty to Dad.

Quickly coming to accept that I have experienced enormous trauma and loss, perhaps the post-traumatic stress disorder suggested by Dr. Martinez, the medical director at Summer Camp, isn't a stretch. But my trauma is different. It isn't a one-time thing; it didn't happen and now it's over. How do I heal from something that's ongoing?

I have to live with the reality of Dad's *situation* every single day until he's dead. And how he might die... that haunts me, too. I have nightmares about his death. When it finally happens, I'll not only have to face the finality while still grieving everything else that was stripped away from us.

Okay, yes, the trauma is raw and valid and soul-crushing, but it still doesn't explain what happened to me in college and my young adult years. I had everything handed to me on the silver platter I used to bash my parents over the head with. Why am I an addict? I knew lots of kids who drank and smoked weed. In the end, they could take it or leave it, whereas I couldn't put it down.

* * *

On day eight, this quiet Sunday, I meet Lara from my Primary Group in the Lodge after breakfast so we can continue working on our Timelines. It's a visual depiction of our lives, sectioned by decades and years. We're supposed to recall significant memories and people from our past, and then overlay a representation of our substance abuse—frequency and duration—as the years went by.

I spent the first week dissecting my childhood, high school, and early college years—realizing that there's nothing exceptional about me. I had a near-idyllic upbringing with parents who were loving and supportive. I discovered that I didn't possess any internal strength or true sense of self. My roots were ripped from underneath me, and I didn't know how to replant them somewhere else. Instead, I retreated into my head and sheltered there. I drank to overcome insecurity and anxiety.

I loved two boys—Braden and Tanner—and I suppose that I let their feelings for me, and mine for them, create and define me. Funny how some things never change. Tanner is everywhere on my Timeline, and I illustrated the status of our relationship with hearts of different colors–yellow (friendship), pink (more than friends), red (love), and grey (confusion). I haven't gotten to the black hearts yet. I'm not looking forward to reliving those moments as I face my twenties.

Lara and I pause every now and then to talk or share a story, but mostly we work in silence, lost in our memories and the struggle to accurately recall where we took our wrong turns in life. My dad calls them forks in the road. He would always say to me, "Every decision you face is a fork in the road. Once you've chosen your path, you might leave a piece of yourself behind as a reminder that you were there, but you can never go back." He was absolutely correct. What he didn't tell me was that sometimes, no matter which path you take, both options lead to destruction.

CHAPTER 2

DECADE THREE: 1992 – 2002
Age: Twenty

My junior year at The University of Arizona kicks off with another year in the red brick historic Yuma Hall. Tanner Rawlings, my friend since the third grade and boyfriend of two years, lives right upstairs. He's a year ahead of me in college because my parents shipped me off to Europe for a year after high school to experience life outside of Pine Ridge.

Instead, I experienced shocking realizations. I'm painfully shy around strangers, beer tastes like shit until I've had at least four, and I should've trusted my instincts when it came to Curt, my asshole German boyfriend, who took my virginity and then called me a fat whore less than twenty-four hours later. I drank my way through a very miserable year.

Late last semester, I applied for an untraditional major called Interdisciplinary Studies allowing me to triple up on my three favorite disciplines—sociology, women's studies, and German. Still clueless about what I actually want to be when I grow up, Tanner keeps cranking through his undergraduate work. He'll be in med school while I'm still throwing darts trying to land on a career choice. Busier than ever, practically living together is our saving grace. Most nights, his room serves as our space to study, while my room smells like sex and sleep—all of which we do as frequently as possible.

Trina, a lifelong friend of mine from Pine Ridge, still shares a small house on Vine Avenue just south of 6th Street with Michele and Violet from our women's studies classes. None of them are lesbians, thus dispelling another myth about women's studies majors. Despite the physical separation of campus versus off-campus living, I see my girlfriends often. We have plenty of classes together, and when I go stir crazy in the dorms while Tanner's off solving the world's problems, I escape to their place or Katie's off-campus apartment. I met blond, blue-eyed, beautiful Katie freshman year in my German classes. She and Trina dragged me to my first frat party last semester. I got stupid drunk and regrettably cheated on Tanner with a frat boy from Sigma Chi.

Frat parties—never again, but I adore the quiet gatherings that take place with smaller groups of students—opportunities to talk and drink wine and smoke cigarettes and weed. I only tried pot a few times last semester, but now it's becoming a regular thing when

I go off campus. Katie does it, and even Trina keeps a steady supply on hand. Katie, I get. Trina baffles me because she and I were so like-minded in high school. *Just say no. Drugs are bad.*

The thing is... this drug doesn't feel bad. It feels like freedom from my neurotic brain. When I sit in a circle of people and we pass the bong, my lungs fill with smoke, I exhale, and within a few minutes my thoughts flow like a river of profoundness. I'll go head to head challenging an idea or belief, and I'm not afraid of what anyone thinks about me.

Well, that isn't entirely true because I'm afraid of what Tanner will think. He'd despise this activity, so I don't tell him. I'm careful to shower the smoke out of my hair, change my clothes, and avoid him when I'm high. Already lying by omission about the night I slept with the frat boy, it's easy to apply that same concept to other things I keep from Tanner. Besides, I don't owe him every thought in my head and a recap of every move I make, right? He doesn't tell me everything—although I can't imagine understanding half the things he's learning in school.

My classes are fantastic—feminist theory, German lit, advanced sociology. Decent grades come easy because my brain naturally peels back layers and spins in different directions. Often undecided in my personal beliefs, I write papers from differing perspectives of an issue. There's so much to think about between the lines in a book or what someone says in class. These alternate viewpoints of society and gender roles and slapping labels on things simply fascinates me.

Instead of sharing my deeper thoughts and burgeoning opinions with Tanner, I make lists and journal often. Trying to explain my interests and passions to him is, for the most part, pointless. Sure, he asks me questions about my classes and thumbs through my books or papers every once in a while, but he doesn't connect with the subject matter. Nothing I care about is based in true science. There are no equations to solve or control groups with studies to produce statistical findings. Theoretical and anecdotal, the social sciences are all about embracing shades of gray. Tanner's brain doesn't work that way. While he believes in Free Will, he's fairly black and white.

Our lives are a contrast, too. It doesn't seem fair that Tanner has to push himself so hard academically and work a part-time job while I have it easy. Never knowing what it's like to worry about money or grades or my class ranking or a sense of security, my parents provide everything I need. Maybe I need a dose of reality because real life can't possibly be this carefree.

Or maybe it can if I go from the security of my parents to the security of marrying a doctor who wants nothing more than to provide a wonderful life for me and our future children—just not six of them. *Please god, not SIX children.*

Jenny, my best friend since the first grade, and I are growing further apart. While I miss her, it seems a natural result of our lives in different cities and my stable relationship with her ex-boyfriend. Even though Tanner was always more my friend than hers growing up, they had a volatile relationship the year I was overseas. To say it didn't end well would be an understatement. She hates him. Since Tanner's tightly wrapped up in my life, it's nearly impossible not to mention him, and so we rarely talk.

I'm sure if one of us really needed the other, we'd step up like no time had passed. History like that never goes away, right? Perhaps one day when Jenny's moved on with a serious relationship of her own, she'll let go of her animosity toward Tanner. Then again, maybe not. Jenny can hold a grudge—another reason why I don't fight the void.

* * *

Right before Thanksgiving break, Luke and I cross paths at the Rec Center. Tanner's counting my reps on the leg press when Luke walks by, does a double-take and, *shit*, stops to peer down at me.

"Mandy from Pine Ridge," he greets.

Ugh. Why didn't I tell him not to call me Mandy? Because hearing that name brought me a little warmth. That name provided a microscopic connection to my first love from high school, Braden McLaughlin. He's now a senior at Iowa, I think. I don't know for sure because he stopped talking to me after Tanner and I became a thing.

Now I'm warm from my own shame of coming face-to-face with my lie by omission—the frat boy I cheated on Tanner with. One stupid, drunken night that I can never take back.

Lowering the press, I sit up hoping Tanner won't notice my discomfort.

"Hi, Luke."

Looking from me to Tanner, Luke asks, "How have you been?"

My reply is cool. "Fine. You?"

"Busy. Surprised to see you here."

"I'm here almost every morning same time. With Tanner, my boyfriend." *Don't you dare go anywhere sordid in front of him.* "Tanner, this is Luke. He's, um, he actually grew up with Braden in Phoenix, before he moved to Pine Ridge."

"Oh?" Tanner extends his hand. *God, Tanner, don't touch him. Why do guys always have to shake hands?* "So you know Amanda from—"

I interrupt before Luke can supply any details. "We met the summer between Germany and Arizona when Braden took me by his old neighborhood."

"Nice to meet you, Luke." *Tanner, it is not nice to meet Luke because I fucked him last semester.* "I used to know Braden pretty well. We had a lot of classes together and played football in Pine Ridge."

Luke looks Tanner in the eye but tilts his head in my direction to unnecessarily remark, "Looks like you have more in common with Braden than classes and football."

Damn it, Luke.

Puffing out his chest, Tanner stands taller. His warning is delivered with one simple word. "Dude."

Luke laughs. "Gotcha. Not funny. Good to see you again, Mandy. Normally don't get up this early. Might do it more often now." With that parting shot, he strolls away.

Tanner glares down at me. "What a dick. He a good friend of yours?"

Continuing my lie by omission, I shrug and say, "I barely know the guy." *Just because I had sex with him, doesn't make us friends.*

"Give me five more and switch places," Tanner orders, getting back to the business at hand.

I spend the next forty-five minutes sneaking glances around the Rec Center, making sure to avoid Luke from Sigma Chi.

Thanksgiving Weekend

Tanner and I come out of the closet over Thanksgiving dinner with my parents. When I confess that we've been in a relationship since my freshman year, Dad laughs so hard tears form in his eyes. Tanner sits bolt upright in his seat, probably wondering if Dad's amused or has gone mad and might turn on him to rip his face off.

"Just how stupid do you think we are?" Dad asks through his laughter.

When I look over at Tanner he shrugs. "Um... I don't think you're stupid at all," I reply.

Dad turns to him. "You've been my son since I coached you in Pop Warner."

Tanner's smile is proud. "I have nothing but respect for both of you."

"That being said," Dad continues through his laughter, "you kids aren't very good at hiding your feelings."

"Oh..." I glance down at my plate and smile. "How long have you known?"

"Since freshman year when we had to call his room if we wanted to talk to you."

"You're not *living together*, are you?" Mom asks.

"No, Mom. Same dorm, separate rooms."

"Might save us some cash if they just moved in together," Dad jokes.

Mom hits the roof. "Michael! We already have one daughter living out of wedlock and making babies with... Oh my goodness, you're being *safe* aren't you? Because you both need to graduate before—"

"—Mom!" Tanner's face is as red as the cranberry sauce. "Please don't."

"Claire," Dad finally stops laughing because discussing our sex lives over Thanksgiving dinner is far from humorous. "This is none of our business." *Thank god.* He continues, "They're adults. This one is starting med school next year. Leave them be."

"When you're under my roof... well, you know how I feel about that," Mom declares.

Sorry, Mom, we've already broken your rules dozens of times, and I have no intention of stopping.

We fall into a brief silence before Tanner breaks it in a huge way. "We're getting married."

Yes, marriage is part of Tanner's life plan, but it's not like he's even asked me to marry him at this point so.... *What*?

"Not before she has her degree," Mom mandates.

"Of course—after Amanda graduates, but I don't wanna wait too long. I love her, and I'm gonna take excellent care of her and our family. You'll have tall, smart, good-looking grandkids." He finishes off that statement with a wink in Mom's direction.

Mom, of course, beams at Tanner. She married Dad right out of college, and they've had a great life. Since my boyfriend is traditional, these grandchildren won't be born outside the sanctity of marriage.

"What if you don't get into med school at Arizona?" Mom voices a remaining concern.

"Not gonna happen, Claire. My GPA is sky high; I don't have the results back yet, but I know I killed the MCAT. I'll get in. Panda will finish her last year of undergrad, and we'll take it from there."

Dad lifts his chin with a smile for Tanner. Mom relaxes back into her seat, and, apparently, Tanner determines my future. Well, it always is just that easy with Tanner, but, still, we just told them we're officially a couple... Maybe he should ask me first before telling my parents we're going to get married.

Territorial Cup—November 1992

We leave for Tucson early on Saturday morning to attend the Territorial Cup game on our home turf later that day. Dating back as far as 1899, Arizona and Arizona State started battling on the football field for bragging rights and the Territorial Cup. In 1964, it became an official annual grudge match held after Thanksgiving, and it gets vicious out there between these arch rivals—often called the Duel in the Desert. The only thing both teams can agree on is that they hate each other. They fight it out on the field until the bitter end.

Even though my parents both hold bachelor degrees from Boston College, I was raised on this rivalry. Mom completed her Master of Education over a series of summers and workshops at Arizona. I was destined to be a Wildcat—programmed by my football-loving father, a six foot five former defensive lineman at Boston College, to root against those Sun Devils.

Arizona leads by six up until the fourth quarter when Arizona State runs the ball fifty-one yards down the field for touchdown and tops it off with an extra point. Stunned into silence, we watch the game clock run out giving ASU their second victory in a row after our nine-game winning streak. *I hate ASU.*

But losing to ASU makes me think of my favorite Sun Devil,

Coach McLaughlin. I miss that gregarious man—both a mentor on the football field and the father of the first boy I loved. Back in high school, I spent all four years working as a student trainer for the Pine Ridge football team. The McLaughlins moved to town my junior year, and I fell hard for Coach's son. When Coach took over the team, he appreciated my love for and knowledge of the game and let me do a lot more than tape ankles and hand out icepacks. He allowed me to correct formations during practice, call plays during games, and chew out the players as I saw fit.

If I'm honest, I never stopped loving Braden—certainly, I haven't stopped thinking about Braden over the years. I probably never will.

CHAPTER 3

Spring Semester—1993
Amanda's Junior Year/Tanner's Senior Year

TANNER POUNDS THE BOOKS HARDER than ever. Even though he has his acceptance from the College of Medicine, he's going for top honors as an undergrad. This means grants and scholarship money because holding down a part-time job will be next to impossible in med school.

We have our comfortable routine, our easy way with each other, and incredible sex. But we also have decisions to make about living arrangements next year because he can't live in undergrad student housing and doesn't want to disrespect my mother's "traditional values" by moving in with me before marriage. Before bed tonight, we have another discussion about this *situation*.

"Tanner, I really don't care what my mother thinks. If we don't live together, we'll never see each other."

"Of course we will. Why would you say that?"

"Because..." Tanner secured a very inexpensive housing option—so inexpensive it's practically free. He can move into a guest house on his study partner's property in the foothills of northwest Tucson. Tyler lives in the main house with his folks, and he and Tanner are as inseparable academically as Tanner and I are in other ways.

Katie offered me the soon-to-be-vacated second bedroom in her apartment because her current roommate is graduating and moving out. Sick of dorm life, no closet space, sharing bathrooms, and slamming doors, I want out. Cross town without traffic, we'll have a thirty-minute drive separating us when we're accustomed to a flight of stairs.

After reiterating our current options, I conclude with a question, "When exactly are we going to see each other?"

"It's workable, Panda. I can't beat zero rent. I just have to pay for my phone line and electricity."

"We could find a one-bedroom right near the College of Medicine, and my parents will cover the rent. You can pick up the utilities if you want—or not."

He immediately shoots me down. "No way. I could never expect your parents to be fine with that."

"We don't have to tell them."

"Have you lost your mind?" he asks. *Maybe I have.* "After everything they've done for me, I repay them by living with you before marriage and trying to hide it from them?"

"We can live together if we want to. Dad won't have a moral objection."

Tanner shakes his head, which is so annoying. Rubbing my hand against my temples, I tax my brain until a viable, albeit premature, option comes to me. I suggest, "We could get engaged now. If Mom knew we were officially committed to getting married, that would lessen the sting."

"I can't afford to get you a ring yet."

"I don't care about a diamond ring. It could be any ring. It doesn't matter to me."

"It could be any ring, but you're not just any woman. I have to do this my way—the right way. Do you understand?"

The volume of my voice rises in accordance with my flaring temper. "No. What I understand is that for the first time in three years you're suggesting that we live miles away from each other when we've basically been living together, sleeping together, every night. And *now* you're worried what my parents might think because we don't maintain the appearance of separate residences? That's beyond ridiculous."

The wheels turning in his head almost creak audibly as he thinks this over. When he finally speaks, he jumps from my premature to his just plain crazy. "Let's get married this summer. I know we told your parents we'd wait until you have your degree, but if we were married—"

"*Married?* I'm twenty years old. I'm not ready to get married. I want to live in sin and have tons of sex."

"I won't live with you unless we're married."

"God, that is so *stupid*." I hurl the words at him.

"It's not *stupid*. It's tradition, and it's respecting your parents."

"Like I said—*stupid*. Brianna is pregnant with her second kid, and she's not married to Marcus. She might never get married." My older sister Brianna's "alternate lifestyle" is an ongoing source of contention with my mother. Lucky for her, she lives far away in Germany.

"Marcus doesn't have the same relationship with your parents. I can't do that to them."

"What about what *I* want? I can't believe you want to separate like this when you're heading into the most stressful time of your life. As it is, we only see each other at the beginning and end of each day. Sometimes we're too tired to talk, but at least we're breathing the same air most nights—which is unavoidable given that we share a stupid little twin bed."

"We're gonna be fine. The living arrangements are temporary. One or two years tops."

"Do you know how many relationships fall apart during med school? A lot of married couples don't make it—like, the divorce rate is astronomical."

He considers my question before answering. "I don't know anyone who has the foundation that we do. Those factors don't apply to our *situation* if we both have a little patience and keep our eye on the end game."

"Patience is one thing. Living apart is a *stupid decision*. I'm perfectly willing to buy an adult-size bed and share it with you every night, but you won't because you're obsessed with tradition and my mother's values. When you're too busy to see me and you stop getting laid on a *very* regular basis, don't complain to me about it." We don't argue as a general rule because there's nothing to argue about, but now I'm full-on yelling at him.

Nostrils flaring, eyes narrowed, he grinds out, "You're the one who doesn't *want to get married right now.*"

"Don't *mimic* me. That's rude."

"It's *rude* of you to disrespect your parents after everything they've done for us."

"This is a *mistake.*"

"This is how it has to be for now." Unyielding. *Unbelievable.*

"You're a *little jerk.*"

He scowls. "Now you're calling me names—like you did back in grade school?"

"Well, you *were* a *little jerk* back then. You with those stupid grasshoppers down my shirt. That time you dumped Spanish rice all over Jenny's head. And let's not forget your bright idea to make out in front of the entire school at Prom. You didn't give a shit what my parents thought when you took me to the lake afterwards and molested me." When I look up to glare at him, he's grinning—*grinning.*

"Yeah, that was awesome. Why don't you shut up and we'll do some more of that right now?"

Angry sex with Tanner sounds more appealing than a conversation going nowhere fast. Out of all the kinds of sex we've had over the years, angry sex isn't on the list. I decide to stay pissed off and see how it works for me.

Flopping back on the bed, I start to wiggle out of my shorts and panties while grumping at him, "Fine. You better get it now while it's readily available."

His eyes turn black. Oh, he's game.

For the record, the angry sex was phenomenal, and I was 100% correct about our living *situation*.

* * *

After Tanner's Commencement Ceremony, my parents take us out to celebrate. Tanner's parents, although invited, didn't RSVP much less show up to see the first person in their family become a college graduate. Tanner's been on the serious outs with his family since his freshman year of college. His parents opened a line of credit in his name, without permission, and never paid it back. Despite knowing Tanner since we were children, I have few memories of his mother or siblings. His dad however...

I'll never forget how he yelled at Tanner from the sidelines of the football field. *Move it, boy! Are you blind!?! A girl could've caught that pass!* The first time he grabbed Tanner by the facemask to chew him out on my dad's field, was the last time. Dad went toe-to-toe with his huge father and laid down the law. He's kept an eye on Tanner ever since.

Not only did Tanner finish college, he graduated magna cum laude. It's such a big deal, and I couldn't be more proud. He worked his ass off for every grade, every scholarship, and every grant that he'll put toward four years of medical school followed by three years of residency. I have no doubts that he'll excel in med school, but I do wonder if I'll be by his side when he finishes.

Summer Break 1993

Tanner moves into the guest house on Tyler's family compound in the foothills, and I head back to Pine Ridge to spend the summer working at Dad's real estate office and kill time with the other college castoffs.

Trina's home for part of the summer before moving to Connecticut to be with her boyfriend Connor and attend grad school. We spend quiet evenings smoking weed at the lake, camping overnight to sleep off the after effects, and having deep conversations about life. I'm going to miss her so much, but I love Connor—such a good guy from a huge Irish family on the East Coast. He left right after graduation to start a job at a stock trading company in the World Trade Center in New York City.

"Do you think it's too soon to move in with Connor?" Trina asks while we sit on Cherry's tailgate—the dependable red Chevy stepside that I received on my sixteenth birthday.

Our small campfire dances while I stare over it at the still lake beyond. "I think that when you know, you know. That may sound trite, but I believe it, T. Connor adores you, and you're absolutely yourself around him which is hard to come by."

Her grin spreads across her face. "Yeah. He's the whole enchilada."

I raise an eyebrow. "Enchilada?"

She shrugs on a shameless grin. "You know how much I love Mexican food."

Giggling, I shake my head at her. "That's so *cheesy.* But I'm happy for you."

"And you have that with Tanner, so we're both lucky."

I hear myself say, "Not exactly."

Her eyes widen in surprise—like mine because I didn't expect to say that. "What? I thought you'd sigh all dreamy-like and say yes."

Sparking up a fresh joint even though I don't need any more, I inhale deeply. Following the exhale, I try to pass it but she declines. "There are things about me that Tanner wouldn't accept."

"Such as?"

After taking another hit, I slide from the tailgate to put the joint out in the sand. Lighting up a smoke, I hop back on Cherry. "Tanner has no idea that I smoke pot. He would hate it. And he thinks my major is kind of a joke."

"Excuse me?"

"Not that he disrespects women or anything; he doesn't understand why I spend so much time dissecting feminist theory and the impact on broader social issues. He doesn't think it's relevant to the real world. And maybe he's right because I don't know how I'm going to use any of this after college."

"That's a big reason why I want to get my MBA now. Is Tanner, like, is he rude about it?"

"No, not at all. He has no desire to clutter his brain with this stuff. To him, people can be whoever they are or do whatever they want as long as they aren't hurting anyone, but that doesn't exactly apply to me as wife potential. He's always been so sure about us, but if he knew that I smoke weed or cigarettes, never mind the doubts I have in my head about getting married so young and," I shudder, "all the children he wants to bring into this world... I don't know if his life plan is going to work for me."

"I can't believe what I'm hearing. I thought you were perfect together."

"Does anyone fit together *perfectly*? I don't think that's possible."

"Are you going to stay with him?"

"We love each other so much. He's my best friend. I'd be crazy to throw that away, wouldn't I?"

Trina mulls this over and says, "A very good friend once told me that when it's right, you'll know. But you... you don't *know*?"

Admitting this out loud for the first time is difficult. "I wish I did. And here's a random thought—I wonder all the time what's happening with Braden. He invades my head every single day. After all these years, isn't that weird?"

"I don't think so," Trina offers support. "It's unresolved. You loved him, he lashed out, and that was it. You're still hurt. Maybe you should resolve things with him."

"He wants nothing to do with me. What's to resolve?"

"Becky's going to live one town over from me in Connecticut. I could ask her about—"

"Please, no. If Braden wants to talk, it's not that difficult to find me." And getting information from Becky Haines about Braden? No thanks. Becky is also from Pine Ridge—just graduated from Yale; however, Becky and Braden's folks have been close friends since their college days at our rival college Arizona State. Becky and I have a mutual disdain for each other.

"And your lie by omission? You never said, but I assume it has to do with Tanner."

"That was like a year ago. You remember that?"

"I've often wondered."

"A lie by omission is definitely a lie, but I'd rather not share. If I say it out loud, it makes it real. No offense."

"None taken," she smiles. "But if you need to get it off your chest, I'm here, even though we'll be a continent apart. I'm going to miss you, Amanda."

"Me too you. But you're going to have a wonderful life with Connor. I can't wait to hear all about it."

CHAPTER 4

Age: Twenty-One

In July, I turn twenty-one which opens new places and possibilities for fun in Pine Ridge. I behave, for the most part. I don't drink and drive, but I am tempted one night by my sixth grade crush—and another one of Jenny's ex-boyfriends—Matt Nielson. He just finished college at Northern Arizona University and moved back to Pine Ridge to help run the family construction business. He looks way hotter than he did in sixth grade and during high school, and, since he never liked me back—well, that just makes a woman curious.

We spend several hours throwing back drinks and two-stepping around the dance floor at The Outpost on Main Street. When we go outside for some fresh air, he makes a move for my mouth. Turning my head, he catches me on the cheek.

"Whoops. I missed."

"I'm, uh... I'm with Tanner."

He blushes at his fumble, which is unusual because he was one hell of a player back in the day. "I'm sorry. I thought I felt something happening here..."

"No apologies. I had a great time with you tonight." I confess, "If this was junior high, I'd be all over you. I didn't mean to give you the wrong idea."

As old friends do, he laughs it off with me and I find a sober ride home from Mike Haines, Becky's older brother, who is now a police officer in Pine Ridge. Still, I keep my distance from Matt for the rest of the summer. He's definitely a temptation, and I don't want to cheat on Tanner or add another guy to the list of men Jenny had in bed before me.

Senior year—Fall 1993

Returning to Tucson for classes in late August, I move into the apartment at The Hollows on 5th Street and Swan with Katie. Dad and Tanner help me haul my things up to the second story unit, and Dad takes the three of us out for dinner that night. His interest in my friends makes me feel good, except when Dad shoots me a smug look as Katie gushes about her year in Germany, declaring it one of the best experiences of her life. To wipe it from Dad's face, I tease her. "Yeah, and how many German guys did you have sex with that year?"

Katie's face turns red, but she recovers nicely. "That's only part of what made the year so memorable. The access to alcohol and nightclubs was also a nice bonus."

Tanner's laughter spills out, and eventually my dad joins in. I'll let Dad keep on believing that Tanner is my first and only. There are no expectations of truth with Dad on this topic, so it isn't a lie by omission.

* * *

Good thing we had that dinner together because after the school year gets underway, as predicted, I don't see much of Tanner. We have phone conversations, and I suggest that we try to meet for lunch a few days a week. Crossing Speedway Boulevard between classes, we find a little time at the main cafeteria at the College of Medicine. Sometimes he eats so quickly, there's no time for conversation. One other time, some guy walked up to me and asked, "Are you Amanda?" I nodded. "Tanner's stuck in lab. He said he's sorry, but he can't make lunch today."

During the third week of school, Tanner takes me into his Gross Anatomy Lab and introduces me to Frank. Poor Frank was sixty-three years old when he died and donated his body to science. Tanner unzips the body bag on the chilled table in the cold room. Frank has a small scalpel wedged between his eyes. If Frank could see himself now, surely he'd change his mind. Also, Frank stinks.

Sinking to the floor, I put my head between my knees. "No more," I beg. "No more Frank."

Tanner, of course, kneels down to laugh in my face. "Okay, babe. I'll put Frank away, but are you sure you don't want to see his junk first?"

"Please no," I protest from my seat on the floor. There are

probably fifty tables with fifty cadavers like unfortunate Frank. The stench is overwhelming.

Frank gets zipped away, and Tanner wants to take me on a tour of the lab after he pulls me off the floor, but I've had enough. In the hallway outside, leaning against the wall, I complain, "Tanner, that was the most disgusting experience of my life."

"It's just a shell, Panda—not a person anymore. That body is one of the most important learning tools we have. And it's so cool. In a few weeks we're gonna crack through his—"

"No." I hold up a hand for the visual portion of my protest. "I can't hear anymore."

His laughter is easy. "All right. Thought you'd be more interested. Sorry."

"Now that I have a personal relationship with Frank, I can't bear to hear what's in store for him."

As he laughs in my face, he crushes his body against mine and leans down to take my mouth in the busy hallway. He must not care who's around because he takes it hard, deep, and toe curling. Breaking the kiss, he says, "I miss you."

I offer him a knowing smile. "I can tell. I miss you, too."

"You're still in this with me, right?" His question hits me out of nowhere.

"What do you mean?"

"You and me. Building a life together."

"I'm with you—even though I'm seldom actually *with* you. When is the last time we—"

"Way too fucking long," he groans pulling me tighter to him.

His body feels so damn good—rock hard. Nipping gently on his earlobe, I suggest, "My place?"

"I have time for lunch in the cafeteria, babe, not an afternoon of—"

"Oh no, I don't need to eat, especially after meeting Frank. Maybe there's a private spot around here where you can examine my anatomy?"

His face lights up. "Yeah. I have an idea…"

Taking me by the hand, he walks me from one building into another and winds down a few hallways before entering a library of sorts. Tanner locates an empty study cubicle in a far back corner. Wedging a chair under the door handle because there's no lock, he twists the blinds on the small window closed.

How many times has this room seen similar action? Walls can't talk, but they are thin, as evidenced by the muffled voices coming from the next room over.

We claw desperately at each other's clothing until it's lying all over the floor. Standing between my legs while I sit on the end of the small conference table, he attacks me with his lips while one hand slides between my legs. Shamelessly grinding against him, I struggle to remain relatively silent when I come apart after a few minutes of getting reacquainted with his fingers.

I'm still pulsing from aftershocks, but he looks miserable as he whispers, "I don't have a condom."

"That's why I'm on the pill. Ninety-nine point nine percent effective when taken as prescribed," I whisper back.

"We've never—"

"It's okay. It's just you and me." *And that one time with Luke, but he wore a condom.*

"Are you sure?"

"Yes, Tanner. Please, just give me that thing." He hesitates and I demand, "Now."

Sinking inside of me, he proclaims, "God... This feels un-*fuck-ing*-believable. No more condoms— ever. But don't move or I'm gonna come right now." When I laugh, Tanner winces and closes his eyes. His desperation over this *situation* becomes clear when he growls, "I said don't move."

"Do you want me to talk about something unsexy?" I offer.

"Please." Eyes shut he remains still inside of me.

"Let's talk about Frank and how bad he smells. How do you handle it without throwing up?" *Maybe Frank was sexy back in his prime. No telling now.*

"We usually wear masks." He opens his eyes and glides in and out a few times testing his ability to go on.

"You had masks in there and you didn't give me one?" I glare while he thrusts with more confidence and laughs quietly in my face.

"Wanted to see your expression. Fucking hilarious." I buck my hips up to meet him. In a flash, he pushes my upper body flat and drags me by my thighs a few inches closer to the edge of the table before pinning my hips down with his hands. "Don't help me. Just lay there."

"Like a cadaver?"

"Yeah, only you're hot and smell wonderful."

"Hey, do you wish you had a female cadaver?" Trying to remain still, I want him so much it's practically killing me not to meet him halfway.

He keeps moving in and out, in and out, and eventually folds his body over mine to suck my nipple into his mouth before squeezing my breasts together trying to get to both at the same time. His lips travel up my skin, lingering on my neck until he takes my mouth and thrusts like he finally means business. He groans quietly after a minute and slows his pace. "Our next cadaver will be female. For obvious reasons."

"Obvious reasons?"

"Boy parts and girl parts." He drives into me hard to make his point clear. "Amazing how they come together."

"Ahhh..." He's hitting one of my favorite spots ever, and I struggle to keep my moan under control. "Lucky that we have each other."

His eyes soften from desire to adoration. "I love how you respond to me."

"Me too," I breathe out between thrusts.

In between kisses and the rhythm he sets, he whispers the sweetest things... Staring up into those chocolate eyes that I've known for thirteen years—a gawky boy, a cocky teenager, and now a young man with a future set in stone—he is so confident that I shiver.

I had drunken sex with Luke from Sigma Chi. I drink too much at parties. I smoke cigarettes and weed. I still think about Braden all the time. I constantly wonder "what if" this or that. If you knew, Tanner, would you still think that God made me for you, or would you run away as fast as you can?

Instead of voicing any of these conflicts in my head, I focus on my heart and tell him the one thing of which I'm absolutely sure. "I love you, Tanner."

His words while making love to me are so magnificent that I die a little inside. I don't deserve him. "I love you. You're so beautiful. I want everything with you. Gonna do this right. Wanna give you a ring, make vows, start my career, build you a house, fill your heart with love, fill your womb with babies..."

"Eww, Tanner." My nose wrinkles at that last one. "Can you not talk about filling my womb with babies *right now*?"

He kisses my nose. "Not right now, babe. One day. I want all of that with you." Covering my body with his, his lips take mine and he controls the pace and tempo. He has a handle on himself because he takes his time until I feel it build inside me.

When I cry out a tad too loudly for the library, he presses his hand over my mouth. Biting at his thumb, I suck it into my mouth like a pacifier. He groans, "I love how you feel, Panda. I love everything about you."

His cock ripples and throbs inside of me, skin coated in a thin layer of sweat. His muscles are tensing. Tanner is close, but, ever the gentleman, he stops before scoring the touchdown and rubs his thumb over my clit, bringing me to the brink again. "Let's finish together."

We do and he remains deep inside me, pressing his body against mine for maximum contact. Unwilling to let go, my legs tighten around his waist as my fingernails lightly graze the damp skin of his backside. While kissing through the afterglow the dark thoughts linger.

If he knew what was going on inside my fucked up head, would he make any promises to me?

***

As the weeks roll by, I'm officially a University of Arizona College of Medicine Widow. I'm not alone. Significant others discarded in the quest to serve the greater good and save lives are always in the cafeteria. Easy to spot, we're well-groomed, our reading materials are all wrong, and we don't appear nearly stressed enough. We should start a support group, but we'd probably just wind up screwing each other.

More than I ever imagined possible, I miss him—talking, laughing, touching, loving, and exercising. *God*, but he is rarely around and it totally sucks.

Living with Katie means that I have both time and pot to burn. In between classes and infrequent moments with Tanner, Katie and I party it up at The Hollows with an ever-expanding circle of new acquaintances. There's always something going on over here. Just open the door and head to the pool or the hot tub, and I'll find someone willing to pass the time with me.

These are not deep and meaningful relationships, but they're easy, especially after tossing back a few drinks or smoking some weed. My inhibitions, my innate shyness, disappear, and pot is preferable to alcohol since I never throw up.

Without a routine and too much time and freedom on my hands, I begin drifting through my days and nights instead of gliding. Off in the distance, a fork in the road is imminent. Without Tanner keeping me on point, I'm moving in the wrong direction.

CHAPTER 5

Late-October 1993

"UGH. I CAN BARELY BUTTON my shorts." Trying to get ready for a rare date with Tanner, I bitch to Katie as I struggle in vain with my clothing. The last time I saw Tanner was three long, lonely weeks ago. He kept cancelling our plans—even too busy for lunch.

He promised dinner and a movie, but, given the *situation* with my shorts, I want to skip both and fall into bed with his mouth and naked body. I'm so excited that I shave my legs all the way up and do some other female maintenance that he loves. My hair is styled in long waves, and I apply actual makeup—that's how much I want to look good for him.

Katie is sprawled on my bed, and my complaint falls on slender ears. Like Jenny, Katie can eat a horse and not gain an ounce. "Your boobs look bigger though." She tries to be helpful.

It's not helpful. "Don't even get me started on my bras. Because my boobs are popping out and," twisting so she can see my backside, I ask, "is that back fat?"

"Maybe..."

"KATIE! I'm falling apart without Tanner. I need a sundress."

Walking back into my closet to look through my options, Katie raises her voice so I can hear her. "He'll take care of you soon. In fact, I can clear out if you'd prefer to jump him when he walks through the door."

"Really? That sounds perfect, actually. I know he feels guilty and wants to make this show of taking me out, but, honestly, I just want to roll around, get pinned to the mattress, and fucked into next week."

Katie busts out laughing. "That much is obvious. No worries. I'll find someone to do tonight."

"Best roommate EVER." Emerging from my closet wearing a stretchy sundress, I beam at her.

"You're a lucky girl, Amanda," Katie grins. "So lucky that you're going to miss me after graduation."

"Jeez, that's only a semester and a half away. Do you have to move back to the Valley? Please stay with me forever."

"You're staying in Tucson?"

"I suppose I have to. I have no clue where I'm going to live or what kind of job I'll have. I mean, I'm assuming Tanner fits into this somehow, but I don't really know how yet." I stop talking because these thoughts send me into panic mode, and I can't calm myself with weed because I'm about to see Tanner. So not ready to get my degree and make life decisions, I want to stop the game clock but have no timeouts.

The phone rings. Caller ID tells me it's the medical school. This can't be good.

"Hi, Tanner."

"How's my girl?"

Chubby and sex-deprived. "Awesome because I'm getting ready to do terribly naughty things with you. What's up?"

He sighs and I brace. "Gonna have to reschedule. We've been working on this assignment since Thursday—all day today. Our conclusion is due Monday, and we're not even halfway through the actual work to produce results."

"Okay." I take a moment to check my temper. In lieu of taking my frustrations out on him directly, I give him something to think about. "But you should know that I put extra care and attention into making sure my skin is silky smooth for you... You know, everywhere." Katie chokes back a snort of laughter as I sit next to her on my bed.

When he groans into the phone, I smile. "Fuck. I'm so sorry. Maybe I can come by when we finish up here."

"When do you think that will be?"

"No idea. Gonna have to work on this all day tomorrow, too, so..."

"So you should get some sleep when you're finished at the lab, and we can try for another time."

"I feel terrible."

You should feel terrible. "Don't. This is what you always wanted."

"Yeah, but it sucks how much time it takes away from us."

"Right." *I told you this would happen.* "Well, there's nothing we can do about that."

He drops his voice. "You totally bare down there?"

"I'm exactly the way you like it."

"Shit," he mutters.

I poke at him for sport. "Try not to think about *that* tonight."

"Wanna put my mouth all over you," he rumbles quietly. "God, I can almost taste you right now."

With a wink at Katie, I tease, "Do you want some quickie phone sex? I'm sure it'll be nothing like actual sex, but I can lie back on my bed and take care of myself while you talk me through it."

His laughter is strained. "If only I had time... It won't always be like this."

My voice is gentle but I'm acting like a *little jerk* when I say, "Just four years of med school followed by your residency, right? That's like no time at all. Seven and a half more years without you."

"I'm sorry about tonight."

"Get back to your assignment, Rawlings."

"Yeah." His sigh is long and drawn out. "Keep the phone by your bed. If it's not too late, I'll come by and get a real taste of you."

"I'm sure you need sleep more than you need other things."

"Calling bullshit on that. Can't stop thinking about doing you."

"Do what you need to do."

"I love you, Panda."

"I love you, too." After disconnecting, I curl up with the handset to my chest.

"The demands of med school strike again?" Katie pouts on my behalf.

"I need him."

"You don't think..."

"Think what?"

Katie's question spills out of her mouth, "Do you think there's someone else in the picture?"

"Sure, lots of someones, and they all wear lab coats. But do I think Tanner is cheating on me; is that what you're asking?"

"Yes."

That's my style, not his. "No way. Tanner is too loyal—and too busy."

"It seems weird that he doesn't have time anymore... I mean, you two have been inseparable for, what, three years now. And suddenly..."

"It's not sudden. He's not about to screw up something he's dreamed about since childhood."

"Are you talking about your relationship?"

"No. God, no. I'm talking about his dream of becoming a doctor. That comes before me. We should have moved in together."

"You want to move out already?" She's teasing but I'm not.

"He won't live with me unless we're married. Besides, Katie... I'm keeping things from him."

"Oh?" She perks up, "Is it time for *Confessions with Katie*?"

I wonder if a confession would be good for my soul. I keep so much inside my head and on the pages of my journal. If there's anyone I can trust with my secret, it's Katie. She's not tied to my life in Pine Ridge.

"Smoke out while we talk?"

"Good plan," she agrees and hops her skinny ass off my bed. "I'll fire up the bong."

I call down the hall after her, "Hide the munchies. I'm fat."

* * *

"So not only did I cheat on him that night at Sigma Chi, I feel like we want different things now. Rather, he still wants the same things, but I might not."

"Luke is your lie by omission. And, by the way, not to gross you out, but I slept with Luke last year—a few times. Luke Sanders, right?"

Choking on my exhale, I hand the bong back to her. "I didn't catch his last name so you're one—or two—up on me. Well, at least we know the man has good taste. But it's gross, so let's not talk about that unfortunate coincidence ever again. Agreed?"

"How did you end up in bed with him? You met him through Braden?"

"Briefly, years ago. You guys ditched me, he found me, and I drank way too much. When he made his move, my body reacted before my mind caught up." She pulls a hit from the bong while I ask, "Being drunk is no excuse, right? And I can't tell Tanner. Am I a sociopath?"

Katie releases her plume of smoke along with a giggle. "Come on, Amanda. That's a little dramatic."

"Is it? I exhibit some classic signs—glibness and superficial charm, lack of remorse, guilt or shame, manipulative, entitled, shallow, promiscuous, and lacking impulse control and a life plan."

"Take this and smoke it." She passes the bong to me. "That's crazy talk. You're none of those things."

Eyebrows raised, I ask, "Or am I? You wouldn't really know because my charm is superficial."

"Sounds to me like you feel guilt and remorse."

"And shame," I add. "Don't forget the shame. Can I get away with this? Not telling him..."

"You already have. The bigger question is, can you live with that?"

"Maybe. But that doesn't address the other issues. Pot would be a deal breaker, yet here I am. And the shit that goes around in my head when he talks about having a litter of children." I quiver. "Yeah, I want to be a mom someday but not tomorrow. And I don't want *SIX* of them."

"That's a lot of dirty diapers."

"*God*, Katie, how many years will it take to have that many children? Like, do I get time off in between for good behavior, or will my vagina function like a PEZ dispenser that keeps popping them out?"

She laughs because, jeez, the mental image alone... "You should decide if this is the future that *YOU* want. Just because you thought you did at the age of eighteen doesn't mean you do now. These years are about changing and trying to figure ourselves out. That's not unique to you. Tanner is an exception to what most people our age struggle over."

"So I'm not unique?"

"Sorry to break it to you, but no. We're all going through some version of this."

"And here I thought I was special. Did you know that sociopaths have a grandiose sense of self?"

Katie laughs at me. "Stop it. I feel really similar things. I just haven't had a constant in my life— like Tanner—that I have to stay aligned with. It's just me and whoever I find interesting at the moment. Yeah, sometimes it's lonely or a total disaster, and I envy what you have. On the flip side, it's easier to try out different personas and ideas because no one is counting on me not to change course."

"That makes so much sense. You're brilliant."

"Yeah, well, I do some of my deepest thinking when I'm high. That whole thing just came to me. I see what you have with Tanner, or what you appear to have, and I want that someday, but I can't handle it right now. Seems like you can't handle it either."

"What should I do?"

"Slow down his schedule or cut him loose."

"*Cut him loose*? Breaking up with Tanner is more like amputating a limb."

"It's just an expression. You need to talk to him, Amanda."

"I can't bother him with this stuff. It pales in comparison to what he's trying to accomplish."

"It's sad you feel that way. The thoughts in your head—your feelings about *your* future—are just as important as his."

"It doesn't feel that way to me," I mumble. "I can't even get the guy to spare time for lunch these days, much less a conversation about our future."

* * *

Later in the evening, sometime around 10:30 p.m., Katie calls it a night. After warning her that Tanner might call—although it seems too late for that—I head down to the hot tub.

Wearing a one-piece because my once toned stomach isn't looking too hot either, the crowd is good-sized when I arrive with my own wine bottle and cup of ice. I talk shit and laugh with the people I know. Sinking into the bubbles, I tip my head back for a scalp massage feeling dizzy, disconnected, drifting...

Jackson elbows me in the ribs. I sit up blinking and trying to clear my fuzzy head—an impossible task. "What?" Jackson points up to a man standing by the side of the hot tub.

"Is this your bottle?" the man asks, gesturing to the white zin sitting on the decking a few feet away. I've never seen this guy before. He has dark hair with a very light sprinkling of gray at the temples and eyes the color of Tanner's—rich chocolate. "Yes. Why? Do you want some?"

"It's a little sweet for my taste." He smiles and his eyes crinkle deeply at the corners—another sign of his yet to be determined age. His smile is warm, teeth slightly crooked on the bottom but straight on the top. He poses a weird question, "Do you know how to read?"

"Um, quite well, actually."

"Can you read that sign?" He points to the one containing all the rules that we never bother to follow. A line item on the sign reads "NO GLASS IN POOL AREA."

"Signs, signs, everywhere there's signs..."

He quips right back. "Fucking up the scenery, breaking my mind."

"Clearly, I ignored that sign."

Kneeling down, still smiling, he studies my face. "You're cute."

"*Who are you?*"

"Jason."

Standing up, I turn around to peer up at him with elbows resting on the concrete. "Jason, why are you harassing me during my time of relaxation? Wine doesn't come in plastic bottles, so it's not completely my fault."

"I'm the night manager here." He points to an apartment right off the hot tub. "I live right there, and you kids are so loud that I had to come out here and do a little noise control. And then I saw the bottle, so I had to say something about that, too."

"You had to? No," I shake my head. "You obviously had a choice in the matter. You can choose to turn right around and leave us alone."

"You've got a smart mouth." His expression tells me that he's a fan of my smart mouth.

"I'm a smart girl. I can read, remember?"

"College girl," he snickers. "How old are you?"

"Why? Are you going to card me, too?"

"Nope, but I'm thinking about spanking you."

My jaw hits my chest. *What?* Jason starts laughing, and, wow, he's better looking after sharing his naughty side with me. "Jason, why are you threatening to hurt me?"

"Oh, I don't want to hurt you." He leans in closer to my upturned face. "But now that I have your attention..."

Jason offers to refill my plastic cup and takes custody of my wine bottle. It will be in his apartment—right over there—when I'm finished in the hot tub.

Drunk, stoned, and sex deprived, I knock on his door about forty-five minutes later in my flip flops and wet suit with a towel around my waist. When he opens the door, I find us standing at eye level. He's about my height of five eleven, possibly a smidge taller, and we probably tip the scales equally. The teasing continues. "Wow, you're tall," he comments, and, really, why do people have to state the obvious?

"I eat all my vegetables," I inform him, even though I rarely eat vegetables anymore. "I believe you have something of mine?"

"Come in." He gestures inside the apartment.

"Uh... no. I'll wait here."

"No?" he raises one brow.

"I don't know you; I'm not coming inside your apartment."

"You forgot my name so soon? I'm Jason."

"Knowing your name doesn't mean I know you. You could be a very dangerous man. I mean, you already threatened to spank me. Maybe that's code for *I strangle college girls in my apartment*."

He snorts out laughter, "I'm into some light kink, but I draw the line way before homicide, sweetheart."

"See, if you knew me at all, you wouldn't call me *sweetheart*. I'm not *sweetheart* material."

"You're smart ass material, that's for sure. What's your name, Smart Ass?"

"Amanda."

"Please come inside, Amanda."

"I'm all wet."

"That's even better." He tries to entice me with a crook of his finger. "Come on. I'd love some company."

Leaning against his door frame, I explain, "It's quite possible that I've had too much to drink and smoke this evening." Tilting my head with squinty eyes to look him over, I make a decision. "You can keep the wine. My gift to you." As I turn to leave, he grabs me by the wrist. Staring at his hand on my skin, once again, my jaw drops open.

"What have you been smoking tonight?"

"*Not* cigarettes." Anyone who smokes weed understands the insinuation. "Please let me go," I request.

He tugs gently at my arm before releasing me and asks, "Do you want some more?"

I want a lot of things—just not from him—but Tanner is nowhere to be found these days. I replay parts of my conversation with Katie tonight in my muddled brain. *Do Tanner and I want the same things? Is he the right man for me? What if he's not—how can I possibly unscramble my life from his? Why didn't we move in together? None of this would be happening if we were together like we used to be. I was right. Why didn't he listen to me?*

I don't have any answers to those questions, but can I hang out with this guy for a while? Smoke some weed, finish up my wine, and maybe make a new friend? Sure, I can. Why not? I walk through the door which should have been marked with a huge blinking neon sign—*FORK IN THE ROAD.*

CHAPTER 6

The Following Morning

WEARING FLIP FLOPS, MY SWIMSUIT covered by Jason's AC/DC shirt, and a towel draped over one arm, I walk into my apartment. On the phone, Katie stops in midsentence to say, "Never mind, she's home. I'll call you later, Nicholas." Hanging up, she shoots a glare at me.

I start to open my mouth, but she brings her finger to her lips in a silent *shut up* motion. Over her shoulder I see one very pissed off and tired looking boyfriend looming in the doorway of my bedroom.

I return the glare as if it's Katie's fault that Tanner is here. "I'm glad you're okay, Amanda. Guys, I have some things to do." Katie grabs her purse and keys and beats a hasty retreat. Wise choice. I'd like to go with her, but...

As the door shuts behind her, Tanner half-bellows the question of the morning, "Where the hell have you been? I've been worried sick."

What the fuck is wrong with me? I lie to him—plausible but far from eloquent. "I drank too much, and I fell asleep on a neighbor's couch."

"Which neighbor?"

Good question. "J- J- Jennifer." I know a lot of Jennifers. "She lives by the hot tub," I add color commentary. "We got to gabbing, I crashed out mid conversation."

Expecting a hug as Tanner moves toward me, I try not to blink when he stops short to inspect my face. Under the scrutiny, my eyes shift to the floor.

He sniffs around my neck. "You smell terrible."

"I... I, um, I'm hungover. And I smoked a few cigarettes last night."

"You were doing more than that." He continues examining me. "What were you doing, Amanda?"

"J-j-just a typical night of college debauchery."

"You're lying," he accuses, or, more accurately, calls me out.

"I... I'm not." *I totally am.*

"You're stuttering."

"Because you're scaring me, Tanner."

"Good. Because you scared the *fuck* out of me."

"What are you even doing here?"

"Called last night. Katie said you were at the hot tub, so I went to find you but you weren't there. I came up to the apartment and you weren't here either."

"Oh."

"*OH*? That's all you have to say when Katie and I spent half the night knocking on doors of all the possible places you could be? Not one person who fucking knows you had any idea where you were. Why is that, Amanda?"

I've never heard Tanner this intensely angry before. Swallowing hard, I try to formulate a response, but he loses it completely and yells in my face. "Fuck! I can't fucking believe you!"

Reminiscent of arguments with Curt the German Cherry Popper, I recoil. Of course, I don't customarily lie to Tanner like a reflex, and Tanner is nothing like Curt except...

"God *fucking* damn it! I don't have time for this shit today!"

"I'm fine." My voice is feeble as my eyes fill with tears of fear and guilt. "I'm sorry."

"If I wasn't so relieved to see you safe, I'd kill you right now! We've been making calls all over town—everyone Katie and I could think of. But not Jennifer." His dark eyes penetrate mine. "She never mentioned *anyone* named Jennifer, but some guy thought he saw you go into an apartment near the hot tub. He just didn't know which one."

"Jennifer's apartment," I lie.

"Why doesn't Katie know this *Jennifer*?" He pins me with his glare. I can barely look at him because *I'm a cheater and a liar*. Damn, this man knows how to read me, and if I don't come up with something fast, I'll cave.

Flipping it around, I offer him a scathing look before asking, "Just what are you accusing me of, Tanner?"

"Not sure yet. I just know you're lying to me."

"I'm not." *I am. God, I totally am.* "I'm a grown woman, and I—"

"Enough!" he roars. "Stop bullshitting me!"

I treat him to dagger eyes before responding, "Don't you dare talk to me that way, Tanner Rawlings. No one talks to me that way." Walking around him, into my room, I slam the door behind me. I need a shower, clean clothes, a nap, and time to figure out *what the fuck is wrong with me*. Resting my head against the wall, I attempt to collect my thoughts.

I'm so pissed at Tanner right now. Why? I'm the cheating liar. It's because Tanner calls all the shots. He's always going to call the shots. His way is always the right way. I can't even cook. I hate cooking. I hate the sound of screaming children. I'm going to wind up with SIX screaming children. God, please get these voices out of my head. Don't ask God to help you now. He doesn't help cheating liars.

Tanner walks into my room without knocking. He appears less irate but fuming nonetheless, and *these fucking voices in my head won't shut the fuck up.*

"I need a shower. Will you be here when I'm finished?" He nods and kicks back on my bed without a word, which is good because the voices in my head are more than enough.

I try to wash away my shame and the voices, but it's impossible. *Cheating once might be called a mistake. Cheating twice is a different story. Tanner deserves so much better than this horrible person I've become.*

* * *

With wet hair, wrapped in a towel and my shame, I curl up next to him and force my way into the crook of his arm so I can rest my head on his chest and avoid his eyes. Second nature, I feel his body relax into mine and he wraps his other arm around me. We lie there together but alone with our thoughts.

"I'm sorry that I yelled at you like that," he breaks the silence. "I was worried out of my mind, Panda—thinking about when to call your parents and the police. I love you."

"I'm really sorry that I worried you and took time away from your studies. I'm so sorry. I love you, too." *I'm sorry that I slept with someone else—again. I'm sorry that I smoke weed and drink to the point that reckless choices don't feel horrible in the moment. I'm sorry that we didn't move in together so I could spend every spare moment you have in your arms. I'm sorry that I don't deserve you. I'm sorry that I don't want SIX fucking kids.*

"Are you sorry enough to tell me the truth?"

"I did tell you the truth." *I'm a fucking fraud.*

He sighs as if resigned and reaches for my chin, forcing my head to tilt up. "I don't like all this partying."

"I'm twenty-one years old and didn't rebel as a teen. It's my time."

He shakes his head. "It's not you."

"What if it is?"

"It is not you." Tanner—always so black and white.

"Maybe it's who I am now. You wouldn't know because you're never around."

"Then we're gonna have huge problems, Panda. Right this minute I should be finishing up that assignment with my lab partners. Instead I spent all this time worrying I'd have to go identify your body at the morgue."

"Tanner," I chide softly. "Come on, it's not like I was driving around town in a stupor. I was safe and sound right here at The Hollows." *In a stranger's bed—underneath him, on top of him, having sex with him... What the fuck is wrong with me?*

"In the blink of an eye, anything can happen. No one is immune. You take risks you don't need to take... I can't go through another night and morning like this."

Straddling him, I smile demurely. "Not even if I make it worth your while?"

"There's nothing you can do to make not knowing you're safe worth my while."

Tilting my head to the side, I run a finger suggestively around the waistband of his shorts. "I bet I can make you forget about it, though..."

He smiles softly. "Now how you gonna do that? I don't have much time."

"If I do it right, this won't take long..."

Kissing him gently, sweetly, like a loyal, loving girlfriend, I trace my lips and tongue down his neck. When I reach for the bottom of his t-shirt he helps me pull it over his head. I spend time exploring his pecs and abs with my mouth. He makes no moves to reciprocate which is exactly how I want him. This is my play, both a distraction and an apology.

Sitting up to unwrap my towel, it gets tossed aside so I can involve bare skin in these caresses. He loves skin on skin, my long hair teasing him while he's sensitive and aroused. I know exactly how to make him forget.

Skating my hands down his torso to the top of his shorts, I shift my weight to the side and give a tug at the waistband. His hips lift off the bed, and I pull his bottoms off. Scooting down the mattress, I use my lips, tongue, and moans on his cock and balls to demonstrate how sorry I am.

Afterwards, I block his attempt at any return sexual favors. Instead, I use the next few minutes to lie in his arms and listen to his pure heart beating inside of his strong and gorgeous body. All too soon, he has to leave—exhausted from wasting his time with my stupid bullshit.

He opens my front door. "See you soon, babe."

"I hope so. I miss you." Wrapped back in my damp towel, I step in for a hug and touch my lips to his jawbone. *You're right, Tanner. I'm a liar.* "I love you."

"I love you, too." He leans down to kiss me, pulling my bottom lip between his teeth, nibbling gently. Sighing in his mouth, I close my eyes trying to lose myself in his loving kiss, but I can't because... *You don't deserve him, Amanda, but you can't let him go.*

As soon as I shut the door behind him my eyes fill with tears. I stop in the kitchen and take a few quick hits from the bong in our pantry before wandering back to my room for a nap. *I'm sorry, Tanner* runs on a loop in my brain as I cry myself to sleep.

* * *

Midweek, early evening a few days later, Katie's out somewhere while I'm reading and smoking a joint. There's a knock on my door, and I'm surprised to see him through the peephole. Smoke billows out into the night when I open the door.

"Damn," he pretends to choke. "You're a professional."

"What brings you by, Jason?"

"You have something of mine—AC/DC." It's just a crappy concert t-shirt, but Jason's using it as an excuse to see me again.

"Right..."

"Shit smells good, Amanda."

"Want some?" I offer because it's rude not to share.

"You talking about weed or something else?"

Certain he prefers something else, I lay it out. "Just weed and something to drink. Nothing else." Once inside, I gesture to the sofa. "Have a seat. Can I get you a drink?"

"You have any beer?"

"Probably." Searching through the fridge, I fish one out. Tossing it at him from a few feet away, I plop myself down leaving a fair amount of space in between. "I'm smoked out, but you're welcome to help yourself."

He lights up the half joint resting in the ashtray and takes a few drags before offering it to me. I shake my head and look over at him while he draws in a few more hits. I know nothing about Jason other than his name and nighttime occupation—oh, and what he's like in bed, sort of, because I was out of it.

"How'd you know where I live?"

"I have my ways. You know, *anyone know where a hot, super tall brunette named Mandy lives*??? You weren't hard to track down."

My correction is swift and biting. "Don't ever call me Mandy again."

"You don't like it? It suits you."

"It doesn't suit me." I shiver as my heartstrings pluck for *stupid Braden* because *Mandy* belongs to him. "It bothers me."

"Okay, *Amanda*. You're a cool one."

"Am I?"

"We had scorching sex. You don't stop by, you don't call... Nothing."

"Maybe I didn't find the sex so *scorching*," I smirk.

"You did. Can't fake that. Most girls would come by for more."

"Oh? Do you often fuck random girls from the hot tub? Like a chick buffet? I felt like a busty brunette last night, but tonight I'll take that little blond spinner over there. Easy pickings, and then they all come right back for more? What a great job you have." Sarcasm drips, but I don't care how often he fucks random girls from the hot tub.

"Jealous?"

"Nope." I'm not.

"To answer your question, no. You're the first girl—woman—I've had sex with since I moved to Tucson. First woman in quite some time."

I feel obligated to ask, "Where are you from?"

"Ohio, originally. Spent some time in LA, Lake Tahoe, Vegas, and now here."

"Tucson's not exactly a mecca of excitement. I suppose Ohio isn't either, but you took a step down when you hit this town."

"I needed some quiet. Seemed like a good place to find it."

"In an apartment by a hot tub full of college students?"

"Worked out for me the other night."

"Yeah." I release a sigh and reach for the roach. Sparking it up, post drag, I inform him, "That's not going to happen again."

"Totally a cool one," he mutters.

"Listen, Jason, I was out of it the other night, and what happened... I'm not a one-night stand kind of woman."

"Are you a relationship woman, because I'm not looking for—"

"I'm in a relationship. A serious one, and I made a huge mistake."

He seems surprised by my interruption, which I was certain would include some spiel about not wanting a relationship. "It can't be *that* serious."

Where have I heard that before? Oh, yes, Luke from Sigma Chi.

"I don't care what you think." I take a final drag—end of joint—and put the roach back.

"Damn, not cool. You're cold."

"Why do you care? You're not a relationship guy, and I'm nothing to you. We're strangers."

"We're not strangers. I had my dick inside of you."

"Stop it," I warn.

He laughs. "What? You loved it when I smacked your ass."

I kind of did when he did me from behind the second time. "Jason..."

"Right now I'm thinking about smacking your ass again."

My eyes roll. "Oh, hell no."

"You've said that before."

He's funny, cute, and harmless with no expectations or clue of what kind of woman I am. I allow myself to laugh for a moment, but this *situation*—how I betrayed Tanner—isn't funny. "I have too much to lose, so there will be no repeat of Saturday night."

"Fair enough," he says. "But I don't know anyone here. Can we, I don't know, be friendly?"

"Yeah, I was already *friendly* with you."

"No, like be friends."

Shaking my head, I stand up. "No. I'm going to get your t-shirt, you're going to leave, and I'm going to forget this happened."

He stares up at me. "Wow. No, not cold—you're ice."

"No. I'm stupid." Grabbing his t-shirt from the back of my desk chair, I walk back into the living room and toss it at him. "Sorry I didn't wash it."

"It's fine," he mutters, staring at the t-shirt in his lap while I stand hands on hips waiting for him to get up.

"My brother died six months ago from pancreatic cancer. He was thirty-six years old. He left behind a wife and two kids, me, my dad..." Fuck, those are tears in his eyes. This guy just wants to talk. I go back into the kitchen, fish out a fresh beer and a new joint, and sit back down in my original seat.

"What was your brother's name?"

CHAPTER 7

AFTER THAT NIGHT, JASON BECOMES a part of my life. Physically, I hold him at bay, but emotionally, we continue to build a connection over long stoned conversations mostly at his apartment. We cover some pretty serious topics. Jason is thirty-two—ancient—and yet we converse with ease because he has a lot to say. We are nothing alike. His life is kind of sad, and not only am I the first woman he's slept with in months, I'm the first person in Tucson who takes time to listen to him. Yeah, sometimes we laugh over stupid things too, but we are never sober together.

* * *

Tanner... my sins are eating away at my soul, but I continue to try and meet him for lunch whenever possible. I get to know Tyler better and meet several of his study group partners, but it's all superficial. They all wear these expressions of varying degrees of dazed and weary, each of their heads filled with too much information to remember and an enormous fear of failure. Occasionally Tanner has time to sneak off with me into a study room. Those are the best visits because we literally reconnect and part ways flushed and laughing.

We spend the occasional weekend night in his studio apartment in the foothills of northwest Tucson. The family compound has significant acreage. The main house is a massive log cabin with high ceilings displaying hunting trophies—antlers, mounted heads, and other remainders of animals taken too soon. There's a huge pool off the back of the cabin, a barn, and arena area that houses several horses, two garages and one workshop.

Tanner's studio apartment is built onto the end of one of the garages. He has a tiny kitchen that he never uses, a three-quarter bath, and space for a desk and an adult-sized bed. When he's home, he takes just about every meal with Tyler's family. His parents have adopted him.

Our time together is scarce and I want to enjoy him, so I retreat inside my head and keep our topics of conversation light. Besides, we're Tanner and Amanda—together for years—and deep conversations aren't required at this point in our relationship. Except deep conversations are more crucial than ever, but he's stressed and I feel guilty about everything. I go through the motions while every day leads me further off course, drifting further away from us.

He has no clue that I spend almost every night in clouds of smoke wondering what my future holds. I don't share that I routinely skip my early classes because I stayed up too late the night before with Jason, or another friend, smoking and talking and falling asleep like the dead when I tumble into bed in the early morning hours. He doesn't know that when I'm with him for too long, I start to feel anxious and jumpy because I can't smoke pot, much less a cigarette, around him.

As we approach Thanksgiving, I'm crumbling—breaking into smaller and smaller pieces, succumbing to a new darkness inside of me. I only show Tanner the light. I keep gaining weight, missing deadlines, make bullshit excuses to my instructors, and throw together papers at the last minute if I bother to do them at all. Two professors call me out on my change in behavior and the subpar quality of my work. In danger of failing two courses, I learn that I can withdraw from both to avoid a D or E. That's what I do. My parents don't check my report cards. They'll never know.

Territorial Cup—1993

The brightest spot heading into December and the end of fall semester is Arizona taking back the Territorial Cup, beating ASU 34-20. I watched the game from my parents' couch. Tanner stayed behind to study and share the holiday with Tyler's family. And, yeah, I was jealous—angry that he ditched my family for Thanksgiving and only spent a few days with us over Christmas. But I didn't tell him that. I kept the peace because, honestly, after everything I'd kept from him, he deserved peace.

Senior Year—Spring 1994

I sign up for 18 credits, but I don't bother trying and drop three classes within a few weeks leaving me with nine credit hours. I won't have enough credits to graduate on schedule, but I figure I can give my parents some sort of excuse about switching out part of my major and make it up over the summer or, worst case, another semester in the fall. My relationship with my folks, once based in trust, is crumbling too. I'm fucking them over—intentionally deceiving them for one of the first times in my life, but I also don't care. I'm not ready to face my uncertain future.

Whatever I decide to do when I grow up, I'll be fat doing it. My clothes no longer fit. I've gone from a very healthy looking size 12 or 14 to an 18/20, and those are getting snug. Exhausted and lifeless, I have new stretch marks on my hips and stomach and faint marks on the skin under my arms where I used to have muscle tone.

Toward the end of February, I drive up to Tanner's place on a Sunday afternoon. In the driveway, I meet his new "sibling," Tyler's older sister Lorraine who moved back home over the holidays. She's finishing her Master of Education at Northern Arizona University and spending this semester student teaching at a nearby elementary school.

Lorraine seems friendly enough, a few years older and taller than me by at least two inches, which is unnerving because tall is my thing. Unlike me, she has the lean frame of a long distance runner, non-existent curves and lanky yet muscular limbs—because that's her thing. She runs. Her light brown hair is short, features quite plain, but her eyes are an interesting shade of green, and her smile is warm and without pretense.

Unhappy about the state of my sorry life and the condition of my bloated body, when Tanner playfully asks if she's making meatloaf for him tomorrow night, my stomach churns. It occurs to me that this woman spends way more time with Tanner than I do.

She cooks for him. Maybe she does his laundry—like I used to do. Hey, maybe she'll start sucking his giant cock, too.

His living *situation* pisses me off more than ever because Tanner is mine. I need him.

"Nice to meet you." I wrap up my portion of the niceties and link my arm through Tanner's. "I'm sure we'll see each other again."

"I look forward to it." Lorraine smiles and walks off toward the main house.

"You," Tanner kisses me softly. "I'm so happy to see you. Let's get naked."

Racing for the guest house, we tumble onto his bed, all hands and lips—always happy to assist the other with the divesting of pesky clothing. When we're skin to skin, Tanner does the unthinkable. He puts his hand on my stomach and gives it a jiggle. "You're packing it on."

"Oh my god... You did not just do that," I hiss. Grabbing his wrist, I throw his hand off, but he immediately moves it right back where it was.

In such a Tanner way, he calls it as he sees it, "Just saying, babe, your body has changed a lot. Are you... are we pregnant?"

"Good god, no. There's no way."

"It wouldn't be the worst thing in the world."

"Yeah, it would. My parents would kill you."

Hand still on my belly fat, he predicts, "Your parents would get over it if we got married right away."

Groaning, I reply, "Great—I'd be like half the girls from Pine

Ridge High School, getting married in a maternity dress while my daddy stands by with a shotgun."

"Your daddy doesn't own any guns."

"Lucky for you."

"Besides, I wouldn't have to be forced into marriage with you. I want to marry you."

"Even though I'm fat?"

"I know how sensitive you can be about your body, and—"

"So you point this out to me by jiggling my fat and telling me I'm packing it on?" Eyes filling with tears, I slide out from under his hand to sit up in bed and reach down to the floor to grab my t-shirt which I pull over my head. I keep my back to him because I don't want him to see the tears spilling down my face.

"Babe," his voice is soft when he places a hand on my back. "If I can't be honest with you, who can I be honest with?"

I stopped being honest with you a long time ago. "You could try being more sensitive—like don't shake my flab while you tell me I'm packing it on. One or other would suffice, not both at the same time."

"I'm so sorry. Will you come here please?"

Wiping my tears, I twist my upper body to look down at his sculpted abs, well-defined muscles, and his huge, perfect cock. "I'm not in the mood anymore."

"Come lay with me. I'll hold you and you can tell me what an asshole I am. Come on..." His eyes plead for mercy. "I'm sorry. I need you next to me."

Knowing Tanner, he'll just force me into the position he wants eventually, so I move on my own into the crook of his arm. Settling in next to his gorgeous body, I feel unworthy in comparison.

"Wanna tell me what a thoughtless asshole I am?" he offers. "I'm listening."

"You're a thoughtless asshole. But you're right. I've gained a lot of weight."

"What's going on, Panda?"

My tears spill onto his skin. Sniffling, I hold back the sobs threatening to escape. "I don't feel right. Like in my head. I'm depressed and unfocused."

"When did you start feeling this way?"

"Med school. God, I'm so sorry because I don't want you to think this is because of you."

"Wish you would've said something sooner." His voice grows softer. "You don't have to keep everything inside. You have me, and I guess I've been too caught up in my life to notice you changing. I'm sorry about that, but don't wait for me to drag feelings out of you. You can lean on me, you know."

"No, I can't." Holding back sobs is now a lost cause. "You're too busy for my crap."

"Shhh." He tries to comfort me. "You always keep shit inside, Panda. Been dragging real feelings and deep thoughts out of you for years. Guess I forgot how far inside your own head you can get."

"So you think I'm what—repressed?"

He cracks a joke. "Not sexually, thank God. But I think you have a hard time asking for what you need emotionally."

"What if I can't have what I need? What if it's not possible?"

"Whatever you need from me, I'll give you," he offers with a stroke of his hand down my face, wiping away some of my tears.

"What if... what if I only kept things together for all these years because you led the way for me? What if... what if, I'm not the person you think I am? Or I'm not the person you need me to be? You don't know this version of me."

While struggling to find the right words to explain, he interrupts. "Babe, it's not like I bumped into you last week. Known you for years and years, and, yeah, you've changed over those years, but you're still my girl—my woman. I love you."

"I don't want *SIX* kids, Tanner." An absurd thing to blurt, sure, but it's the first thing that came out.

"How many do you want?"

"I don't know. Maybe two? I don't want them tomorrow. I don't feel ready to get married and have kids right away, but I know that's what you want."

His voice catches ever so slightly as he asks, "Are you saying that you don't want to get married and have a family with me? Or you just need more time to go through whatever it is you're going through?"

Raising my head to look into eyes that usually ground me in truth, I find those gorgeous eyes killing me softly instead. "I can't lose you."

He adjusts his body so we're each curled on our sides but face-to-face. "I'm not going anywhere. I'm worried about where all of this is coming from."

"Me too," I whisper my confession. "I feel dark... I'm so lonely without you. It's like I need you to make me feel like a whole person. That isn't normal, is it?"

This revelation makes me cry even harder. Tanner has a stranger in his bed—a fat stranger who smokes weed, drops out of classes, and has sex with other men while in a committed relationship with him. My Tanner deserves so much better than this pitiful, cheating woman in his arms.

Because he doesn't know any better, he holds me while stroking my lumpy skin and pressing his lips to my forehead as I cry. When I start to calm down he tells me, "I need you, too. You're the other part of me, Amanda."

"Without me, you still have your goals and dreams, and you're making things happen. You always make things happen. If I got hit by a bus tomorrow, you'd go on. As for me, you put some distance and time between us, I fall to pieces. Who the hell am I without you? Shouldn't we both know the answer to that question before we commit to a lifetime together?"

"I don't get it. You can do or be anything you want. You wanna stay home and raise a family? Great. You want a career? Great. What's important to you—that's for you to decide. While you're figuring it out, I'm here for you."

"What if I don't figure it out?"

"What if you do get hit by a bus tomorrow?" He laughs softly. "That would suck, by the way, but it doesn't mean that I love you any more or any less because you don't have your life mapped out in front of you right this second. Damn, get outside of your head, babe. Have faith that you're strong enough to figure it out. Have faith that I'll support you no matter what you decide."

Even if I tell you that I cheated on you? Even if I tell you that I do drugs? Even if I tell you that I'm not going to graduate this spring? Even if I tell you that I'm not sure I want to follow your lead for the rest of my life? Even if I tell you that I've fallen into such a pathetic hole of despair that I've lost faith in myself?

Instead of saying any of this, I respond with, "Okay. I'll try." I know—*know*—I want and need this man. In this moment, I almost believe we can have a beautiful life together, but Tanner is making deals with the devil right now. None of what he promised was based in truth. He deserves the truth, but I'm not ready to lose him.

"You know what's good for the blues? Depression?" His eyes dance. He wants to bring me back from the edge of misery.

Willing myself to step away from the edge, I smile at him. "What?"

"I'm not making this up. It's a scientific fact which means there's unquestionable evidence, and since I'm in medical school, you should probably listen up."

I break out into a full grin. "I'm listening."

"Physical activity. Specifically, endorphins. They're like Mother Nature's stimulant. Now, we could go for a jog or hit the Rec Center, but the quickest way to achieve this natural high is to use what we have at our disposal right now."

"Which is?" I ask fully knowing where this is going.

"I love you and your body, and I happen to love loving your body. Ditch that t-shirt and let's roll around. Give me two minutes, I'll get your heart rate up. Five minutes tops, your lungs will be filling with oxygen that you'll need to scream my name. In about forty-five min-utes, I'll have you lightheaded and worn the fuck out."

With feigned uncertainty in my eyes, I ask, "You're sure this is all based in science, Dr. Rawlings?"

"Didn't graduate magna cum laude because I'm a dipshit, Pan-da," he retorts. His hands snake under my t-shirt to gain access.

Turns out, Tanner is right. I fall asleep completely worn the fuck out. When I wake up in the morning, I'm alone in his little guest house with a note from him.

Panda,

Thank you for coming to me (and for me) last night.

I love you always and forever. – T

CHAPTER 8

One Week Later

TANNER DOESN'T CALL FOR SEVERAL days, and I don't try to reach him. Instead, I think a lot about what we said to each other, and, having a colossal decision to make about confessing my sins, I spend time working on my list inside my journal, lining out the pros and cons and potential forks in the road.

Perhaps I shouldn't discuss the pros and cons with Katie while taking hits from the bong and eating pizza, but that's how it happens. No matter which fork I take, I can't have Tanner and weed. But I can have bong hits right now because I haven't reached a decision.

"Oh my fucking god," Katie says when I finish telling her about my night with Jason and everything that followed. "Amanda! *What the fuck were you thinking*? That dude is old and sketchy—totally beneath you. I've heard he hits on young girls like us all the time. And, *damn it*, that entire night we were both freaked out about where you were. You scared me *and* left me trapped in this apartment with your *terrifying when seriously pissed off* boyfriend. He paced the apartment like a caged beast and acted like it was my fault. You totally suck." She tops off her rant with a bong hit.

"I'm sorry that I put you in that position."

"Are you? Or are you actually a sociopath? Because you kept this from me for all these months skipping around like a goody two-shoes when you banged the fucking maintenance man."

She passes the bong to me. Post-exhale, I ask, "Would you find my behavior more or less abhorrent if I'd slept with some drunken frat boy?"

"You already did that, remember? But to answer your question, way less disgusting because we all know that I've done my share of drunken frat boys." She snorts out a laugh. "Especially the one I shared with you. Luke is hot."

"Eww... shut up. So you're judging based on Jason's socioeconomic status?"

"No... Maybe... Okay, yes. I'm from north Scottsdale for god's sake. It's ingrained behavior to judge based on socioeconomic status. But either way, what a shitty thing to do to Tanner. Again."

Agreeing with a nod, I hand her the bong. Before taking a hit, she asks, "Are you sure that you're not going to graduate this spring?"

"There's no way. I checked with an academic advisor, we ran the credits, and maybe if I do two full summer sessions I can pull it out, but it looks like I'm going to have to take this into next fall."

"You screwed up."

"I know. I can't live like this, Katie. I have to tell him."

"He has no idea," she mutters.

"None."

"Are you prepared to lose him?"

I look to the floor. "No, but it kills me to look at him—to have him love me when he doesn't know what I've done."

"You better be willing to tell him anything he wants to know."

My eyes fill with tears. "I'm going to lose him, aren't I?"

Katie presses her lips together and offers me her sympathetic blue eyes. "I don't see this ending well—at all."

Coming Clean—Saturday, February 26, 1994

Tanner sits on my couch, his eyes growing darker and narrowing with each stilted word I choke out. I start with the easier things such as the state of my diploma this spring, or the lack thereof, and how I needed the summer or another semester to pull it out of my ass. The natural segue of the conversation turns to why—which is way more difficult.

After a deep breath I keep talking, "I've been partying, Tanner. A lot. Not just drinking, but... smoking marijuana."

His eyes snap open. "What did you say?"

"I started smoking weed about a year ago."

He demands on a glare, "Define a lot."

"Pretty much daily at this point."

"This isn't a joke?" I shake my head. "And you hid this shit from me?"

"I know how you feel about drugs."

He shakes his head slowly and stares me down. "Thought I knew how *you* felt about drugs."

"I'm sorry."

"You do this with Katie and Trina?" I nod before he looks at the ceiling, perhaps worried that the sky might be falling. "Right now, in this apartment, you have drugs here?"

"Yes."

"Your mind's in a dark place and you have no energy; you're skipping class, eating shit food, and busting the seams on your old clothes."

"Hey," I protest the rudeness of the busted seams comment.

"Truth, Amanda. You smoke weed every day, eat shit, stop moving and taking care of yourself, you're gonna get fat and feel dark inside."

The truth hurts.

"What else are you doing besides drinking and smoking weed? Any other drug habits you've picked up while I'm busting my ass to become a doctor and give us a stable future?"

"No."

"You have to stop. It's disgusting. In all the years I've known you, you never wanted to do this shit."

"I like it."

His eyes thunder along with his voice. "Look at what it's doing to you! I can't be with a *stoner*. If I got caught up in any of your shit even accidentally as a bystander, I'd get kicked out of med school. And after med school, I could lose my license to practice. I could lose everything. Do you get that?"

The thought of costing Tanner everything *he's* ever wanted never crossed my mind—not like this. It's sobering—serious. "I do now."

"So you're gonna stop?"

"Yes."

"Today?"

"Yes. Today. I'll never touch it again, but—"

"Thank fuck," he mutters. "No more drugs. No more keeping shit from me. Do we have a deal?"

If only it were this simple. I wish that I could tell him yes and the conversation could stop right here. Of their own volition, more tears and snot stream down my face.

"Why, babe?" Tanner moves closer and tries to pull me into his side with his arm.

Resisting, I swallow hard and croak, "I need you to forgive me."

"I do, Panda. Of course I—"

"You don't know why I'm asking for forgiveness. You don't know everything."

"There's more?" I can't even look at him. He says, "Just tell me and we'll deal with it."

Don't do it. Don't do it. Don't do it. You have to. You have to. You have to.

Throwing myself off a cliff, I might not survive when I hit the bottom but Tanner will—eventually. "I cheated on you."

He heard me but doesn't respond. I look up to find him staring at the floor. Watching it sink in and burn through him, I know there is no going back. I have to look away again because I cannot bear it. We sit there in silence, save for my sniffles.

When he speaks, his voice is loud, an unrestrained rumble. "What did you say to me?!?"

"I cheated on you."

"*YOU* cheated on *ME*?"

"Yes." My voice is barely audible but Tanner's just warming up.

"ONCE?"

"Does it matter?"

"Fuck *YES* it matters, Amanda. Did you make a mistake one drunken, stoned night, or do you make fucking other men a habit? One guy? Two? Twenty? Fifty? *ANSWER ME*!" he bellows.

"Twice."

"Same guy?"

"No."

"I don't know if that makes it better or worse," he scoffs. Then he shouts, "*FUCK! FUCK ME! I CAN'T BELIEVE YOU DID THIS TO ME!!!*"

Cringing, my tears continue falling. "I'll tell you whatever you want to know."

"I don't want to know... *FUCK*, Amanda, we haven't used condoms in months. You're doing drugs *AND* sleeping around on me, and *WHAT THE FUCK! WHO THE FUCK ARE YOU*???"

I assume he isn't expecting an answer. Trying to prepare for whatever happens next, I sit in silence save for my sniffles.

It takes a while, but when he speaks it's with incredible self-control. His question is three-fold. "Start with the first one. Who, when, and fucking why."

"That guy we ran into at the Rec Center last year, Luke."

Tanner's eyes flash with anger and recognition. "Braden's friend from Phoenix?"

"Yes."

"You fuck his little buddy before or after I met him?"

"Before."

"I stood there like a *fucking* asshole in front of a guy who *fucked* you?"

"I'm the asshole, Tanner. Not you."

"You're something else, Panda. Not sure what that is yet..."

"Do you want to know the rest?"

"No." He cradles his head in his hands for a moment, then looks back up at me. "Yes."

"It happened about two years ago at a fraternity party. As for the why... I'm not sure. I was really drunk and had to use the bathroom. He let me use the one in his room because there were these huge lines, and when I came out of the bathroom he was all over me."

"He force himself on you?"

Hesitating, I ponder this question before deciding that Luke and I share equal responsibility for what happened. No, I didn't plan on or want to have sex with Luke that night, but we were both drinking. "He made a move; I wasn't thinking straight, and I... I didn't try to stop him."

"And I brought you breakfast in fucking bed the next morning, didn't I?"

I nod.

"You were hungover and I brought you *FUCKING BREAKFAST* after you *FUCKED LUKE*."

"Yes."

"Never went back for seconds with *FUCKING LUKE*?"

"No," I whisper.

"It's taking everything I have not to call you a *FUCKING BITCH* right now."

"I think you just did, Tanner. It's okay. I deserve it." My voice is still soft and my tears are still rolling, but I'm one confession closer to the end of this conversation.

"Why are you telling me this shit? Never would've guessed it on my own, Amanda. Never would've fucking occurred to me that you're capable of this."

"If we're going to have a future, you need to know the whole truth. I can't deceive you for the rest of my life."

"I don't even want to have a *present* with you," he grinds out. "So this is about you not wanting to live with guilt? *Fucking hilarious.* If this didn't hurt so fucking bad, I'd laugh my ass off. But let's go. Number two..."

Fumbling because this is the worst betrayal—so fresh, and I didn't lie by omission. I absolutely lied to his face. "There was this guy who lives here at The Hollows. Just one time. I was drunk and stoned. Last fall, and it was the night that... it was... oh god, it was that night when..."

It takes Tanner approximately five seconds to fill in the blanks. "It was the night you fucking lied to me about falling asleep at *Jennifer's* apartment. There is no Jennifer. I lost my fucking mind looking for you when you should've been in bed with me. Fuck, I even told you I was gonna try and stop by, and you went out and screwed some other guy... I *knew* you were lying. You're a fucking liar."

"I'm sorry, Tanner."

"Fuck you, Amanda. *FUCK YOU!*" Tanner stands and heads for the door. For a moment I think he'll keep going but instead he hits the door—literally pounds it with his fist and stalks back to the sofa. He paces, repeating the motion over and over while I sit with my hands folded and pressed tightly against my mouth. I want to smoke a joint, curl up into a ball and cry. Forever.

He stops. "Condoms?"

"Yes."

"I hate you right now." His glare blisters my guilty skin. "You know... My entire group got a shit grade on that assignment because I wasn't there to do my part. I let down three other people, not just myself. *BECAUSE OF YOU!* Every single grade affects me—my ranking, my scholarships, where I can apply for residency. I'm busting my ass for *our future,* and you're a lying, cheating, drugged up *FUCKING BITCH, AMANDA!*"

We're over, I know it—but maybe if he takes some time away to digest this he'll eventually calm down. "I think you should go, Tanner."

"You gonna kick me out now? *REALLY*?!? You drop this *FUCKING BULLSHIT* on me and ask me to leave?"

"I told you everything, and maybe you need some time? If you sit here with me, you're going to get more pissed off."

"Don't *YOU* FUCKING TELL *ME* what I need!" He yells as tears spill from his eyes and roll down his cheeks. I have *never* seen Tanner cry. *Oh my god.* I made him cry. Standing, I place one hand on his shoulder. He flings it off and drops my wrist. "Don't *YOU* FUCKING TOUCH *ME* ever again!"

He paces and paces until he has enough control to walk up to me, get in my face, and put an end to Option Two with eerie restraint. "You gutted me, Amanda. Do you get that? You fucking gutted me tonight. Didn't think I could ever hurt this bad. Didn't think you had it in you to do this to me. I don't need time. I need to get the *FUCK AWAY FROM YOU!*" The front door slams shut behind him with such force that dishes in the kitchen cabinets rattle.

Sinking to the floor on my knees, I beg God to take the pain away. He is busy or maybe I deserve to suffer for hurting my Tanner. My body lands face first on the carpet. Fists pounding the floor, I sob and wail. Yeah, I gutted Tanner all right, but right now it feels like murder/suicide.

Eight Days Later

For the past week, I inhaled smoke into my lungs and released it into the air along with hope, faith, and my will to go on. After a week of nothing but silence, I drive to the compound. His truck is there, but he's not in his studio. I try the main house.

Tyler answers my knock at the door. His eyes narrow into slits at the sight of me, but he calls over his shoulder, "Tanner. Amanda is here." The door shuts in my face.

When Tanner walks outside a few minutes later, he heads straight to the guest house with scarcely a look in my direction. Sitting on his bed in the dim light of the evening, he looks at the floor.

I speak his name softly, "Tanner."

His gorgeous eyes are dark and cold when they slam into mine. "Why are you here?"

I wasn't invited but I sit cross-legged at the foot of his bed. "Fourteen years—that's how long we've been friends. Since our senior year of high school; that's how long we've had feelings for each other as more than friends."

"One week," he retorts. "That's how long ago you eviscerated me."

"I'm so sorry. I will do *whatever* it takes to earn your trust again. I love you. That's all I have to give you."

He's silent for a few beats before shaking his head. "Not possible. I've tried to figure out how we can get through this, but I can't. There's no way."

"Maybe with time you'll—"

"There's not enough time in the world for me to trust you again."

"Do you still love me—at all?"

His bite of laughter is embittered. "You want me to talk about *love* after what you did to me?"

"If there's still love, there's still hope... maybe."

He looks at the ceiling. "God, Panda wants to talk about love, so please forgive me for how I'm gonna say this." His eyes come back to me and it doesn't take a magna cum laude graduate to know how this is going to end. "I can't help but love you, but right now I hate you more. I don't have the space in my head to deal with you."

I'm definitely not too proud to beg. "Please, Tanner. I'm so sorry. I love you. God, I'm so in love with you. Please don't leave me. Please just give me another—"

"No. We're finished." He attempts to soften his expression before delivering the harshest blow. "Don't wanna hash this out, talk this out, try to work this out. If I wanna talk, I'll come to you. Don't come by, don't call, and don't think you can do anything to fix this. I have to focus on school right now, and if you fuck with my head anymore, I'm gonna lose it. Do you understand me?"

The lump in my throat prevents me from speaking.

"I asked you a question. Do you understand me, Amanda?"

"Yes." I choke on that word because while I understand, *my life without Tanner in it at all* is beyond comprehension.

"Anything I say to you just now require clarification?"

What will I do without you, Tanner? "No."

"Please leave."

Feet encased in concrete, heart shattered, tears blinding... I stand and walk to the door. He doesn't stop me. *Why would he?* Still, I turn around before I close the door on Tanner and Amanda forever because what I have to say bears repeating, "I love you, Tanner. I am so, so sorry for hurting you."

CHAPTER 9

Mid-April 1994

"You need to take a shower and get out of this apartment," Katie orders from the doorway of my room.

From my bed, I stare with dead eyes and mutter, "No."

"You stink, Amanda, and I don't know if you've moved from that spot in over a month."

"Where would I go?" I whisper.

"After you shower, how about to school? Or to the laundry room to wash your sheets and clothes? Maybe just outside the front door to get some Vitamin D? Just get the hell out of bed."

"I can't."

Katie crosses the room to my bed. She takes a seat and reaches a hand out to stroke my forehead. The simple gesture, the warmth of her touch, causes me to break out in fresh tears. "Amanda, I'm really worried about you. I'm moving out in six weeks. If you don't move, eventually you're going to die here. Your parents keep calling, classmates are calling—Nicholas thinks I buried your body in the desert somewhere—and I've fielded calls from two of your instructors. What can I do to get you out of this bed?"

"You can bring me the phone."

"Gladly." She reaches over one foot and hands it to me.

"Please stay while I make this call."

"Okay."

When Jenny answers, I'm too overcome with emotions to get the words out over my sobbing. Pointing to the graduation photo on my nightstand—to Jenny—I give Katie the phone.

"Jenny? This is Amanda's roommate Katie. Listen... She needs you."

* * *

Jenny should've told me to go to hell because I've been missing in action for years. But that's the thing about history—connections rooted so deeply in friendship and fond memories and true affection, love for another human being. Years had passed with few conversations between us, but when Katie asked her to come to me, she did.

That evening, Jenny sits on the couch with Katie and me, listening to me pour my guts out while I take in hit after hit of pot. She picks up my snotty Kleenexes, grabs takeout menus in the kitchen, and asks what I want to eat. After assessing the state of the refrigerator, Jenny makes me a deal. "I'll go get you some Diet Pepsi, but only if you agree to take a shower while I'm gone."

I agree to her terms because, seriously, Katie's right—I stink, and ice cold Diet Pepsi sounds like Heaven to my cotton mouth.

Katie remarks to Jenny, "Now see, I didn't know that Diet Pepsi was her currency."

My voice is flat when I reply, "It's like you don't know me at all."

The shower does me some good. When I step out, my skin is scrubbed pink and fresh, legs and pits are shaved, and my hair is no longer in danger of turning into dreadlocks.

Sitting with my girls over Chinese food and ice cold Diet Pepsi with shit tons of ice, we talk and talk, and, god, Jenny—I almost let her slip through my fingers...

"I'm not going to say *I told you so* because this is a totally different *situation*," Jenny says. "But, Amanda, you fucked up huge. You massively screwed over Tanner." I wince, forgetting that she doesn't mince words. "If I know him, he's already moving on, and you have to do the same."

"I don't know how to do that."

"You better figure it out because it's over with him. He's not coming back."

"God, Jenny, maybe you could break this to me gently."

"Gentle won't get your ass in gear. You need to talk to your parents because they're expecting a diploma in six weeks. You need to figure out if you're going to stay in this apartment or find somewhere else to live while you finish school. And... you need to shower more than once a month. Speaking of which, we should probably wash your bedding before you go to sleep tonight. Let's do that first. Then you call your parents, and I'll hold your hand while you break the news."

Summer 1994

My parents weren't livid—exactly. They were disappointed, but I wasn't forthcoming with the extent of my fucking up. I explained that after Tanner and I broke up, it hit me so hard that I became depressed and unfocused. For added measure, I threw in that I was thinking about augmenting my major with some additional classes. Bullshit. Still, they trusted me and accepted what I told them. If I ever have kids one day, I'll know they're capable of leveraging trust to deceive me.

Without having to find another roommate, I keep the apartment for summer school and one semester in the fall. Dad even joked about his second senior year at Boston College. Sadly, I just talked my parents into financing further self-destruction.

Most of my close friends are gone. Katie moved into a townhouse in Tempe and started an entry-level accounting position with the city. She promised that there would be a room for me if I decided to move up there. Michele and Violet are gone. Nicholas is still in town, but he's getting ready to start law school. Basically everyone I know got their diplomas on schedule and split or moved on to the next phase of their education in pursuit of a grown up life.

I force myself to attend class three days a week and complete my assignments—albeit not very well. Summer school moves at a rapid pace, but my brain does not. I'm high and mostly dead inside. Jason—god... He's around way too much and so not a relationship guy. Not relationship material at all. We latch on to each other over the summer, and there's no reason not to fuck him now. I'm lonely and he's there. He's there with demons that I can't begin to understand.

Jason left Las Vegas because he crossed some sort of drug cartel and owes them money. If they find him, they'll kill him—which sounds fabricated or fucked up. He used to do some heavy drugs—cocaine and then crack—because, apparently, crack is cheaper. He assures me that he's been off of them for over a year but thinks smoking pot and getting drunk are full-blown sobriety.

He works afternoons into the late evening as a waiter at a fairly upscale Italian restaurant. Sometimes after work he'll come to my apartment and use my body. Other times, days go by and I don't see or hear from him. Either way, I don't give a shit.

Occasionally, I head over to the hot tub because I still have some friends around The Hollows, although no one who matters. It's all the same to them because I don't matter either. I screw a few random guys because, who cares. I don't. They can't fill the wretched emptiness in my heart.

Age: Twenty-two

I turn twenty-two alone and high save for a few phone calls that go to my answering machine. I pick up for my parents. Since my mom went through the effort of having me, it's the least I can do.

"You don't sound like yourself," Dad observes a few minutes into the call.

Tears. *Stupid fucking tears.* "I miss him, Daddy,"

"Call him, Brown Eyes."

"He told me not to. Do you still talk to him?"

Dad sighs. "Yes. He usually calls on Sunday night." Of course he does. That's a tradition in our family. It's when my sister Brianna called home when she was away at college, and she still calls most Sundays. When I'm not high, I call on Sundays too. I've probably missed a lot of calls over the last year.

I ask, "How is he?"

"Focused."

"Does he ask about me?"

There's a long pause before Mom answers, "No, Honey."

I sniffle into the phone. "I have to go." And I do. After hanging up, I ignore their immediate return call. Before drifting off to sleep in front of the TV, I smoke a few bowls.

Happy birthday, Amanda. You're a worthless dumbass.

***

By the end of the summer, barely passing two of my four courses, I have 12 more credits toward finishing my degree. Credits are credits despite my falling GPA. And, god, what I wouldn't give to go back in time and keep my legs shut. Since I can't do that, I write for hours on end in my journal—recording memories with Tanner as far back as I can remember so I'll never forget what I lost in him.

Senior Year—Take 2, Fall Semester 1994

When Jason loses his job and rent free apartment at The Hollows, he's sketchy on the details with me. Rumor has it that he screwed a barely eighteen-year-old freshman. Her parents called the leasing office and raised hell. Still not a relationship guy and most definitely not relationship material, I take him in because he has nowhere to go and I feel sorry for him.

Now he uses more than my body. He uses my apartment, my parents' money, and my truck without asking because he has no car. He was sketchy on the details of what happened to his car, too. He claims it was stolen, and because it wasn't exactly insured he couldn't report it. He still waits tables at night and comes to my place night after night for the first month, but by mid-September, his return to the apartment after work is unpredictable.

I know what he's doing and grow increasingly concerned for his safety. Often waiting up until he stumbles through the door sometimes at the break of dawn, I'm grateful that he didn't overdose or get into a car accident—in my truck.

I want to scream some sense into him, but his brain is vacant. There's no point yelling at a zombie. When he flops down on my bed and reaches for me—perspiring, limbs twitching, eyes rapidly moving beneath his closed lids—he's disgusting, yes. I try to slip away, but he holds on tightly and begs me to stay. He needs me, but I can't help him anymore than I can stop him.

* * *

One afternoon in late September as I load groceries in Cherry's extended cab, I catch something shimmer in the sunlight under the back of the driver's seat. Upon investigating, I discover a long, narrow, dirty glass tube. *A crack pipe? Oh my god.* Slipping it into my pocket, I walk to the nearest public garbage can and drop it inside. Closer inspection of Cherry reveals small burn marks on her interior carpet. The fucker smoked crack in my beloved Cherry, and that is unforgivable.

The second I walk through the apartment door, I yell at him, "You're smoking crack in my truck!"

While sitting on my couch, stoned on my weed and drinking my white zin, he stares at me with those lifeless brown eyes I'm growing to hate. He is such a worthless loser. A fucking asshole. My skin crawls thinking about all the times I let a guy like him touch me. "Just once."

"I want you to leave," I announce as I put the bags of groceries on the kitchen counter. When he doesn't reply, I walk over to him. "I'm serious. Get out of my apartment. Now."

"Amanda, baby, where am I going to go?"

"How about rehab?" I suggest. He doesn't move an inch. "You're sick and you need help," I tell him, and *seriously, look who's talking here...* "I can make some calls. I'm sure there are places around here where you can get help."

"I don't want help." He lights up a Marlboro Red, saturating my apartment with more smoke.

"Then leave, because I can't live like this anymore. What if I'd gotten pulled over and a cop spotted that pipe in my truck? I'd go to jail. Or what if you killed somebody behind the wheel of my truck?"

"My mom is dead, Amanda. I don't need a lecture from you."

"Fine. Get off your ass, and get out of my apartment."

"I get my mail here," he says while his ass grows roots into my sofa cushions.

"So?"

"So that means I live here."

"You don't live here. You crash here."

"No, I reside here."

"Your name isn't on the lease." I'm breathing fire. *Where is he going with this*? "Do I have to call the leasing office and have them remove you?"

He chuckles at me. "You can try it, but they won't do shit."

"This isn't your apartment. It's mine."

"Then you'll have to call the police and prove to them that I don't live here. Impossible to do when this is where I get my mail and my clothes are hanging in the closet."

Oh. My. God. Can this be true? "I don't believe you."

"Call the police and let's see what happens. Better hide your stash first."

"You're a fucking parasite. I hate you." And I totally do.

As I put the groceries away back in the kitchen, I try to think. *Think, Amanda. Think...* Nicholas is in Law School this year. Later tonight, I'll send him email to see if he can help with a remedy for this *situation* I'm in.

With a plan, my voice takes on a level of calm that surprises me. "It would be easier on both of us if you just left."

"I'll look for a place. I'll ask around at work tonight."

"You're going to work like that?" He shrugs, and what do I care if he serves plates of pasta stoned off his ass? Except I do. I have to set some sort of boundaries. "If you drive my truck again for any reason, I'll report it stolen and press charges."

When he doesn't respond, I poke my head around the corner. "Did you hear me, Jason?"

"I heard you. I'll call someone for a ride, and I'll try not to come home tonight."

"This isn't your home," I remind him.

"It is for now."

Well, apparently he's got me there.

* * *

It takes Nicholas a few days to respond to my email, and when he does the news is not good. Even though the lease is in my name, Jason established residency, and I have to follow very specific steps to have him evicted from my own fucking apartment where he doesn't pay one cent of rent *because he smokes crack with his tip money*. I imagine this isn't the first time Jason played this game.

God, I'm so stupid.

CHAPTER 10

EVICTING HIM TAKES TIME, EFFORT, and the authorities—plus, he keeps promising to leave on his own. I haven't taken any steps to throw him out. Afraid to leave the apartment because I'm worried about what he might steal, he comes "home" every few nights and falls asleep on the couch. The one and only time he crawled into bed with me, I threatened to cut off his dick when he passed out. He never tried that again. In fact, he comes back here less and less, but he hasn't returned my key or moved out.

A few weeks later when I open my credit card statement—a joint line with my parents that I have for books and emergencies—the balance is over five thousand dollars. I haven't used it in months, and all the charges are from the same place—Jason's employer, the Italian restaurant where meals are not cheap. Racing to my purse, I dig through my wallet.

He stole my fucking credit card.

I get high to calm myself down before rooting through email to find Nicholas's phone number. A familiar female voice answers the phone. "Amanda?"

"Michele?"

"Yes!"

"Oh my god! I thought you went back to New Jersey!"

"Yeah," she laughs. "I had a last-minute change of plans. Nicholas and I moved in together."

Michele with her jet-black hair and New Jersey attitude and sweet Nicholas, the gentle and thought-provoking guy from Nebraska—they are an unlikely couple, but I can see it. "I can't wait to see you, Michele."

"Let's do that. I'm in nursing school, though, so no more fun like we used to have."

"Got it. Hey, um, I'm having a little problem over here."

"With your *roommate*?" Her tone says it all. She knows.

"Yeah... um, is Nicholas around?"

"Sure. Come over for dinner soon, okay?"

"Deal."

After I explain, he teases me, "You know I'm not a lawyer yet, right?"

"Yeah, but you're the smartest person I know—aside from Michele—in Tucson, you know, who's still speaking to me. What should I do?"

"Call the credit card company. Tell them what you know and let them handle it. For your safety, say nothing to the dirtbag about being onto him and, for fuck's sake, start the eviction process. I can draft a notice and make it sound all legal, but you still have to file with the local court—and your leasing office. Where did you find this shithead again?"

"Nothing good happens at the hot tub at The Hollows. Trust me."

"Listen, once you report the card stolen, the bank will take over. When you see that guy again, play dumb—"

"That's not hard to do these days."

He laughs because, even financially screwed, he still finds me amusing. "The next time he tries to use the card, he'll know you cancelled it, and then he might react. Do you think this guy would hurt you?"

"I don't think so, but he smokes crack and was smart enough to pull a *Pacific Heights* on me. Have you ever seen that movie with Matthew Modine and Michael Keaton? God, Matthew Modine is so hot, but what happens to him during that movie is really terrible. I mean, Michael Keaton moves in and he seems perfect at first, but then all this terrible shit starts happening and poor Matthew plays right into his hands. And next thing you know—"

"Are you high?"

"How did you know?"

"Stoned Amanda has a hard time staying on point." He chuckles. "I can't do that shit anymore—too many details to remember."

I mumble, "Might explain why I'm a second year senior."

"If you don't feel safe, you're welcome to crash over here. Call if you need us."

"Yeah, so... How'd you make that happen underneath our noses?"

"I'm persuasive."

"Yeah. It's kind of difficult to argue with a guy like you."

"As I recall, you can hold your own. Put down the bong and join me at law school. Man, with your analytical brain and the way you look at things from every angle—not to mention your enthusiasm for debating—you'd make a fantastic attorney."

"My high school boyfriend used to tell me that all the time."

Braden. God, where is Braden? What is he doing right now?

After I finish talking to Nicholas, I report the card stolen and call Dad. Hell no, he doesn't get the whole story. Dad doesn't even get half of the story. He has no idea his once responsible daughter is stoned off her ass and shacking up with a crack head.

I'm a nervous wreck waiting for some sort of confrontation with Jason. Dropping my remaining classes, I shelter in my apartment except for the occasional outing for food, wine, or weed—because you can't have one without the others. I'm royally fucking my parents. The semester is a total loss, along with my outlook on life.

Jason doesn't work at the restaurant anymore. I have no idea where he's hiding out, but I toss his shit into the spare bedroom hoping that *out of sight, out of mind* is actually a thing. It isn't.

Vacillating between absolute humiliation and full-blown despair, I rarely experience an emotion between these two. I am nothing but the darkest thoughts in my head and on the pages of my journal. Endlessly, I document the forks in my road—each fork leads to another and another, and there's no going back. Playing mind games, sometimes I plot out a series of different forks and imagine that I wound up somewhere else entirely. No matter where my mind takes me, I find myself in the same place—my stagnant apartment with no forthcoming degree and a very broken life.

* * *

As October continues, so does the darkness in my soul until I find myself contemplating how best to put an end to the misery. After making a list of options in my journal, I cross them off one by one until I'm left with the two most viable—driving my truck off a cliff or slitting my wrists.

Winding up paralyzed is a huge fear, so I nix "Death by Cherry." I wander into the kitchen to consider which knife will make the sharpest, deepest cut. I know that I need to slice vertically into the veins—not horizontally across it because it will take much longer to bleed out.

I select the knife and test it out on my finger, and then I run a warm bath because I read in some novel—probably in Freshman English—that a person bleeds out more quickly in water. Plus, if the loss of blood doesn't kill me first, I'll drown once I lose consciousness. I guess my Freshman English TA's reading assignments were helpful after all.

From the edge of the tub, I run through a series of questions.

Do I want to be found naked when I'm so fat? *No, leave your clothes on.*

Should I burn my journals first? *No, your written words will give them insight into how fucked up you became.*

Should I write them a letter? *Maybe... No, they'll understand when they read your journals. But you should leave a letter for Tanner. He might think it's his fault when it's all on you, Amanda.*

Tanner. Jenny. Trina. Katie. My parents—*god, I love my parents.* I'll never see them again because death is a done deal. No second or third chances—nothing but the end. I'll never finish my degree, have a career, fall in love again—if that's even possible. I'll never get married and have fucked up little children of my own because they might take after me. I'll rot away in a box in the ground.

Do I want to be cremated instead? *Yes, you do. Put that in Tanner's letter so he'll tell your parents.*

With knife in hand, I stare at the bathtub as it fills with water. But I have to write that letter and go in search of paper and pen. While wandering the apartment, I open the pantry and take a few hits from my bong.

Once back in the bathroom, I sit on the closed toilet seat. Keeping an eye on the water level, I start on Tanner's letter. Putting my thoughts down on paper is harder than I thought it would be. I keep scratching things out, balling up the paper, and starting over. Nothing is coming out right.

Eventually, I turn off the faucet and keep writing. There is so much to say, but I can't find the words because...

I don't want to die. *Why not? You're already dead inside.*

Can I change that? *Yes.*

How? *You need help.*

Who would help me now? *Anyone, dumbass. Call your parents or any one of those people you just said you'd miss.*

I wish I was dead already. *You don't. You want to feel alive again. You still want everything, Amanda—a degree, career, love, family, friendships. You have to stop smoking that shit and figure this out. The water is getting cold.*

This is the desert. Draining and refilling the tub is a waste of natural resources, right? *So is killing yourself, dumbass.*

I'm too chicken shit to go through with this. *Or maybe there's an ounce of sanity left inside your fucked up brain.*

I need him. *He's probably not home.*

I have to try. *He told you not to fuck with his head.*

Leaving the knife on the bathroom vanity, I make my way to the telephone and dial the one phone number I will never forget. When he answers, I'm so shocked it momentarily takes away my power of speech, but I feel warmth roll through my body upon hearing his deep voice again.

This is good, Amanda. It's a sign of life.

Warmth is replaced by sobs of despair when I start speaking. "I know you said not to call, but, Tanner, I... I..."

"Amanda? What's going on?"

"I... I... I need you, Tanner. Please. I need you to help me..."

"Where are you?"

"My apartment..." I choke out.

"Same place?"

"Y... Y... Yes."

"What's happening?"

Howling into the phone, I confess, "I hurt so much. I wanted to die."

"Die? I'm calling 9-1-1."

"No." I cry while begging, "Please, no. You're the only one who can help me." Catching my breath, I whisper, "My head hurts."

"Are you hurt? Did you fall down, hit your head? I don't understand."

"I'm fucked up. I'm sick in the head," I sob. "It's all in my fucking fucked up head. Please, Tanner. Please help me."

"Panda, it's gonna take me thirty minutes to get to you. What am I gonna find when I get there?"

"Me. Just fucked up me."

He hesitates. "If you're thinking about hurting yourself, I need to call the—"

"No!" I interrupt with a yell. "I promise. I'll unlock the door and wait for you. Please. I need you."

"I'll be right there."

* * *

As with Jenny, here's the thing about history—connections rooted so deeply in friendship and fond memories and true affection, love, for another human being. I gutted Tanner, and I'm sure a part of him still hates me, but maybe a part of him will always love me because he shows up twenty minutes later. He must have broken a number of traffic laws.

Walking into my dark, stinky, dirty apartment, he finds me on the floor by the front door—back to the wall, arms curled around my legs. Dropping to the floor, he begins asking questions, but I have no answers. I'm too busy wailing and shaking, tears and snot pouring down my face.

He grabs me under my stinky armpits, forcing me to stand, but I fall back on the wall for support while he inspects me—for obvious signs of injury, maybe? No need. Just like I told him on the phone, everything that ails me is inside my fucked up mind.

Having determined I'm not gushing blood, he leads me to the sofa where I curl up on my side, head on his lap, face buried in his stomach. Strong arms comfort me until I can speak, and, when I form words, they all come pouring out—every fucked up sordid detail. He holds on tight until I finish, and then I feel his legs twitching underneath me. He's trying to figure out what to do with me now.

"You ready to pull your head out of your ass, Panda?"

"Yes."

He tells me to stay put—and I do—while he calls all the plays because I have nothing left.

When he calls the rental office and demands someone come over and change my locks, he uses words like *liability* and *lawsuit* and f*ailure to properly background check an employee who has access to vulnerable young women.*

For another phone call, he walks down the hallway murmuring softly into the handset. He calls that person *babe,* and my face falls into my hands. Eight months after I gutted him, Tanner has indeed moved on. I catch fragments—*Amanda, Pine Ridge, day or two, off the rails, bad, knew you'd understand.* He ends with *I love you, too.*

You love her*, too? Who do you love? Damn it. I love you, Tanner.*

Striding back into the living room, he eyes me wearily before calling the next person on his list.

"Michael, it's Tanner."

Oh fuck—Dad. This shit is real.

"I'm fine, thank you. But Amanda isn't. I'm driving her home to Pine Ridge today."

He listens before responding. "No, it's not that. She's having an emotional breakdown. I've never seen her like this. You need to start making calls. Find her a good therapist who can see her tomorrow."

Dad is probably rapid firing questions. Calm and collected, Tanner responds with short answers—*a while, therapy, medication maybe, serious help.* Finally, he ends the call with, "Five hours tops. We'll talk when I get up there." More silence, then, "Don't worry, Michael. I've got her. She's safe."

He peers down at me still curled in a ball on the sofa. "You need to take a shower before we pack a suitcase."

"Fine." In no position to argue, I follow him into the bathroom, forgetting about the tub full of water and the knife on the edge of the counter top. His face and entire body clench in the bathroom mirror reflection.

His eyes close tight while he groans, "Fuck, fuck, fuck." Spinning around, he grabs me roughly by the shoulders but says nothing. He just stares into my eyes.

"I called you instead, Tanner. I wasn't going to... I couldn't do it."

Breaking eye contact to reach into the tub, he releases the drain and wipes his arm on my towel. He turns on the shower, picks up the knife, and asks, "Do I have to watch you in here?"

I try to explain. "No. I just felt dead. That's it."

"Get in," he directs.

My shower is long because it's been a while. Tanner leaves the bathroom door open and checks in with me frequently. By the time I'm clean, he's completed a sweep of my apartment—filling three trash bags with my shame. While we finish waiting for the locks to be changed, he helps me pack a suitcase, even reminding me that it's a lot cooler in Pine Ridge and I need winter clothes.

I get dressed inside my closet and walk out wearing Braden's horrifically gold Iowa sweatshirt—an immature act of defiance. Tanner's eyes narrow on sight. "Seriously?" He may love another woman, but he still hates seeing me wearing Braden's sweatshirt.

Instead of answering, I add more clothes and my stack of journals to the suitcase. After locking up the apartment, he tosses the trash bags with Jason's belongings over the balcony onto the grass below. We step around Jason's baggage, which is no longer my problem. On the way to the parking lot, he throws away my alcohol, pipes, bong, and remaining stash in the dumpster. Loading my suitcase in Cherry's extended cab, he buckles me into the passenger seat and proceeds to return me to sender.

CHAPTER 11

WE DON'T TALK MUCH ON the four-hour drive home. He sings along to country music while I weep against the window in between naps. I want to know who he loves, but I'm afraid to ask.

Arriving well after 9 p.m., I ignore my parents and keep walking until I'm curled up in the fetal position once again—only this time on my childhood bed. I just can't deal. Whatever Tanner decides to tell them, I'll face it in the morning.

When he joins me later, I'm surprised. For sake of appearances, he used to set up camp in Brianna's old room, and I certainly wasn't expecting him to crawl into bed with me ever again. As he spoons me from behind, his body and arms lock around me. Melting into him while he strokes my hair, he tells me that everything will be all right.

"If you want things to change, Amanda, they will. I know you can do this."

My heart thumps triple time. "I feel so anxious. I need something to quiet my brain."

"Shhh," he soothes and traces a lazy path from my shoulder to my hand with his fingertips. "Take some deep breaths and try to think about good things."

"Nothing is good," I whisper.

He captures my hand and squeezes hard. "You called me. You're home now. That's good, Amanda."

"What did you tell my parents?"

He brings our joined hands up to my chest. "I told them that I'm sleeping in here with you tonight." Laughing quietly, he shares, "Claire didn't even put up a fight."

"Did you tell them about the marijuana?"

"No. You'll do that tomorrow. Promise me."

"What do they know?"

"I told them that you got in over your head with an older guy—a piece of shit. You haven't been going to classes, and you're in such a bad place that you thought about killing yourself. I told them what I saw in your bathroom."

"Well, I suppose that's more than enough for one night." My laugh is small before I state the obvious, "I lost you."

"I'm right here, babe."

"I miss you."

"I'm here now."

"Do you still hate me?"

"No."

"Do you forgive me?"

He hesitates before answering. "I'm working on it."

"I'll never get you back, will I?"

"Amanda, I'm with... listen, we don't have to do this right now."

"Who is she?" I whisper. "I heard you say that you love her." He doesn't provide an answer so I state more obvious things. "I fucked up everything."

"You can fix that."

"But not with you."

"We can't go back in time."

I release my breath into the quiet room and ask, "Why are you sleeping in here with me tonight? Why are you holding me like this?"

"So you don't do anything crazy until we get you some help tomorrow. For as long as I live, I'll never forget the state you were in today." Letting go of my hand to stroke my hair again, his voice becomes softer, sweeter. "I'm sorry that you're suffering, but you're gonna get better, okay? Your parents will get you help, and I'm gonna help you. You're surrounded by people who love you."

"And you? Do you still love me?" I regret the question because I'm afraid of the answer.

"Panda, you're the best friend I've ever had. I will always love you. Always. Now, let's get some sleep." With those words and in the comfort of his safe arms, I relax until sleep finally comes.

* * *

In the light of day, humbled but feeling more alive than I have in months, I reluctantly untangle myself from Tanner to use the bathroom before climbing back into bed. He does the same and settles us back into our earlier position. It's easier to talk to him when I don't have to look him in the eyes. Maybe it's the same for him.

"Thank you for taking care of me. You scraped me off the floor."

"Don't wanna do that ever again. I will if I have to, but please don't make me."

"I have a lot of work to do."

"You do, but you're not alone. Don't forget that."

"You should probably go back to Tucson," I offer. "You're missing class."

He laughs in my ear. "I should probably go see what Claire is making for breakfast. I hope it's pancakes."

"Please tell me who *she* is." He sighs and I press for an answer, "I need to know"

"Lorraine."

Tyler's sister who lives in the main house less than fifty yards away from Tanner. I called it the minute I laid eyes on her. I steady my voice. "That's... um, convenient. You're in love with her?"

"It doesn't matter."

"It does matter. We're really over."

"We haven't talked in eight months."

"You told me to stay out of your life."

"I'm sorry."

"Why are *you* sorry? I'm the one who screwed everything up."

"Yeah, but I own some of that, too."

"How?"

Instead of answering the question, he whispers, "You have a huge piece of my heart. It's yours forever."

"You can choose which piece of mine you want to keep. Just pick one up off the floor on your way out." I laugh without humor.

"Listen... the only thing that should matter right now is finding your way back to you." His gentle voice assures me, "You and me—we can talk through our stuff later. Unless this breakdown is all about me, which I don't think it is."

"I think there's something wrong with my brain."

Tanner tickles me in the rib cage. "Known that since the first day I met you."

For the first time in I don't remember how long, I laugh for real, and that in itself feels amazing.

* * *

Over breakfast, Tanner and my parents keep things light. I don't know how they manage because I'm a train wreck with weepy eyes and sniffles, but they all give that to me by talking around me about med school, how much Tanner misses Mom's cooking, the upcoming Territorial Cup—which makes me think of Coach. He offers to stay another day, but Dad tells him that he's done more than enough already and needs to get back to school.

After he says his goodbyes to my grateful parents, I walk him outside and attempt a smile.

"You already look better. I see light in your eyes."

"That's good because I only feel darkness in my cold, dead heart."

He gathers me in his arms and I wish I could stay there forever. "Take the help. Take the time. I'll put your apartment on police watch when I get back down there. And when you're ready to come back, I'll come get you."

"You don't have to do that."

"Um, I'm taking Cherry, Amanda."

"No, I just meant that I'll have my parents drive me down."

"Whatever you want. You need to talk while you're figuring things out, you need to talk to someone who believes in you, call me. If you don't call me, I'll call you."

I cling tighter and sniffle into his ear, "Thank you."

"Yeah..." When he pulls his head back to look at me, his eyes are filled with tears. "Don't do anything stupid." He thumps his chest. "I chose the sweetest piece of your heart. You're right here inside of me forever. I need you to get better."

Rolling up on my toes, I place a cautious and chaste kiss on his lips. "I love you, Tanner."

His hand touches my chin and he tilts my head to place his lips back on mine. For a beat or two, he captures my bottom lip between his teeth and nibbles. "Old habits," he explains with a small smile. "I shouldn't have done that. And I love you, too."

With a final squeeze, I watch him get into Cherry and drive away—back to Tucson and back to Lorraine, that lucky, lucky, woman who is probably smart enough to know that she has a man worth keeping forever.

* * *

Mom takes a sick day at work and my parents attempt to engage me in conversation, but I ask them to leave me alone in my room with my thoughts and a box of Kleenex. They allow it but insist that I leave the bedroom door open. I cry quietly into the sleeve of Braden's Iowa sweatshirt until I fall asleep again. Without anything to numb my pain, losing Tanner is a fresh wound all over again.

After lunch, which I decline to eat, Dad drives me to the office of a psychiatrist named Dr. Anderson. She's probably in her mid-forties with a pleasant face, comfy couches, and plenty of Kleenex. We have two hours together, which seemed like a long time when Dad told me, but the time flies by. She wants to know if I still feel like hurting myself.

"No. I just hurt in my heart—my head. But I don't want to die. I just felt dead already... Because... because... God, I can't believe how low I sank. All these *stupid decisions* that are so unlike me. I wasn't raised this way. I don't know what happened to me."

"Think back and tell me when you first felt like you started making decisions that were so unlike you."

I talk to her about my relationship with my parents—all the freedom and trust. I tell her about Pine Ridge High School, my friends, the football team, and my love for Coach's son. I transition to Germany, where I retreated into myself instead of finding my way, that I drank to be outgoing, and I was so desperate to belong and desperate for affection.

"And that's when I got into a relationship with Curt. I gave him my virginity. I knew it was wrong, but I did it anyway. Then things got ugly—like he thought he owned me and he called me horrible names... He told me I was fat and a whore and I stayed with him. We had a pregnancy scare, and when I got back home, I threw myself into Braden's arms because I needed to feel special again. Braden and me—we loved each other, said the words for the first time and spent three weeks in this bubble before he went back to Iowa and I started at Arizona. I still felt out of place, at first, but I had friends there from Pine Ridge and, of course, Tanner was there. He wanted a relationship with me—something Braden wouldn't offer—and it's totally possible to be in love with two guys at the same time. Two amazing guys and I lost them both. Tanner and I were really good together until..."

I talk about my classes and the way I started to look at gender roles and wonder what I wanted to do with my life. "But I didn't speak up in class, really, or around other people until I went back to the keg, and then one night I decided to smoke pot. My mouth opened and all this stuff came out, and I liked it. So I kept doing it, but I hid it from Tanner because I knew how he'd feel. It wasn't a part of me he knew existed. One night, I got so drunk that I found myself underneath a frat boy—so cliché—a drunken coed cliché of what not to do at a frat party. And, of course, I was mortified. I mean, I'd just slept with Tanner right before that party. Two guys in one night? Who does something like that, Dr. Anderson? A slut?"

"Someone whose decision-making ability is gravely impaired by alcohol."

"I tried to pretend it didn't happen and lived with the guilt. And maybe Tanner and I would've been okay except... I moved off campus a year later, and he did, too, and we were separated by our living *situations,* and he was so busy with med school that I just wafted away..." I shift gears and share, "I love how I feel when I'm high."

"How do you feel?"

"I feel like nothing. Not a care in the world. Until Jason..." And

I relive that shameful night in Jason's apartment, our unnatural friendship, the escalation of drugs and alcohol, the weight gain, and the ensuing darkness. "And eventually I came clean. I told Tanner everything. He exploded—of course he did. I've never heard someone use the word fuck so many times in the course of one fucked up, fucking horrible conversation." I stop and look at her. "I can say fuck around you, right?"

She smiles. "Yes, Amanda. You can say whatever you'd like around me."

"He told me that I gutted—eviscerated—him, and he wouldn't take me back. I stayed in bed for like a month. I got up to take bong hits and pee. I tried that summer to put myself back together, but Jason was there."

I talk about Jason's demons, our entangled fucked up relationship, the lying and stealing. "I sheltered in place like a fucking slimy slug... I got so dark, and it was scary because I stopped feeling nothing. I felt less than nothing. In that moment in my apartment, I did want to die. I thought, why bother anymore? But when it came time to go through with it... I couldn't do it."

"What stopped you?"

"Thinking about my family and friends... and Tanner. And I thought about it for so long that the water in the bathtub got cold." I laugh at the crazy thoughts that rattled through my head that afternoon. "And I didn't want to waste water, so I called Tanner."

"And he was there for you?"

I start to cry. "Yes. After everything I did to him, he brought me home last night, and here I am. I'd really kill for a bong hit or five right now."

Her smile is warm. "I appreciate the honesty. What do you want to accomplish with me, Amanda?"

"I want my life back... The one where I felt good about myself."

* * *

We do this for several more days in fifty minute increments until I have a prescription for an anti-depressant and a short-term plan. This is followed by a family session with my parents who've been watching me like a hawk and holding back—big time—with specific questions.

Getting me healthy enough to finish my degree is their top priority. Everything else comes second. So first—or firstly—I have to call the university and figure out what stands between me and that diploma. Once I know what it will take, hopefully just a full load in the spring, we'll tackle the rest.

Mom and Dad are adamant that I move back on campus, and I feel like arguing—which is a good sign. Dr. Anderson also encourages my parents to take things one step at a time with me. I have two months to pull my head out of my ass and get back to school.

There are many more sessions with Dr. Anderson, and, as she helps me wade through my shit, she's convinced that I've lived with a chemical imbalance in my brain caused by depression—the social anxiety being a byproduct—for many years, and the drugs became a coping mechanism. In addition to the anti-depressant, she prescribes abstinence from marijuana, along with doses of sunshine and exercise.

As the days roll by, Mom is teaching but rushes home right after school. Dad is sticking close to home. I love their big, fat cat

Sylvester. We spend a lot of time together in my room where I read books and journal. I make lists and plans for the uncertain future. I also go into the attic above the garage and break into a sealed box which contains journals from my earlier years. Most of it makes me laugh, some of it makes me cry, and it's clear that from the age of fifteen to eighteen, Braden was my drug of choice.

I can't tell if the antidepressants are helping, but Dr. Anderson says that it might take up to a month before I feel the full benefits. I'm not sleeping at night, so she prescribes an additional medication to take at least an hour before bed.

I make every effort to follow her orders. I walk down the hill each evening with Mom or Dad, or sometimes both, to walk around the small lakes at the town park. While we walk, we sometimes talk, but more often we don't because there's so much that I don't want them to know.

CHAPTER 12

Tanner calls a few weeks in, although I know he's been talking to Dad almost every day since he brought me home. We need to wade through our shit, but, first or firstly, we talk about my sessions with Dr. Anderson and my plans for finishing school. He's on the same page of the playbook as my parents. He insists that I move back on campus and suggests Gila Hall because it's small and generally quiet.

When I protest, he throws down. "You need to be close to your classes and cut ties with that part of your life." He's vehement and bossy. "You need structure, and it'll make it easier for you to get up at the ass crack of dawn to meet me at the Rec Center."

"You have time to work out with me?"

"Gonna make the time. But I'm not gonna work out with you."

He laughs. "I'm gonna work you out. You want your firm ass and tight abs back; you're gonna do everything I say."

"Well," I laugh in return, "that'll be a first."

"I can come up this weekend," he offers. "Maybe we can go watch the Bobcats play or something."

"That's really nice, but I'm not strong enough to be around you just yet."

"I don't understand."

"It takes next to nothing to set me off, and finding out about you and Lorraine—it's like losing you all over again. I'm still processing everything."

"Process this," he says. "I always said that I'd give you what you needed, but I didn't. Too caught up in my own life, I stopped paying attention to yours. Didn't even see this coming. I took you for granted, babe. Waited years to make you mine and I didn't protect what I had."

"Now I don't understand."

"My whole life, you were a challenge—so damn determined to get your point across. You had all this fire and a smart mouth, gave as good as you got, and I wanted that for myself. Couldn't have you, though. For years I was too short, too skinny, too poor, and then you were too in love with a guy who was all the things I wasn't. That only made me want you more."

"And when you had me?"

He chuckles softly. "Just covered that. Didn't give you what you needed—time, attention, understanding. You're a lot more sensitive than me, and I shoulda been way more focused on your needs."

"I barely remember who I was before you."

"Before me, with me, after me—you're Amanda Harrington. She's someone I'll always love."

"Are we really over?"

After several beats of quiet, he says, "I've learned some things about myself since we broke up. Not only do I like to run the show, I have to run it. It's my nature. School, women, sports—you name it, I wanna be in charge. A woman like you, Panda, you weren't made to follow a leader—at least not without questioning the leader every step of the way."

"But we rarely argued. It was easy."

"At first, yeah. Look at the classes you take and the things you're into now. And that's fine, it's your deal, but it never made much sense to me why you'd get so into that instead of going after something practical to do with your life. I don't understand half the shit you think about or why you bother worrying about it. I guess you needed something that I can't give you. That's why you wanted out."

"You broke up with me, remember? I wanted to stay together."

"You knew cheating would end us, so you found your way out and made me say the words to you instead of the other way around." He chuckles warmly and teases me. "That's just like you, Panda—make me do all the tough stuff. Seriously, the only reason you think that you want back with me is because I'm who you know, not who you want. Think about it. It's not because you'd be happy with me and a houseful of kids that I want and you don't. You're not gonna allow me or any other guy to take point in a marriage. It's not in you."

I sigh into the phone because, damn it, he might be right. "Do you really think that we can be just friends? I don't think people who break up can go back to how it was before."

"It's never gonna be how it was before. It'll be different because we shared something deep, but, Panda, I fucking miss you. My life isn't the same without you in it. Let's get back to the parts of us that made us such good friends to begin with."

"I just... It's raw. It hurts."

"Stop overthinking this. If we want this, it's simple. No flow chart required."

This cracks me up, and I allow myself a moment of pure laughter. "Okay. I'm willing to try," I say. "Your friendship after everything I did to you probably isn't deserved, but—"

"Process that with your shrink and put it to rest. If we're gonna enjoy any time together, we can't dwell on all the heavy stuff, okay? We said a lot of shit today. Let's deal with it and move on."

"How does Lorraine feel about our friendship? Does she know that you want to, um, spend time with me?"

"Of course she knows. She's fine because it's what I want."

"You're in love with her?"

"She's good for me. I don't want to hurt you, but there's no struggle with Lorraine. She's docile by nature. She was born to follow, not mouth off."

"That's kind of fucked up, Tanner."

He laughs. "Yeah, but it's the truth."

Yes, the truth still hurts, but I'm going to have to live with it.

Territorial Cup—1994

It came down to the wire, but Arizona pulled it out in the end—28 to 27. It was ugly, but a win is a win, and I'll take it. Now I have Coach on the brain. I call first, and he greets me with boom and zest and tells me that he'd love to see me. I ask permission to borrow Mom's car and head across our small town.

In retrospect, I should've tried to meet him somewhere in town, because pulling into the driveway floods my gut with nausea. Braden and I spent so much time here together as teenagers. This house holds a thousand memories of kisses, heated groping sessions, and sweet words combined with the occasional argument—promises never made, thus never broken.

When Coach opens the door, he takes note of my U of A sweatshirt. "You and Fiona," he grumbles as we hug. "I should disown you both."

I ask about Braden's older sister, "How is Fiona?"

"She's here somewhere—you can ask her yourself."

"Great."

"Fiona," he hollers. "Get your Wildcat ass out here. I have one of your kind here."

I laugh and it feels amazing to see Coach again, but when he leads me through the formal living area to sit in the family room where Braden and I used to watch movies and make out on the brown leather sofa, my stomach seizes and my skin crawls. "Can we sit out here—in the living room?" I ask.

"We can sit wherever you want," he replies good-naturedly. "Would you like a drink?"

Whiskey. "No, thank you."

Once we get settled in a room that holds very few memories, Coach asks, "What's going on in your life? Hit me, Harrington."

I always love it when he says that to me. "I'm sorry that I haven't stopped by or at least called to rub in our previous wins."

He chuckles, and god does Braden take after him. "That's okay. I know things get busy, but you're here now and that's a good thing."

"Not really... I mean, it's good to see you, but it's not a good thing that I'm in Pine Ridge right now. I sort of..." I sigh. "I'm in a really weird place right now, and I'm home to—"

"Mandy?" Fiona grins at me before crossing the room. "Gosh, it's been *years*."

I stand to give her trim frame a quick hug, and she plops down on the sofa next to Coach. "I know. I can't believe we haven't run into each other on campus." *Of course, the odds might go up if I actually visited campus once in a while.*

"So what are you up to these days?" she asks.

"Finishing my undergrad. Last semester, in the spring."

Coach's eyebrows contract. "I thought you'd be done by now."

"So did everyone, but apparently I'm, uh, taking the scenic route. How about you, Fiona? What are you up to?"

"No good." She laughs, and I feel fenced in by Braden's blue eyes. "I'm working on my PhD, and I instruct several classes in the Sociology Department."

"Wow, that's great. And it's totally weird that I haven't seen you at all because Sociology is part of my major."

"I know why this one is taking the scenic route." Coach gestures to Fiona. "She's a professional student. But why are you still down there?"

"Oh, um... I made some... bad decisions, I guess. I took a little time off this semester to regroup here at home, and then I'll finish up."

"You do that, Harrington. Go back. Once you have that degree, they can never take it away from you." Coach comments, "Rawlings is in med school, I hear. I ran into his father a while back. He's proud. You must be, too."

"Yes. Second year." I beam at Coach as if I have something to do with Tanner's success. "He's working so hard. I knew he was determined, but I had no idea until we, um... Did you know we were together?"

"Yes." His chuckle is dry. "That was big news in our house a while back."

I feel my face warming, and I share, "We're not together anymore. It didn't work out."

"Seem to recall that boy not leaving your side much on those bus trips."

"Yeah, as if the front seat you made me sit in wasn't enough to protect my virtue on the road with the team, I had Tanner standing guard." Even though I say this with a smile, now I wonder if Coach is questioning my *virtue* because of all those sleepovers I had with Braden in this very house.

I press my lips together in a straight line. "That was a long time ago, but sometimes it feels like yesterday. My years here were so easy—uncomplicated."

"That's a good thing for a kid," Coach says. "Strong roots."

"Sheltered. Protected. Encased in bubble wrap," I respond. "That was life in Pine Ridge, but when you have strong roots somewhere it makes it tough to dig them up and plant them elsewhere."

"Is that what happened to you?"

I try to lighten the mood. "Gee, Coach, this conversation is getting kind of deep."

"I blame Fiona—she brings out my deep side."

"Hey," Fiona pretends to protest, but the look she gives Coach is one of daughterly admiration. It's the same one that I reserve exclusively for mine.

"What have you decided to do after college?" he asks. Then he winks at me. "Or is that too deep?"

"Probably. Because I don't know. Um, I guess I'll decide in May," I reply. "I keep hoping it will come to me, so if you have any ideas..."

"I thought you'd go into sports medicine. But Braden was convinced you belonged in law school—said he never met a girl who liked to build an argument more than you."

There's my opening. I take it. "How is Braden? Where is he these days?"

"He's good," Coach launches in. "Great, actually. Still in Iowa freezing his ass off. They bought a starter home outside of Iowa City last fall, staying near Jessica's big family. We're hoping for grandkids before we get too old to enjoy them."

"What?" I whisper the question and bring my hand to my mouth so I can pull nervously at my lips and chin. I read the pity in their matching blue eyes when they realize that I had no idea.

"He's married."

Braden married the *pig farmer's daughter*??? When I was in Germany, we both lost our virginity—just not with each other. To make matters worse, Braden refused to have sex with me after I returned home and we spilled our guts to each other. He said it would be making a promise to me that he wasn't in a position to keep. I guess he took those words—and his promises to Jessica—to heart. She wound up with *everything*.

"Um, when did that happen?" I can't help myself—I might as well ask all my questions now so I can cry over the answers with Dr. Anderson on Monday.

Fiona's voice is gentle when she answers, "Last summer—after they graduated from Iowa."

"Oh," I find myself dabbing at the tears that form in the corners of my eyes. "I'm... I'm sorry." I shake my stupid, stupid, stupid head and try to pull off a laugh but it falls flat. "Well, this is really awkward, right, guys?"

He pats my knee. "Always thought you'd make an excellent daughter-in-law."

"Dad," Fiona cautions and tries to recover his fumble. "We're sorry, Mandy. I assumed that you knew."

"No. I don't know anything about him because, you know, Braden hasn't talked to me since Tanner and I... But I thought maybe one day we'd have a chance to talk or whatever, but I guess that's not going to happen now—or, like, ever." My scrap of laughter is laden with hostility, and I think about the last time I laid eyes on him—in front of my dorm freshman year. We'd spent three weeks reconnecting after a year apart and had to say goodbye again. And, while some things are better left unsaid in front of Braden's family, it spills out anyway. "I loved him so much."

Braden pulled up in front of Manzi/Mo and helped me unload my shopping bags from Coach's truck.

"Do you want me to help you take that upstairs?" he offered.

"No, I got it." I put the bags on the ground. "If I take you upstairs, I'll want to keep you with me always."

He gave me a long hug in the blistering heat. "I wish I could stay with you."

"It's not too late. You can tell Iowa to fuck off."

He laughed and kissed my neck. "I might think about that when the weather turns to shit and I can't get you off my mind. I love you, Mandy."

"I love you back."

Sighing, he pulled me closer. "Listen, if you and Tanner—"

I looked up at him. "Please don't."

"If you do, I want to know. I mean, I don't want it to happen, but I need you to tell me. Promise me."

"I will, but if you and the pig farmer's daughter... I don't want to know because it will break my heart."

"I'll call you next week. We'll talk and write, and I'll see you over Christmas break."

"Are you sure you don't want to make any other promises?" I offered. "It's not too late."

He shook his head. "I promise that when we're ready to make promises, I won't break them."

Fiona tries to reason with me. "Just because he's married,

doesn't mean you can't talk to him. He loved you, too, and some-times it's therapeutic to get closure."

"Yeah... You know, they used to say that about shock therapy." I'm not strong enough to hear this—I'm about to lose it, and it's going to be ugly. Scrunching my face to ward off more tears, I stand on shaky legs. I need to be alone so I can fall apart. "I have to go."

Coach stands and places a hand on my shoulder. "Honey," he starts.

"I just... I can't deal with this. I'm sorry." I take a deep breath and swallow hard. "Nice to see you, Fiona. I'll call you, Coach."

Beating a hasty retreat out the front door, I somehow manage to get down their harrowing driveway without sliding off the mountain. I pull over in front of Robert's old house—another one of Jenny's ex-boyfriends, and it's exactly like the evening Tanner told me that he was finished with me. I can barely see through my tears, can hardly breathe through the sobs that wrack my body. I'm not sure how long I spend sitting in Mom's car crying my heart out. How pathetic to cry over a guy I haven't talked to in years.

What the fuck is wrong with me?

When Coach calls the house a few days later, after I hear Dad greet him over the phone, I shake my head and slink away. Dad makes an excuse about why I can't talk right now and chats with him for a few minutes. I don't call Coach before I leave town. In fact, I wonder if I'll ever call Coach again.

CHAPTER 13

Senior Year—Take 2, Spring Semester 1995

I HAVE TO TAKE TWENTY-ONE credit hours—seven classes. Dad drives me back to Tucson in January. Tanner meets us at The Hollows with my beloved Chevy truck Cherry, and he brings muscle in the form of med school buddies—including Lorraine's younger brother Tyler. He also brings Lorraine, which we'd discussed well in advance.

Tanner wants us to get to know each other, so I suck it up and put on a brave face when I feel anything but. It's not like he expects the two of us to become best friends, and I know that if she has problems with me that will cause troubles for him. I'm no longer his priority.

Lorraine and Tyler's parents offered to store my furniture in their barn until I decide where I'm going after graduation. I've been talking to Jenny and Katie, and I'll probably move to the Valley because there's nothing for me in Tucson after I get my degree.

After all the heavy lifting, packing, and cleaning up, Lorraine and Tanner are the last to leave. Hell yes, it was awkward. Dad and Tanner hug it out, and on their way to Lorraine's car, Tanner calls out over his shoulder, "Get some sleep tonight, Panda. Six o'clock in the morning comes awfully early."

I stifle my groan but not my smart mouth and call back, "I'll be there before you."

Tanner and I have standing Rec Center appointments at 6 a.m. on Monday, Wednesday, and Friday, and 8 a.m. on Saturdays and/or Sundays depending on his schedule. The early days will leave me no time for evening debauchery—not that I have plans for any, but, with me, it's both possible and probable if I don't stick to the plan.

Dad follows me and Cherry in his car over to Gila Hall. I have a single on the first floor. Like Yuma Hall, it's an older red brick building in close proximity to the majority of my classes. It's typically reserved for honors students, but someone in Student Housing made an exception. We unpack quickly and move my truck into the assigned parking garage. Dad takes me out for a late lunch before heading back to Pine Ridge.

"I worry about you, Brown Eyes."

"Well, I've given you lots of reasons to worry, haven't I?"

"Your mom and I feel like we're missing critical pieces of information."

"Dr. Anderson isn't. There are things I can't share with you. I hope you know how thankful I am for all of your support—financially and emotionally."

"This is the last dance, Brown Eyes. If you don't pull it out this semester, you're going to have to support yourself."

"I know. It's part of our agreement, and I'm not going to let you or Mom down this time."

"You can't. I need you to get your hand out of my wallet so I can keep saving for retirement. Your mom will probably teach for another five to ten years, and I want to travel with her."

I smile. "That sounds like a wonderful plan. Good thing I didn't fuck up like this at Stanford. That would've been five times as expensive."

"I have a feeling this wouldn't have happened to you at Stanford."

"I'm a nut job, Daddy—chemically imbalanced with loose screws, and it's genetic so you should keep a close eye on yourself."

He grins before his expression sobers. "Tanner grew up to be a fine young man." I nod and wonder where he is going with this. "I like Lorraine. She seems like a good match for him, but I have to say—"

"Do you? Do you have to say it, Daddy?"

He chuckles. "You don't even know what I'm going to say."

"Oh, well, I assume you're going to give me some speech about how I really screwed up with Tanner, and if I'm ever lucky enough to catch the interest of another doctor again, I should hold on tight with both hands."

"No. I was going to say that you're damn lucky to still have him on your side—we all are. I try not to think about the scene he described in your bathroom a few months ago, but it's never far from my mind that you felt so hopeless and alone you considered taking yourself out of this world."

I shake my head. "I wouldn't have done it, Daddy. I was too scared."

"Ending it all is for cowards, Brown Eyes. Remember that."

* * *

My agreement with my parents has several stipulations, and I follow them all. I meet with Dr. Anderson for fifty minutes twice a week by phone, I call my parents at the same time every Sunday night and whenever the mood strikes me during the week. I take my medications as prescribed. I attend every single class. I do all of the required work and then some.

In my downtime, I occasionally visit Nicholas and Michele off-campus for dinner and debating. When I'm not studying, I leave my dorm room door open—a sign that visitors are welcome, and I have some of those. I wander down the halls and poke my head into other open doors and meet most of the students on my coed floor. I venture into the common areas to watch TV and strike up conversations with whomever is around. Yes, it's difficult for me to put myself out there like this, but I don't have many friends left down here. I need to feed off the energy from other people, chatter, and normal activities.

Occasionally I feel the urge to do something reckless and stupid. It would be easy. I still have connections and a desire to check out of my head for a while. When those times hit hardest, I call Jenny, Trina, or Katie, and they take my mind off of my crazy by sharing their crazy. Still, even with them, I've kept the worst of my crazy all to myself. My girlfriends don't know how far I fell.

I meet Tanner faithfully at the Rec Center four, sometimes five, mornings a week. He's going drill sergeant on my ass, but I leave him with a natural high from the endorphins—both from the workout and the laughter. Tanner is playful, and when we aren't exchanging smart ass barbs, we're talking about the usual things—classes, new people and experiences, and plans for the future—just not a future together which stings. I mask it—smile it away—and refer often to the drawings of alternate forks not taken in my journal.

Eventually, after weeks of routine, I have it down, and—bonus—I found someone to roll around with. Noah lives on my floor several doors down, and he's adorable with thick dark hair, a tall husky build, and dark eyes with a heavy fringe of lashes. He's also young—a nineteen-year-old sophomore from Orange County.

I'm not going to fall in love with Noah because I'm not ready to hand over my heart, plus we have an expiration date. He's smart and funny and an exceptional kisser, but he's totally clueless about certain *situations*. That becomes painfully obvious the first time he slips his hand into my panties. Poor kid has no idea what to do down there. It's practically a Law of Sisterhood to pass along some *wisdom* for the next girl who comes along.

Noah's been with women before me; I just don't think they walked away very satisfied. I provide coaching and shit tons of positive reinforcement during my lessons on the female anatomy. I pass along a few tricks from Tanner's playbook, and I let him try and try again until he elicits moans and stammers from me. It's a little tricky up there, but end result is tried and true. Noah is a quick study, and now he can multitask and find *that spot* on the very first try.

He also understands that the woman should always come first, during if possible and most definitely after. To Noah's future women, you are welcome. In the meantime, I plan to keep this player to myself and enjoy the end results of my coaching until the game clock runs out in May.

* * *

"Push, Panda," Tanner barks down at me. "You leg press like a girl."

My glare meets his smirk.

I grit my teeth and fully extend my legs with a push of air from my lungs. Locking my knees, I retort, "Fuck you, Tanner." It's six-thirty in the morning—*fuck you* is the best I have to offer at this time of day. I haven't even had coffee yet.

He laughs in my face because some things never change. "Give me five more," he orders, and, damn, he's bossier than usual this morning. Bossy and busy all the time, but he's here for me as promised and it's paying off.

A few weeks ago, Lorraine helped me dig through the barn and locate my size 18/20 boxes. She clapped her freaking hands, jumped up and down on her trim athletic legs, and complimented my progress. No, we'll never be best friends, but I couldn't hate her if I tried. I may never fit into those twelves again because that body was the result of daily workouts and more sex per day than was realistically possible in a normal person's life, but my fourteens—along with my dignity and diploma—are the end goals.

He helps me lock the weights back in place after I give him an extra two because I can. As we rotate machines and trade off counting reps, his smack talk comes with a biting edge.

"What's with the bad mood?" I call him out. "No time to get any lately?"

Tanner spills a shocking secret. "Except for my right hand, I haven't gotten any in over a year."

"*What?*" Because *WHAT???*

"Lorraine is saving herself for marriage. Haven't been with anyone since you."

Since he doesn't look amused, I stifle my laughter and seek clarification. "Um—has she been saving herself for marriage her entire life?"

"Yup."

"A virgin... How fascinating. Has she done much of anything?"

He groans out, "No, not really."

"Blowjob?" And, really, it's disturbing to ask questions when the answers might give me nightmares, but I'm intrigued with the limits of a twenty-four-year-old virgin.

"Out of the question."

"Hand job?"

He responds with full agitation, "You gonna keep running through the list of *jobs* I can't have, or are you here to work out?"

Now I laugh in his face. "I think I covered the two most obvious *jobs*... Unless you can think of one that I forgot." Tanner finishes his bicep curl and glares at me. "Oh wait... there's a *rim job* but even I wouldn't do that job. Receiving one however... totally different story." My grin is *shit*-eating because I wouldn't but Tanner would.

He snaps at me, "Should make you switch to cardio. You can't talk when you're *winded*."

Oh, hell yes, this is too good to pass up, "You wanna get *winded*, Tanner?"

"You suck," he glowers.

"I totally do." Nodding, I take the easy and most obvious one-point conversion. "And I swallow."

"*Enough!*" He points in the direction of the free weights. "No more rotating. We're both doing free weights because you can't mouth off counting your own reps."

As we walk, he tries to regain the upper hand by saying, "Only your weights will be much smaller because I'm so much stronger." He flexes to make his point, but, too bad for him, he uses his right arm and I'm on a roll.

When we hit the mat, I offer him a charming smile. "Will you flex for me with both arms? I think your muscles are a lot bigger." At this time of the morning, we don't have a lot of company, just a few older professor-looking types working out on some cardio machines.

"Yeah?" God, he's making this too easy, puffing out like a peacock complete with a double flex.

Eyes narrowing in fake meticulous scrutiny, I also give both arms attention with my hands. "Impressive." I take a step back before delivering the line. "But totally uneven. Looks like you're favoring your right side—a lot."

Quick as a former fullback, he lunges. Averting his forward motion is not in my skill set, and I release a laughter-filled squeal as he hooks a leg behind my knees and takes me down to the mat.

Flat on my back with my thighs and arms pinned to the mat, my smile disappears. He leans over me, way too close for comfort. My body catches fire. *Whoosh.*

"You gonna behave?" he taunts. His lips curl into a devious grin while his brown eyes dance with... *Oh my god! Are those naughty intentions?* If he wasn't straddling my thighs, my legs would spread for him on spontaneous reflex.

"Tanner, let me go."

"No." He smiles, and, *oh hell*, it is naughty. "Not until you promise to behave. Do you promise?"

My eyes dart around before landing back on his. "I don't think proper behavior is part of my DNA, but I'll take it easy on you."

"Not good enough. I need assurances."

"Please let me up." My request sounds as weak as my resistance.

"No. Forgot how much I enjoy it when you're powerless underneath me." He's still grinning, but this is no joke because his eyes are dark and breathing labored. *No, no, no—oh shit*, I feel his erection growing against my body.

He wants me. *I love him. We can't do this.*

My voice drops to an urgent whisper, "You need to let me up right now because this is really turning me on."

He stares down at me, the grin turning into a thoughtful expression as he considers his next move above me.

"Tanner, get off me." He doesn't budge. "*Please.*"

"I can't get off you," he whispers back. "I have a raging hard on."

"Yeah, um, I can totally feel it."

"This is so wrong... and so fucking right."

"It's just, um, a biochemical reaction. It's what our bodies know."

"Fuck," he mutters. "It's way more than that. I need you back with me."

As his mouth drops to my neck, I struggle with my head and my heart. Except for the power of words, I can't stop this play.

"Stop!" If a whisper can be yelled, I pull it off. "You don't want to do this." *But I sure as hell want to.*

He freezes before his lips make contact with my skin. Pulling back slightly—our chests rising and falling too quickly—he studies my face.

"You're going to get off me right now, Tanner, and we're going to sit here on the mat until you don't scare people away with the size of your giant cock."

"Talking about my giant cock is not helping the *situation*, Panda."

I turn the conversation to Lorraine. "And you're going to stick that thing inside a virgin without, like, having her try out a fun-size penis first? She needs to work her way up. That sex shop on Grant Avenue probably sells starter dildos. You should get one of those little things and a gallon of KY."

With eyes the color of the darkest night, he cracks a smile. "You don't need KY. You're always soaking wet. Hot and dripping," he punctuates those last three words as he watches me. "I bet you're wet for me right now."

You are 100% correct, Tanner.

With his eyes pinned to mine and my wrists pinned to the mat, he shifts his position and slides one muscular leg between mine until the bare skin of his knee makes contact with my soaking wet, hot and dripping center. And, damn it, my legs spread for him. *Stupid spontaneous reflex.* "Fuck, Amanda," he whispers on a growl. "So fucking hot—nothing like it."

It takes every ounce of self-restraint to choke back a moan, not grind into his knee or wrap my free leg around his back. I want to taste his mouth and feel him inside of me again. I want to go back to a time and place when life was simple and good.

You want Tanner back.

I close my eyes and take a very deep breath. It doesn't help, so I take two more.

This is not going to happen, Amanda. Put a stop to it now.

When my eyes open, I order at full volume, "Get off me *right now*."

That does it. He finally shifts off me right onto his ass and brings his knees up to his chest. "Son of a bitch," he mutters turning his eyes back to mine. "What have I done?"

"Averted a giant mistake."

"Would you *please* stop using the word *giant*?" He groans quietly. "I'm such a fucking dog."

"No, no..." I sit cross-legged a few inches across from him. "Why would you say that?" I whisper again so we don't shock the professors who still look a little concerned after the whole *get off me right now situation.*

"Because I want you back. Right now, let's fix this. We can get back togeth—"

"Shh... Shush... Listen to me. We have a lot of fucking history together or a lot of history fucking... however you want to look at it. *Oh my god*, that is so fucking funny." I can't help myself and give in to a minor giggle fit. Tanner doesn't laugh but he does smile because it is really funny.

After composing myself, I try to explain *ourselves.* "God, Tanner, your blood is probably equal parts water and testosterone, and you aren't getting any right now. Our bodies just responded to the *situation* because it's familiar. We didn't *do* anything."

"Lorraine..."

"It's okay. You're sure about her. You love her, right?" I question him in a soothing tone.

"Yes."

"Okay then. Nothing hap—"

"I'm still in love with you."

Shit.

"Panda, I can forgive you. I do forgive you. Spending all this time together made me realize that you and me have a once in a lifetime kind of love."

All you have to do is tell him, Amanda. Say it. I love you, too, Tanner. Let's try again.

Instead, I rub at my temples before meeting his eyes. I remind him, "I wasn't born to follow the leader. Tanner... I, um..." *Damn, trying to do the right thing isn't easy.* "Why do you love Lorraine?"

His eyes widen for a fraction before he looks down at the mat to compose his thoughts. "She was there for me when you broke my fucking heart... She listened and cared, and along the way I found out that we want the same things in life."

"What's she like? As a person? Like, what qualities does she have?"

He doesn't even have to think about his answer. "She's honest, open, and uncomplicated."

"And you get along well, right?"

"Yes."

"I hurt you." I smile gently with tears in my eyes. "She helped you heal, and you don't have to be anyone but yourself when you're with her. Did I get that right?"

"True."

"You need to trust your heart—your instincts—because... You said it best—I'm fire with a smart mouth, and you want—"

"I want you."

I want you, too, Tanner. "How would you feel about losing a woman like Lorraine if we can't make it work? I'm all kinds of complicated." I nudge him with my foot to make sure he's listening. "I hid things from you, lied to you. Yeah, I think we'll always have feelings for each other that linger, but..." *Shut up, Amanda. Just tell him that you want to try again.* "It doesn't mean I'm the right woman for your future. Lorraine seems like that kind of person for you."

"Then why do I feel—"

"Because we're part of each other, remember?"

"Yeah." Relieved to see his gorgeous eyes returning to their normal shade of brown, he asks me, "Now what?"

"We meet here on Friday and work out, right? Because I'm still one size away from my target."

"This is gonna kill Lorraine because I told her that—"

"That's why you're going to keep this morning to yourself." His eyes fly wide open along with his mouth, but I quickly reason, "You don't need to say anything to her about this because thoughts are not actions and thoughts are private."

"Right," he mutters but still looked wrecked. "But I shared those thoughts with you."

"So what?" I shrug. "That's what friends are for. Think of it like an informal brainstorming session. We threw out some ideas, but decided not to use them."

He chuckles—a good sign. "Friends."

"Forever." I smile. "I need you to be my friend. Please."

"All right." He looks to the ceiling tiles and sighs. "As soon as I have this under control, we should call it a morning. Thanks for helping me get this figured out because—"

He has to stop wallowing so I interrupt, "Jeez, it's not like we could've banged right here in the middle of the free weights. If I didn't wind up in jail for drugs, I'm certainly not going there for indecent exposure at the Rec Center."

His body relaxes and his easy smile returns. "You're fucking hilarious, Panda."

"Right? I am. Hey, I'm going to go. I'll see you on Friday."

Standing to make my way to the locker room, I need a cold shower. I'm dripping wet after that *situation* on the mat.

CHAPTER 14

I RUN INTO FIONA THAT afternoon in the main Social Sciences building. "Mandy," she greets me with a smile and a hug. "It's good to see you, and so soon."

"Finally, our paths cross in our natural habitat," I jest half-heartedly. "It's about time."

"Are you coming or going from class?"

"Going. All done for today except for the 500 pages of reading tonight." *Homework AND taking my sexual frustrations out on Noah.*

"Do you have time for coffee?"

Since I do we walk over to the Student Union and settle into a seating area with two iced coffees. I ask her a lot of questions to keep the conversation focused on topics that I can handle. She discusses her PhD program, and I learn that she has a live-in boyfriend named Jeremy, but they have no plans to marry or have children—ever. Fiona wants to teach, travel, and have the freedom to do as she pleases.

"I'm really sorry about Thanksgiving weekend," she broaches the touchy subject. "Dad and I thought that you knew."

"Can we not?"

She probes regardless. "Braden hasn't talked to you since... when?"

"Christmas break of my freshman year."

"I asked him why."

While I want to know what he said, I also don't. My brain has reached maximum capacity with *stupid feelings* over two boys from Pine Ridge. I'm taking twenty-one credit hours. *Eyes on the goal line.*

"Fiona. Please—I can't talk about Braden." I choose an alternate topic. "But I can talk about my nephews..." Digging in my backpack, I locate my wallet to share pictures of the boys and chat about Brianna's life in Germany and the ever-changing politics and landscape of East and West becoming one.

As we talk about anything but Braden, he might as well be sitting there with us because my heart weighs one thousand pounds. Every single time she calls me Mandy or smiles in a certain way, I see him in Fiona's beautiful blue eyes, and it stings like a bitch. As we part ways, I give her my personal email address when she asks for it and share that I'll likely move to Phoenix after this semester. When I ask her to please keep in touch, I hope that she doesn't.

After walking back to the dorm, I dump my backpack on the bed and hit the shower again. Washing myself from head to toe, I shave my legs until they're soft and smooth. Back in my room, after locating sexy underwear and a matching bra, I slip into a light-weight robe and saunter down the hall to Noah's room. His door is open, and he's lounging on his bed reading a book.

"Hi, handsome." I smile suggestively from the doorway and ask, "You busy?"

He marks his place in the book and tosses it to the floor. "Not for you."

I shut and lock the door behind me. By the time I reach his bed, I've left him only the sexy undergarments to remove. Yeah, sure, I'm using him—but this *situation* is a win-win.

* * *

I keep working my ass off—classes, papers, appointments with my shrink talking about my feelings and my progress. And, yes, I discuss Tanner with Dr. Anderson. She quizzes me long and hard about my stupid feelings for that gorgeous man, and I invest way too much time working and reworking my *Getting Back Together* list of pros and cons.

Tanner keeps our Rec Center appointments, but our interactions are no longer playful and light-hearted. He's all business in the gym, and that hurts even more. I wonder if I'll always regret not taking advantage of that morning on the mat.

I thought it might help the *situation* if I share that I've been seeing someone.

"Why didn't you say anything to me? Too weird?" he asks.

"It didn't seem fair to tell you I'm getting it regularly while you're waiting for marriage. I mean, that's not considerate behavior, is it?"

I jest while adjusting the weight pin on the Lat Pull Down machine for him.

"Is it serious?"

"No. I can't handle serious, remember? He's a cute boy from my dorm. No big deal. I'll probably never see him again after I move."

"A cute *boy*?"

"He's kind of young—a sophomore. Nineteen," I admit. Attempting levity, normalcy, I grin, "But he was willing to learn."

Tanner laughs in my face which makes me feel so much better. "Well, at least he's legal."

I give him the stink eye, but I don't care. "Whatever. It's only three years, which seems like a lot now but it wouldn't if we were, like, in our forties—which is ancient and depressing to think about. Noah is really sweet, and he doesn't smoke crack."

"That's definitely an upgrade."

Telling Tanner about Noah is the most normal conversation we've had in weeks.

* * *

Late on a Friday afternoon just two weeks out from graduation, I visit the compound to retrieve my size 14/16 boxes. I root around in the storage room in the massive barn making stilted small talk with Tyler. I know he can't stand me, but, since I interrupted him working in the barn, he's cordial and offered to help me move boxes around.

"I got it from here, Dude." Tanner makes his presence known.

Jumping at the sound of his voice, I wanted to be in and out of here before he got home. Too bad for me, my timing was off.

"Nice to see you again, Amanda," Tyler says, although there's no possible way he means it. On his way out of the storage room he pointedly tells Tanner, "Lorraine should be home any minute."

Tanner nods and waits for Tyler to leave before looking at me. "Last full week of classes, yeah?"

"Yup."

"I wanna see you get your diploma so I know it's for real."

"Funny guy. You and, um, Lorraine are invited to dinner two weeks from tonight. My parents are taking me out to celebrate. I'm not going to the actual ceremony, but if you're around on Saturday, you can help Dad and me load up my furniture."

His eyes quiz mine. "Why aren't you walking for graduation?"

"Why should I? I'll take my diploma and run off to stupid Tempe before they change their minds. That's good enough for me."

He laughs, but it doesn't reach his eyes. "We need to talk."

"About?"

"Us."

An exhale escapes my lips. "What about *us*?"

"I've been thinking..."

I fake a smile. "Oh, I wish you wouldn't do that."

"Before I let you go, I have to know something."

My head shakes slowly although he hasn't told me anything yet. "No, Tanner."

He closes the door to the storage room turning us into muted shadows. "Yes, Amanda."

There's nowhere for me to maneuver as he makes his approach. Heart pounding, emotions raw, senses tingling like a numb limb coming back to life, when he palms the side of my face I feel the tears escape my eyes.

"You're crying."

"Yes," I whisper in the dim light.

"Why?"

"In case you haven't noticed, I cry a lot."

He cracks a smile before cupping my chin in his hand. "Hard to miss, Panda."

"Don't touch me. Please."

"Why?" he brings his face closer still.

"I love you."

He places a kiss on my forehead. "I love you, too."

My arms instinctively wrap around his waist. "I will *never* be able to undo what I did to you."

His arms wrap around my shoulders; my head rests against his beating heart. "I forgave you."

I remind him, "You said that we can't go back in time."

His lips drop to my face, dotting my skin with tiny kisses and love. "We can't, but we can go forward—have something better."

On spontaneous reflex, our hands explore familiar terrain, moving up and down each other's torsos. Crossing the line and breaking all the rules of *just friends*, our lips meet and we lose control. As we share hot and deep kisses in the darkness, I never want to stop. But the voices in my head—they won't shut up. They want me to stop.

Why are you torturing yourself like this, Amanda? Yes, you love him, but this isn't what's best for Tanner. Or you. Not really.

He speaks against my lips. "Stay here. Have a future with me."

Everything I hold inside—guilt, regret, fear—releases like a compromised dam when I start sobbing on his t-shirt. Time seems to stop as I try to purge these feelings in his arms.

The game clock resumes its countdown when I realize that I'll never be able to forgive myself for what I did to him. I finally utter a word in the dark room. "Lorraine."

"This is about you and me, Panda. You tell me there's a chance, I'll handle the rest. I promise—you won't regret staying."

Resting my head on his shoulder, I give him my best effort at the truth. "I want to say yes, but I can't."

"Why?"

Before answering, my lips touch the skin of his neck. Kissing him tenderly several times before moving along his jawbone, I seek his lips again. Groaning, he pulls me closer and we give in to this kiss, to our love.

Finally, I tear my lips away from his and try to explain. "I haven't forgiven myself. I have a lot of growing up—and healing—to do. I don't trust myself to make good decisions right now—except, maybe, where you're concerned."

Sniffling, I continue speaking my truth, "I have no idea when I'll be ready to get married, and, *god*, you'd have to be insane to trust someone like me with small children."

He smiles at me, but he shouldn't. I'm not joking. "We can slow this down. Nothing needs to happen tomorrow. Just stay and be with me. Please."

"I love you too much to risk letting you down again."

"So you're gonna walk away, Panda?"

I look up at his gorgeous face. "Don't you get it? I have to walk away. The thought of losing you again is more than I can bear."

"You're not making sense. If you don't stay, you're losing me—you're leaving me."

"God, Tanner, don't be stupid." And I have to laugh because I've said these words to him so many times in exactly the same tone since the third grade. "Think about how horrible it was when we didn't talk for all those months. For me, it was like missing a limb."

"Me too," he confirms quietly.

"I can't let you gamble your future on a woman like me."

"I always pictured my future with you."

"Say it out loud. Tell me what you want in the future."

He sighs. "You already know this. Finish med school, get married, start a family, complete my residency, and go into practice. I wanna give my kids the life I never had—except where your parents stepped in and helped me along. They still do."

"They're your parents, too, Tanner. No matter what happens with us, we've *chosen* to be family. Family by choice, buddy. My parents love you like a son."

He squeezes me tight and my head rests against his heart once again. "I know. Thank you for saying that, though."

"If we start over and I let you down... What then, Tanner?"

He mutters, "You'll break my heart—again."

Wow, that hurts—but it's exactly my point. "We'll lose the best parts of each other. Who makes more sense for the future you want—Lorraine or me?"

"You're part of me. I'm willing to take the chance on us."

"I'm not ready, but you are... That's kind of the story of us in a nutshell, don't you think?" I look up at him and laugh inwardly followed by a sniffle. "You're steady, I'm unpredictable. You're confident, I'm full of self-doubt. You're ready to be a husband and a father, and I'm clueless—and the sound of screaming children makes me want to slit my wrists."

"Too soon," he reminds me.

"I thought about killing myself," I whisper. "I went so dark that... No, Tanner. I'm not the right woman for you."

We stand there in each other's arms in silence except for the muted sounds of horses on the other side of the door. It's time to end this conversation and move forward. "As long as we live, Tanner, we'll hold pieces of each other's hearts, and this way we'll always have our friendship and each other." I choke back more tears and say, "If I had only one friend left, I'd want it to be you."

"Prom night," he whispers.

"Junior or senior?" I poke him in the ribs and he laughs.

"It didn't suck, Panda."

"No. It didn't suck."

"If you walk away from us, I'll marry her," he says.

It isn't meant as a threat. It's simply his truth, and I let that hang in the air between us while I think this through one last time.

I respond slowly, "I know. When you and Lorraine decide to get married—if she survives the wedding night—" Tanner interrupts with laughter. "I'm not kidding. Do *not* slam it up in there. And I hope—I know—that you're going to have a good life with a woman like her."

"I hate this."

"Me too, Tanner."

"We're going to be okay, you and me, right?"

"Yes, we are." I loop my arms around his neck and pull his face close to mine. I steal another kiss from his gorgeous mouth before promising, "If you *ever* need me, which you probably won't because you've got your whole act together... but if you do, I'll drop everything and be there for you."

"So that's it?" He releases me and steps away. "You're moving to the Valley. I'm gonna settle down with Lorraine and try not to feel guilty that I just asked you to try again."

"It'll be easier when I'm gone."

"Doesn't change the fact that I put you first."

"Maybe in this moment, but once you build a life with her, she'll always come first. And if you think for one second that the idea of that is easy for me, well, you're crazier than I am."

"That's a scary thought," he attempts humor. "You wanna try and fake *just friends* over dinner with your parents, my girlfriend, and your boy toy?"

Yeah, that makes me laugh. "We have to get used to *just friends*, Tanner, because I don't plan on ever losing your friendship again."

He clears his throat. "How many boxes?"

"Five."

"Let's get to it." Tanner steps away to open the door. When the daylight floods in, I take in his face like I've never seen him before. "Why are you staring at me?"

"Because I want to remember you."

He chuckles. "You just said I'd always be in your life."

"You will, but it'll be different."

"Honey," her voice rings out.

"Right here," Tanner calls back.

We put even more physical distance between us before Lorraine appears in the doorway. Looking from his face to mine she says quietly, "Tyler said you two were out here." I wonder what's going through her head as she takes us both in—my face streaked with tears and our matching brown eyes that give away every emotion.

"Just need to help Panda get some boxes to her truck," Tanner tells her. "Won't take but a few minutes, babe."

That *babe* is a slap in the face because, for all my bravado, I just gave that *babe* to Lorraine—likely for the rest of her life. As much as I know it's the right thing to do, I fucking hate it.

CHAPTER 15

Commencement—May 1995

IT ALL CAME TOGETHER IN the end. I finished with four A's, one B, and two C's. As the saying goes, C's get degrees, and now I have one. Nope, there is no magna cum laude or anything special about mine, but it's done, and my huge sense of accomplishment makes it special to me.

I called Lorraine a few days after my conversation with Tanner in the barn, and personally invited the two of them out to dinner with my parents and Noah. I made sure to mention that my parents think of Tanner as one of their own children, and Mom really wants to meet the love of Tanner's life. I almost choked on those words.

Before my parents picked up Noah and me outside the dorm, I slipped on a pair of heels and Noah surprised me with a red and white corsage that he pinned to my dress while he copped a feel and stole a few kisses. *I'm such a good coach.* It was the perfect color-coordinated accessory for any Arizona Wildcat.

While initially awkward, our dinner out is mostly festive and cheerful. Lorraine looks beautiful in her little black dress with a bit of makeup. My sundress is blue with a flattering cut. We order drinks and a few appetizers, and Dad requests a round of champagne for the table. Thank goodness the waiter doesn't check IDs because one of us should not be served. Tanner, though, he can't resist. His eyes dance before he throws it out there, "Hey, Noah, you gonna break the law and drink that champagne?"

"Tanner—" I warn.

He shrugs with a playful wink in my direction. "What? Just looking out for the kid."

"What's this about?" Dad asks.

"Noah isn't twenty-one yet, Daddy, and Tanner thinks he's funny."

"I am funny," Tanner retorts. My eyes roll at him—spontaneous reflex.

Dad smiles. "Oh, well, I didn't hear that. Besides, it's a night for celebration."

Yes, it is.

When our champagne arrives, Dad asks for quiet and makes a toast. "Brown Eyes, we weren't sure this day would ever come." Everyone laughs—even me. "But five years later—not that we were counting—here you are with a diploma that is yours to keep forever. The word Commencement stands for the beginning or dawning of a new time in your life. And so, in honor of your accomplishments and our Irish heritage, your mother and I are sending you off into the world with a traditional Irish Blessing... *May the road rise to meet you, may the wind always be at your back, may the sun shine warm upon your face, and may the rains fall softly upon your favorite football fields turning them lush and green and ready for game day."*

We crack up at Dad's modification of the last line and bring our glasses together over the center of the table. "Now, of course," Dad continues, "we're not sending you off into the world with just an Irish Blessing. We're not really sending you off into the world at all because you're moving even closer to home. You have ninety days before the Bank of Dad closes its doors, and your mother and I got you a gift." He slides a small box across the table.

"You didn't have to do that. You've already done so much."

"We know," Mom chimes in with a rare and funny quip.

I open the box and find a delicate gold chain with a beautiful charm inside. It looks familiar but I'm not sure. "Is this a Celtic Trinity Knot?"

"Yes." Mom's smile is big. "I know you aren't very religious, but the trinity knot has different meanings depending on what you believe in. In the religious sense, Catholics see it as a representation of the Father, the Son, and the Holy Spirit. When given as a graduation gift, it traditionally represents Past, Future, and Present. *Do not cry over your Past because you cannot change it. Do not fear your Future because it hasn't happened yet. Live in the Present and make it beautiful."*

I choke up. *How can I not?* Jumping from my seat, I hug Mom. Sure, sometimes she passes along faulty information, but this time she's right on target. She said exactly what I needed to hear tonight. "Thank you," I whisper in her ear. "I love you so much."

"I love you, too, Amanda. I'm very proud of you."

With eyes full of happy tears, I approach Dad who stands for his hug. "I love you, Daddy. Your arms are the safest place in the whole world—except for that one time when you used them to shove me onto an airplane. I still haven't forgotten about that."

He kisses my forehead. "My beautiful baby girl, you are so much like me it's scary."

I wisecrack, "Yeah, you should be scared now that you know what I'm capable of when I'm not medicated." *You don't know the half of it, Daddy. I'm too ashamed to tell you.*

* * *

The following day, after my dorm room is cleared out and I kiss Noah goodbye, Dad and I stop by U-Haul to hitch a trailer to Cherry and drive to the compound for my furniture. Lorraine's mom serves us sandwiches, and before we drive to Tempe, Tanner asks me for a few minutes alone.

We step into his guesthouse and a shiver runs through me thinking about the last time we were in this room together and the harsh words he had for me after what I'd done.

"Thought a lot about what you said, Panda."

"I hope you didn't think too hard."

He laughs in my face before sobering. "You were right."

"Oh... Say that again, please," I tease.

"You were right," he repeats with that grin I love so much. "Call me when you're settled. Keep your shit straight up there with Katie."

I mock salute. "Yes, Sir."

"Before you leave I want one last thing from you."

"Anything."

He touches his hand to my chin and lifts my face up to his. His trademark grin and those eyes—god, they are deep pools of chocolate and everything that is good in this world. These eyes love me, laugh with me, and turn black with anger and desire. I could drown in them, but instead I return his grin until he says, "I want one last kiss."

"What?"

His arms tighten around me, and spontaneous reflex dictates that mine hold him. "You heard me. One last kiss—better than the first time."

We kiss and it sucks—which it won't—we laugh it off and go on. It doesn't suck—we do it again. Have our whole lives ahead of us.

If it makes me selfish to do this, I don't care. I gave Lorraine a shot at an incredible future, and this will never happen again. "One last kiss," I whisper my consent.

He locks my head into place with one hand and the other hand drops to my ass so he can command full body contact and control the *situation*. With a level of intimacy that only exists between lovers, we tilt our heads, mouths parting the second our lips met. Our mouths give and take, tongues tangle and mate, and our bodies press together like they are meant to be one. But they aren't.

We kiss like our diplomas depend on it, only they don't. It is way better than our first kiss, and it so far from sucks it takes us way too long to stop. When it ends, it's over way too soon.

Deep in Sun Devil Territory

The townhouse in Tempe was built in the 1970s, but it's in decent condition and far roomier than our apartment at The Hollows. We have two stories with the living room, kitchen/dining area, and half bath on the main floor. Upstairs, Katie has the master suite for an extra contribution of rent. I move into a smaller bedroom with a shared bath that I don't have to share because it's just the two of us, and we use the third bedroom for our computers and extra storage.

We settle right back into our friendship and roommate ways, only this time around I'm not broken-hearted and high all the time, so I shower every day, do my laundry, and wear clean clothes. Yeah, it's funny *now* when Katie teases me about how low I sank right after losing Tanner, but, it's only funny because Katie doesn't know the half of it, and I feel relatively stable despite all the recent life changes. Plus, she knows my currency—ice cold Diet Pepsi.

Katie works an entry-accounting job for the City of Tempe, and her boyfriend Nathan, a fellow Wildcat just a few years older than us, works in information technology. He spends a few nights a week at our place, and she stays several nights at his place so I have alone time. Nathan's a good guy—easy-going, quick with a comeback, and he likes to cook. I don't mind having him around at all.

Age: Twenty-three

It takes about six weeks of job searching before I land a receptionist gig through a staffing agency at a healthcare company that delivers home health supplies to homebound patients. I start just before my twenty-third birthday. I still have no idea what I want to be when I grow up, but at least the job gets me off of Dad's payroll and, except for my health insurance and car insurance (I'm still on the family plans), he closes the Bank of Dad. It's a satisfying milestone for both of us. We celebrate the new job over dinner, but, of course, I let him pay.

My job is just a few miles away—Monday through Friday, 8:30 a.m. to 5:00 p.m. with thirty minutes for lunch. I'm not saving lives, but I'm starting mine. I don't meet our patients face-to-face, but they sure do call a lot. The phones ring constantly.

I answer cheerfully, park calls, bark out call holding warnings over the intercom for different staff members, and when the calls ring back to the switchboard after three minutes on hold, I take messages on two-part forms and place them in a spinning wheel on the counter of my desk. I'm tied to the phones and have to ask the General Manager's Administrative Assistant, Kelli, for permission to use the bathroom so she can cover for me.

It's not a glamorous life by any stretch of the imagination, but after ninety days working for them via the staffing agency, the company offers me a full-time position with medical benefits. I gratefully accept and Mom drops me from the school's health insurance plan.

I'm making work friends. We have about eighty people in our branch office, and plenty of twenty-somethings work here in various jobs—pharmacy assistants, patient care reps, delivery drivers, warehouse workers. I fall "in like" with Philip, a cute Hispanic guy in the warehouse. He's too short for me so it's nothing romantic, but he makes me laugh, and he's the first to roll out the welcome mat by including me in happy hours at a nearby dive bar.

I also become unlikely friends with our marketing director, Patrick. He stops by my desk late afternoon on a Friday and asks, "Do you babysit, Amanda?"

"Um, not since I was about thirteen, but I could probably handle it."

"Tonight? After work? Please say yes. Please. I'm in a bind, and my wife might divorce me if I don't get her out of the house."

"Sure." I have no plans, so why not?

* * *

Why not? I should have asked a few more questions before deciding to do this. I follow him to his house after work and walk into utter chaos. Patrick and his wife Caroline have FIVE children under the age of eight. Number SIX is in the womb. The house is a large rambler on the Scottsdale/Tempe/Phoenix boarder in a well-established neighborhood. The inside is a wreck—dirty dishes, scattered toys, and piles of laundry—oh, and children. Everywhere.

So relieved to have dinner and movie night out with Patrick, Caroline throws her arms around me when Patrick introduces us. She sticks a gooey baby in my arms, gives me a quick tour of the house, and points out a list of cell phone and pager numbers by the phone. She races for her bedroom followed by several children to change into some clothes that aren't stained with baby juices. Patrick and Caroline ditch me soon after, promising to return around midnight.

I take stock of the *situation* and quickly realize I'm well out of my comfort zone. The kids are running the asylum, so I round them up and ask them to take turns picking their favorite games to play. We do that while I try to memorize their names. Mackenzie, the eldest at age eight, becomes my ally. She's like a miniature mother and knows how things go down in the house.

Patrick and Caroline left money to fly in a pizza delivery, and Mackenzie helps me change diapers, find plates, and reminds me to lock the baby gates behind me. Eventually, I settle them all in front of the TV, rocking the littlest, Vanessa, in my arms until she falls asleep and I place her in the crib inside the master bedroom. The children remind me of a litter of kittens. They're curled up, piled on top of each other. Some are asleep, some still watching the movie, but they're relatively stationary, so I pick up the scattered toys and go into the kitchen to scrub it clean. I load the dishwasher and do several rounds by hand, wiping them dry and setting them aside on the clean countertop. I locate the washer/dryer in a hallway, and get a load going.

Sinking back on the sofa in exhaustion, I take a moment to give thanks that I'll never have this many children of my own—ever. I don't know how Caroline does it day in and day out. When they return home just after midnight, the children are now passed out on the living room floor. I just left them in heap, but Caroline beams when she sees the tidied living room and clean kitchen. They pay me $100 for the evening and ask me to come back next Friday night.

* * *

Tanner and I share occasional phone calls. During one very tough call he breaks the news that he asked Lorraine to be his wife and, of course, she said yes. Hell yes, I broke down after that conversation, but I kept it together while we were talking. I tried—I did—to wish him well and mean it.

As the months roll by following the engagement, I often find myself at the intersection of *What If* and *If Only*. I'm still in love with Tanner and have so many regrets, but I love him enough to keep these thoughts to myself.

He does laugh his ass off when I tell him about my recurring babysitting gig taking care of Patrick and Carole's now *SIX* children. "Tanner, I swear, this is the best reality check, because if I had to be responsible for that chaos every single day, I would blow my head off. No joke. I'm not cut out to raise a litter of children. It's also the best form of birth control. There is no way in hell I'm getting knocked up before I'm good and ready."

Not that I'm in any danger of getting knocked up. I haven't been with anyone since sweet Noah, but Tanner doesn't need to know about my dry spell. He's still having a long one himself.

In the meantime, I spend plenty of time with Jenny and her boyfriend Paul, whom I adore. They live together about thirty minutes away just north of downtown Phoenix. God, I hope she marries this one because he balances out her crazy.

Jenny finished an Associate's degree a while back, and she works full-time doing insurance billing for a physician's office. She hates every second of it and lives for the proverbial end of day whistle. Paul, an ASU grad, is five years older than us and works with his father running an established (meaning they have a ton of clients) financial planning/accounting firm in Phoenix. Paul talks to me right away about putting money into my company's 401K plan. "Every penny you save at this age will be there times five when you reach the age of retirement," he preaches. "Start saving young. I promise you won't regret it." I take the Sun Devil's advice.

CHAPTER 16

Age: Twenty-four

AFTER A YEAR ON THE job, the GM's assistant resigns from her job, and I'm asked to step into her role and train a new receptionist. I still have no idea what I want to be when I grow up, but I get a fairly decent raise with the new responsibilities.

I have new friends, Katie and I are getting along perfectly as roomies, I grow closer to Patrick, Caroline, and their children, and I talk to and see my parents often. But I have no love life to speak of, and it's getting a little lonely out there. Late evening after a day of work in August, it gets even lonelier.

My parents call to say that they received our invitation to Tanner's wedding in the mail. The big day is December 15, 1996. Of course, the invitation came addressed to our entire family, but there is no possible way I can sit there and watch Tanner pledge his love and fidelity to Lorraine.

"RSVP for yourselves. I'm not going," I tell them.

Dad starts, "After everything you've been through together over the years you—"

"Because of everything we've been through, I have no business being there, Daddy. He included me to be polite."

"He included you because you're his friend," Mom pipes in over the speaker phone.

"I'm not going. I can't handle it. Please, just accept my decision, and I really have to go. I'll call you later." I hang up and the walls cave in.

Fuck, it's really happening and, fuck, it hurts. Katie isn't home, so I drive to the dive bar in search of work friends. I find Philip, Carlos, and Justin—*thank god*. I need sympathy and a drink. One drink turns into six because I need a lot of sympathy. They keep me plied with whiskey while I cry out my *woe is me* tale. Shit-faced drunk, I leave Cherry at the bar and Philip drives me home.

When I walk in the back door of our townhouse, I throw myself on the couch and burst into fresh tears. I sob all over Katie's shoulder as poor Nathan wisely takes his leave. After he's gone, I curl up on the couch with my head on Katie's thigh, and she strokes my hair while I wail pathetic things like: *I know he wasn't the one, so why does this hurt so fucking much? I shouldn't have told him that I cheated. He has the biggest cock I've ever seen. What have I done?*

I blubber incessantly until Katie breaks out the bong to calm me down. It's been so long—what's the harm? A little hit (or five) does the trick. By hit three, my brain quiets, and I don't feel as distraught.

A few minutes later, I feel nothing... sweet nothing. I've missed nothing. But I promise myself then and there that I will only smoke once a week. Saturdays might be a good night, and Saturday is just two days away. I won't slip into that dark place again.

* * *

The months between the invitation and the wedding pass by. I'm working on a project at work—making sure the personnel files are 100% perfect for an upcoming JCAHO audit. It's an accreditation process that's critical to healthcare companies. Getting all the required documentation in place and catalogued is like herding cats. There are dozens of conference calls with Craig, myself, and our HR contact at the corporate office in Seattle, Camille.

Camille sounds like a nice person. I have to interact with her every time we have a new hire or termination, and I become more curious about her job. There isn't a position like Camille's available for me at a branch location, but she's willing to share her knowledge and give me some extra responsibilities at the branch.

And when someone complains to the Director of Nursing that one of the guys in the warehouse is making sexual comments, I find myself helping Camille out with this process called an investigation. I enjoy the fact finding—the he said, she said, so and so might have overheard what was said. After gathering all the information, Camille asks me to refer to the company's policy on anti-harassment.

"What do you think, Amanda? Did Carlos violate the company policy by saying these things in front of Barbara?"

"No."

"Interesting take. Why not?"

"I mean, he shouldn't have said those things out loud at work, but he wasn't saying them to her. If nothing else, Carlos should be reminded that this is a place of business, not a locker room, and apologize for offending her. And Barbara should've told these guys to shut it down before she took it up the food chain. These aren't bad guys, Camille. If Barbara had simply told Carlos to watch his mouth, he would have, and all of this could've been avoided."

"That's exactly what I think," Camille affirms. I'm thrilled. My interest is beyond piqued. I have an idea about what I want to be when I grow up.

Territorial Cup—1996

ASU kicks our asses 56 to 14. I don't know why Arizona bothered dressing out, much less hitting the field. I've delayed the game clock on another *situation* for several months. I call Tanner shortly after the game.

"Hey, Panda. What a shit-fest today, right?"

"I can't decide if I'm more disgusted or embarrassed. I'll go with both right now. I have to drive around this stupid city with U of A license plates on my truck. Usually, I just get flipped off. Now they're going to point and laugh. I think that's worse, don't you?"

Tanner laughs. "Oh yeah, I'd rather be flipped off, but we deserve to be laughed at after that disaster."

"So, um, the actual reason I called is to tell you that I hope your wedding day is amazing. I wish I could be there, but—"

"You're not coming?"

"Um... can we not make this a deep and heavy conversation?"

"Say what you need to say."

"My parents are coming, of course, but I can't."

"Can't or won't?"

"Both. I wish you all the happiness in the world."

He sighs heavily and cuts me some slack. "I understand."

"Thank you. Take care of yourself."

"You, too."

"Bye, Tanner." I disconnect the call and head for our pantry where we keep our bong because some things never change. And, besides, it's Saturday, which is probably why I picked today to make this call. It is also how I plan to spend Tanner's wedding day—even though it's on Sunday.

* * *

Kicking off the New Year, I have one goal in mind. My dry spell is approaching twenty months. I haven't gone this long without action on my field since there was action on my field. I miss rolling around. I am practically dying to roll around. To that end, I'm going to a house party with Katie and Nathan where I'm assured that I may find several viable options.

After tricking out my dark mane of hair, which falls way below my shoulder blades but is usually in a ponytail or a sloppy updo, I apply dramatic makeup and select a red dress that shows some skin. Nixing heels, I opt for flats because if he—whoever *he* might be—is attractive enough, five foot eleven will do. Besides, when you're horizontal it doesn't really matter.

When we arrive at a huge stucco house on a man-made lake in the city of Gilbert around 10:30 p.m., the party is in full swing.

The house is packed and this isn't my scene at all—too loud, too crowded, too many strangers. It reminds me of an adult frat party in the boonies because the freeway hasn't even been built out this far. Instantly, I want to go home, but Katie is determined. She brings me liquid courage and helps scan the crowd for viable options.

"Oh, that one," Katie points—*freaking points*—at some dude.

"Um... could you stop pointing? God, you suck at this. How did you manage to get laid so much in college?" I grumble.

"I'm hot."

I agree, "This is true."

"What? You don't think he's cute?"

"I think you should stop pointing. Or is that how it works in Adult Land? I point at a guy, crook my finger, and he falls at my feet?"

Katie grins at me. "Maybe... You want to try that out?"

Braden crooked his index finger at me, "Come here—I'll keep you warm." I was fifteen years old when he crooked that finger at me and, hell, I fell at his feet. I crack up laughing and share the memory with Katie. "So maybe it does work. How did you meet Nathan anyway?"

"He picked me up at a bar after work."

"Very classy," I tease. "Maybe you should dress that story up before you tell it to your children."

"Wait, I see a good one—and I know him. He works with Nathan. This is perfect..."

"Don't point; describe him to me." I follow her eyes but discover that she doesn't need to use her words. "By the fire pit—dark hair, big shoulders, black shirt..."

"His name is Dave. Let's go say hi."

Katie helps break the ice. He's cute. He has a great smile, and he's absolutely my type—physically anyway. As we talk, Nathan approaches and brings us a fresh round. It's going well, and warmed by alcohol and the fire pit, I start to think *maybe*... We talk and drink and I make a few jokes, and eventually Katie and Nathan slip away to mingle.

Dave kisses me at midnight. He drives me home that night even though I already have a ride. Dave breaks my twenty-month dry spell, but he's a huge disappointment. Dave obviously didn't have a good coach in his early years. He gets his just fine, but I don't get mine. He doesn't even try to make that happen. There's no cuddling. He gets up, puts his clothes on, and tells me that he had a great time.

That makes one of us. Thanks for leaving your condom in my bed—there was a trash can in the bathroom. Don't worry about me, Dave. I'll finish myself off.

* * *

Changing up my game plan, I wonder why I didn't think of this before. Katie got picked up in bar and I go to a certain bar several times a week, but I'm usually surrounded by male coworkers. That doesn't exactly say *I'm single, come hit on me.*

Instead of sitting in our booth for a few hours, I slip away from my pack and linger at the bar making small talk with Adam, the dive bar's owner. He's a crusty sort with a full gray beard and tattoos everywhere. His Harley is always parked on the side of the building under the security camera so he can keep an eye on it from the monitor behind the bar.

I know what I like. I have a type. When I see a viable option, I smile and flirt a little, and, damn, this is easy. It's just a matter if *he* thinks I'm attractive, too. We exchange phone numbers, kisses in dark corners, and often more if the feelings are good enough.

With a renewed sense of energy after a few good experiences under my belt—pun intended, I mix casual flings into my work weeks when Katie is at Nathan's or over the weekends sometimes. Unfortunately, that means I'm spending more time drinking, and I start to feel it in the waistline of my clothes.

Catching myself, I change the play by joining a gym near the office. While I miss my favorite workout partner, I know my way around a gym. I get up early and work out, and moderate the alcohol and weed-induced munchies until I have control over my clothing *situation* again.

But what am I looking for as I approach the age of twenty-five? Love? Commitment? Happily ever after? Hell if I know. Not even the really good experiences—the ones with chemistry and laughter that seem like there could be more—none of these guys become more to me. There are weeks at a time where I'll see just one man and think maybe we're heading somewhere. I become hopeful, but when *he* stops calling—and *he* always stops calling—I don't chase after *him*. That's not my style.

I do wonder why *he* loses interest and drifts away. Am I not interesting enough, pretty enough, smart enough, or good enough? Did *he* find someone more interesting, prettier, smarter, better? Do I really care?

I've spent the majority of my young life in long-term relationships, and it's hard to comprehend why my door that once opened and shut now revolves in an endless circle of bullshit.

While thinking about the revolving door one evening in June, I pull out my journal and start a list of men who've passed through along the way. It starts out easy enough: Curt (the German Cherry Popper), Tanner (the One I Screwed Over), Luke (the Sigma Chi Mistake), Jason (the Crackhead), and, of course, Noah (the Rookie). In between Tanner and Noah there were three, or was it four, guys. I can only come up with two out of the three or four names. That's at least eight, possibly nine.

Since the twenty-month dry spell, I jot down six names, but that's not all. Those were just the guys that were memorable in one way or another. Then it gets scary hazy because it's all totally recent—two, three, no four—definitely four—others, so that's a total of eighteen... maybe nineteen. I think? I don't know. *What the fuck? How can I not know who I've slept with?*

This isn't something to be proud of; in fact, I feel more discouraged than I have in a very long time. *Stupid lists.* I could've been any woman—any vagina—and it all would've been the same to the vast majority of these guys.

I'm not alone in this world, but I am very lonely. Trying to fill the void in my heart with random penises isn't helping. I need to stop the madness before I end up with herpes and my phone number written on bathroom walls all across the metro area.

That reminds me, I need to schedule my annual checkup with the gynecologist and make sure I don't have anything horrible going on down there. It is time to slow my roll—or slow my rolling around.

CHAPTER 17

Age: Twenty-five

SHORTLY AFTER MY TWENTY-FIFTH BIRTHDAY, following an action-packed Friday night with my SIX children, Patrick—as he always does—walks me out to Cherry. As we often do, I drop the tailgate, and we take a seat and light up a cigarette before I drive home. Caroline hates the smoking, but she loves me, so she allows it. At this point in my life, Patrick, Caroline, and all of their children are an extension of family—*family by choice*.

This night on Cherry's tailgate, Patrick shares that he's leaving our company for a better position—large company, more responsibility, etc. He recently finished up an Executive MBA program at ASU, and he's ready for more.

We've talked about my interest in Human Resources as a

potential career path, and I'm actually going to start an MBA program myself, although not at ASU. It pains me to admit that I most likely lack the GPA requirement to get into ASU's business school. My GPA might matter after all. But that's all right—I have another viable option, and I'm ready to go.

After Patrick describes his new job at this Fortune 500 technology company in downtown Phoenix, he asks me to join him as his Executive Assistant.

"Are you serious?" I reply.

"Absolutely. I can offer a good bump in pay, full benefits, and I commit to you that after year one, I'll have done everything in my power to position you for a move into human resources—if that's what you still want to do. There are HR-liaison responsibilities in this role, so you'll get experience and exposure. Then you can hire your replacement," he laughs.

I release a stream of smoke into the hot desert night air. "Patrick, this sounds too good to be true."

"Did I mention they have a tuition assistance program?" He sweetens the pot, although it's completely unnecessary because his offer is a fork in the road. I'd be stupid not to take this job—especially with someone I respect and trust.

"I'm in," I tell him.

"I thought you'd have more questions for me."

"When do I start?"

* * *

I stopped sleeping around after the journal *situation*. It is important and helpful to make lists. Lists aid in the decision-making process.

For example, if you can't list all of the men you've screwed on your *Men I've Screwed* list, it's time to stop screwing around. See? Lists are totally helpful, and I feel much better after my Pap and blood work came back clear.

I do not, however, stop going to the dive bar. I like hanging with the warehouse boys, and I'm going to miss them when I hand in my resignation after the terms and conditions of the job offer at CompuWorld are finalized.

It's early September on a Wednesday evening, and the next round is on me. I slide out of our booth and head to the bar. "Be right with you, doll." The owner/bartender Adam has his hands full but jokes, "Keep your shirt on."

"Okay, Adam. I'll keep my skirt on while I'm at it."

"Feel free to change your mind any time," a deep voice rumbles in my right ear.

I turn my head, and *oh my god, where have you been since May of 1995? You are delicious.* At least six foot four, he's built out of muscles and testosterone with dark brown hair cut short, deep brown eyes with honey flecks, straight white teeth, chiseled features, and a nose that's probably been broken at least once to add rugged character. If it wouldn't be too obvious, I'd check out his ass right now because I'm positive it fills out those worn Levis perfectly.

My physical response to him is so intense that I have to take a moment before responding to him verbally. "You're at least going to have to take me out on a proper date first." *I want to bring you home with me right now.*

Grinning, he asks, "Is that all it takes?"

No. Just crook your finger and I'll fall at your feet. Grateful that today is an exceptional hair day, I slowly shake my head with the soft curls falling over my shoulders to signify that it's not that simple. "It takes more than that." *It absolutely does not, but you don't need to know that.*

He extends a hand. "My name is Shawn. You are?"

"Amanda." Taking his hand, I pray mine isn't sweaty because my hormones are on heightened alert.

Are you kidding me right now? Amanda, you racked up a list of nameless nobodies when a guy this freaking hot was out there in the world? It's fine to have a type, right? I mean, I prefer Diet Pepsi to Diet Coke. I more than prefer it—I don't drink Diet Coke, like ever.

"Amanda," Adam shouts out. "What'll it be?"

"Later, Adam," I call back without taking my eyes or hand off of Shawn. *I want to climb you, Shawn. I want you to drag me into a dark corner, shove me against the wall, and pop all the buttons off my blouse when you rip it off of me. I really love this blouse, but I could love you more.*

Eventually I have to look away because Adam has seen every play in my book since January. He knows this crowd, and he's warned me off more than one man with a nay gesture. My eyes find Adam's who is amused by my antics. Unfortunately, he offers me a shrug which means he doesn't know this guy at all.

"You must come here often. Bartender knows you by name." *That grin... your eyes... Shawn, please don't be an asshole. Can you give me that?*

"Is that a play on the *do you come here often* line?" I smile coyly, play with my hair, and try not to jump him.

"Uh..." *I rattled you, Shawn—you're blushing.* "I'm a little rusty with lines."

I offer an assist and nod my head in the direction of the booth. Philip is smirking at me. "I come here a few times a week, actually. I work up the street with that crew over there. You don't come here often." Deliberately scanning his handsome face, I raise the Flirtation Scale. "I'd definitely remember you."

He leans a hip against the bar. "Rare night out—spending it with the guys. I don't normally come to this side of town."

"What's your normal side of town?"

"Central Phoenix—streets, north of Glendale."

"Well, I'd personally like to thank ADOT for the 51 and Red Mountain Freeways."

He laughs. "Me too, babe." *You babe'd me, Shawn, and I love that.* He catches Adam's attention by raising his hand. "Are you running table service for your boys over there?"

"It's my round."

"What are we drinking?" Shawn asks as Adam approaches on the other side of the bar.

We both place orders and talk as we wait. Shawn's a police officer with the city of Phoenix and so are most of his hot friends in the booth next to ours. I make a mental note to tell Philip and Carlos to lay off the weed talk. I'm on weed sabbatical since the job offer from Patrick. I have to drug test in the next week or two, and Katie isn't allowed to say the word *weed* much less smoke it around me. Just to be safe, I had her remove it from the townhouse.

When the drinks arrive, Shawn pays for both of our rounds and helps me carry everything back to my table. He smiles down at me.

I love that you have to look down to smile at me. "I know it's not a proper date—yet, but can I pick you back up in about fifteen minutes for darts?"

You can pick me up for anything you want, Shawn. Just, please—pretty, pretty, pretty please—do not break my heart.

We play darts with our friends, cracking one-liners and picking out songs on the ancient jukebox, and we all laugh—a lot. My guys peel off around 9 p.m., leaving me with Shawn and three of his friends. Regretfully, I also need to get going. Tomorrow is both a work day and a school night, and I haven't finished my reading.

"Hey, I should probably head out too," I tell Shawn. *Please ask for my phone number so I can see you again.*

"Can you stay for a few more minutes?"

"Just a few because I have to hit the books before bed."

Eyes widening in shock while taking a step backward, he asks, "Wait, are you still in college? Christ. How old are you?"

"Easy, officer. I'm perfectly legal except when I intentionally choose to break law." *No joke—I'm giving you a heads up.* "I'm twenty-five. I started an MBA program at Thunderbird a few months ago."

"Damn," he whistles. "That's a hike from here."

"Isn't it? And don't even ask me why not ASU. I'm a card carrying Wildcat." He laughs at his understanding of that *situation*. I continue, "But it'll get easier soon. I'm starting a job in downtown Phoenix in a few weeks, so I can head up to class from downtown at least. I can't believe I live in Tempe. Did I mention that I hate ASU?"

"Think you covered that, babe." He grins at me. "What are my chances of walking out of here with your number?"

Yes!!! Yes!!! Yes!!!

Like a cool cat, I ask, "What are my chances you're going to use my number if I give it you?"

"I promise that I'll use it, and I'm a man of my word."

"We'll see." I pull my flip phone out of my purse. "What's your cell?" Typing in the numbers as he calls them out, I hit send. Within a few seconds, his pocket rings. "Now you have it."

"Smooth, Amanda. I see how you did that to get my number."

"Make no mistake; I won't call you first. That's not how this works."

"How does this work?"

"If you want to see me, you'll make an effort. If you don't, you don't." I finish with a casual shrug, but *I will die a little inside if you don't.*

Shawn keeps making small talk as he takes my elbow and guides me away from his friends toward the back of the bar. There are some dark corners in here—I know because I've spent time in all of them.

As soon as the song floods over the speakers, I know why he asked me to hang around. He picked this song out for me. Since 1986, I've had numerous men lip-sync these lyrics to me. Tanner, of course, all the freaking time, the players on the team bus in high school would bust it out over a boom box, it spilled out over the lake on a summer night and my friends would sing to me, and, occasionally a guy drops me line or two from the song thinking that he's clever.

This hot cop might be recycling a tired play, but his originality and execution are inspiring. "One dance before I walk you out?" He requests and reaches for my hand.

No one dances in this crappy bar, but tonight we're the exception. Sliding his arms around my waist, he pulls me flush and that makes me *flush*. I wrap my arms around his broad back and rest my head on his shoulder while he guides me in a dreamy clinch. During the second chorus, our lips meet. By the end, we're making out like there is no tomorrow because we can't wait another day.

Since 1986, I've never enjoyed *Amanda* by Boston more than I did tonight.

At the end of our dance, he walks me out to Cherry. I smile and wave at his grinning friends as we pass. In the parking lot, he takes the keys from my hand, unlocks, and opens the door for me. *You are such a gentleman. I want to keep you.*

Far more modestly than he did during our dance, he leans down and touches his lips to mine before I slide into the seat. He waits for me to put on my seatbelt before saying, "I didn't expect to meet a woman like you in bar like this. An unexpected pleasure, Amanda. I'll call you soon."

October 1997

I join CompuWorld and a few hundred thousand commuters heading from the East Valley to downtown Phoenix at the same time every Monday through Friday. The office sits right on Central Avenue, and I work on the eleventh floor. The environment is new—big, corporate, shit tons of *Directors of This* and *VPs of That*, but the responsibilities aren't new. I pick things up quickly and, of course, Patrick and I work very well together. He is more *friend* than *boss*, and I plan to keep it that way.

In the midst of all these changes on Monday afternoon during my third week at CompuWorld, Jenny drops a bomb on me. I pick up my line and she launches right in. "Here's the deal, I'm a little bit pregnant, and don't interrupt me, Amanda, because, no, it wasn't planned and, yes, I know how birth control works. But it's all good because we're in love, and I don't have time for a bunch of questions or one of your lectures right now." She pauses to take a breath and I remain silent.

"We're getting married two weeks from next Saturday at Paul's parents' house off of 44th and Camelback. It is freaking amazing, by the way. Their backyard is huge, and it's going to be beautiful. Anyway, I need you swing by the bridal shop with me after work on Wednesday to have a fitting for your maid of honor dress. No bridesmaids—it's just you and me up there. Well, and Paul and his brother—and a minister. I already picked out your dress, but it's probably going to need a few nips and tucks because it's off the rack and maybe a size too big. I'm not sure. Oh, and I need to invite your parents. Remind me to do that. I hope they can make it." She stops talking. I'm still speechless. "Well, Amanda?"

"Well what? Which part of this conversation are you *welling* me about?"

She sighs as if I'm supposed to know the answer. "Can you meet me after work on Wednesday at five-thirty?"

"Where's the bridal shop?"

"Near the Biltmore. I'll email you the address."

"I'll be there."

"Great—I'll see you then."

"Wait—Jenny?"

"Yes?"

"Congratulations. I'm honored that you want me beside you on your wedding day. Don't forget to call my parents."

"We've only been talking about this since the first grade, so who else would be by my side, genius?" The phone clicks in my ear and our conversation is over. I hang up the receiver and stare at the phone.

Did that just happen? I hope she remembers to call my parents.

* * *

Shawn, as it turns out, is not an asshole. He called as promised, and we're making progress. Shawn claims that he hasn't hit on a woman in a bar since he met his ex-wife back in college at Northern Arizona University in Flagstaff, but he couldn't resist making a play when the door was wide open—what with the whole keeping my shirt and skirt on... or not.

Everyone has a painful past. Unfortunately, Shawn is still reeling from his. He's thirty-six, and after twelve years of marriage and three children, he caught his wife in the act with one of his brothers in blue when he stopped by his house during the middle of a shift.

Obviously, she wasn't expecting him. From the sound of it, the fact that his kids were in the house at the time prevented Shawn from committing homicide. Their divorce was finalized on the very day we met. His friends insisted on taking him out to celebrate, and he found me.

We talk on the phone several times a week, and, between the distance of our homes and our very busy schedules, we've managed to see each other four times. *Yes, I'm counting.* After the third date he took me in my bed. No, I didn't say that he took me to bed—he actually *took me in my bed*. Shawn is an assertive and attentive lover whose prior coach deserves a trophy, even if she did cheat on him.

An insanely amazing kisser. I could do that for hours, but there are better ways to spend our time together. His hands—*god his hands*... And his body—*god his body*... I came undone before, during, and after. Speaking of after, he promptly disposed of his own condom in the bathroom and returned to my bed where we cuddled, talked, and laughed until we fell asleep. Demanding and forceful during the act, but tender in the afterglow.

I feel myself falling—definitely infatuated, bordering on doodling *Amanda Barton* all over the pages of my journal and drawing hearts around it, high school *Mandy McLaughlin* style. Holding back, I try to play it cool because he *is not ready for anything serious* and he *wants to take things slow* because he *didn't think he would meet anyone so quickly*. If he disappears into the wind tomorrow without a word, it will cause me to wallow in self-pity for months.

Between my job, school, and Jenny's wedding, I don't have time to wallow, or babysit for Patrick and Caroline. *I will not fall in love with an emotionally unavailable man. I will not fall in love. I will not fall in love.* I need other options—more than just Shawn so I don't lose my heart.

CHAPTER 18

CompuWorld relies heavily on America Online for instant messaging. It's something I've never used before, but I sign up with a screen name befitting a Wildcat and add colleagues to an ever-growing list of contacts. IM is quicker than making phone calls or sending an email, but it's also a distraction.

I discover that inside of AOL there are these things called chat rooms. Chat rooms can be about any topic under the sun and most are public. I can pop in and out at different times during the day and converse with strangers all over the place. Apparently, I'm late to this AOL party. It's been around for years, and I've been missing out.

Sure, I should probably spend more time working, but my day job isn't complicated. Patrick travels a lot. I coordinate his travel arrangements and meeting calendar, stop people from barging into his office when he's around, fill out his expense reports, shuffle and file paperwork, forge his signature at his request, answer his phone, and screen his work emails. Easy. And I'm glad it's easy because I can surf the web and work on school projects all while making a very decent living.

In the meantime, this whole AOL thing opens up an opportunity to enter chat groups for people of a certain age in and around the metro area. If someone seems interesting, it's easy to break off into a private messaging session, have more in-depth 'conversations', and wonder who is really behind the screen name.

I haven't met anyone in person yet, but I'm considering a few options because I need to get Shawn off the brain.

October 18, 1997—Jenny & Paul's Wedding

The backyard of Paul's parents' home makes an elegant venue. I can't believe everything came together considering the tight time-frame. Jenny picked out a flattering gown for me—black satin with a navy velvet empire waist bodice. I love it, but I will probably never wear it again. She, of course, looks incredible and not one day pregnant, but she's just eight weeks along.

My parents are able to attend, and Mom loses it just a little bit as she snaps a few photos of the two of us together before the ceremony. She sniffles, "It seems like yesterday you were just little girls, and now look at you two—beautiful young women and still by each other's sides." When Mom glances down to adjust the camera, Jenny and I use the opportunity to roll our eyes at each other because some things never change.

But other things do change. As I listen to Jenny and Paul pledge their lives to one another in front of their families and closest friends, I think of that graduation photo of the four of us—Jenny, Braden, Tanner, and me—at Pine Ridge High School and the once connected pieces of the Berlin Wall that we each have. I wonder if those four pieces will ever fit back together again.

"Braden, you obviously understand that we have pieces of history that fit together. And I think it is a perfect metaphor for—a symbol of—our friendship. Even though we're going off to separate places again soon, when we come back together, I hope that we will always fit."

He reached for my hand across the table, squeezed it, and then used both of his hands to cradle mine and play with my fingers. "Thank you for the gift and the sentiment. So sweet, Mandy."

I always wanted to fit back together with each of them, and no single bond made another any less meaningful.

The thought is ridiculous. Braden hasn't spoken to me in almost seven years, he's married to the pig farmer's daughter, and it's quite possible that they have children by now. Tanner found Lorraine, and six kids are in his future plans. Now Jenny has Paul with their first child growing strong and healthy inside of her at this very moment.

The common denominator in the photo is me. The pieces of the Berlin Wall came from me. I'm the one who brought these friendships together, and I'm the one who almost lost them all. It seems fitting that I'm the one who is still alone.

* * *

Saddened by my very single status and the thoughts I had during Jenny's wedding, I want more. I'm considering a dating spree—not a screwing spree—but I don't want to screw things up with Shawn. Over the phone one night I *casually* (I hope) ask his opinion about dating other people.

"I thought we had this talk, babe. I don't have the time to run all over town trying to meet women, and I'm not ready to jump back into another long-term relationship."

"I was also kind of asking your thoughts about me dating other guys." *Please tell me that you don't want that.*

"I don't like it, but I get that women around a certain age aren't looking for a date to prom anymore. That's why I avoid women."

It is funny, maybe not for me exactly, but I laugh anyway. "Um... you do realize that I'm a woman right?"

"That's hard to miss, Amanda. No pillow talk about other men. If you find someone special, I'm either going to have to be ready for a woman like you or I'm going to watch you walk away."

I might not be looking for a date to prom anymore, but this all sounds way too familiar. It didn't work out so well for me the last time I fell in love with a guy who wouldn't make me any promises but was more than happy to kiss me stupid on a regular basis.

Venturing back online, I make some dates. Dating sucks. It's a concrete jungle out there, and I find myself sprawled on the pavement more often than on the receiving end of something good. A mental connection—a sense of humor, easy conversation, fun—is just as important as physical attraction. Both have to exist in the first place. Neither can be forced, and both take a hell of a lot of trial and error to find when the point of origination is an online chat room.

Eventually I meet two guys who are interesting enough to serve as distractions from Shawn. I have three *potentials*? Three *regulars*? Three *friends with benefits*? Basically, I'm dating three guys at the same time, but there are no commitments and certainly no promises of something more. It's not where I'd hoped to end this little online social experiment, but I'm a busy woman. My life and bench are full.

When I share my *situation* and the associated analogy with Katie, I fear she might die laughing.

"It's like this, Katie. If I combine all these guys into one man, I'd pretty much have the ideal boyfriend. But I can't, so I'm going to rotate them as needed. I'll keep at least one in play and the others can sit on the bench until it's their turn. Bench players can get a lot of play or get cut from the team if they aren't, you know, performing."

Choking hard on her bong inhale, I whack her on the back. She hacks and sputters, and I bring her some water and Kleenex because she laughed so hard that she started crying—and drooling. "What am I going to do with you, Amanda?" She wheezes out.

"I have no idea, but this whole dating thing... I hate every second of it. I'm exhausted, and I'm ready to settle down with someone special. Where is he? Did he marry Lorraine?"

"Stop it. He didn't marry Lorraine. He's out there. And my vote is for Shawn. I love him."

"Please," I moan, "don't say Shawn and love in the same sentence."

"Speaking of love, and not to rub salt in a wound... Nathan asked me to move in with him when our lease is up."

I widen my eyes even though I'm not all that surprised. "You're breaking up with me?"

"We can still be friends. You can keep the townhouse. We just have to get everything transferred to your name, or we can give notice if you want to skip Tempe."

"Ah, yes." I smile at her. "I'm very familiar with the *let's be friends* speech, but I think *you* might actually mean it."

Her return smile is enormous, and her face flushes when she shares, "Nathan started talking about how diamonds are cut—solitaire, princess, cushion, emerald, and I think maybe—"

"No guy would *randomly* bring that up." I sigh wistfully—lucky Katie. "Are you ready to say yes if he asks?"

"I totally am."

"And which cut do you favor?"

"Princess, of course."

"I wouldn't expect anything less from a girl raised in north Scottsdale." I wink at her. "Just remember that you can't book your wedding date for Saturday, June 27th. It's circled in a red heart on our calendar."

She laughs. "We'll be in Pine Ridge making sure Trina makes it down the aisle to Connor."

"That's a stretch, Katie. We're going to make sure she looks amazing before she sprints down that aisle. We should probably remind her to walk slowly so she doesn't trip on her gown," I snicker and reach for the bong.

"When is Jenny due?"

I exhale. "May 26th. God... Jenny's going to be a mom, Trina is getting married, and there's a ring in your near future. It's almost like too much of a good thing!"

"You can never have too much of a good thing."

You can't have too much of a good thing? I guess if what I actually want are *three* guys who aren't *the one* that would be a good thing. But that's not what I want. I want Shawn.

Instead, I'm also dating James—a general contractor. Eight years older than me, he's also a big guy with dark hair and brown eyes. Probably not the brightest bulb on the string of lights, but he's good with his hands and has an easy-going nature.

James loves to laugh, smoke a bowl, curl up and watch movies. He isn't looking for anything serious because he, too, is divorced and she wiped him out. He is "starting over," which includes living in a crappy apartment and not having enough money to go out on lavish dates. I don't hold that against him because it really doesn't matter to me. I'm more content at home and I enjoy his company.

Alan the Chef... Well, he too is more than a few years older than me, divorced with the dark features and big build, but this one is a deep thinker—broody and kind of artsy. He works crazy hours at this restaurant in Scottsdale, and sometimes as much as a week will go by before I hear from him. He usually meets me for drinks or invites me over to cook. Even though, or maybe because, he's a chef, he loves to create and try new things in the kitchen. He buys all these cool ingredients and explains what he's combining and why. I help with the prep work, but I also drive him crazy because *that's the wrong knife, I said dice not pulverize, you're supposed to slice it horizontally, whatever*. The end result is almost always a very delicious meal, and I get to bring home leftovers.

Alan's also a fan of weed, but I'm starting to suspect there might be more to that story. There are times he has way too much nervous energy or his *equipment* fails him. But I keep him on my bench because I enjoy our conversations, and when his equipment works, it is industrial-sized—and he knows how to use it.

Territorial Cup—1997

I work, study, and rotate my bench as one day turns into another until I celebrate Arizona's 28 to 16 victory over Arizona State. That victory is never too much of a good thing. Dad and I turn off the television with huge smiles and small whiskey buzzes. No one is going to laugh at my license plates now. Arizona took the National Championship in NCAA Men's basketball in March, and now we've shattered hearts and ruined Thanksgiving weekend for Sun Devil fans everywhere. Bear Down, Arizona. It's a great year to be a Wildcat.

CHAPTER 19

March 1998

IN LATE MARCH, TANNER SURPRISES me with a phone call and some big news. "Panda," his deep and happy voice greets in response to my hello.

"Hey there, stranger. How are you?"

"Awesome. How are you?"

"You first," I reply. "How's your residency going?" Tanner is specializing in pediatrics, and he's currently working at University Medical Center.

"Busy. Tons of hours. Really rewarding but there are terrible moments, too, and I'm still learning how to deal with all of that."

"Do you have a good support system—like, people you can talk to? Please don't stuff that shit inside and not deal with it or you'll turn into one of those asshole robot doctors. Or a serial killer."

He laughs at me. "Yeah, I have plenty of people to talk to here. It's just that little ones are so helpless."

"I can't even imagine. Tanner, I'm so proud of you." Because I'm his *friend*, I ask, "And how is Lorraine?"

"She's good. Has a rowdy class of eight-year-olds, but she's a trooper. This'll be her last year teaching though."

"Oh? Career change?"

"Sort of. We're expecting," his voice is excited.

"Expecting what?"

"Babies. Twins."

"Um..." As with most big news, I need my ass on the sofa to absorb it. "Did you just say twins?"

"I did!"

"That's, um... That's... Wow, Tanner. That's amazing. Congratulations to both of you. How is Lorraine feeling?"

"Not great, but she should perk up soon."

"How far along are you?"

"Twelve weeks. We're due in the fall, but there's more risk with multiples. She could go early. It's a scary thought."

"I can't wait to meet them, but not until they're fully... um, cooked. Do you know what you're having, other than twins?"

"No, it's too early, but we both wanna know. I'll pass that along if it's okay with her."

"Yes, it's always helpful to know what color blankets I should knit."

"You don't knit, Panda."

"That's right, I don't... Um, well, it's helpful to know what color blankets I should purchase—from Target or something. No, for you guys I'll shop somewhere nicer. So, uh, any other big news from Tucson?"

"This is pretty big, so I'm good for now. Gonna call Michael and Claire when we hang up, but I wanted to tell you first."

"Tanner, are you even talking to your own parents?"

"Kind of. Rarely. They were at the wedding, which you would've known if you'd—"

"So you have some sort of relationship with them again?"

"It's not much, but I'm not expecting much either." His voice takes a turn for the authoritative. "Your turn. I got your email about the new job and the MBA. How's that going?"

"It's all good. My job is fine with promotion potential, and there's even a gym in the building. I'm staying in shape."

"Good for you. And the MBA program?"

"I fell into this awesome study group at school. We do tons of project-based work, and the five of us can divvy up an assignment over a pitcher of margaritas. Everyone comes back together with their part finished. It's unbelievable, actually. I've seen some ugly finger pointing in some of these study groups. Me? I'm drama free."

"How about your love life? Is that drama free too?"

"You're nosy."

"I'm not nosy. You never talk to me about this stuff."

"Because it's weird."

"Come on, Panda. Tell your old friend a few stories."

"Fine. There's no *one* special guy at the moment. I'm rotating my bench until I find just the right player."

"You gonna explain that?"

"Ugh. I don't want to explain, but since I opened my big mouth... There are a few guys, nice guys, but none of them seem to want an actual, you know, commitment, relationship. Jeez, they're all kind of the same—just different names, faces, and occupations—but it's kind of like that guy Noah in college. I have needs so..."

"You're still dating nineteen-year-old boys?" Tanner teases.

"No, they're actual men. Like the village people, but not gay. There's a general contractor, a chef, and a cop—currently, but my roster could change at any moment. I'm looking for a house in Phoenix so the GC skillset is crucial, if you think about it. He can hook me up with electricians and plumbers and landscapers if I need to outsource anything else."

Tanner goes off in a fit of laughter before asking, "Wait, you're looking for a house in Phoenix?"

"Katie and I are breaking up. She and Nathan are getting married in September, and our lease is up soon. I'm working with an agent that Dad suggested, although he's really against the idea of me buying an actual house."

"Why's Michael against it?"

"Single woman, lots of responsibility, I can't even keep a houseplant alive, blah, blah, blah. But I want resale value, equity, and no shared walls, so there's not much chance he's going to talk me out of it at this point."

"Hard to talk you outta things when your mind is already made up," he cracks, but it's the truth.

"Speaking of which, I need to call my realtor Patty back and get on the hunt this weekend because the clock is ticking... *stupid clock is always ticking.*"

"I'm proud of you, too, Panda."

"Why? I haven't created life or saved a life, so it's all basic stuff on my end."

"Everything good that's happening to you makes me feel proud. I hear a lot of good, and I'm glad to hear you're all right out there."

I'm all right out there, I guess, but when we finally hang up the baby *situation* burns like a bitch. I numb it the best way I know how, and it's not even a Saturday or Sunday. Saturday and Sunday are now more of a guideline. I favor pot over white zin, but I keep it in check. I am an adult after all.

May 1998

My new neighborhood is iffy, built in the 1950s in downtown Phoenix just off 7th Avenue and south of Camelback. It has the potential to go historic in the future if it's not taken over by the gang activity that runs rampant just west of 15th Avenue.

My 'hood is an eclectic mix of skin tones, ethnic backgrounds, and ages—including the elderly who built their homes originally and raised their own families, lower middle class families, young professionals like myself, and a healthy population of gay men. My office building is a quick drive south, school is twenty minutes north, and Jenny and Paul live within ten minutes.

The bungalow-style tract home is white with light pink trim

and is fully renovated inside—except for the parts that should remain retro—by the previous gay owner who has fantastic taste. I have 1,300 square feet with three bedrooms, 1 ¾ baths, and a huge backyard with citrus trees, but it was the kitchen that sold me even though I'll rarely use it.

The white kitchen cabinets are original with scrolling trim work. I have grey concrete countertops that match the floors in the rest of the home, but the kitchen floor is decked out with black and white checkered tiles like you'd find in an old diner.

My oven is the showstopper. It's original to the home—a turquoise 1953 Maytag with beautiful lines like a classic car. It even came with the original owner's manual, which kills me. Page five advises the housewife to freshen up her hair and lipstick and don a clean apron before her husband returns home from work. *Remember to greet him with a smile and his favorite drink to put him at ease after a long day at work.*

I have plenty of help moving in. Shawn calls on some friends from the PPD who work for pizza and beer. Nathan and Katie help us load the U-Haul in Tempe, and Paul and Jenny meet us on the other side to unload. Well, Jenny sits on a chair rubbing her enormous, about to burst belly, while barking orders at the men who have the good sense not to argue with a very pregnant woman.

After changing our minds a few times, we finally have the major pieces of furniture in place. I feed my helpers and send them on their way because now it's time for proper organization—which is a very important life skill.

Shawn stays behind with Jenny and Paul, and we make good progress unpacking boxes and setting up the kitchen. When we move on to the wardrobe boxes, Shawn teases me relentlessly about my shoe and handbag collection because I fill every closet in the house. Walk-ins weren't a thing back in 1950s.

I'm just grateful he doesn't come across my bong because... I wonder, would he actually arrest me, or would he let it slide? I have no idea. Best case, if he busts me, he'll force me up against the wall and make me spread 'em while he frisks me thoroughly before placing me in cuffs. I'm not ashamed to admit that play *never* gets old.

* * *

After Jenny and Paul call it a night, Shawn and I shower off in my retro master bath and christen my new bedroom. Bossy sex with Shawn *never* gets old either. He's extraordinary, and I want to keep him. Sadly, since he has an overnight shift, he has to get ready for work.

He makes a quick trip to his cruiser to grab a few things. "I should've brought this one in," he says putting the black duffle bag on my bed. "I won't forget next time."

"What's in there?"

"Tactical gear." My blank look leads to further explanation, "Service items—Kevlar, belt, spray, flashlight, gloves, mags, cuffs." He catches my eye with a smirk because I love handcuffs so much that he carries an extra clean and shiny set just for me. "You know, the usual stuff. I left my service weapon in the coat closet. Whenever I'm here, coming or going from a shift, I'll store it there. And..." He pulls out *my* handcuffs and twirls them once around on his big fingers. "You have a lingerie drawer where I can stash these?"

I think I love you, Shawn.

As he changes from hot bench player into hot cop before my very eyes, I'm fascinated and ready to go again even though he just took me in my bed. It's so much of a sight to behold that I can't contain myself.

My ovaries twitch, and I blurt, "Eights months! I've known you for eight months and you've been keeping this from me?!?" His eyes flash with concern. Perhaps that came out a tad too forcefully... "Shawn, you're so hot. I can't wait to take all of that off of you, demand you do indecent but awesome things to me, and watch you put it all on again."

He busts out laughing and turns slightly red, but he stands a little taller, so I know he's feeling good about himself. "You're such a nut, babe."

I've only just begun to divulge the depths of my nuttiness. "If you pulled me over, I would jump out of my car and beg you to frisk me. I mean, how many women hit on you during an average night?"

"First of all, if you get pulled over, stay in your car. If you rush an officer, you'll wind up on your face in the street with a knee in your back until he can slap the cuffs on."

"Yeah," I grin at him. "If you're the one doing that to me, I don't see a downside."

"God, babe," he shakes his head and chortles. "Second of all, the only traffic stops we make in this area involve active suspects and scum. Male or female, they aren't exactly happy to see me."

Clapping my hands together, I share, "I am so happy to see you right now." I punctuate this statement by pumping my fist in the air and adding, "Yay for me!"

"Yeah, I'm getting that loud and clear." He shows his appreciation of my enthusiasm by giving me possession of his mouth.

Possession is nine-tenths of the law, Shawn, and my ovaries will not stop twitching. I want to breed with you. Thank God you can't read my mind.

When we come up for air, Shawn says, "We need to talk about your windows. Some of those locks are flimsy, and you need a security system in here."

Nope, you definitely can't read my mind, Shawn, because I want to talk about making babies not home security.

"I can come back over tomorrow afternoon after I wake up and replace the latches that need it, and I know a guy who does security systems, so I'll have him call you to set up a time. I want it installed within a week—don't wait any longer."

I furrow my brows. This is all very sweet, but James is coming over tomorrow to help me hook up my electronics and hang bookshelves in the bedrooms. "I can't do tomorrow. I have plans."

"Monday I have an admin meeting. Tuesday? I'm off."

"I have school. Wednesday?"

"I have the kids." He's never asked me to meet his kids, and I know better than to go there. "Thursday? No, you have class on Thursday..."

"Friday after my work but before yours?"

"Friday it is, Amanda."

"I'll make you dinner." *Um, Ovaries, we don't cook dinner for our bench players.* "I'll be home by five-thirty."

"Sounds good. We'll stay in." He locks his arms around me and gives me a hot cop kiss. "And after I fuck you, you can watch me get dressed for work."

"Oh my god," I groan, which makes Shawn laugh and blush again.

Give it a rest already, Ovaries. We're too good for his ego.

On his way out, Shawn lectures me about using the deadbolts on both the security door and the main door. "Never," he warns, "open the front door to someone you do not personally know unless that security door is dead-bolted. Promise me."

I roll my eyes. "I promise."

"I'm serious, Amanda. I work this area, and shit goes down—shit I don't want you to know about, much less experience firsthand. I *never* want to respond to an emergency call at this address unless it's for sex."

I laugh. He does not. "Okay, Shawn, I promise." I give him a final kiss on his way out the door. Then, damn it, I forget to lock the security door before I shut and lock the front door. My doorbell rings immediately. "Who is it?" I call through the door.

"Damn it, Amanda, open the door."

"I can't—the security door isn't dead bolted." Hearing his laughter, I decide that he can't be too upset. I swing open the front door to find him glaring at me. "What?" I shrug feigning nonchalance. "I personally know you, so it's all right."

"I'm leaving. You might not know the next person who comes to your door," he bites out each word.

Holding up both hands, I drop him a cheeseball line. "Sorry, Officer. Please don't shoot, but you are more than welcome to search my body cavities because I might be hiding evidence."

Amusement replaces agitation. "I've already searched your cavities." Taking a step toward me, he stops. "Shit, I don't have time to do it again." He locks his face down to one befitting a humorless law enforcement professional. "Secure the deadbolt," he barks and lets the steel door fall shut behind him. He stands there watching me until I click the lock in place, but he's not finished being bossy. "And the main door."

"Jeez, got it, Officer Bossy." I salute. "Please be safe out there."

"I always am," he responds.

CHAPTER 20

JAMES COMES OVER THE NEXT day with a toolbox, weed, and a hard on. I take care of the hard on first. While we're doing it, I close my eyes and try to pretend he's Shawn, but he is no Shawn. After we smoke a little weed on the back patio, I give him a tour of the rest of the house before he gets busy hooking up the TV/VCR and speakers. He shows me how to use a stud finder—which, come on, makes me laugh so hard I almost wet my pants.

We hang the first set of shelves together using a stud finder, pencil, level, wall anchors, screws, and a power drill. The power drill is my favorite part. I fall in love with it and insist on doing the second set of bookshelves myself while he observes and tries to keep his mouth shut.

"I have to learn how to do this stuff, so thanks for sharing your drill with me," I say with a wink.

"Oh, I have a drill for you."

"One more set of shelves, buddy. Focus."

We hang the last set together and smoke a bowl while we wait on pizza. I don't want to use his other drill again, so we watch a movie.

He leaves for work early on Monday morning, giving me a peck on the lips and a *see you later, gorgeous*. How much later? I have no idea. I like him, but I have it so bad for Officer Barton right now that he's all I can think about.

* * *

I menu planned with Jenny midweek and stopped by the grocery store on my way home from school last night. By the time Shawn shows up on Friday evening, I have everything I need to prepare a simple dinner of spaghetti, sauce from a can spiced up with Italian sausage that I need to brown, garlic bread, salad fixings, and bottle of wine. *How hard can it be?*

Shawn arrives with his work bags in hand and places everything in the coat closet. Yes, I carved out a space for his things, which is practically the equivalent of giving him a dresser drawer. My ovaries twitch at the thought of watching him put all that stuff on later tonight. As he walks the house and does a window latch count, I change out of my business attire into a breezy sundress and sweep my hair into a quick updo.

Shawn finds me coming out of my bathroom. "I like your hair better down, babe."

Slipping my arms around him, I offer up my neck. "Easier access this way." He takes the bait and my neck is rewarded. "Besides, this way you won't be eating my hair with your dinner tonight."

He chuckles and asks, "Is your toolbox out in the shed?"

No, but my bong is out there. "Um... toolbox?"

"Do you have any tools—screwdrivers, wrenches, pliers, a drill?"

I blink my eyes at him, "Um..."

"You own a house. You need tools."

Isn't that why I have a bench? "I have a hammer and a screw-driver or two... Will those help?"

"Phillips or slot head?"

"What's the difference?" *Please, Arizona, do not revoke the women's studies portion of my diploma.* "Slot head sounds kind of dirty..."

He tries to suppress amusement. "I have to run over to Ace. I need some hardware for a few of the windows, and I need to get *someone* a basic toolbox."

"Do you want me to come with you?" I offer.

"No, you'll just distract me talking dirty about slot head screw-drivers."

He's right, but I frown because I'm not sure how much window hardware costs. "Let me give you my debit card."

"You can pay me back later with dinner—and in your bed."

"I don't exchange sex for household favors, Shawn," I protest, although that *might* be just a little bit true.

"Consider it a housewarming present. I'll be back in twenty." He heads toward the front door, turns and orders, "Get over here and lock the doors behind me."

* * *

While he works on the windows, I get to work in the kitchen. I brown the sausage, drain the fat, and leave it to simmer mixed in with the sauce on top of the range. I mince the garlic, cut the Italian bread roll down the middle and slather on the butter and garlic before sliding it in the oven on a baking sheet. While the pasta is boiling, I start chopping the vegetables for our salad.

I'm not wearing an apron, but I'm June freaking Cleaver. This cooking dinner stuff is easy. Maybe next time I'll try something a little more challenging. As I chop, I may have lost track of time on the pasta because when I tip the contents of the boiling pot into the strainer, my spaghetti immediately forms clumps. Clumps? *How is it possible to screw up pasta?*

"Jenny, my pasta is clumpy," I whisper into the phone. "What did I do wrong?"

"Did you overcook it? Use enough water?"

"How would I know? It's clumpy. I can't serve this."

"Boil some more, use lots of water, and keep an eye on the time."

"I don't have any more."

"Hmmm... you could turn it into a pasta bake. Roll the pasta in a bit of egg white, parmesan, and Italian seasoning, slice through it so you cut up the clumps, mix in the sauce, and bake it in a casserole dish for about thirty minutes."

"Thirty minutes? But my bread is probably done by now." I check on the bread *situation* and shit, *really*? "Never mind, I forgot to turn on the oven."

Jenny cracks up and makes a suggestion. "Maybe you should order out, Amanda."

After I tell her to shut up, I disconnect and follow her advice. I put the whole concoction into the oven—which I turn on, set a timer, and go back to my vegetables. Sometime later, Shawn strolls in, "Windows are in good shape. Smells good in here. How long until it's ready?"

Like a vixen-version of June Cleaver, I bat my eyes with a smile and glance at the timer. "Thank you. About ten minutes. Do you want wine with dinner tonight or something nonalcoholic?"

"I have enough time before my shift to have a glass. For future reference, though, I prefer beer."

"Name your label and I'll keep some on hand for you."

He kisses my cheek. "That's nice, babe. Heineken or Sam Adams will do. Where's the corkscrew? I'll open the bottle," he offers as he snags a cherry tomato.

Please let me have your babies, Shawn. Or at least ask me to be your girlfriend. I want more of this.

"It's a screw top."

While laughing, he reaches for the bottle. "Well, that makes it easier, doesn't it?"

I sip my wine, finish the salad, and set the small retro diner table in the corner of the kitchen where Shawn sits flipping through the sports section of today's Arizona Republic like the hottest version of Ward Cleaver *ever*. I love this dynamic inside my cozy 1950s kitchen. *Maybe I should freshen up my lipstick like the Maytag manual says.*

Or maybe I should take a freaking cooking class because Shawn raises his head and asks, "What is that smell?"

I sniff the air. *Shit, what is that smell?* I rush to the oven and when I drop the door pungent smoke billows out and fills my ridiculously cramped kitchen. Eyes burning, I cough and try to wave the smoke from the air when *BEEP BEEP BEEP BEEP BEEP*. My eardrums are practically bleeding. "Shawn?" I yell.

He heads for the kitchen windows to crank them open even though it's over 100 degrees outside, and the smile on his face is *HUGE*. "Good news is your smoke detector works. Step stool?" he yells back. I grab it from the utility area off the kitchen and watch him climb up and push a button until the incessant beeping ceases—well, in the kitchen at least. The rest of the house is still beeping. "Must be wired together," he says. "I got it." He takes the stool, and as he moves through each room, the beeping grows quieter and quieter until, at last, it's over.

Meanwhile I assess the *situation*. My garlic bread is black, my spaghetti bake is now a clumpy yet runny failure, and I'm no June Cleaver.

I have wine and salad which is not going to fill up 250-pounds of pure man. When he returns to the kitchen, step stool in hand, I rub my temples and look at the floor before asking, "Pizza or Chinese?"

* * *

I eventually hear from Alan a week after my kitchen disaster. This time when he invites me over for dinner, I describe my new kitchen and classic Maytag oven and invite him to come to me. He brings all the food and wine and critiques my prep skills before pulling off a perfectly-timed, delicious-tasting, and beautifully presented meal.

After dinner, we smoke a bowl (or three) and decide to head to a nearby bar to have a few drinks and listen to a live band. We return to my place, smoke another bowl (or three) and fall into bed. Alan loves to kiss and grind and say filthy things to me while we're doing it. That part of us is very compatible, but I have a feeling that if he had to pick between me and my Maytag, he'd choose the latter. If I had to pick between him and Officer Barton, there'd be no contest.

May 21, 1998

The phone rings just before midnight on Thursday.

"It's Paul. We're at the hospital. She's definitely in labor."

"Should I come over now or wait?"

"Come now. She won't stop swearing at me, and I could use another target."

Jenny and I discussed me being there, and I wanted to, but now that I'm here, I can't watch anything going on down there. Paul holds one leg, and I take the other while concentrating on Jenny's face as my best friend struggles for a few hours to push this new life out into the world.

Humbled at first sight, Paul kisses Jenny and thanks her for his new daughter. Goosebumps dot my skin, and happy tears roll down my face as I watch them become a family.

Sitting out of the way of the activity, I observe with wide eyes while the baby is tagged, weighed and measured, foot-printed, cleaned up because she was covered in yuck, and I'm not sure what else is going on over there, but she is not happy about it.

Eventually, after Jenny and Paul have had their first cuddles, Paul offers me his precious girl wrapped snugly in a white blanket with pink and blue stripes, wearing a tiny pink cap on her head. Her eyes are closed tight, and her little lips are puckering even in slumber.

"Jenny, would you like to do the honors?" Paul asks.

Worn out from her ordeal, Jenny turns and smiles softly at me. "Amanda, we'd like you to meet your niece—Maisy Grace Castillo."

Tears fill my eyes again. They *Graced* their baby with my middle name. I am honored beyond belief. I whisper to Maisy because this is just between the two of us, "Auntie Amanda will never *Maisy Grace* you in anger. I will love you and look out for you forever. I don't care if you get kicked out of the Brownies or raise hell like your mommy did. I love you, but right now *you are making my ovaries twitch, Maisy.*"

June 27, 1998—Trina and Connor's Wedding

There are few things worse than a hometown wedding with a high-visibility role in the festivities and no date. Shawn couldn't swap his shift, Alan is working, and James doesn't own formal attire. What good is a freaking bench if all my players are lame during my time of need?

Instead of renting a male escort, I drive up to Pine Ridge on Friday afternoon before the Saturday wedding with Katie and Nathan who assure me on a loop that there's nothing *wrong* with being single. Easy for them to say with their wedding date approaching in September. I don't even have Jenny because she's busy with breastmilk and diapers and having a whole lot of sleepless nights.

Because Trina and Connor are taking the show from Connecticut to Pine Ridge, we don't have time for all the traditional things before the ceremony. We swing by my parents' house to change before meeting the wedding party and families at the Lutheran Church for a rehearsal. Dad is delighted to see Katie and warms to Nathan immediately.

Mom makes a face at me after I return from showing them to Brianna's old room. "I thought you girls would stay in your room," she criticizes.

"Dad, is she serious right now?" I pose the question while glaring at Mom. "For god's sake, Mom, they already *live together*. Do you expect me to tell them that they have to sleep in separate beds the next two nights?"

She glowers. "I don't like it, and don't take the Lord's Name in vain."

I might be on the verge of my twenty-sixth birthday, but age doesn't always equal maturity. Rolling my eyes most disrespectfully, I bite out, "No wonder Brianna doesn't come back here to visit. You'd probably make her and Marcus sleep in separate rooms even though they have two children together."

"Enough, ladies," Dad steps in. "They're adult guests in our home, and the sleeping arrangements are fine."

Vindicated, I shoot Mom a victory smirk. Like I said, age doesn't always equal maturity.

* * *

I squeal with glee at the church. We're together again! Trina and Connor—yay! Nicholas and Michele—soon to be married. Woohoo! And Violet with her, um, *girlfriend,* Lindsey? I mean, whatever, but when did that happen? I'll ask her later, but love is love and she looks happy.

Trina had to have a big bridal party to offset Connor's five older brothers serving as groomsmen. I'm her maid of honor. Katie, Michele, and Violet are bridesmaids, and the fifth and final bridesmaid hails from both Pine Ridge and Connecticut—Becky Haines, now Becky Haines-Peterson. Trina and Connor live in Norwalk, and Becky is in the neighboring town of Stamford with her lawyer husband Henry. They spend a lot of time together.

Becky's putting her degree from Yale to good use by volunteering for a few charities while five-months pregnant with her first child. Yes, there's still a *rub* all these years later. She eyes me head to toe and pretends to hide her scorn under the guise of a syrupy voice. "Amanda, it's so good to see you."

"You, too, Becky. You look lovely. Glowing."

"Didn't you have those boots in *high school*?" Attire for the evening is country casual. The east coast stiffs are dressed in polos and khakis while the Arizona crowd read and followed the memo. Trina should have included illustrations because Becky, who is *technically* one of us, is wearing a stuffy sweater set with a strand of pearls.

"Yup. You remember how hard it is to break in a pair of boots, don't you, Becky?" I paired them with an above-the-knee cotton sundress which will transition nicely from church to dancefloor later in the night.

"Red boots in a church," she mutters.

"It's Pine Ridge, not a scene from *Footloose*. Boots, regardless of color, are welcome anywhere in this town."

"If you say so," she sneers.

I lower my voice, "Do you want to take swings at each other for the next two days? I'm game, but I'd rather play nice and support Trina. Wouldn't you?"

Her eyes narrow, but she smiles sweetly before taking another swing. "Henry and I were just at the lake house in Michigan with Braden's family."

My face goes up in flames. "How lovely for all of you." *Direct hit, Becky.*

"How is Tanner these days? Is he here somewhere?" That Becky. She doesn't want to take swings at me; she wants to watch me bleed.

I glare at her and hiss, "You know perfectly well that Tanner is married."

She feigns innocence with a casual shrug. "Guess I forgot. Sorry."

Leaning down, I speak directly into her ear, "Cut the bullshit, Becky. We're here for Trina, and I'd really hate to shove a tiara up a pregnant woman's ass." I stand up tall to look down on her. "Are we clear?" I'll give Becky credit—she still knows when it's time to get the hell of my way.

CHAPTER 21

AFTER THE REHEARSAL, WE HAVE dinner at the family-owned Italian restaurant with a banquet room large enough to accommodate our party—and the Rotary Club—and then we're off to The Outpost on Main Street for a Friday night of drinking and dancing with anyone invited to the wedding who wants to come, and anyone from Pine Ridge who happens to be there. Poor Becky. Bar smoke isn't good for the baby, so she and Henry go back to her parents' house.

Katie and I cackle at a corner table for a while with Trina, Michele, Violet, and Lindsey. It's sort of like Trina's bachelorette party except all the men are here, too. "Who brought the weed?" Trina asks.

"Would I let you down, Trina?" Katie grins. "It's out in the car, but where are we going to do this?"

"Oh, there's a ranch behind the bar. We can slip through the barbed wire and sit on the fire pit logs on the back edge," I suggest. Everyone appears shocked except Trina. "What? You don't have barbed wire fences in north Scottsdale?" I tease Katie.

"Let's go after Connor's brothers leave." Trina wiggles in excitement. "I'm giddy at the thought—it's been so damn long."

"Take it easy, T. We don't want you forgetting Connor's name at the altar tomorrow," I jest.

"Oh, the minister will remind me, I'm sure."

* * *

As the night goes on, Connor's brothers are wearing on my last nerve. From their position of self-appointed superiority at the bar they are shit-faced drunk and making fun of the bar, town, church, hotel, and *whatever*. Katie and I wait on our drink order, and I listen in on Donovan, Aidan, Quinn, Dylan, and Declan. I shoot one of them a dirty look. I have no idea which one because I can't tell them apart except for Donovan, the best man. I have to walk next to him tomorrow, and he's three inches shorter than me.

"What?" Aidan/Quinn/Dylan/Declan asks me.

"You better keep your voices down, boys. You piss off the wrong local, you're going to be in a world of hurt," I warn.

"Piece of shit town. I can't believe Connor is marrying into this upbringing. His first kid might come out wearing spurs," scoffs Aidan/Quinn/Dylan/Declan.

"And now you pissed off the wrong local." I breathe fire and prepare to defend both Trina and this town. "You think pressed khakis and penny loafers make you better than—"

"Who's that?" Katie interrupts, grabbing my arm with one hand,

and, of course, *she is pointing* with the other hand at the guy who just walked through the swinging saloon doors.

I immediately lose interest in the feckin' gobshite the O'Hara brothers are dishing out. Hopefully a local deputy will pop them for DUI on the way back to their hotel and haul them off in the paddy wagon.

He is a sight for my sorely single status this weekend. Light brown hair with soft hazel eyes—he's tall and broad, fit and tan from working outdoors in the sunshine with his hands. I haven't seen him in years, and he's never looked more tempting. As he scans the bar for familiar faces, I ditch Katie and watch his face break out into a smile when he recognizes me. After we hug and exchange a few words, he takes my hand and leads me out to the dancefloor.

We start with a quick two-step to Lonestar's *Come Cryin' to Me* already in play. We slow our pace when *Carried Away* by George Strait blares over the speakers. Our bodies lock tight, and our dance is in perfect precision because some things never change. I won't get carried away for longer than a night or two, but sixteen years is a long time to wait to make out with Matt Neilson, my sixth grade crush. I don't wait another second. I tip my head up and Matt smiles down at me.

"Are you still with Rawlings?" he asks.

"Nope. And I feel something happening here."

"Oh yeah," he grins, and our public display of affection is on.

* * *

I spend the rest of the evening with the University of Arizona wedding party and dancing with Matt—when we aren't busy kissing and groping each other, that is. Once the O'Hara brothers head out, we stumble across the back parking lot and slip through the barbed wire fence onto Fisher's Ranch to smoke a few joints, making sure to keep our voices down so we don't wind up on the wrong end of a rifle or the wrong side of the law. I'd hate to use my one phone call to ask Dad to bail us out of the Main Street jail.

I throw the flag on Trina and Connor, who are now amateurs, and we trip back to the bar in the dark for another round and a few more dances. After returning home with Katie and Nathan, I make sure they're settled and, like a teenager, sneak out of the house—even though as a teenager I never had to sneak out.

Hopping into Matt's idling truck waiting at the bottom of the driveway, he slides a hand up my leg and, as if it were an actual question, he asks, "My place?"

We spend a naked and sexually rewarding night at his house. I plan to rotate him back in next time I'm in Pine Ridge. I have him drop me off before dawn and sneak back in before my parents wake up. I'll see him this afternoon because now I have a plus one.

Exhausted from no sleep—but it was totally worth it—Katie and I spend the day with the bridal party at the one spa in town. We get massages, hair, and makeup done before returning to Trina's house to get dressed for her big afternoon. I ignore Becky but delight in the fact that her gown is so snug we can barely get the zipper up.

Our gowns are a beautiful shade of deep purple. We ordered them from the same dressmaker in Connecticut, and they were made from the same lot of fabric, but Trina gave us Free Will on selecting the cut. I chose the most flattering for my curvy frame. I love the gown, but I will never wear it again.

The ceremony goes off without a hitch. Trina remembers Connor's name and her vows. I hold her bouquet and mine—which makes it tough to wipe back my tears while they join their lives together. We traverse to the Indian casino on the outskirts of town for the reception and spend the evening in a transformed-to-magical back room eating, drinking, dancing, laughing, and celebrating. Matt and I have another sticky, frenzied night together. I fall asleep on the drive home because I've been awake for forty-eight hours straight. Totally worth it.

Age: Twenty-six

About a week after my birthday in July, the phone rings out ten minutes before my alarm is set to go off. Still groggy, I pick up, and Tanner announces flatly, "The babies were born last night."

I sit upright with an initial thrill until it hits me that the babies aren't due until early fall. Fear instantly replaces joy. "Tanner, how early are they? Is everyone okay?"

"Lorraine's fair on her way to good. The babies were twenty-nine weeks gestational."

"What does that mean?" I ask quietly. He is silent and, dear god, he said *were* not *are.*

My voice becomes more urgent. "Twenty-nine weeks. What does that mean for the babies?" He remains silent, but I can hear him sniffling. "Tanner—speak," I order.

"My head hurts." I can hear the pain in his voice. "I have to be strong right now."

"You do. You are strong. Do you want to call me later? Do you need to talk? What do you need?"

More silence before, "I need you here."

"Are the babies... okay? Tanner, how are they...?"

"They're alive. I need you *now*. Can you get down here?"

I glance at the clock again and estimate, "I can be there in under three hours. Are you at UMC?"

He gives me a few more instructions about which entrance to use and what floor they'll be on.

"I'll be there as soon as I can."

After getting dressed, I leave Patrick a voicemail and head down the I-10, calling my parents from the truck. I have plenty of time to mull over worst possible scenarios, but I also have plenty of time to pray to God to watch over these babies.

When I arrive at UMC, I'm allowed into Labor & Delivery because Tanner left my name on a list. I show ID, sign in, and I'm issued a badge and given a room number. As I approach, I recognize the timbre of Tanner's voice coming from inside the room. Poking my head around the doorframe, I see Lorraine lying in a hospital bed, face streaked with tears and caked with exhaustion.

Her mother sits on chair next to the bed wearing the same expression. Lorraine's father is on the couch under the window looking grim, and Tanner is pacing the small room while speaking in a gentle voice.

I feel like an intruder—so uncomfortable, but it's not about me. Knocking softly on the open door before crossing the threshold, I offer Lorraine a meek smile and turn to Tanner. With barely a glance in my direction, he announces to the room, "I'll be right down the hall off the nurse's station."

I follow him into a small room with plastic sofas and an old TV. Once the door clicks shut behind us, I turn to face him with a million questions on the tip of my tongue. Before I can get a word out, he breaks down—tears followed by body wracking sobs. My arms snake around his waist and hold tight. His arms lock around my shoulders and my hair absorbs his tears. I know exactly why I'm here.

As he cries, I run my palms up and down his back to soothe him, but I don't try to quiet him with words. I want him to let it out, however long it takes. In all of our years as friends, I've never been in a position to comfort him like this. He's always been the strong one.

When he regains the power of speech, we sit on the sofa, and I hold onto his hand. "I needed to lose my shit," he explains unnecessarily.

I nod. "Happy to be of service. Do you want to talk?"

As he speaks, I watch his expression carefully, trying to take in every word. I notice that he sounds like several different people—a doctor, a freaked out father, and a terrified husband—and those personas come and go in no particular order. "The babies... We don't have names yet. A girl and a boy—1 pound 8 ounces and 1 pound 3 ounces, respectively." I smile softly thinking about the best of both worlds. "Twenty-nine weeks gestation means roughly 80% chance of survival."

I breathe an audible sigh of relief. "That's good news."

"It happened so fast—cramping, pain, she was screaming. There was nothing we could do to stop it. I couldn't even go in with her. They wouldn't let me, and I *work* here, Amanda. God damn it, I wasn't there for Lorraine when they took them from her."

He doesn't explain why, but I imagine they didn't want him to interfere. "The babies are in the NICU, and even with 80% odds there are so many risks for complications." His face crumbles again and more tears fall.

I put my other hand over his and squeeze. He details potential complications while the lump in my throat grows. "Risk of infection from poking and prodding—feeding tubes, antibiotics, breathing machines. Then there's cerebral palsy, brain impairment, vision, hearing, motor control, chronic asthma, learning disabilities, chronic lung disease, I could go on..."

I can hardly comprehend the magnitude of what he said, but I'll take more if he needs to let it out. "Do you want to go on?"

"No." His gaze is vulnerable. "Just tell me everything's gonna be okay."

"I can do that." I sit up on my knees and cradle his large body against my chest. While he cries on my t-shirt, I stroke his hair and whisper, "Everything is going to be fine. It's going to be okay. I promise, everything will be all right."

After I repeat those lines over and over, I change my talk track and tell him stories about the future. "Your babies are going to grow up strong and healthy. I bet Lorraine will bake amazing birthday cakes. If you leave the kids with her parents, they'll ply them with ice cream behind your backs and return them to you on a sugar high. Oh, and wait until I—their Auntie Panda—buys them the loudest, most obnoxious toys on the planet—birthdays and Christmases. They'll draw on your walls with permanent markers, so you should probably store those somewhere up high. But your son will be a climber, so it won't matter. It's inevitable."

"They'll fight with each other but defend one another. I hope they are huge pains in your ass. Your daughter's going to have a smart mouth, and your son is going to wreck his first car, but he'll be okay. They'll both be wicked smart—way smarter than you. Except that your daughter will probably get felt up on prom night by a guy who's totally handsy, and you're not allowed to kill him because orange is not a good color on you—and you were that guy once." Tanner snickers at that one, and I continue talking.

"They'll have long, beautiful lives and be the luckiest kids ever because Lorraine is their mom and you are their dad. You'll be an incredible father, Tanner. The best—like, Michael Harrington awesome. Those babies are so, so lucky...."

When I trail off, I look down to assess his state. His eyes are closed, and while he's still leaking tears, he has a small smile on his gorgeous face.

He opens his chocolate eyes and blinks up at me. "Please keep talking," he requests softly, and so I do. I hope that I'm not lying to him when I make my stories about their futures very beautiful and creative.

* * *

When I tell Tanner that I'll find some magazines and stay close by for a while, he protests but I won't have it any other way. "I need occasional progress reports so I can keep my parents updated. Otherwise they're going to drive down here, and Mom's going to force feed everyone chocolate chip cookies." I smile even though levity is a stretch right now. "Now—go. I'm staying here."

He checks in with me throughout the day, and I take notes so I can relay the updates correctly to my parents. As early evening approaches, he tries to give me my walking papers, but I refuse.

"I'm going to spend the night with Michele and Nicholas. Call my cell phone if you need anything. I don't care what time it is. If I don't hear from you, I'll swing by in the morning before I head home."

"You don't have to."

"I want to. It would make me feel better, Tanner, so really, I'm just being selfish."

He shakes his head. "You'll spend the night with Pam and Dale."

"Um... who?"

"My in-laws."

"Oh," I chuckle, "I didn't realize they had actual names."

He smiles with his lips closed. "They do. Pam and Dale. If you're gonna stay down here tonight, you can make yourself useful. Tyler's backpacking in Yellowstone, and we haven't been able to reach him yet. Drive them home, please. They're exhausted. Make sure they eat dinner, make small talk, but whatever you do, don't talk about Abigail's prom night."

"Abigail," I beam at him. "I love it. And what shall I call the boy child who's going to wreck his first car?"

"Andrew."

I nod and confirm in a serious tone, "Very good. I will commit the names of your children to memory and use them accordingly."

His lips split into the first full smile I've seen on him all day. "I'm a father, Panda."

"And those babies are so lucky." I match his smile, but his disappears.

"If anything goes wrong and they need to come back in the night, I'm gonna call your cell. I need you to handle them with care. Wake them, drive them back here. Will you do that for us?"

"Of course, but you're not going to call because those little Wildcats are going to be just fine tonight, tomorrow, and every day and night after that."

"From your lips to God's ears."

"Yeah, I've been chatting Him up all day. He's listening."

"If I had only one friend left, I'd want it to be you," he says, kissing my forehead.

"You're going to eat those words when I start sending those babies annoying Christmas and birthday presents. No hurry with the in-laws. I'll be here when they're ready to go home."

He gives me a tight squeeze and another kiss on the forehead. "Thank you for letting me cry on you today. You have some of my crusty snot in your hair," he says with a grin.

I chuck his chin. "You've had more than your fair share of my crusty snot on you over the years. Now get. Go tell Abigail and Andrew to Bear Down, and I'll see you in the morning."

Thankfully, after dinner and some conversation with Tanner's exhausted in-laws, we all sleep through the night—no emergencies.

I deliver them back to the hospital after breakfast and stop by Lorraine's room to say goodbye to them. Tanner and Lorraine both look in better spirits. I hope they got some sleep last night.

"Have you seen the babies, Amanda?" Lorraine asks, and I shake my head. "Tanner, go introduce her on the way out."

I could go inside the NICU, but that would involve scrubbing down and gowning up and, really, the *situation* is too tenuous. I'll meet them when they're stronger. Tanner doesn't need to see me fall apart. I can hardly keep it together seeing them from a distance through the glass window.

The incubator they share is wound with wires and tubes. Their *situations* will be touch and go for several months, and there might be unknown complications down the road, but, as of right now, the twins are Bearing Down like good baby Wildcats. I head back to Phoenix, and I pray to God for their good health and futures.

CHAPTER 22

I'M LONELY OVER THE FOLLOWING months, but I shouldn't be. I have good times with my bench players, great girlfriends, conversations with and visits from my parents. I have my job and classes, and plenty of ways to pass the time. I receive positive email updates from Tanner about the twins. He invites me down several times, but I don't go because I plan on seeing him over Christmas with my parents.

My life appears to be FULL, but my heart feels empty. I want more. I want to love and be loved by *the one*, but he is nowhere to be found. Instead, I drive to the Humane Society and adopt an adorable lonely little kitten. I name him Squirt and have high hopes for a beautiful future together.

I'm a single woman—why not become a full-blown cliché? *Here you go, Ovaries, we have a little baby kitten to love.* My ovaries are not impressed.

September 1998

Katie and Nathan's wedding in mid-September is at a fancy resort in north Scottsdale. I give Shawn plenty of notice to swap his shift, and he is so freaking hot in a suit. He's an attentive and charming date after the ceremony while we eat, drink, and dance in my Kelly green satin bridesmaid's gown.

The higher neckline and slim cut across the hips doesn't make the most out of my curves, though, and I will never wear it again. Getting to see Nicholas and Michele and Violet and Lindsey again is worth wearing an unflattering dress.

I drink too much white zin, and Shawn has to drive me home even though he met me at the venue because I was busy before the ceremony. I'm a happy, friendly, handsy kind of buzzed, but he protests big time when I try to take him in my bed. I have to cajole and entice him with sweet talk to convince him to stay on his back and let me have my way. He draws the line with me using the handcuffs on him, and after I come on top of him, he flips me to my back and finishes things his way.

The words... *those three small but very meaningful words...* are on the tip on my tongue as we cuddle together and laugh about the evening. As much as I've tried to keep my *stupid heart* out of this *situation*, my heart is in this. I'm ready to clear my bench, marry, and make my own babies with Shawn, but he's given no indication whatsoever that he wants more than what we have right now.

What we have seems so right, but I'm too scared to ask how he feels a year into this... If he wants more, wouldn't he tell me?

Quit twitching, Ovaries. We're still looking for the one. Maybe it's that guy Max that we've been chatting with online for the past two months, but that's probably too much to ask.

October 1998

True to his word, Patrick made introductions, gave me HR-liaison responsibilities over the past year, and I'm welcomed into the Human Resources Department at CompuWorld at the beginning of October. Business is booming as Y2K approaches.

The entire world is freaking out about the new millennium. Doomsayers predict everything from digital clocks no longer working to a total loss of electricity across the globe—even spontaneous combustion of our planet. We have IT teams working contracts at client sites all over the country. Truth be told, I'm put into a role that I'm not quite qualified for, but my new boss Alisha has faith in me. She's not just teaching me the ropes, she's mentoring me.

With seven thousand employees in all fifty states, there are multiple HR disciplines to explore, but I want to be in the trenches. I like the crazy drama and employee/manager challenges. I'm focusing on Employee Relations, which is basically helping managers (and the company) get away with hiring, firing, and treating employees however they please without breaking any labor laws or violating company policies.

When a *situation* arises, I explore all sides of the story, take good notes because people lie and contradict themselves, and often the truth comes out. After the investigation, I study the fine print, talk it over with Alisha, and sometimes we call a kick ass employment law attorney we keep on retainer before rendering a decision on how to handle the *situation*. These areas are gray, though. Everything is open to interpretation, whereas Collective Bargaining Agreements for unionized labor are more cut and dried. I love looking for loopholes and finding a solid technicality on which to proceed.

* * *

Shortly after my promotion, I decide to accept a date with Max Masterson—a potential bench player who might be something more. We've been talking online for months before making plans to meet IRL (in real life). I have such high hopes for him. He has such a quick wit that I find myself stifling giggles as we type away.

At thirty-five years old, he has nine years on me chronologically, but he's never been married because he's married to his job. I'm familiar with Max's work because he's a sports reporter for a larger newspaper in the metro area. He writes with honesty served with a side of snarky. He travels the country covering the Cardinals. Going by the picture next to his byline, I know he's adorable. After speaking with him on the phone, I know that our banter translates verbally, and he has a sexy voice and laugh.

Max fits my modus operandi with the dark hair and brown eyes. He says that he's six foot one, so IRL that probably means six feet. I'm willing to sacrifice heels for the rest of my life if he turns out to be the real deal. And because I figure a media personality won't rape me and dump my body in the desert, I allow him to pick me up at my house for our dinner date on Friday night. Of course, I give

Jenny all the pertinent details in advance and promise to call her in the morning.

Wanting to look my absolute best, I prepare for this date with a nervous feeling in the pit of my stomach. Even though I've shared several pictures of myself with him, I'm still self-conscious about my overall size and worry that will be a turn off for him. There's such a strong mental connection, I would hate to see it all fall apart if there's no physical attraction when I open that door.

I go all out with the hair and makeup. Wearing my favorite black dress with a deep V-neck and flattering A-line cut that lands a few inches above my knees, I keep my jewelry simple, letting my cleavage speak for itself. Of course, I wear flats because I don't want to tempt fate.

I'm glad that I put in the effort but sorry I wasted time worrying about his reaction to me. When I open the front door (and unbolt the security screen) and take him in, the air crackles with potential. His smile warms me all the way down to my belly. He is unbelievably adorable.

This ember has potential to turn into a bonfire as he eyes me from head to toe like a Popsicle and states, "Not sure I'm supposed be this attracted to a Wildcat."

Oh yeah, there is a *rub*. Max is a rabid Arizona State fan and proud alumnus—although I don't understand why anyone from ASU feels proud about that.

Daring him with my eyes, I deliver the verbal challenge, "I'm perfectly willing to defy the laws of nature if you are."

"I'm in." His grin is *devilish* (pun intended) as he steps through my front door.

I offer him a beverage and he declines. I offer him a tour of my humble abode and he declines. I try to offer him something else but he interrupts me, "If we don't leave for dinner right now, our first kiss is going to happen in about five seconds."

My jaw drops open. I'm tempted, but I want things with this man to be different. I'm also legitimately famished and need to eat dinner. My expression makes him laugh—rich laughter. "Up to you, Wildcat," he teases.

"D...d...dinner," I stutter. Completely flustered, I manage to pick up my handbag, set the alarm, and my hands shake as I dead bolt both doors.

**

On the quick drive over to my favorite seafood restaurant near the Biltmore, he rests his hand on my bare leg, his thumb lightly stroking my skin. I release a sigh because, god, I swear my panties are already drenched and he's only touched my leg.

"What's with the sigh?"

Oh, you know, I'm just totally turned on right now, Max. "Your hand is warm."

"You mean my hand is making you warm?" He flashes those baby browns innocently before turning his attention back to Camelback Road. His hand slides over my knee and up my leg but stops well before the inappropriate zone. "This is nothing. We'll have plenty of time for hanky-panky after dinner."

"Listen, Max, there might be some *hanky*, but I can assure you there will be absolutely no *panky* tonight."

His laughter comes easy. "We'll see how much the bill is and then I'll decide."

Inside the restaurant, we take a seat at the bar while waiting on our table upstairs. He's a complete gentleman—opening doors, sliding out chairs, sweeping his hand underneath my hair and skating his fingers across the back of my neck. *Wait, that last thing wasn't gentlemanly, but it certainly made a lasting impression.* He slides into the seat next to mine, our legs press together, and his hand moves immediately to my knee like it was born to be there. *This man... help me... I'm melting.*

"What would you like to drink, Wildcat?"

"I'll have a Riesling." *That sounds a little classier than a glass of cheap white zin, right?* "And are you going to call me by my given name at any point this evening?"

He snickers. "Don't count on it."

We fall into easy conversation over drinks, banter laden with double entendre. I love every second, but I'm really hungry. Wine and goosebumps on an empty stomach cause my eye to wander when a man on the other side of me is served an appetizer that smells better than it looks—which is saying a lot. Emboldened, I make conversation with him. "That smells absolutely incredible. What is it?"

"Crab cake bites with a jalapeño sauce." He has food *and* he's cute. Picking up a bite-sized piece, he offers, "Would you like a taste?"

Um... Before I can respond, Max stands up to look over the bar at this man with a nonthreatening expression. "I'm sure you're a nice guy, but if anyone's going to handfeed this woman tonight, it's going to be me."

The guy backs off immediately with a *no harm, no foul* wave of his hand and a nod to my date. Max sits back down and gently squares my shoulders. "Are you trying to start a fight tonight, Wildcat?" I smile sheepishly and shake my head. He looks right into my eyes and says, "When you're out with me, you keep your eyes on *me*."

My stomach does a thousand cartwheels, and I wish I had a fresh pair of panties in my purse. I like my men a little bossy. So what? I'm not ashamed. But I kind of wonder why...

Dinner is delicious, tête-à-tête stimulating, and I'm so primed for Max that I want him for dessert. Seriously, I wave the menu away and suggest we go back to my place. After he glances over the bill, he states dryly, "Someone's going to have to get naked tonight."

* * *

Fumbling with those stupid deadbolts getting back into the house, I have to dig into the deep recesses of my brain to remember the alarm code and lock the deadbolts behind us.

"You're pretty serious about security," he comments.

"Ah, yes, well, I took a vow of safety when I moved in here on my own in May."

"And yet," he moves into my personal space and runs his fingers lightly across my collarbone, "you locked *me* inside all alone with *you*."

I laugh nervously. "I'm safe with you, right?"

"Oh, I'm going to take good care of you." He moves in for the first kiss. His lips are full, and the kiss is the perfect mixture of hot and wet without too much or too little of anything. The first kiss turns into a second, third, fourth, and then I lose count because our mouths, tongues, and hands become a commingled tangle of *oh my god...*

When he pulls back to smile at me, I'm short on breath and rational thought. Ten steps stand between us and my bedroom door. Tempted to drag him in there and further defy the laws of Wildcat/Sun Devil nature, I hesitate. Taking the *Jump the Guy* fork in the road won't lead me anywhere new.

Calling a play of his own, he leads us to my sofa and gestures for me to take a seat. Max smoothly crooks his arm under my knees and sweeps my legs onto his lap. After slipping off my flats he proceeds to massage my right foot. As he hits different pressure points, he asks questions about my affinity for football, my poor choice in universities, my MBA program.

I respond to his questions and ask many of my own while he massages, slowly and methodically, working his way from my foot to ankle, ankle to calf, calf to knee, knee to mid-thigh, mid-thigh to... nothing. He stops right there. "Are you relaxed, Amanda?"

"Mm hmm..."

"Do you want me to do the other leg?"

"Mm hmm..."

"Good to know." Moving my legs, he stands up and carefully places my limbs back on the couch. Smirking, he informs me, "I only do left legs on the second date. I have to get going tonight."

What? Did he just throw the flag? Is this where it ends?

"I'd let myself out, but I don't think I can work all those locks."

Glowering up at him from my position of bliss interrupted, I ask in disbelief, "You're really going to leave now? As in—*right now*?" He has an early morning flight to Houston—*stupid football*, and I love football.

That *devil* grins at me. "Yup, but I'll be back in town on Monday. I'll call you then to schedule your left leg massage."

The Next Day

"Oh my god, Jenny... Who walks out on a first date like that?" I just finished giving her the play-by-play from last night.

She's laughing her ass off, holding a sleepy Maisy in her arms. "That dude's playing with you, Amanda. He's probably pulled that move a few dozen times."

"Shit," I mutter and look at Paul. "Is she right?"

Paul is clearly amused. I'm a constant source of entertainment for this man. "Yeah. Gotta say, that was an epic move to lock down a second date. Wish I'd thought of that back in the day."

"Ugh..." I bring my hand to my forehead and try to rub some common sense into my brain. "So, he likes me, right? You don't think he's a player?"

Paul says, "It sounds like he's into you. But if he doesn't call you on Monday, he's probably a player."

I grind out, "I do not need any more players on my bench."

"Why not?" Jenny asks. "If you like him, put him in rotation."

"Because I'm tired... so, so tired of screwing the same man. Like, the only guy I can see a future with is Shawn, but he's still... we're still exactly where we were one year ago because he's so messed up from his divorce. Please, you guys, don't ever get a divorce or mess each other up. Everything is on hot cop's terms. I've never been to his place, never met his children—he's just content to bang me with his nightstick a few nights a week. I mean, that's awesome, but I think I'm in love with the guy. And he might have to arrest me, right? Like, what if he catches me with weed? I'd look totally fat in Sheriff Joe's horizontal black and white stripes."

I pause to take in a gulp of air because I'm nowhere near finished. "I think Alan's on meth—did I tell you that? Because something is not right with that guy, and people in restaurants are known for doing that shit. And James... James is cool to hang out with, but he's," I wrinkle my nose, "not as smart as me. He's flat broke all the time. Does that make me sound like an asshole? I'm such an asshole. But mostly, I'm just sick of being single. I haven't had a real relationship since college, and that was like *A MILLION YEARS AGO*! I've been *ALONE FOR ONE MILLION FREAKING YEARS*! Why doesn't anyone want to keep me?" I'm angry, but here come the *stupid tears*.

I need to calm down. "Give me that baby. I need a hit."

Jenny complies immediately. Once I have Maisy nestled in my arms, I inhale deeply, taking a hit from her baby head, and coo at her, "Auntie Amanda wants to find a man who will marry her and give her babies. Auntie Amanda is sick of my bench players. And I'm just dating them, baby girl. I didn't mean it when I said that I was screwing them."

Paul and Jenny break out into laughter. Paul says, "I don't know what's more disturbing—you talking about yourself in the third person or talking to my baby about your freaking bench."

"I want Max to be different. I want him to be *the one*. Maisy, why can't he be *the one*?"

Maisy has nothing for me but a bubbled drool smile.

CHAPTER 23

I SPEND THE REST OF the weekend cocooned in my house, watching movies, smoking a little weed, drinking white zin with shit tons of ice, and trying to make Squirt cuddle with me. He'll have none of it. Worse than aloof, he's an asshole cat who will probably eat my rotting carcass when I expire from *aloneness*.

I'm so uncommitted, it might take days for someone to notice that I'm missing. Maybe Shawn will sweep the perimeter and catch wind of the foul stench coming from inside my house. Maybe I'll never hear from Shawn again. Who knows? No one owes me any-thing—except for Max. He owes me a phone call.

At work on Monday, I wait and wait and wait to hear from that Sun Devil. Not only does Max not call, he isn't on IM at all. After work, I come back home and wait and wait and wait. In between waiting, I smoke half a joint on my back porch, and I might have cried a few times.

Paul and Jenny called it; Max is just another player. But when my doorbell rings out at 8:30 p.m., hope springs alive. Would he be so bold and just drop by? Will he massage my left leg?

Throwing open the door, I'm thankful my security screen is dead-bolted because Shawn stands on the other side in his uniform carrying his gear bag. And, too bad for me, I probably reek of weed—and now I'm going to jail.

"You going to let me in?"

"Yes. I need two minutes." I call over my shoulder as I head for my bedroom, "Be right back. Don't worry—you'll be safe out there. You have a gun."

I change my shirt in a flash, spritz myself with perfume, and make a mad dash for my toothbrush. I also wash my face and hands making quick work of hiding the evidence—as long as he doesn't go into the backyard where half a joint rests in the ashtray on the patio table. *Damn it.* I would not make a good criminal, and Shawn really needs to call before he comes over.

When I rush back to the door and throw open the deadbolt, I try to look cool but probably fail.

"What's up with you tonight?" he asks stepping inside. Here's the *rub* about dating (or banging) a cop—when Shawn asks me a question, no matter how trivial, he watches my eyes and reads my face like he's conducting a lie detector test. It's an occupational haz- ard that I find totally annoying. My goal is to tell him no lies—ever, so sometimes I tell half of the truth.

"Girl stuff." I attempt nonchalance and meet his eyes. "I wasn't expecting you, and my breath wasn't suitable for your company. I was doing you a favor." I grin and tip my face up to kiss his hot cop jawline.

He buys it. "Babe, you're a nut."

Is that why you won't keep me?

With no additional small talk, he puts his big hands on my shoulders and starts walking me backwards into my bedroom. When my legs hit the mattress, I fall back and assume the position. Straddling me, he leans over to kiss my mouth and *cop* a feel. My ovaries are delighted, but then he rolls off and settles next to me. "I'm taking this weekend off. I have a thing—a wedding. I'm sorry for the late notice, but I wasn't sure I could get the time off. I was hoping you'd be my plus one."

"Oh… When?"

"This Saturday, 5 p.m. Reception after. And I need you to look extra hot because my kids' mom is going to be there."

Rolling to face him, I prop up my head with one hand. "Well, this is an unusual request."

"I was your plus one at what's her name's wedding."

"Katie—my former roommate you've met at least a dozen times. God, you'd think a cop would remember little things like details."

"Will you come with me?"

"Is there an open bar?"

He chuckles. "Yeah, I think so."

"Top shelf or just the cheap shit?"

"Babe, you drink the cheap shit, so does it matter?"

"I guess not." I roll to my back. "How hot? Dressed up and classy hot? Slutty hot? Arizona-casual wedding hot?"

"The first one—dressy and classy hot. And heels. I want you to tower over her."

"Are you *using* me?"

"Only in good ways, Amanda. Oh, I forgot to mention the wedding's in Sedona, so it's a twenty-four-hour commitment."

It might only be twenty-four hours, but it's the first time he's asked for any *commitment*. "Okay," I agree. Max is a player, but at least he didn't score with me. "You could've just called."

"Then I wouldn't be able to make you come before my shift."

"Nice one, Officer Barton." I smile in appreciation of his naughty intentions. As he resumes his earlier play of *copping* a feel, it occurs to me that he doesn't work Mondays. "Did you swap your shift?"

He pauses—lips on my neck, one hand between my legs—and answers, "Yeah, so I could swing the weekend off."

"You on at ten?"

"I am which means I need to get you off by nine-thirty at the latest."

Well, crap. Every day, I fall a little more in love with him.

* * *

Max pings me via IM on Thursday. *Thursday.* He's only FOUR DAYS late (who's counting) and this is not a phone call.

Max: *Wildcat*

Me: *What?*

Max: *Where have you been?*

Me: *Not sitting at home since MONDAY waiting for the phone to ring.*

Max: *You're angry.*

Me: *You're awfully smart for a Sun Devil.*

Max: *Ouch. I was sick.*

Me: *How sad.*

Max: *Really. I've been down for days. Just starting to feel human again.*

Me: *Can Devils feel human?*

Max: *How are you feeling? Maybe you got me sick.*

Me: *Maybe you should just stick with saying you're sorry.*

Max: *Can I make it up to you?*

Me (after pondering because I so wanted this guy to be different, my bench is full, and I have a lot on my plate between work and school): *No.*

Max: *I can't make it up to you?*

Me: *I can't do this with you.*

Max: *???*

Me: *Never trust a Sun Devil – defies the laws of nature.*

Max: *I was sick.*

Me: *You should have called.*

Max: *I'M SORRY.*

Me: *A SHOUTY CAPS apology doesn't count as an actual apology.*

Max: *I already apologized without SHOUTY CAPS. I want to take you out Saturday night.*

Me: *I already have plans.*

Max: *Washing your hair? ;)*

Me: *I won't be in town. I have an overnight date in Sedona.*

Max: *You're dating someone?*

Me: *Yes.*

Max: *Damn, Amanda. You could've told me.*

Me: *Why? I don't owe you anything. You don't owe me anything either – not a phone call or a left leg massage. You owe me nothing.*

Max: *I owe you a left leg massage.*

Me: *I'll get one from my date on Saturday night. Don't worry about it.*

Max: *That's harsh, Wildcat.*

Me: *So is leaving a woman twisting in the wind after an amazing date and NOT CALLING her as PROMISED.*

Max: *I thought our first date was amazing, too.*

Me: *I meant to type mediocre – a mediocre date.*

Max: *I'm going to have to work for this, aren't I?*

Me: *Don't bother.*

Max: *Are you serious?*

Me: *Yes. And I have actual work to do – there's a pile of it on my desk. Bye.*

Before he can respond, I close the chat box and sign off IM. Biting back tears, I hop on the elevator and ride it down to the lobby. In the outdoor atrium, I light up a cigarette and suck it down.

When that doesn't do the trick, I go back upstairs and pop my head into my boss' office, begging off for the afternoon citing a painful headache. I take half the pile of work home, but I don't touch it. I smoke a joint, watch TV, and lick my Max-inflicted wounds.

***

Shawn picks me up mid-morning on Saturday. We're going to check into the resort and change into our semi-formal attire before the ceremony. The groom is a mutual friend of Shawn and his ex from their college days at NAU, which is like Switzerland for Arizona and Arizona State fans alike. None of us hate the Lumberjacks.

"Debbie is the name of your ex-wife, right?" I have to ask because he primarily refers to her as *My Kids' Mom*—which is generous, considering.

"Yup."

"Is it going be awkward or get ugly between the two of you?"

"I don't think so. The kids are with her parents this weekend. She'll be there with her husband."

"She's remarried already?"

"Right after the ink dried on the divorce papers."

"You never mentioned that. Did she marry the guy she... you know, the affair guy?"

"Oh yeah. Guess she prefers her man working day shifts."

"Is that why—"

"I'd rather not talk about her. I don't want to lay this shit on you, Amanda. Let's have some fun this weekend."

Because I've never broached the subject and he's a captive audience right now, unless he decides to drive his truck off a cliff on the I-17, he has to answer. "Why don't you lay any of your shit on me? I mean, you help me with my stuff all the time. We've been seeing each other for over a year now and," I hesitate. I need to shut up, but my ovaries are dying to know. "Is this all it's going to be between us?"

He lets the question linger in the air way too long before muttering, "Here we go..."

My eyes narrow. "I think it's a valid question."

"Babe, I deal with the dregs of Phoenix night after night. You are like sunshine after darkness—smart, pretty, so funny. You can't cook, but that's okay." He spares me a sideways glance and snickers. "I'm definitely not dating you for your cooking."

"Well, that's a relief."

He laughs at me. "Yeah. I'm with a woman like you because you're not complicated. I care about you more than I should, but..." *There is always a but...* "I'm stretched thin and my two biggest priorities are my kids and my job."

"Am I ever going to meet your kids?" *God, shut up, Amanda.*

"I'm not even a part-time dad. What little time I get with them is ours."

We fall into silence, and it isn't one bit comfortable. My mind is regurgitating his words, trying to process what this means for me and my *stupid ovaries.*

"I don't want a never-ending one-night stand. Eventually I'm going to need more, and I'm not asking you to give that to me right now." *Yes, I am. Please offer me more.*

"This conversation isn't a surprise to me. I don't like having it because I'm happy right now, but I get it—I've been married, already have a family, and you haven't done any of that yet."

"Right."

"I'm not ready to go there again."

I sigh. "You want status quo?" *And, did you just call me* uncomplicated *earlier? Aren't cops supposed to be good judges of character?*

"Please."

"Forever?"

"Not necessarily, but it's too soon."

"Fine. I won't bring it up again." *Not even if my ovaries beg me.* "It has to come from you."

We drive many miles in silence—although it's not quite as uncomfortable. I know where he stands, and he hasn't budged an inch in over a year. As the desert landscape changes to scrub brush and eventually to the beautiful oaks and pines and mammoth red rocks of Sedona that take my breath away, Shawn and I resume conversation when I ask him about his college days at NAU.

I'm surprised to learn that he played college football. *Me and football players... It figures.* We talk and argue about our favorite teams and players, and, by the time we pull into the resort and check in, we are so back to normal that we get very dirty before showering off together and getting dressed up for the wedding.

It's a touching ceremony even though I don't know the happy couple. The venue is stunning, and the indoor/outdoor reception sparkles with bright white lights and candlelight. Shawn keeps me close to his side all evening. He introduces me to the woman who gave him his children and broke his heart. She's tall and brunette like me, just not as tall or as curvy. She's polite but very reserved and won't let go of her husband's arm.

I can't believe you cheated on a man like Shawn. Then again, I cheated on a man like Tanner so who am I to judge?

We have a lovely meal, and I drink wine to quell my *forced to make small talk with strangers* nerves. We dance close and kiss often, and as I play the part of his doting plus one, I wonder how much of his affection is for show. Every once in a while, I pretend that this is more than what it actually is. When we return to the hotel room, he takes me in the bed. He's passionate and confident, and I love everything about him—save for the little fact that he doesn't love me.

When we finally curl up to fall asleep, my bare back pressing into the slick skin of his front, his arms holding me close, I'm grateful that he can't see my face because I cry silent tears onto my pillow. He is everything I want, but he is not mine to keep.

CHAPTER 24

The Monday before Thanksgiving, five days before the Territorial Cup grudge match, Max hits me up on IM.

Max: *Care to make a wager, Wildcat?*

Me: *You again... You can't see me, but I'm rolling my eyes right now.*

Max: *Come on... Let's make a bet on the game.*

Me: *No.*

Max: *Pussycat???*

Me: *Your track record isn't that great. We got you last year, skipped a year, and had three in a row before that.*

Max: *I love and hate that you can rattle off football stats without even blinking. Makes me hard.*

Me: *Right. I didn't blink, but I'm still rolling my eyes.*

Max: *Here's the bet... Arizona takes it—you get the restaurant of your choice, a left leg massage, and anything else you want.*

Me: *((((Rolling eyes))))*

Max: *ASU takes it—I plan the date and you give me whatever I want.*

Me: *Sounds like I lose either way.*

Max: *Come on. You can't stay angry forever. I'M SORRY. Please see me again. I'll even sweeten the pot with some Cards tickets.*

Me: *Not a Cards fan.*

Max: *Come on, Wildcat. Let's have date two.*

Me: *Maybe.*

Max: *December 4th. I'll pick you up at 6:30 p.m. Winner's choice.*

Me: *Fine, but I swear to god, if you no call, no show, I will NEVER speak to you again.*

Max: *I'll be there. I promise.*

Me: *FYI—you better start saving up. I'm picking the most expensive restaurant I can find.*

Max: *You have to win the game first, Wildcat.*

Territorial Cup—1998

From my parents' living room, Dad and I jump up pumping fists and screaming for joy. It was one hell of a fight. Arizona—50; Arizona State—42. Either way, Max structured the bet so he'd win.

Friday, December 4, 1998

He shows up with flowers. He grovels, just a little bit. His brown eyes dance with mine, and he takes me out to the restaurant of my choice. It's expensive. After all, he has to pay for dinner and for not calling when he said that he would. Over dinner, I forgive him, because—*god*, this man makes me laugh, and he makes me wet, and all of it is way too enjoyable for my own good.

Until he asks me about the other man in my life. When I tell him that there are three, I get raised eyebrows followed by a glare.

"What?" I shrug. "What's wrong with dating more than one guy?"

"Are you sleeping with all of these guys?"

"Is that any of your business?"

"Shit." He sighs. "You are."

"I didn't answer the question because it's none of your business."

"I won't share a woman with anyone else," he states.

I smile. "I'm not going to clear my well-rounded bench after one and a half dates. You've seen my neighborhood—it's practically a necessity to have a cop in my rotation."

While he laughs, he doesn't find it funny, because his eyes are still giving me attitude. "A woman like you... I like what I see here. Wildcat thing aside, you're interesting, attractive, love sports. I don't know if I'm going to enjoy your brain or your body more. We could both have a good time exploring that."

Right back at you, Max. I drain my Riesling and shake my glass by the stem indicating that he should order me another one before responding, "That's what we're doing."

"Yes, but..." *There's always a but with these guys...* "I'm not going to sleep with a woman who's having sex with other men."

Now it's my turn to glare. "I never answered your question, and you're quite presumptuous assuming that sex is on the table. I should be offended, don't you think?"

His lips quirk into a smile. "It's not a stretch of the imagination, Amanda. Even if you plead the Fifth, juggling three guys at once means you're not exactly a rookie player."

"I'm pretty sure you've already gone pro."

"I don't claim to be innocent, Wildcat. I'm just telling you that I have a hard line on this one."

"I heard you, Max. There will be no *panky* on the field."

There is plenty of hanky, however. In fact, there's hanky at the dinner table, in the parking lot, and back at my house. He starts with my left leg which does not get the same level of attention as my right, because he has other things on his mind. He's all give, no take—proven by the fact that I only manage to get his shirt off while my entire outfit, drenched panties included, is scattered all over my bedroom floor.

His lips travel from my mouth to neck and stop to nibble on my earlobe. His fingers are between my legs, toying with me, and he whispers, "You're so wet for me. I can't wait to taste you."

He pulls me to the edge of the bed, spreads my legs wide open, and drops to his knees on the floor. Before he tastes me, he kisses the insides of my thighs, delivers soft bites and suction; his nose rubs against my clit followed by his mouth and this, *holy fuck*, combination of tongue, lips, teeth, and fingers.

Sure, I've had guys go down on me before, but Max is like no other. He went pro quite some time ago and, screw football, oral sex is his favorite sport. We're not rivals on the field—I'm totally on his team.

The orgasm starts in my brain because I carefully consider the fact that it might actually kill me. I clench every muscle trying to fight it off. He senses my struggle and hops to his feet; I lose his tongue but not his fingers. He drops over me, and sexier than anything in my life is his mouth finding mine. His face and mouth are saturated with me, and I fucking love it.

His calm voice tells me how this play is going down. "I'm going to make you come harder than you ever have before, Wildcat. Relax, let go, and scream my name so your neighbors know which guy on your damn bench is here tonight. Do you understand me?"

I'm certain the question is rhetorical. Instead of answering, the sensations thunder through my body—massive and agonizing in the best possible way. My nails dig into the skin of his back, my toes curl, and I do scream his name. Hell, I would've screamed *GO A-S-U* if he'd told me to. Every fiber of my entire being is rocked into an alternate universe.

I'm still pulsing and shaking when he calls the next play. "That was outstanding, Amanda. We're going to do it again." *We are? Oh, hell, yes we are*, because his fingers don't let up, they slide deeper inside and find that spot—*you know the one and if you don't that's really too bad for you*. Within seconds, the second one rips through me, almost as brilliant as the first.

My pro isn't finished with me. He takes my mouth, adjusts his magnificent fingers and challenges, "What else do you have for me, Wildcat? Give it to me."

I'm in tears and protest, "No more."

The *devil* has other plans. "I'm going to make you do this all night."

Yup, I'm totally on his team. In fact, the colors that flood my vision might as well be maroon and gold because this Sun Devil pulls off something I've only read about in dirty books. I'm so loud that every neighbor within a two-mile radius has to know what's happening over here. This must be how legends become renowned.

He rolls one orgasm into the next into the next into the—*oh my god*—next until the neighbor's dog is howling, my bed is soaked, and all I can do is shake and cry.

"Hey... hey..." Moving to my side, his hand slides over my breast. He toys with my nipple before taking it in his mouth and sucking hard. I gasp and then immediately groan when his hand moves back between my legs. *God help me, the* devil *wants to kill me.* The coroner will declare *death by orgasm* and stamp it on my death certificate. Jenny will cheer, but my mother will be very ashamed of my behavior.

Exhausted and ruined, but he wants more. He changes tactics and kisses me so tenderly, sweetly while his fingers slow their tempo inside me.

He whispers, "Amanda, watching you come undone is incredible." His kiss is gentle like his whisper. "It's like you're in another world. Your face and your body all the way down to your toes... every part of you gets in on the act. It makes me feel like such a man knowing I can do that to you."

Lips trail down my body, and he slides back to his knees on the floor. As tenderly as he kissed my mouth, he kisses and licks my lips, sucks gently on my clit, and coaxes two more out of me with his tongue and fingers—slow and spectacular.

After this one-sided encounter—after all I won the bet, and I'm too weak to reciprocate—we lie in my bed together under the covers well away from the wet spot. He spoons me from behind, playing with my hair and stroking my skin. "You feeling okay, Wildcat?"

"Mmmm hmmm..."

"So is this what it takes to get you to shut up?"

"Mmmm hmmm... Hey!" I try to throw an elbow back, but I lack the strength to do it at all, never mind effectively, so I let it slide. I mumble, "Didn't know that was possible... Can't believe it's not a myth...."

"What's that?"

"Mmmmultiples..." and that's all I have left to give before this player passes out on the field.

Christmas Eve Day, 1998

I go to Pine Ridge for Christmas. It's just the three of us—quiet, relaxing. I have a brush with my past when I run into Fiona and Mrs. McLaughlin at Safeway. Mom needs butterscotch pudding mix for her sticky buns, and I cross paths with them in the baking aisle. After exchanging hugs and pleasantries, Mrs. McLaughlin invites me up to the house to see Coach. I decline when I learn that Braden is home with the pig farmer's daughter.

"I'll come by next time I'm in town, and Braden's not, you know, visiting with his wife. Way too awkward."

"Amanda," she offers after exchanging glances with Fiona, "it's been years. Perhaps a visit with Braden wouldn't be as awkward as you think. You were such good friends, and I know Braden's curious about what you've been up to. Nick hasn't seen you in years."

"I'm sorry. It has been years, Mrs. McLaughlin, but I'm going back to the Valley right after Christmas. I'm taking my parents to the Cardinal's game on Friday, and then we're going to Tucson to visit Tanner and meet his twins."

"Tanner has *twins*?" Fiona asks with a smile.

"Abigail and Andrew—they were born this summer," I share. "We can't wait to meet them. Tanner's busy doing his residency at UMC. Please tell Coach that he's doing great. And so am I."

"I'll be sure to tell him," Mrs. McLaughlin responds.

"Well, I better get going... Mom needs this for her sticky buns," I wave the box of pudding.

"Wait, let's exchange info. Jeremy and I bought a house last year. Maybe you can stop by when you're in Tucson," Fiona suggests.

"Sure, but not this trip. We're just going down for a few hours." Digging in my purse for paper and a pen, I scroll out my address, number, and email. "I just bought a house, too. Hopefully I'll be there for a while." I smile at Fiona and rip the paper in half so she can give me her information. We end the conversation with hugs and promises to see each other soon, but I have no intention of contacting Fiona.

Back in Cherry, I tremble at the thought of being so close yet so far from Braden. He's at his house just ten minutes from this parking lot, and I want... *What do you want? He married the pig farmer's daughter and hasn't spoken to you in EIGHT YEARS.*

He'll find out soon enough that I'm in Pine Ridge, and if he wants to see me, he can call. He should be the one to call after what he said to me eight years ago.

I heard Braden sigh into the phone and it was a big, broody one. "What?" He said.

"Are we... are you..." and the stammering was back because I wasn't sure what I wanted to ask him, much less how to ask. I took a deep breath and expressed a coherent thought, "Can we get together and talk?"

"No."

No? How could he possibly say no to me? Didn't I matter to him? *"I understand that you're upset about me and Tanner, but, you know, we talked about all of this over the summer, and I thought our friendship would survive. I thought that's what you wanted."*

"Not anymore."

"So that's it?" I asked. Nothing. *"We're not going to be friends anymore?" The silence was deafening, and it was breaking my heart. "Braden..." I searched again—for words, for hope, for an end to this excruciating one-sided conversation. "After everything we shared over the years, you have nothing to say to me?"*

After another prolonged period of more awkward silence, he finally spoke, "Yeah. I have something to say."

"Thank god. I'm listening."

He went in for the kill. "I should've just gone ahead and fucked you when you spread your legs for me." The line went dead.

After eight years, you'd think it wouldn't hurt anymore, but it does—so, so much.

Friday, December 27, 1998

The Cardinals beat the Chargers 16 to 13. Dad loves the free box suite tickets, beer, and buffet. Mom could've stayed at my house with Squirt and had a better time. Her football knowledge is pathetic, and she doesn't care to learn. It feels utterly creepy to watch our pro team play at Sun Devil Stadium. They really need their own digs. During half-time, Max pops in to say hello and meet the parents. He is, of course, charming, and my dad falls in love with him.

After Max leaves, Dad turns to me and says, "If you don't marry that guy, you're doing a disservice to the entire family."

"Yeah," I laugh. "You'd love to see me with a sports reporter with access to free tickets who is willing to talk football twenty-four seven. Maybe you should marry him, Dad."

"I'm already taken, but you... You're not getting any younger."

"Um... *thanks*? It's still a really new thing, Dad, and, well, he's a Sun Devil so..."

CHAPTER 25

The Next Day

TANNER MEETS US IN THE driveway and dispenses warm hugs to the three of us. Before we meet the babies, who are with Lorraine and the in-laws in the main house, he takes us on a tour of their newly constructed home on the family compound. It's small, but he breaks out some blueprints to show us where and how they plan to add on as their family grows. I linger in the doorway of the nursery and take in the blue and pink bedding in each crib. It smells like baby heads in here. Heaven.

Stop twitching, Ovaries.

In the main house, Lorraine and her family roll out the welcome mat. I stop in the hallway to take in a collage of wedding photos. I'm more curious than sad, and I break out into a grin when I see the traditional shot of the bride and groom with their parents. My parents are by Tanner's side. The pit in my stomach during the drive down fades away. *We are family by choice.*

We all wash our hands before we're introduced to my new favorite Wildcats. They have Tanner's brown eyes, and, as with Maisy, I fall instantly in love. Mom and I trade off between Abigail and Andrew. I take hits from their Heavenly baby heads and whisper my private promises to each of them.

Conversation and good feelings flow freely around their large family room. We visit for several hours and have lunch before heading back to the Valley. Mom can't stop gushing happy baby thoughts. I wish she would've stuck with that for two hours, but she changes her tune and laments the fact that she barely knows her grandsons and starts talking about advanced maternal age, that Max seems like such a nice boy, and *shoot me now.*

* * *

My parents are staying one more night with me, so Mom and I—okay, mostly Mom—get dinner ready. I make a great salad, though. After dinner my doorbell rings. Elbow deep in dishes and suds, after Dad opens the door I hear him ask, "Can I help you, Officer?"

Oh my god. Worlds are colliding. I wipe my arms off with a dishtowel and pop my head around the corner. "Hi, Shawn. Please come in," I greet.

"The security door isn't dead bolted." He glares at me as he steps through the door, his gear bag slung over one shoulder.

"You can take that up with my dad—if you dare," I tease and

introduce them. "Shawn, these are my parents, Michael and Claire Harrington. Parents, this is my, um, friend Shawn, otherwise known as Officer Barton, Officer Bossy, and/or Officer Obsessed with my Deadbolts. But you can call him Shawn."

Dad quirks a brow at me before returning to his perusal of Officer Shawn Barton. They shake hands, and Shawn apologizes for not calling first. "I didn't recognize the car in the drive. I probably shouldn't have stopped."

"No worries. Are you on at ten?" I ask.

"Am I always on at ten?" he responds with a smile.

"Put your bag away and stay."

"I don't want to intrude, but I haven't seen you in a while."

"You're not intruding at all. We're pretty much sick of each other after days of togetherness," I joke. "Store your gear and come on in the kitchen." He follows my directions. Back in the kitchen I offer, "We just finished dinner—lemon chicken breasts, wild rice, and salad. I have plenty of leftovers if you're hungry."

"That depends." He quips dryly, "Who cooked dinner?"

Dad snorts out a laugh and points to Mom. "Claire."

"In that case, yes, I'd love something to eat."

As I fix him a plate, Mom sets a place for him at the table, and I grumble, "You know, I'm glad you all feel comfortable taking cheap shots at my kitchen skills. Go right ahead and mock me. I don't care."

"Babe, that *one time* you made dinner for me... Remember we had to fly in Chinese?"

I roll my eyes at him. "Of course I remember, because you won't let me forget it, and you won't give me a do-over."

"I don't want to die," he shoots back.

With a mild glare, I plop down the plate and ask, "Water or lemonade? It's too late for beer."

"Water, please. Thanks, babe."

Mom's confused. "How long have you known each other?"

Shawn glances at me. "What... well over a year by now, right?"

I explain, "Um, Shawn is the man who helped me move most of the stuff into the house this spring. He also hooked me up with the guy who installed the security system, and don't even get him started on the whole deadbolt *situation*. He takes safety very seriously."

Mom blurts out, "Are you *dating*?"

"We go out on dates, so I guess we're *dating*. I went to that wedding with him in Sedona back in October."

"Oh." Mom's eyes register the event, but my parents are still puzzled by the sight of this manly cop in uniform thoroughly at ease in my house eating Mom's chicken.

Dad starts asking him questions about his job and carries the conversation during Shawn's meal while Mom and I finish cleaning the kitchen. After he declines seconds, I scoop up his empty plate and silverware to rinse and put in the dishwasher.

During a brief lull in the chatter, Shawn stands. "I should probably go and leave you to your family time."

"Please stay," I request. "Really, we are quite sick of each other."

"If you don't mind, I have more questions about this neighborhood," Dad says.

The conversation moves into the living room. I learn that Shawn is very concerned about the nightly *situations* west of 15th Avenue, which is just a few blocks down, but he doesn't elaborate too much.

He reassures Dad that my pocket is relatively safe as long as I remember to lock the security door and use my alarm.

He adds, "I wish she had a garage instead of that carport. I worry knowing she's coming back from class in the dark."

You worry about me, Shawn?

"But she's on a well-traveled street, not tucked back into the neighborhood. We patrol this corridor routinely, and the unit members have eyes on Amanda's house every time they drive by."

This is news to me. While the thought of being watched over by the Phoenix Police Department is comforting, it also makes me queasy. As I rotate bench players, the cars in my driveway rotate. He's never stopped by unannounced before when I've had company over, but he did tonight.

Can he run plates? *Um, yeah, he's a cop.* Did he run my parents' plates? Has he run other plates? Can he name the players on my bench?

I'm slightly disturbed in more ways than one, but Dad is beyond pleased. "We really appreciate that, Shawn. I was against this neighborhood for a young single woman, but this puts me at ease."

"Crime can happen anywhere, Michael. I'm just glad she's east of 15th Avenue. It's a gang boundary so, like I said, just about everything I never want Amanda to know about happens on the other side."

Before Shawn leaves, he takes his bag into my room and puts on his belt and gear. My parents stand to bid their farewells, and he politely states that it was his pleasure to meet them.

I walk him to the door and send him off onto the streets of Phoenix with my usual parting line, "Please be safe out there."

"I always am." He surprises me with a hug and a tender albeit brief kiss on the lips in front of my parents. Before I even have the security door shut, he barks out over his shoulder, "Lock the deadbolts."

"Yes, Officer Bossy," I bark back, and do what I'm told.

When I turn around, my parents are both beaming at me like I introduced them to the Pope. *Great, my ovaries and my parents want me to have babies with this guy.*

"I'm on the fence," Dad declares. "I don't know which one I like better. Which one do you like better, Claire?"

I caution, "Dad, don't get your hopes up because..." My eyes sting with tears. "Ugh. Crap."

"Brown Eyes?"

"I could use some parental guidance." Without any sordid details about my sex life, we sit back down and I spill my current *situation*. I tell them about the men I've been dating—just dating, not screwing, but I become more emotional when I share how discouraged I feel. "My friends are pretty much married off, we just spent the day with Tanner's family, and everything is *fine* but I want more. Do I get a shot at this happily ever after crap, or do I have to do this forever?"

"I don't understand," Mom says.

"What?" I ask.

"When I met your father in college, he took the lead and the next thing I knew, I was married. And I don't regret it, honey." She makes doe eyes at Dad but there are none of those for me. "I don't understand why you kids make things so complicated."

"I think," Dad interjects, "that when a man is ready to commit to a woman, he doesn't mess around. He'll move heaven and earth to make it happen."

"Where is *that man*, Daddy? Is he out there?"

"There are lots of clichés about love, kid, but most of them are true. Maybe you're dating him right now or you haven't met him yet, but when it's right for both of you, he'll make it happen and you'll know. When the time is right, you'll find what you want. Timing is everything."

* * *

Timing might be everything, but timing has a sick sense of humor. Between work and school, I don't have enough of it. In March, I cut Alan from my bench and I give James the *let's be friends* speech. Even with no expectation of sex, James and I become *friends* and spend the occasional evening having conversations or watching a movie—stoned, of course. And he's willing to fix things around my house, but I return the favor with food and weed.

Max, the sarcastic, funny, giver of the best oral sex ever... Well, it turns out that professional hockey season runs concurrently with football season and continues relentlessly into late spring. Hockey teams play about six times as many games as a pro football team. I've never given any thought to hockey before, but now it's a huge part of bad timing. Max goes on the road with the Coyotes. He shares coverage of some home games with another reporter, but Max prefers the road.

Max and I "talk" almost every day over IM. We see each other every few weeks, but it isn't enough to take us to the next level. I really enjoy the hell out of that *devil*, but I can't decide if my feelings are the real deal because every occasional reunion feels like a honeymoon. It's all sweet talk, lips, hands, and a lot of tongue with heavy doses of ridiculous side-splitting banter.

We engage in plenty of hanky but no panky because I'm still seeing Shawn, and my ovaries and I have all kinds of feelings for that hot cop. Neither guy is moving heaven much less the earth to be with me, but I want them both.

* * *

Heading into late spring of 1999, I'm awarded a shiny new diploma. My MBA is complete, and I paid for and accomplished this one all on my own. My parents invite me and *the man of my choice* out to dinner to celebrate. Max is traveling nonstop for *stupid hockey*, but Shawn is game and joins us out on a Friday evening before his shift.

With three nights a week now free, I have more time for Jenny and Maisy. She turns a year old in May. I feel like I blinked and Maisy grew from a tiny baby into a toddler. Her head no longer smells like *Essence of Baby*. It's like she lost that new baby smell, but she gained mobility. Take your eyes off Maisy and she's gone in a flash. She is Jenny's daughter for sure.

Shawn and I have more time together, but he doesn't use it to—you know—move our relationship forward. Every time I'm tempted to push or ask, I think about our conversation on the drive to Sedona. He knows what I want, but, what's that saying—*why buy the cow when she gives the milk for free*?

By the time Max comes up for air on his beat in early summer, I'm promoted to a Regional Labor Relations Specialist, and I have to hit the road myself. Up and down the west coast, I support over one thousand employees in Arizona, Nevada, California, Oregon, Washington, and Alaska. Wow, Alaska—breathtaking, the nicest people I've ever met, and I experience my first earthquake. I'm grateful for upward mobility and more money, and the opportunity to travel the coast on CompuWorld's dime.

Age: Twenty-seven

I celebrate my unremarkable twenty-seventh birthday in Portland with a few of my colleagues. Returning in time to make a quick trip to Tucson with my parents for the twins' first birthday, I, of course, bring them obnoxious toys. It is my duty. I adore my honorary niece and nephew. They are exquisite works of art, and they completely fascinate me even though Abigail and Andrew have also lost that new baby smell. Oh, and speaking of babies, Jenny and Paul are expecting baby two.

At work, we have teams of IT professionals working around the clock, around the country in preparation for Y2K. Finally, fully staffed, I take a deep breath, check the calendar—*stupid timing*—and it's football season once again. Fuck. As mentioned, football players don't have to work nearly as much, so Max and I are able to carve out time, but he still won't sleep with me because I still won't cut Shawn from my bench.

In September, there are two major announcements. Trina and Katie are both knocked up. I'm excited for them, but my ovaries are angry because—*what the hell*? I just burned through another year with Shawn and a whole bunch of weed without making any progress on my own love life.

CHAPTER 26

Early October 1999

ON AN EARLY SATURDAY AFTERNOON, Cherry and I are returning from meeting Katie at the mall. Cruising along the I-10, nearing our exit in the far right lane, we're listening to Garth Brooks when we find ourselves in a horrible *situation*. I see brake lights ahead and start to slow down, but the car in front of me is at a dead stop. By the time I realize it, I have an instant to swerve, but it's not enough time. *Stupid timing.* Cherry crashes into the back passenger side of the Nissan.

My seatbelt locks; however, it's not enough to keep my head from flying into the steering wheel before it whips back into the seat rest. Ouch. That freaking hurt... *SMASH!* We're hit directly from behind in another grinding clash of metal on metal. My seatbelt is no longer locked, so my body hits the steering wheel. Cherry comes to rest at an odd angle, like we're heading down an incline instead of sitting on a flat piece of highway. There's one more impact, although nowhere near as violent as the first or second.

Stunned, I try to sit upright in my seat and gather my wits as traffic slows to a crawl, but I feel like I got punched in the *everything*. A man knocks on my closed window and asks me if I'm all right. Blinking thickly, I try to turn to him, but my *everything* really hurts.

He calls out, "There's one in here. She's conscious but bleeding."

I'm bleeding? God, I hope my ovaries are all right.

Sirens. Lots of sirens... firetrucks roll up. One blocks several lanes of traffic on my left, and the other pulls to the right side off the freeway. Department of Public Safety officers arrive along with a few City of Phoenix units. As I taste the blood trickling down my face, I wonder how many cars and people are involved in this accident.

There's another knock at my window. Since my *everything* hurts, it takes a superhuman effort to turn my head. By the time I manage to look to my left, Cherry's passenger window shatters. A hand reaches in to unlock the door and it's pried open. I blink at the man peering in at me. He looks like a fireman. *Why does every man on the face of the earth look sexier in a uniform?*

"Ma'am, don't try to move. Just stay put. What's your name?"

"Amanda."

"Hi, Amanda. I'm Chris. What day is it?"

"Don't you know what day it is?"

"I do." He smiles at me. "I want to know if *you* know what day it is."

"It's Saturday."

"Where are you, Amanda?"

"Phoenix."

"Can you be more specific?"

"I-10 before the Deck Park Tunnel."

"How old are you?"

"Twenty-seven."

"Are you pregnant?"

I glare because—*what the hell?* Chris seemed like a nice guy, but now I hate him. "Do I look like I'm pregnant?"

"No, Amanda, but I need to ask."

I mumble, "Maybe you should preface that question with, *you don't appear to be pregnant, but I'm required to ask....*"

He smiles. "You don't appear to be pregnant, Amanda, but are you?"

"Much better, Chris. No, I'm not."

"What happened today?"

"I crashed my truck."

"Good, Amanda. That's good."

Are you crazy, Chris?

He leans across the cab and pops the lock on my side. Remaining in my personal space, he looks at my lower body. "Stay as still as possible, but I want you to move your legs for me."

My legs work but my *everything* hurts. My face, my side, taking a breath...

"All right, let me see you move your arms." I know they work because my hands are covered in the blood I tried to wipe away earlier, but I move them for him anyway. "Excellent."

He scoots out the passenger side, stands, and shouts, "One female. Green. Spinal precautions." Popping his head back into the cab, he instructs, "Sit still, Amanda. We'll get you out as soon as possible." Before he walks off, he slaps a green sticker on Cherry's mangled windshield.

I close my eyes and wait—each breath more painful than the last—until Cherry's driver's side door is pried open with an unnatural squawk.

"Do you remember me?"

"You're Chris, the guy who asks rude questions."

He chuckles good-naturedly. "That's me. We're going to move you out of here." He explains as he works, "I'm going to put a collar on you as a precaution to keep your neck and spine as stable as possible." Ugh. Is this how Squirt felt wearing that *cone of shame* after I had him neutered? *Stupid asshole cat.* "We'll slide you onto a board and take you for a little ride over to the side of the freeway. Are you with me?"

"Yes, but, the other drivers? Is anyone..."

Chris relieves my worries right away. "Between the seat belts and the airbags, we're all green. Green is good, Amanda."

I'm with him, but the backboard hurts worse than lying on my concrete floors at home. I'm on the opposite side of the firetruck and can't see much of anything but the blue sky above me. Chris bandages my forehead, and I start to cry, which makes it more painful to breathe.

"Where do you hurt the most, Amanda?"

I stop short of informing him that my Cherry hurts the most. "It hurts when I breathe."

"You need to keep doing that for me, okay?" he quips and offers me the occasional hit of oxygen as we wait.

A moment later, I find myself looking up into the eyes of a female DPS unit member. "I'm Officer Silva. You were driving the red Chevy pickup?" After I confirm, she asks for some basic information and then, "Can you tell me what happened?"

There's not much to tell—crash, boom, bang. She takes my statement and asks where she can find my license and insurance information. "You're going to be transported to get checked out, Ms. Harrington. I'll finish talking to you at the hospital."

"Wait... please." I need a hug. I need to be consoled. I need a ride home from the hospital. My brain is fuzzy, but I have a logical thought. Law enforcement is a family in itself. I give her Shawn's name and badge number. "I'm his... he's my...," *I don't know what he is to me, but my* everything hurts and I need him. "Will you please find him for me?" Officer Silva calls into dispatch from the small radio on her shoulder and relays the information along with the name of the hospital where I'm going.

* * *

Inside a curtained cubicle lying on that stupid backboard on a gurney, huge collar still around my neck, I've been here for about an hour—I think. Commotion hums all around me, but since I can't see through the plastic panels, I pass the time making up stories in my head and counting ceiling tiles.

When Shawn peers down at me in his hot bench player clothes, I'm so happy to see him that my eyes swell with tears. "Baby, you look..." He stops himself and locks down his alarmed expression to one of concern. "Are you in pain?"

"Everywhere. It hurts to breathe."

"Have you been seen by a doctor?"

"No."

He opens his mouth to say something, but a crotchety old nurse-looking woman grouches at him, "Sir, you can't be in here,"

Shawn produces his badge and the grouching stops. Apparently, that means he can be in here. He asks Nurse Grouch, "Why hasn't she been evaluated by a physician?"

"We've taken vitals."

He growls, "Her breathing is labored. She's in pain and could have a punctured lung. She needs attention now." Nurse Grouch glares. Shawn glares back then barks, "Ma'am, I do not see you moving. If I have to go locate an attending myself or have her transported somewhere else, I will."

Nurse Grouch decides not to argue further with 250-pounds of riled up cop. She walks away, and fifteen minutes later we're meeting a physician. Even though my *everything* hurts, I can still appreciate that Shawn's Hotness Scale is off the charts.

I'm x-rayed for spinal injuries and fractured *whatevers*, and finally they remove that awful collar and I'm allowed to get off of that torture device called a backboard. The rundown is two sets of sutures on my forehead, a broken nose, two broken ribs, risk of concussion, and, apparently, I'm going to feel a whole lot worse tomorrow because local numbing agents and morphine are helping my *everything*.

In the midst of sutures and bandaging and trying not to cry, Officer Silva arrives. Shawn shakes her hand and introduces himself with his hot cop title and as my boyfriend. He thanks her for making sure that he was contacted so quickly.

Did he say boyfriend? I must have a concussion. Ovaries, why aren't you excited?

Officer Silva is all business quickly adding *insult* to *injury*. She returns my insurance, registration, license and purse, and presents me with a citation. My first ticket and it's a big one.

In Arizona, the rear-ender is always at fault. I was driving the third vehicle in a five-car smash up. I'm responsible for rear-ending the car in front of me at a dead stop on a busy freeway because she'd just rear-ended the car in front of her. That makes me responsible for car two and partially responsible for further damage to car one. On the plus side, I was rear-ended twice so the blame gets passed around. Poor car number five. That dude is totally screwed.

I sigh and frown then look to Shawn. "I suppose you can't *fix* this for me, right? Like make it go away."

Shawn laughs and says to Officer Silva, "She's joking."

"So that's a no?"

He shakes his head at me, "Afraid so, babe. I'll be right back. I'm going to walk Officer Silva out and get information about your truck."

"Thank you for my purse, Officer Silva, but not the ticket. No offense."

Shawn grins at me because he's right; I am a nut. Officer Silva cracks a smile. "You're welcome, Ms. Harrington."

* * *

Many hours later, I'm discharged with pain medication and after-care instructions. I hope Shawn was paying attention because the finer details are a little hazy. Back at the house, he runs me a warm bath, carefully removing my crunchy dried blood clothing before helping me into the tub.

He washes me cautiously, cleaning me up as best he can while I choose to breathe instead of cry. Draining the rust-colored water in the tub, he refills it and repeats the process.

"My truck?" I ask while he's rinsing shampoo from my hair a second time, trying to hold the water back so it doesn't trickle onto my bandaged forehead.

"I haven't seen it myself, but Officer Silva said she'll be surprised if your insurance doesn't total it given the damage, model year, and depreciated value."

"I love Cherry. You have no idea what we've been through together or you wouldn't use hurtful words like depreciated value." *Which is sort of how I felt about my actual cherry after Curt was finished with it.*

"It's just a truck, Amanda. Hold still while I finish your hair."

As he rinses my hair, a montage of Cherry's greatest hits floats through my foggy brain. *Shiny and new with a silver bow across her hood, coed camping at the lake with a boom box on her wheel well watching the campfire burn out over the lake... Rolling around with Tanner on prom night, my first and second orgasms with Braden on high school graduation night, and his branding until we meet again kiss... Trips up and down I-10 and the winding highway home. Spring breaks in Mexico, conversations on her tailgate, blasting music... Tanner returning me to sender, starting my adult life* in the Valley—147,342 miles traveled over the last eleven years... *Smashed, shattered, and completely destroyed in a matter of seconds...* Jeez, it's almost exactly like losing my virginity. I really want to cry, but it hurts too much.

He puts the plastic cup down on the side of the tub. "You have a lot of hair. I'm not sure I got all the suds out, but you can take a real shower in a day or two. Let's get you in bed."

Normally those words would excite me. *Ovaries, are you still with me?* He helps me stand and dry off. I need to keep my ribs wrapped for another day or two, and while Shawn is doing that for me, I catch my reflection in the mirror. I lean in for closer inspection and, *damn that hurts*, I start to cry, which, *damn that hurts even more*, but I can't help myself. I look like a horror show.

"Don't you dare tell me it's just a face."

"You'll heal. Meanwhile, you'll look like a badass," he jokes and winks at me in the mirror as he finishes with the bandage. "Start working on the line, 'you should see the other guy.'"

I laugh and, *ouch*, that was not a good idea either. It would seem this is not a time for any emotion whatsoever. I state the obvious, "I'm not a badass. I'm ugly and my *everything* hurts."

"You're a gorgeous badass, and you're lucky to be standing here right now. Bed," he orders and turns me gently away from the mirror.

From my seat on the edge of my bed I tell him where to find a clean nightie. He picks out a semi-sexy one—of course he does—and helps slip it over my head and get my arms through the straps. Looking up at him I tease quietly, "That's a first."

"What's that?"

"You've never helped me put *on* my clothes before."

He belts out a laugh. "Such a nut, babe. But that's not entirely true. I've zipped you into a dress plenty of times over the last couple of years."

Two years, Shawn... TWO YEARS. Why haven't I met your children? Why don't you love me?

After I'm tucked in, Shawn doles out a pain pill that they prescribed for me before leaving the ER. Looking down at me from his perch on the edge of my bed, he strokes my hair. "Thank God you're not seriously injured. That's all that matters right now. That and getting rest."

My injuries might not be serious, but my *everything* doesn't know that.

"You're on duty tonight," I mumble as my eyes struggle to remain open.

"I'm on Amanda duty tonight. I'll stay right here, but you're going to need someone overnight with you tomorrow at least. Do you want me to call your parents tonight?"

"Yes," I mutter. "Don't scare them."

He chuckles. "It's not the first time I've had to share news like this. Before you pass out," he brushes my hair with his fingers, "I'm going to have to wake you up several times tonight for pain meds and ice packs. Doctor wants me to check for signs of concussion."

"Okay." My *everything* wants to sleep now.

Sleeping fitfully in small doses, when I wake up Shawn is there to offer me sips of water and pain meds and fresh ice packs. In the light of morning, I can't seem to pry myself from the mattress, but I need to get to the bathroom. I wake Shawn up and ask him to help me. As I sit and then stand, I discover he was right last night—my *everything* hurts so much worse. Stiff and sore, bruises are darkening under both eyes.

CHAPTER 27

I GIVE SHAWN A SPARE key to my house so he can come and go. He cleans out Cherry and returns with a box and his opinion that she'll be totaled. Between my parents who spend a few nights with me, Jenny, and Shawn, I'm well-coddled during my time of need.

Max—well, he's sorry to hear about the accident, but he's a busy guy with constant deadlines and pressure, and, while he hasn't said, I'm under the impression Max might have a bench of his own because he hasn't asked about mine in a while.

Shawn handles me with such tenderness, and he's with me as much as time permits. He makes me dinner, we watch TV, and we spend a lot of time talking and laughing, but not too hard because that hurts. He doesn't ring the doorbell—he just uses his key.

Within two weeks' time, I'm still sore but ready to go back to work. Shawn takes me to pick up a rental car covered by insurance until I can cope with the decision of how to replace my officially totaled Cherry.

A week after I return to work, Shawn makes love to me for the first time since the accident. At least it feels like we're making love because he doesn't take me in my bed. He's uncharacteristically gentle with whisper-soft caresses and sweet words.

The last man who actually made love to me was Tanner and that was so long ago. How sad is that? But still... I love this hot cop. No doubt about it; he makes me feel beautiful, safe, and protected—except for my heart...

Perhaps I should've borrowed his Kevlar because in his strong arms, in the darkness of my bedroom, in the afterglow of all that he's given to me over the past few weeks, I say those three words to him. "I love you."

His frame tightens. I hear his sharp intake of air before he releases it on a sigh. "Babe..." he starts. *Babe* means all sorts of things; it depends on the tone, the *situation*, the moment in time. Timing is everything. This *babe* does not sound promising, and what follows will probably not be a good time.

I instantly regret calling the play. I wish I could take back the words, but, then again, I'm sick of hiding my feelings in this relationship of uncertainty with Shawn.

"I'm glad I could be here to help you after the accident, but..." *Stupid buts. Stupid me with my stupid ovaries and the stupid last two years of my life waiting and hoping for more.* "I think it's time we have a talk about what we're both looking for in the future."

Better two years later than never.

"Okay," my voice is tentative. "Since I'm the one who just bared my soul, why don't you start?"

He releases another sigh into the dark room before speaking, "Spending time with you is the best part of my day. When I leave you, I walk out that door feeling like a superhero instead of a thirty-eight-year-old cop."

"That's good, right?"

"It's very good, but I am a thirty-eight-year-old cop—not a super-hero. I already have three kids. You're so much younger than me. Having children of your own is still on your mind, right?"

"Yes," I whisper into the dark while my ovaries twitch with the possibility of coming in handy.

"I pay child support, but I also do everything I can above and beyond because that's what a father should do—provide. There's a reason I haven't invited you to my apartment. It's a shithole—embarrassing at my age, but I have three kids to take care of. I can't have more, babe. I don't have that in me."

"If this is about the cost of children, I have a career, we'd have my income too, and—"

"There's all the time and energy it takes to get through the early years. That's behind me now. I'm good with what I have."

"Not even one more? Just one tiny little baby?" I'm still whispering, but my ovaries are begging to be heard.

"No," his voice is gentle but firm. "That's what I need you to understand."

"And it took you *two years* to tell me this?" My words fly out on a hiss. I'm not proud, but my ovaries made me do it.

His reply is calm, cool, and collected with his *stupid ability* to control his emotions. "It took me a fair amount of time to recover and rebuild my life, and you've been a huge part of that. Before things get any deeper between us, I can't go down the baby road again."

"Is there anything else you can't do?" I ask through the *stupid tears* welling in my eyes and spilling over. "You *can't* have kids with me, but what else? Can you make a commitment to me? Can you see a future with me?"

"I can see all of that. Coming home and waking up to you, having you get to know my kids, and us having a solid chance at something good which would lead to more time with my kids because I'd have a partner in my family life." *This is all good except I don't even know his children. They could be little monsters.*

"But, Amanda, can you see that with me without bringing a baby into this world?" *This is all very bad. No children of your own, Amanda?* If we can't blend the *family by choice*, it is game over. I lose Shawn and precious time to find a man who wants a family with me. *Two years. TWO YEARS.*

Shawn interrupts my internal dialogue. "This is really hard for me to say because we've been seeing each other a long time, but—"

"No more *buts.*"

"But, Amanda—"

"I said no more *buts.* Just be quiet, please. I'm thinking."

Dad's words spin through my mind. *When a man is ready to commit to a woman, he doesn't mess around. He'll move heaven and earth to make it happen. When it's right for both of you, he'll make it happen and you'll know. When the time is right, you'll find what you want. Timing is everything.*

This is not what I want. I want children. And, what the hell, I went down the I LOVE YOU fork in the road, and he didn't follow my lead.

Does Shawn love you? If he loves you, he'll take a stand, make a declaration, hold a freaking boom box over his head like Lloyd Dobler winning the heart of Diane Court in Say Anything.

"I told you that I love you."

I can hear him breathing in the dark. God, this sucks, but I force myself to keep my mouth shut. "I think that's what I feel for you," he finally says.

That's neither a stand, declaration, nor Peter Gabriel's *In Your Eyes* blaring from a boom box.

"You *think* so? What the hell does that even mean, Shawn?"

"It means that I need more time before I'm ready to say those words again. I've only said them to one woman, and she destroyed me."

Timing, you are a son of a bitch, and I hate you. I make up my mind and blurt it out before I have *time* to change it. "I can't do this anymore." My words are solid but my voice cracks.

"Babe—"

"No more *babes* either. No *babes*, no *buts*, no *babies*, and no *boom box*."

"Boom box?"

"Forget it. My point is, no more. We have to be over because you're right—if that's behind you, it's still ahead of me. I want *every-thing*. After two years, you can't even say that you love me."

Fight for me, Shawn. Tell me what I need to hear. It's not too late.

Shawn reserves the right to remain silent, and it's awkward, long, and excruciating.

I've had enough. I need to cry. "You should leave now," I whisper in the dark.

"That's really what you want?"

No, I want you to love me, marry me, and have a baby with me. "Yes."

Sighing, he flips on the nightstand light. I turn away because the light hurts my eyes and I can't stand to look at all that I'm losing—even though he can't give me what I want and he was never mine. I listen to him get dressed from my fetal position. After a few minutes, I feel the weight of his knee on the bed behind me. Leaning down he speaks softly into my ear, "When you're ready to talk, call me."

"I won't call you." I say this out loud because I'm making a promise to myself.

"Just so we're clear, Amanda, I don't want to break up. I think we should take a day or two to think things over and figure this out."

I keep my back to him. "What's to figure out? Are you going to realize how much you love me and want children with me in the next day or two?" His silence is my answer, and not the one that I'm looking for. "Please leave my house key and make sure you grab your extra clothes and stuff."

Fighting the urge to take back everything I just said as he moves around my room and bathroom, finally I hear the jingling of keys followed by the soft clink of the key to my house meeting the nightstand. "You need to get up so you can lock the doors behind me."

Officer Bossy is as obsessed with my freaking deadbolts as my *stupid ovaries* are obsessed with him. I groan quietly but comply, wrapping a blanket around me before I follow him to the door.

"You really don't want to see me again, Amanda? We can't talk this out?"

I can't even look at him because the *stupid tears* are burning my eyes. "There's nothing to talk about unless you change your mind," I murmur. "Please don't come back here unless you change your mind. Will you do that for me?"

"I want to come back, babe."

"And I want *more*. So... that's it. Please be safe out there," my voice is barely above a whisper, my eyes still unwilling to look at him as I fight back *stupid tears*.

He releases a heavy sigh before dropping a kiss on my lowered head. "I always am."

Locking the deadbolts behind him, my body sinks to the entry-way floor. Tears pour down my face and mingle with the snot running out of my nose as I sob. I miss him already, and my *everything* hurts.

Eventually, I pad into the kitchen and wipe my face with a paper towel. Still wrapped in my blanket, I pour myself a glass of white zin and fish out of a pack of cigarettes in the back of a kitchen drawer. I walk outside and sit down alone.

Sliding a cigarette and a joint out of the pack, I alternate between the three—wine, cigarettes, and weed, until my body feels heavy and my heart hurts a little less than it did twenty minutes ago. I haven't sparked up since before the accident, and while it hurts like a bitch to inhale with cracked ribs, it's worth it. It settles into me like a mass of nothing.

Back inside, I set the house alarm and crawl into bed naked and alone with nothing but the lingering scent of him to keep me company.

Aside from going to work and follow-up doctor appointments, I spend the next month of my life trying to feel nothing inside, but my *everything* still hurts.

Territorial Cup—1999

Arizona State kicks our asses 42 to 27, and takes back the Territorial Cup. I watch alone from my sofa in absolute disgust. I've spent a lot of time on my sofa crying and a lot of time on my back porch smoking.

I even begged off Thanksgiving in Pine Ridge telling my parents that I was spending the day with Jenny. Instead, I spent it curled in a ball trying to nurse a broken heart. And that asshole cat still won't come near me. He hates me.

Max calls from his hotel room in New Jersey to rub it in. The Cards are playing the Giants the following day.

I answer, "I don't want to talk about."

"Of course, we're going to talk about it."

"I haven't heard your voice in *weeks*, and you call to give me shit now?"

"Uh... yeah, Wildcat. What else did you expect?"

"Don't you have anyone else to harass?"

"Nope. I'm all alone at the moment."

"It's my lucky fucking night."

"Wow, she's a sore loser," he pokes the Wildcat in me.

"She's not used to losing, remember?" I grumble in return. "And my back hurts, my cat hates me, and I can't get my nose fixed for at least another two months, but thanks for coming by to check on me, or, you know, calling."

"Is the nose that bad?"

"Yes. I'm hideous, and now I'm a loser. What do you want, Max?"

As he talks, I relocate to the back patio—to my weed and cigarettes. "I was hoping I could take you out next Saturday night, but if you're too hideous to be seen with in public, we can stay in."

Lighting up the joint, I inhale and exhale slowly before responding. "I'm not in the mood to be good company."

"You can be bad company, Wildcat. I'd just like to see you."

"I've stuck close to home the last six weeks convalescing and licking my wounds, you know, from the car accident where I totaled my truck."

"Yeah, I stopped by at least three times when I was in the area."

"And I wasn't home?"

"You weren't alone."

"What are you talking about?" Inhale...

"Police car in the driveway every time. Either you're in trouble with the law, or you're still dating that cop." This is surprising news— maybe he does give a shit. Exhale... "Are you smoking, Amanda?"

"So what if I am?"

"I didn't know you smoked."

I snap, "There are a lot of things you don't know about me, including my enjoyment of an occasional cigarette. Go ahead and judge me for it, Devil. I don't give a shit."

"You *are* in a mood."

I want to cry because that's all I do these days... Drink, smoke, cry, miss Shawn, and feel sorry for myself. Oh, I also work, but my head hasn't been in the game since the accident. I need to call Dr. Anderson. I feel myself succumbing to the darkness.

Max throws me another lifeline. "Let me see you next Saturday. I'll come by around six. We can go out, stay in, whatever you want... Unless the cop lives there now."

"No," I reply. "Officer Bossy and I recently parted ways."

"Oh? Do you want to talk about it?"

I scoff, "Not with you, no."

"Good. I only offered to sound like a nice guy. You're a free agent now?"

I think about James, but he doesn't count. "It's more like my bench is empty, and I have no interest in new recruits."

After a beat he says, "You know I'm not a team player. If I have you one-on-one maybe we can finally take this thing in a more meaningful direction."

My heart beats with potential. "If we're going to try for something more meaningful, I need you to promise me two things right now."

"What's that?"

"That we'll continue to speak in sports metaphors and you'll call me Wildcat as often as possible."

He laughs. "I promise, Wildcat. That's a yes to next Saturday?"

"Yes."

"You made that almost too easy."

I snicker and smart off, "You're not the first guy to say that to me.

Plus, I'm buying a new car that day, so maybe I'll be in a good mood by the time you get here."

"Do you need any help with that? I could go with you."

"That's a nice offer, but my dad's coming down. He has mad negotiation skills."

"It might be a good time to swap out those loser license plates for Sparky and a pitchfork."

"I'll do that when hell freezes over, Max."

"Tough loss today, Wildcat. Not for me—it's a great day to be me. I'll make you feel better next week."

"I'll hold you to it."

I'm still grieving the loss of Shawn and our beautiful babies, but Max Masterson is way more than a consolation prize. We've been crushing on each other for over a year now. Maybe it's time for *stupid timing* to stop screwing with me.

CHAPTER 28

Saturday, December 5, 1999

DAD HAS MAD NEGOTIATION SKILLS because he makes me walk away from my first choice at the Chevy dealership on McDowell Road in Scottsdale even though I knew I'd found *the one*—at least in terms of a vehicle. Eventually after visiting three other non-Chevy lots and having lunch, we saunter back to the first dealership. Dad cuts immediately to the chase and doesn't give an inch until he's behind closed doors with the finance director.

I'm outside the door because Dad doesn't like to say the F-word in front of me even though it's one of my favorite words. I really want this SUV, but as I wait outside for over an hour and the salesman paces by every now and then, I foresee a trip to another Chevy dealer in our future.

Finally the volume drops, but another twenty minutes go by before I'm invited to step inside the office. Prepared to write the biggest check of my life for the down payment, instead I'm presented with paperwork to sign. The Bank of Dad already paid in full.

"Dad? No... This is way too much to ask."

"You didn't ask. Save your money to fix that nose." I open my mouth and he stops me with a finger. "The deal is done, Brown Eyes. Merry Christmas—and don't tell Brianna."

After hugs and more thank yous, Dad heads back to Pine Ridge, and I drive home in my brand new 1999 Chevy Blazer. She was a close-out model—white, 4-door, and fully loaded with electric everything, airbags, leather, sunroof, dark windows, a kick ass stereo system, 4-wheel drive, and a tow package. My new University of Arizona plates should arrive in the mail in two to four weeks.

* * *

Max and I decided to stay in tonight, and he's bringing over dinner and *You've Got Mail*. My movie choice was met with resistance over our IM chat midweek because...

> Max: *Wildcat, that's a chick flick. Let's watch something with gratuitous nudity or senseless violence or both at the same time.*
> Me: *I am a chick. Have you forgotten about my large, juicy breasts?*
> Max: *And... I'm sporting wood in the newsroom.*
> Me: *Plus, I'm still recovering from my injuries from the car accident and the football game.*
> Max: *You win. You had me at large juicy breasts.*

With some creative use of concealer and makeup, I'm able to

hide the faint sickly-looking yellow bruises that linger under both eyes but not the crook in my once perfect nose. Now I have to deal with the clothing *situation*.

I've put on a little weight since the accident and the break-up, which is no surprise since I've been hitting the bong and munchies and haven't been able to hit the gym because of my back and neck problems. With some creative use of clothing choices, I attempt to conceal the extra 15 pounds underneath a flowy but casual red sweater dress. No shoes, because we're staying in and Max barely breaks the six-foot mark.

I open the door to his warm smile and meal, and he quips on the way in, "It pains me to admit that I think you look especially beautiful in red, Wildcat."

"Confirmation that I went to the right university," I banter back.

"I like the new ride outside. Country girl—I thought you'd buy another monster truck."

"I like it too. It's different having all that, you know, seating and storage back there, but I decided it's more practical at this stage in my life." *One day I'll need the space for infant car seats and diaper bags, Max. You should probably know that.*

He heads into my kitchen to put down the Chinese takeout. Once his hands are free, I greet him properly with a hug. He leans in for a kiss while latching a hand on my left breast to give it an enthusiastic fondle.

"Max," I protest his play. "I haven't seen you in almost two months. You don't just get to pick up where we left off."

The *devil* came ready to play. He grins and slyly replies, "We left off with my mouth between your legs, Wildcat. You seemed pretty happy about that at the time."

I blush at the memory. "Hmm... yeah, you're right about that." I laugh. "Then you might as well grope them both." Max is happy to oblige, and two months is a long time to keep the lid on our combustible chemistry.

The motion on the field starts in the kitchen but moves immediately to the bedroom where my carefully chosen outfit lands in a heap on the floor followed by most of his. "You wore that for me?" he ogles my red lace demi-cup bra and matching panties.

I shrug on a smile. "You said you like me in red."

"I love a good lingerie show. I also like you in nothing at all." He starts to reach for the back clasp.

He's skilled enough to unhook it in two seconds flat with his eyes closed and ten broken fingers. I block his pass and call a timeout. "This is all very fun, but I want to know where you think this is heading now that I'm a free agent."

"I promise you tonight won't end on a handshake, Wildcat."

"It never does, but I'm serious here."

He gauges my Bullshit Scale. "Okay, let's talk."

"Over dinner," I decree. "With all of our clothes on."

He grumbles good-naturedly, "Wildcat, you should've called the false start back in the kitchen." He reaches down and starts sorting through our clothes, tossing my sweater dress up in my face with a devilish grin.

"Right." I slide the dress over my head. "I'm off my game." Kissing his adorable mouth, I say, "Thanks for being a good sport."

**

Over Chinese food, I explain the turn of events in my bedroom. "I don't think we really know each other. I mean, we know certain things about each other, but we're pretty much all about verbal one-upmanship and our unfinished sexual business."

Max surprises me by responding with little wordplay. "I agree. I'm a little surprised to find myself here with you and no bench." His *devil* wit kicks back in, "You don't have anyone waiting down the street for me to leave do you?"

"No." I grin. "There is no one left on my bench—by choice because I'm really worn out from all the games I've played since my last serious relationship."

"When was that?"

Squinting my eyes, I mull this over. "My college boyfriend, I guess. It was the last time I was with a man who was my best friend and loved me as much as I loved him. What about you?"

Dropping his fork, he loses himself in thought before answering. "I was twenty-five, I think... That was what... twelve years ago." He looks so sad. "Mary was her name. We lived together for two years after college, and I put a ring on her finger, but we broke up six months before the wedding."

"Why?"

"I started working at the paper about a year into our living together. She couldn't handle the travel and she cheated on me—more than once. I stayed after the first time."

I nod and ask, "And since Mary... what's the biggest reason why you haven't had another serious relationship over the last twelve years?"

"I'm on the road sixty to seventy percent of the time, and when I'm home there's still a daily grind." The grind includes the franchise, business, and human interest angles of covering the NFL/NHL, and the players who provide never-ending examples of men behaving badly.

"Do you foresee that changing?"

He looks puzzled. "Are you asking me to change?"

I offer him a sincere smile. "I don't have an ulterior motive. I'm getting to know you better—for who you are, not who you think I might want you to be. And, if there's anything you care to know about me, you're more than welcome to ask. Does that put you more at ease?"

"Yeah... I think we should make this a game—alternate the Q and A."

"Sure." I laugh. "You owe me an answer. You travel up to 70% of the time for a job you clearly love. Do you foresee that changing?"

"No. I love my career, and I've yet to find a woman who can handle the separation. When I've had to choose between a relationships and work, I choose my job. Always will. Scared off yet?"

"Is that one of your questions?"

He chuckles. "Yes, Wildcat."

"Yes, because I know that dating you is challenging enough... the road, the nights and weekends... That's a big reason why I hung onto my bench. You're not around much, and we never seemed to pick up many yards on the field."

"What happened with you and the cop?"

"It's my turn to ask a question."

He calls a technical foul. "You got a head start. Besides, he's been in your life since we met. And after the accident, you turned to him—not me."

"True," I mumble.

"What happened with you two?"

"He's older, divorced, and doesn't want more children. Deal breaker." *I want kids, Max—did you catch that?* I ask my next question, "What are you looking for at this stage in your life?"

"This feels like a job interview."

"Well, I am a Human Resources professional," I tease. "What are you looking for beyond excellent banter and insanely incredible blowjobs?"

"A woman who can give me those two things and handle my career. I haven't found her yet, but, for the record, you're two out of three." He takes a bite of beef and broccoli before asking me to spell it out. "What are you looking for, Wildcat?"

I lay it out for him so there are no "gotcha's" down the road. "Marriage, children, the whole thing—plus excellent banter and great sex. And, no, I'm not asking you to propose, but I need to know if you're opposed to any of the overall concepts. Are you? Do any those words scare you—*marriage, children,* the *whole thing*?"

"In theory, no. In reality, it hasn't come together for me. My future wife or mother of my children will be doing a lot of it on her own. Summers are good for me unless they change my beat again. I've done the NBA and MLB, too. I hate the summer heat, so I'll take you, um... her on some great vacations. You wouldn't believe how many frequent flyer miles and Hilton points I have. We could go anywhere in the world." He catches me with a mouthful of Kung Pao chicken. "How serious did it get between you and the cop?"

While I finish chewing, I decide on full disclosure. "I fell in love with Shawn." I don't like the expression on Max's face because I can't read it. "Does that bother you?"

During the entire conversation, we've pretty much been looking at each other between bites of food and during the back and forth of questions, but Max looks to the ceiling and his eyes close. He sighs and looks back to me. "I thought this whole bench thing was you being young and fooling around, but you're just getting out of a relationship."

"Technically, Max, it wasn't an exclusive relationship. I fooled around and fell in love." He catches my classic rock pun and smiles. "But I'll get over it." I shrug like it's no big deal.

"What should we do here, Wildcat?"

"See where this takes us."

His *devilish* grin is back along with the play in his eyes. "Even if it works out, we still have one hell of an obstacle to overcome."

I take the bait. "What?"

"A Sun Devil and a Wildcat, both loyal to the core. Now, we could have some creative bets with each other every November and celebrate our wins between the sheets, but how would we raise our children?"

Max is hilarious, and I break into laughter before answering, "I guess they'll make up their own minds when they're old enough to understand how much your college sucks ass."

He laughs. "Or we can send them to NAU. No one hates the Lumberjacks."

Right? Max and I aren't so different after all, or maybe we're more alike than we'd ever care to admit.

"In all seriousness, Wildcat, once you're finished crying in your Kung Pao chicken over the cop, I want to see where this goes between us. You know what my schedule is like—there's no mystery there. The unknown is whether or not we can handle it together and apart when we're both putting our best foot forward. And you know my deal breaker. I'm absolutely serious about that."

I narrow my eyes in confusion and ask, "Deal breaker?"

"Now that your bench is clear, it needs to stay that way. If we do this, we're exclusive."

"Are you asking me to go steady?"

He snickers. "I guess I am. I expect you to only be with me, and you can expect the same from me. No other players."

"Did we decide to do this, or are we still talking about doing this?"

"That's the problem with you, Wildcat. Everything has to be repeated and over-explained because college dumbed you down." He flashes those mischievous brown eyes at me, and I can't help but laugh.

"When you're over the cop, you're going to tell me, and we're going to seal the deal in the bedroom. Once we go there, that's it. We're together until one of us kicks the other to the curb. Did you follow me, or do I need to dumb it down some more?"

I smirk at him. "No, I've got it."

We continue asking and answering questions, but we ditch the serious talk after dinner and opt for *You've Got Mail,* during which Max grumbles and protests the level of chick flick exposure. His hands and mouth start to wander until I'm forced to give up on the movie.

Max is correct. We do not end the evening on a handshake, but there is no touchdown either. The hanky, as always, is insanely good for both of us. The panky is yet to be determined.

* * *

Over the next few weeks, Max works and travels, and we spend time together in between. I haven't finished crying in my Kung Pao chicken, so there is no sealing of the deal. It occurs to me that I should figure this out soon because hockey season is already in full swing, and the Cardinals are almost finished with the regular season.

I can't blow off Christmas in Pine Ridge, but I spend a fair amount of time sneaking weed and cigarettes in the freezing cold off the side of the garage while I think about my future. I make up a bullshit excuse about CompuWorld requiring all hands on deck leading up to Y2K to get out of the *family by choice* visit with my parents and Tanner.

I don't have to work. With Max on the road to Atlanta, I wallow in self-pity with my bong and white zin while rotating my collection of John Hughes' movies and all of their *stupid happily ever after endings*. Max goes directly from Atlanta to Green Bay after the New Year.

CHAPTER 29

A New Millennium—Y2K

THE WORLD DOESN'T END WHEN the clock strikes midnight. All Y2K conspiracy theories are dispelled. I spent the night with Jenny and her family. We played with Maisy, cooked dinner for Paul, watched movies, and I felt her second daughter doing in utero gymnastics. Jenny's due date is just two months away. I packed an overnight bag because some things never change—we're not too old for slumber parties. If I'm going to end up childless and single, my relationships with my girlfriends and their children are more important than ever.

Max's hockey schedule hits me squarely between my eyes like a saucer pass gone bad, and I wasn't wearing protective gear. He goes from a football game in Green Bay on January 2, 2000, straight into a twelve-day hockey away-game spree in Detroit, Ottawa, New

Jersey, and New York. Back home for a week, he's so exhausted that I'm not sure he realizes which city he's in before he heads back out. Seriously, we are not off to a good start, and I really hate hockey.

In February, I get an email from Tanner with a minor guilt trip about not seeing them after Christmas. He also shares the news that Baby #3 is on its way. I write back wishing them all the best for a boring, healthy pregnancy. Everyone—*everyone*—is having a baby. Jenny, Trina, Katie, and Lorraine. My ovaries are not amused.

I do call Dr. Anderson, and we start meeting weekly over the phone again. She's concerned that I've been smoking marijuana over the past few years and that I feel dark after my split from Shawn. I downplay the frequency and assure her that it is recreational—like a glass of wine with dinner, but she has plenty to say on the topic.

"Amanda, marijuana changes the chemistry in the brain. We're trying to regulate your levels of serotonin to treat the depression, so while it may be recreational for some people, because you have depression and anxiety you're jeopardizing your mental health. The medical research is iffy about whether marijuana can cause depression, but many regular users—"

"I said I do it every once in a while."

"Many regular marijuana users with a history of depression run the risk of dependency or addiction. You might think you're using it to relax, but are you really?"

"Yes, really."

"And do you *relax* to disconnect from reality? When something happens that you don't want to process, do you rely on marijuana to escape those feelings?"

Yes. "No."

"Are you being honest?"

"No. Okay, I'm lying to you. I don't know why. I mean, I pay you a lot of money to dig around in my brain—why am I lying to you?"

"Why do you think you're lying to me?"

"Because I have to hide it from almost everyone. My parents would be so disappointed in me, my ex-boyfriend would arrest me, and Max—well, he has no idea I even touch the stuff. It's not part of my image. No one would expect a woman like me to do this stuff. The only person I smoke with anymore—besides myself—is James. And I'm not sleeping with him. Max and I are trying to spend more time together, but James still comes over and we get high, watch TV, and hang out."

"You're in a committed relationship with Max, the reporter, right?"

"Almost. Do you know anything about hockey, Dr. Anderson?"

"I love hockey. I'm a huge Coyotes fan."

"Hockey sucks. I think I'm ready to move on after Shawn, but I haven't found the right time to tell Max that I'm ready to, um, progress our relationship. And once we do that, he made it very clear that we'll only see each other."

"Meanwhile, you're associating with another man because he uses drugs with you?"

"When you say it like that, Dr. Anderson, it doesn't sound like a very good idea." My laughter is forced.

"Not only that, Amanda, it sounds eerily familiar to what happened in your life during college. What brought you to me in the first place?" Damn, she's good— she remembers names and everything.

"You were in a very healthy relationship with Tanner and doing well in school. You started experimenting with alcohol and drugs which led to some reckless sexual behavior, and you chose to break up with Tanner, which is how you ended up with Jason, continuing to use more and more until you contemplated suicide. Did I get that right?"

I'm stunned. She got that so right after so many years, except Tanner ultimately dumped me, but I'm willing to overlook that minor detail. *This is different, right*? "It's different," I say it out loud to test my theory.

"How so?"

"Jason sucked me dry—he used me. He stole, cheated, lied... James is just a friend. He doesn't make me miserable. We just hang out and he helps me fix things around the house. You know, he's a general contractor and this is an old house."

I have to give her credit—she doesn't laugh at me. However, she probably has to bite her tongue before responding. "James is a friend who supports your drug use, engages in it with you. Why do you think that's a friendship you choose to maintain?"

Because he gets me killer weed. Because I can kick back and lose myself with someone who doesn't judge me for... Oh, shit...

"Dr. Anderson?"

"Yes, Amanda?"

"I don't like where this conversation is going."

"Why is that?"

"Because I don't do it *all* the time. I don't feel like I have to do it. I finished my MBA program, I have a great job, I pay my own bills.

Yeah, my love life isn't ideal, but I'm totally a productive member of society. Is it really a problem if I can do all these things and enjoy some weed here and there?"

"I think you need to ask yourself why you hide the behavior from the people who are most important to you. And, also, remember that every time you use a substance to dull a real emotion, not only are you not dealing with that emotion, you're altering the chemistry of your brain making it very difficult to keep the depression and anxiety in check. It's risky behavior, Amanda—not just a slippery slope; it's like walking along the edge of a cliff."

I take all of this under careful consideration. I've walked on the edge of a cliff, and I didn't stumble. I jumped and lost Tanner, my dignity, and my mental health. I decide to behave like a grownup. Even if I am a hockey widow, I want Max in my future, and I can't risk losing him or myself again. I have self-control, but not complete control. I cut way back on the weed, and I also cut James from my life.

March 2000—Sealing the Deal with the Devil

In early March, I have plastic surgery on my nose which results in two black eyes. Even with black eyes, Max has a ten-day travel reprieve and is not covering any home games. There's no better time for hanky to turn into full blown panky. We've spent well over two years waiting to score a touchdown, and in that critical moment when we're ready to seal the deal in my bedroom, Max calls the timeout.

"What's wrong, Max?" I'm bewildered. My hand is still on his pitchfork where I had him positioned to penetrate the slot.

He looks down at me with thoughtful eyes. "I've had my share of fun." *That makes two of us, Max.* I release my hold on him and listen up. "But this means something with you. It's not just sex. Do you get that, or do I need to dumb it down for you, Wildcat?"

My *devil*... always ready with the Arizona dig which might get old.

"Dumb it down," I reply because I want to know what he's really thinking.

"Amanda, we need more time to make sure that we're three for three, but I was invested a long time ago which is why I wasn't going to share a woman like you with anyone else. I've had a lot of relationships end while I was on the road. Please don't do that me. If number three isn't working out for your life, be honest."

Damn, Max, I'll sure try, but I keep shit bottled up inside and sometimes I lie on reflex. Oh, and I like to smoke weed and I kind of smoke a lot of cigarettes during the work day. How do you feel about that?

Instead I say, "I will." I might be a Wildcat, but he's not the first man to make a deal with the *devil* inside me.

We spend the next ten nights together at both my place and his patio home near Tempe. Not only does Max hate Wildcats, he's allergic to actual housecats. Like me, he's not a fan of Squirt. With a concentration of time together and no distractions from his work or my former bench, Max starts to reveal his deeper side that includes a very long, convoluted history of trying and failing to find the elusive three for three. I thought I was exhausted from my trials and errors—he's been on the losing end of love for twice as long.

While he's invested in me, he seems cautious. And he should be, because I'm not sure about number three. I am sure that our panky leaves absolutely nothing to be desired. I've had my share of sexual partners, and it's no surprise that the more my heart is invested, the better the physical relationship.

* * *

But timing is still a bitch... Heading into the late spring, when Max finally has time for me, I have little to no time for him because CompuWorld is spinning off its axis. Our rapid growth heading into Y2K came to a screeching halt. Our clients now feel secure that they are in good shape, and as contracts expire, the amount of onsite support is cut in half or more. Some contracts are simply not renewed, leaving us with an expansive inventory of idle IT workers on staff. This leads to layoffs into the thousands, and it's the worst part of being in Human Resources.

I pore over lists of people across the country—name, age, gender, race, tenure, and performance rating—and we narrow down the field to an unlucky 1,250 people. We send out W.A.R.N. notifications, and I start traveling. On the verge of turning twenty-eight, I'm a grim reaper that rips away incomes and hopes and dreams from loyal employees, and I leave them with the fear of uncertainty. There are tears, of course. Sometimes I'm called horrible names as people react in shock, and twice we had to call local police because an employee threatened physical harm.

Through it all, I try to treat people with the utmost compassion—reviewing their severance packages line by line, answering questions, even speaking with spouses over speakerphone if the employee wants them involved in the discussion. I also encourage them all to utilize our "Outplacement Partner" who can provide counseling, assistance with resume retooling, and job searches. It is beyond unpleasant, and I find myself thankful for my evenings at home where I fire up the bong to quiet my whirling brain.

Age: Twenty-eight

When I turn twenty-eight, it's alone in my hotel room on the road in the Bay Area. I eat dinner from the room service tray and talk to my parents and Max. Max wanted to join me, and, in retrospect, I should have let him tag along, but killing dreams is not sexy work and it doesn't feel right to have hot sex in my hotel room after informing thirty people that they no longer have jobs.

There's no lull in the activity. I'm constantly boarding planes and navigating rental cars through strange cities all over the country well outside of my defined region because HR people are getting cut as well. We have to do more with less, and I wonder when I'll find myself on the other side of the severance package table. I think I'm surviving because I'm single, childless, and willing to travel at a moment's notice. It's not exactly fair, but that's the way it is.

In late August, Max and I carve out time for a long weekend getaway. We fly to San Diego and stay in a beautiful Hilton right on Pacific Beach. We spend a day at Sea World acting like two kids, take strolls on the beach watching the sunsets, and make up for lost time in the bedroom. On our third and final night together, after eight orgasms—because Max loves to keep score, he rolls off of me and expresses his own frustrations about getting a dose of two out three with me.

"Your travel schedule is almost as bad as mine," he says.

"Not so fun when the shoe is on the other foot, is it?" I tease.

"You're all kinds of fun, Wildcat," he says spooning into my back and skating his fingers down my bare skin. "When I get to see you. This weekend was beyond necessary. I wish we had time to do it again, but—"

"You're in the middle of pre-season."

"Are we going to make it?"

I roll over to face him and answer honestly, "I don't know. We can't seem to catch a break when it comes to timing, can we?"

He sighs, and his normally playful eyes are humorless. His lips touch mine, and he deepens the kiss before pulling back. "I want us to make it. I love you, Amanda."

I've been in love four times in my life—Braden, Tanner, Shawn, and Max. I wonder if a part of me will always love them in some way, shape, or form. Does the heart ever forget how it felt to love that man, or does it just adapt and adjust in order to love again after that man has moved on without me?

Max makes me laugh, challenges my mind, our attraction is palpable, and his sexual prowess has taken my body to levels of physical pleasure that I didn't know were possible.

We have so much more than a physical connection, though. We have a foundation of friendship and fantastic conversations, and I wish we could get the timing right, but our careers have ensured that all these months later we are still just two out of three.

"I love you, too, Max." I absolutely mean it going down the I LOVE YOU fork in the road with Max. I leave the rest unsaid because I'm pretty sure that it's just a matter of time... bad timing... before it catches up with us.

CHAPTER 30

Thursday, October 7, 2000

I PULL UP TO MY house after midnight following an overnight trip to Las Vegas. I'm exhausted. I helped close down an entire branch topped off by a mechanical delay at the airport. Parking under the carport, I make my way to the front door. The security screen is unlocked. Unease rolls through me. I know I locked it. I ALWAYS lock it—the habit is so ingrained. I try the main door, and it's also unlocked.

My heart plummets to my gut. Something is not right... I try to think. *What to do, what to do*? Whoever got into my house could still be inside. Even panic stricken and freaking like a character in a scary movie, I certainly don't run into the house, or if this were an actual horror movie, run upstairs. I jump back into my car and drive a few houses down the street before pulling over. Making sure my car doors are locked, I call 9-1-1.

"9-1-1, state your name and address please," a soothing female voice directs. After I give her the information she asks, "What is your emergency?"

"I... I... I just got back from a business trip and my security screen and front door are both unlocked. I locked them before I left—I'm sure of it. And I have an alarm system, but I'm not sure that I set it."

"Does anyone else reside at this address?"

"No, just me. No one else should be inside except my stupid, worthless cat. Oh my god, I hope he's okay."

"Did you enter the residence, Ma'am?"

"No. I got back in my car, and I'm parked a few houses west of the house right now."

"Make, model, year, and color of your vehicle, Ma'am?" I give it to her. "Are you safe?"

"I suppose I'm as safe as anyone can be in this crappy neighborhood."

"Do you see any movement in the house?"

"No... Nothing."

"I've dispatched a unit to your home address. Do not approach or enter the residence until a uniformed officer makes direct contact with you in your vehicle. Stay inside your vehicle, Ma'am, do you understand?"

"Y...Yes..."

"I'm going to stay on the line with you."

"Okay. How long do you think it will be?"

"As soon as they can get there."

"God, I hope they hurry because I really have to pee."

The woman on the other end of the line playfully asks, "Would you like me to dispatch that information as well?"

"Good god, no." I'm horrified before I realize that she's teasing.

"I'm going to ask you a few more questions. Do you have a dog in your house or backyard?"

"No, just my asshole cat inside the house."

"Do you see any unusual vehicles near your house?"

"No... I don't think so."

"What's the house number that you're parked in front of?" I squint and give it to her. "Do you have any stickers or anything on your vehicle that will make it easier for the officers to identify the car?"

"Yes. I have a Wildcat sticker. It's a U of A football helmet in the lower left rear window."

"Don't worry. I'm not going to judge you for that." *Very funny, Lady.* "You said no one else should be inside the residence, but does anyone else have access to your house that could be inside? A friend, family member?"

"Yes, but no one planned on coming by. Not at this hour."

"And what do you look like—hair color, height, weight."

"Long brown hair, five eleven, and I'm not telling you how much I weigh. No one but my doctor is allowed to know that truth."

She laughs. "Okay, Amanda. We'll just stay on the line together, and I want you to tell me if you see or hear anything else."

About fifteen minutes later a marked unit pulls up, shining a huge spotlight from the roof of the cruiser onto my house. I see two unit members exit their vehicle. They split up to walk around the outside with flashlights. Returning a few minutes later they enter through my front door together. I wait on pins and needles, and I really, really have to pee.

I jump in my seat when headlights flood the Blazer from behind. Emergency lights flash for a few seconds before they stop again, but the glaring headlights stay on shining through my back window. From my side mirror, I watch a backlit figure approach. In the lighting, he looks like a superhero, but he is actually a thirty-nine-year-old divorced cop with three kids.

Pressing the power window button, I look up into his hot cop face. "Shawn, I'm glad you're here." Even if he did break my heart, the sight of him is just as comforting as it was the afternoon he showed up at the ER. Maybe I do have a superhero complex. I tuck that thought aside to discuss with Dr. Anderson.

"Babe." His greeting is casual like he saw me yesterday instead of a year ago. "Stay in your car. Nice choice, by the way. I need to get some information from you. Before I do, are you all right?" He places his hand on my arm as he asks the question, and, *Ovaries, would you please calm the hell down?*

"No." I overshare, "I really, really, really have to pee. I should have gone at the airport, but I just wanted to get home to my stupid asshole cat."

"Still a nut," he mutters on a chuckle before talking business. "I'm staying out here with you. My partner is checking on the other unit, but your house is unoccupied, so it shouldn't be much longer." He grins roguishly. "While you try not to think about trickling water faucets or running rivers, walk me through your schedule and be specific. When were you last home, how long were you gone, what time did you return?"

Looking up at his impossibly handsome face while he jots down notes, I explain my activities over the last forty-three hours. "I left the house at five yesterday morning, took a seven o'clock flight from Sky Harbor to Las Vegas. I laid off about forty-five people over two days—which really sucked, by the way. Like, I handed out pink slips with Kleenex because I'm a corporate assassin of hopes and dreams now."

I stop to take a breath and find myself gripping the steering wheel. Staring at my hands, I continue, "All I do is fly around the country and fire people. Beyond horrible, although I suppose you could make the argument that dealing with gangs and criminals is a tougher job."

"Amanda." The sound of his voice brings me back to the topic at hand. When I look up, he's grinning down at me, and my *stupid ovaries* throw a fucking parade.

The Hotness Scale is code red. I have to look away. "I was supposed to be home around eight this evening, but my flight was delayed for *HOURS*—some sort of mechanical bullshit. You'd think it'd be fun to be stuck in an airport with slot machines, but it's not, Shawn. It's not fun at all. The noises are totally annoying—all these bells ringing and dinging and chiming and the sound of quarters falling from the machine into the doohickey catcher things. And there were all these Canadians getting pissed off about missing their connecting flight out of Phoenix to Edmonton. I didn't know

Canadians got pissed off. You always hear about how nice they are, but not during hockey games or when—"

"Babe, focus. Eyes on me."

I follow his instructions. *Sigh... god, your eyes are gorgeous. Your shoulders are so broad, and I love your thick forearms. Your hands are HUGE and those fingers of yours... You are so tall and strong and unbelievably hot. Our babies would be so beautiful. Shut up, Ovaries, he doesn't want our babies.* Who the hell am I kidding? I can't focus with my eyes on him.

"What time did you arrive home tonight?"

I shake my head to clear it. "After midnight—around 12:15. Both of the front doors were unlocked, and, before you ask, I'm positive that both doors were dead bolted."

He is pleased with my security efforts, but that's about to change because, "And the alarm?"

"That I'm not so sure about... It was so early, and I don't remember if I set it."

His grin turns to a glare and his voice is stern. "*Amanda.*"

"I know, I know, Officer Bossy. Did I mention it was really early? I hadn't even had coffee, so I wasn't fully awake yet. Spare me the lecture."

"I'm not going to spare you the lecture, but I'll save it for after you empty your bladder."

"Great." I smile at him and then, hoping to deflect a lecture with my charming personality, I ask, "Did I mention how happy I am to see you?"

"I heard the call go out. I got here as fast as I could. Didn't I tell you that I *never* wanted to respond to a call at this address unless the emergency was sexual in nature?"

I heat up from his words, the memories of how he'd take me—the manhandling, the orgasms, the handcuffs, his strong body and talented appendages. The sensations roll through me and pool right between my legs, which is really uncomfortable with a full bladder.

As he stares me down, I swallow hard and say, "And I told you not to come back unless you changed your mind."

He continues looking intently into my eyes in that *I can read your mind* kind of way. "My job is to ensure the safety and security for each person in our community. You know, protect and *serve*, and if you think I'd pass up an opportunity to protect and/or *serve* you, you have a seriously deficient recollection of what you mean to me."

"Stop," I release a groan. "Please."

My ovaries can't handle this.

"I've really missed you, and I—" He stops when we hear a voice call out from my front door. His body turns to the house where I see one of the officers raise his arm. "All clear. Let's get you inside."

* * *

In the brief seconds from the front door to the hall bathroom, I can clearly see that this *situation* sucks. After I take care of business, I inspect my house. Tossed, trashed, my shit is everywhere, and anything of any value is gone—electronics, jewelry, Mom's twelve sets of actual silver silverware that she'd given me as a housewarming gift. Thankfully, whoever did this didn't realize that I had thousands of dollars in handbags in the office closet. They were stored in their dust bags but wrapped a second time in nondescript plain white pillowcases. It pays to be overly organized sometimes. At least I have Louis and Chanel and all of their friends—oh, and Squirt is still here. He's glaring at me for causing a ruckus in his house.

When I finish the initial walk-through, I sink to the floor in my living room, holding my head in my hands and taking deep breaths so I won't swear and/or cry. No amount of deep breathing helps, and the words *motherfucking sons of bitches* fly out of my mouth. I'm not quiet about it, but my hands may have muffled my choice of words.

Shawn tells the other unit that he and his partner will take it from here. "I took her initial statement and she's *mine*," he asserts ownership of... me? Oh hell no.

Thanking the other two officers before they leave me alone with Shawn and his partner, Officer Cute Buns, I'm seething. *She's mine*? I glower and remind him, "I am not *yours*. I could've been but you didn't want me, remember?"

Officer Cute Buns fails to choke back laughter while Officer Barton drops to one knee next to me on the floor. "Oh, I want you." His dark eyes flare.

I growl—*yes, growl*—at him until he gets his hot cop face out of mine.

After we take inventory of the most expensive and obvious items missing, Shawn and his partner drill a piece of plywood into the slump block wall on the inside of my house to cover my bathroom window until I can get it replaced. I'm certain that the plywood is above and beyond the call of duty, but it's the least Shawn can do since he killed my dream of bearing his children.

The thief/thieves broke in through that window on the side of the house, hidden from the street by my property fence. I didn't set the alarm before I left for the airport. They had time to do a thorough job and walk my shit right out the front door—which, of course, they didn't lock behind them.

Shawn and Officer Cute Buns check all the windows and other exterior doors before they prepare to leave. "You can work on a complete inventory over the next few days, Amanda. You're going to need it for the insurance claim anyway, and you can give the list to me. It's highly unlikely we'll recover anything. Whoever did this was looking for items to fence to buy drugs."

Oh, yeah, Officers, the fuckers stole my weed and my favorite bong. I'll leave that off the inventory.

"We don't have the resources to look for items of lesser value. We might have some luck with the silver, though. Higher value and more easily identifiable at a pawn shop. Detectives won't care, but I'll see what I can do on my own time."

"I appreciate that, Shawn."

"Are you going to be all right tonight? We'll have units driving by throughout the night, but you're cleaned out. It's doubtful you'll have a repeat visit."

"Do I have a choice? I have to be all right, but I feel so... violated. Like this house is tainted now. I should've listened to my dad and never moved here."

Shawn lifts his chin at Officer Cute Buns who steps outside. He puts his arms around me, and I melt into his big protective body. "I'm really scared," I confess. "They went through my—"

He runs a large hand down my face. "I know, Amanda. It's

normal to be scared after something like this. I'm glad you weren't home, and it's just stuff you can replace, right?"

I look up and meet his eyes with a tiny smile. My voice is soft when I say, "It's just a truck. It's just a face. It's just stuff."

He pulls me closer. "That's all true. You have a sweet new Blazer with airbags, your face is prettier than I remember, and, if you want some help with your stuff, I can come back after my shift tonight. I'm on until six, but I'll swing by before I head home."

Alone time with Officer Bossy is such a bad idea. Say no. "Yes, please."

"Okay," he continues, comforting me with his voice and arms. "Then that's what we'll do. I'll help you with the inventory and clean-up, but please don't try to make me breakfast."

I snicker. "I have cereal and milk—unless they stole that."

"Perfect. You can make me some cereal." He bends down and gives me a quick peck on the lips meant as a gesture of concern and reassurance, I'm sure, but my lips are controlled by my *stupid ovaries*. I go back for more until our mouths and tongues are beyond reacquainted.

God, Max... Max is rarely here, Amanda...

"Damn, Amanda," he whispers in my ear. "I've missed that sweet mouth of yours."

My ovaries force a wistful sigh from me before I take a step back. FORK IN THE ROAD.

Don't do this, Amanda. "I'll see you in a few hours." I walk Shawn to the door, and my parting words are routine, "Please be safe out there."

He smiles and replies, "I always am." He gives me another toe-curling kiss and waits outside my door while I lock up behind him.

After setting my alarm, I close my curtains before leaving a voicemail for my boss Alisha. I brief her on Las Vegas and the robbery, and tell her that I'm taking tomorrow off. Luckily Monday is a holiday, so I'll have a long weekend. Since I traveled with my work computer, I still have a computer. I fire it up to check the Cardinals' schedule. We have a home game on Sunday, so Max is in town. Going on 2 a.m. and feeling guilty about the *situation* with Shawn, I send Max an email providing some details about the break-in and saying that we need to talk about our stupid travel schedules. I promise to call him at some point after I get some rest.

Opting to deal with the mess in the morning, with no TV or music or weed to keep me company, I take a quick shower to wash off the airplane germs. After putting on a nightie, I take to the couch with my journal. I have plenty of time to contemplate the fork in the road ahead and draft a list of pros and cons while Squirt judges me from across the room.

"What?" I ask him. "Why don't you like me, Asshole Cat? I make your *stupid cat life* really easy. You don't have any decisions to make—eat, shit, sleep, and lick yourself. The least you could do is let me scratch you behind the ears since cuddling is too much to ask."

Tail twitching as he shelters in place under the rubber tree plant, I don't hold back. "I knew I should've adopted the gray kitten with the loud purr. I always choose the wrong guy—even the feline variety."

I love Max. He is almost everything I've been looking for all these years. I envision a lifetime of battling wits, laughing our asses off, and having steamy reunion sex. If our gene pools produced children, they would be wicked smart sarcastic little assholes torn between two arch rivals. Having little dark-haired, brown-eyed, smartass children with Max would be wonderful—except for all the lonely days and weeks stretching out in front of me without him around to run defense with our uber-sarcastic offspring. I absolutely understand why all his relationships end in failure. His schedule is nothing short of brutal, and, even with our best efforts, I hate it.

Shawn scrambles my senses. Tall and built, he's such a freaking man that I feel protected, feminine, and sexy by his side. He accepts—even appreciates in an amused sort of way—that I'm quirky. Our personalities complement as opposed to compete. Sure, the only thing that brought him back into my life now was the line of duty, but he could've easily let someone else handle it. He didn't, though, and he admitted that he still has feelings for me. It's highly unlikely he's changed his mind about the whole baby *situation*, but the pull between us is intense. If I let Shawn inside my front door, I know exactly what's going to happen. And, *fan-freaking-tastic*, my ovaries want him.

You could have a fling, see where Shawn stands, and, if nothing has changed, Max would never be the wiser. You could have your cop and keep your devil, too.

CHAPTER 31

JUMPING UP AT THE SOUND of my doorbell in the early morning, I realize that I fell asleep with my journal and my twisted thoughts. I call through the door, "Hold on. I need to turn off the alarm." While punching in the code, I'm resigned to the fact that my hormones are going to call this play.

"Glad to hear you actually used that alarm last night." He smiles and steps inside, locking the deadbolts behind him.

I don't return his smile. I'm deep in thought. Hell yes, I feel guilty about Max because, as it turns out, I'm not a sociopath. But I can't help myself where Shawn is concerned. He is sensory overload—there in my time of need, and, really, I do need to talk to Dr. Anderson about this superhero complex thing.

Studying my face, he asks, "Did you get any sleep after we left?"

"Not much—maybe a few hours."

"Do you want to talk about last night?"

Stepping into his personal space, I tilt my head up. "No. I don't want to talk." I touch my lips to the skin on his neck and ask, "Do you want to *talk*?"

He answers me with his familiar crushing kiss. *Whoosh*. I'm on fire from head to toe as he walks me backwards into my bedroom without uncoupling our mouths. My nightie is whisked over my head, and I'm flat on my back with Shawn's body covering mine. I groan as one talented hand slips into my panties, and his fingers hit the magic spot.

He makes an observation and issues an order. "Soaked—for me. *For me*. Tell me how *I* make you feel, Amanda."

I manage to whimper, "So, so good." Tangling with his mouth while rotating my hips in rhythm to his hand, he knows exactly what to do with every inch of me. When the orgasm rips through me, I make sure to cry out the correct name so my neighbors know which guy on my damn bench is here.

The release was so intense, I'm in danger of bursting into happy tears. Instead I crack a joke. "Is that your nightstick, Officer, or are you just happy to see me?" While it's a joke, it is also a valid question because he's still in full uniform including his belt and all his service gear.

Bursting out into laughter as he untangles himself from me, he replies, "Both. Let's even things out." Removing the belt, he places it on top of my dresser. I reserve the right to remain silent as I watch him take off his shirt and the Kevlar underneath. As he kicks off his shoes and strips off his pants and socks, I appreciate the fact that very few men can rock a wife beater and briefs.

He announces, "I'm going to take a quick shower."

"Why? Do you have brain matter or bodily fluids, besides mine, stuck to your skin?"

He smiles. "Not this shift, but that vest is hot and I want to clean up for you." I lose him for a few minutes while he rinses off. Meanwhile, I ditch my soaked underwear and crawl under the covers.

I contemplate my next move because even though no one hates a Lumberjack, this Lumberjack is most definitely a deal-breaker for me and my Sun Devil.

Strolling out of the bathroom—naked and clean—he shoots me a grin and walks over to my underwear drawer. *Oh my god*, he pulls out my handcuffs which are right where he left them a year ago. On instinct, I scoot closer to the headboard and raise my hands over my head in complete submission.

Click on the left wrist. He loops the other cuff around the metal slat of my headboard. *Click* on the right wrist. I squirm in anticipation while my ovaries perform backflips. His eyes, darkened with desire, are full of bossy intentions. Grabbing the top of the covers, he flips them aside and scans my body. I'm nervous but not scared because some things never change. He'll do amazing things to me—with me—and I've missed him.

If I pull too hard, the cuffs cut into my skin. Pain mixed with pleasure intensifies the rush, and Shawn's an expert at bringing me right to the brink of too much intensity and pulling me back again until I beg him to finish what he started. This reunion is no exception.

We take a nap, wake up a few hours later; he flips me to my stomach and grabs my hips, dragging me to my knees. I use my arms to brace while he thrusts inside of me, hitting the perfect spot every single time. Thanks to Max, I've learned how to allow my body to roll the first release into another and another and another. By the time he comes, I've lost count. While I'm sure that Max won't appreciate my perfection of the multiple playing out in bed with another man, he taught me a very important life skill.

After our next nap, I make Shawn oatmeal because the man needs fuel for round number three, which is a departure from rounds one and two. His touch—soft and methodical; his kisses—tender and deep. The words he speaks while he looks me in the eyes and moves inside of me are brilliant. "I'm not losing you again. I love you, Amanda."

He collapses on me, and I wrap every limb around him, taking his weight until I can't anymore. "Can't breathe," I protest after a few minutes. He laughs and rolls to his side and takes me with him so we're facing each other.

"Do you still love me, babe?"

Breaking into a smile, I kiss his mouth and tell him, "Yes." I never stopped loving Shawn. I put those feelings aside so I could focus on Max. And, damn it, I love Max...

Ten years later, I'm still torn between two men. And, seriously, what does this say about the kind of woman I am?

You're indecisive? You love too much? You're incapable of fidelity?

I'm an idiot.

"I need to hear you say it."

"I love you, Shawn." *Let's get married and have just one tiny, little baby.*

Smiling warmly, he strokes my face, ending on a tender kiss. "I love you, too."

We fall asleep cuddling and wake up later for sandwiches. He helps me try to restore order to my bungalow while we work on the inventory for the insurance company then heads back to his place to get clean clothes for his shift. I'll see him in the morning. My ovaries have some very important questions.

* * *

I shower and call Jenny to spill out the entire *situation* while she gasps in surprise and relays bits and pieces to Paul.

"Jeez, Jenny, just put me on speaker phone so he can get all the facts straight."

"Good idea!" She missed the Sarcasm Scale, but it's okay. They're married, and she tells him everything anyway. Besides, they get to lead the single life vicariously through me, and I probably make them feel damn grateful to have found each other. "What if Shawn still doesn't want another kid?"

I sigh heavily. "Then I'll have to figure out if I want to be a step-mother, I guess. But not like the ones in the Disney movies. That never works out well. Or maybe he's changed his mind. He said that he loves me. Maybe that means... I don't know."

"And Max?" she asks.

"He's my next call. I have to break up with him."

"You don't want to know what Officer Bossy has to say about the baby *situation* before you break things off?"

"I broke things off ten seconds after Shawn showed up at my house this morning. Max just doesn't know it yet. I was thinking about back in college with Tanner—"

"Hey, Paul, did I ever tell you that Amanda and I slept with the same guy?"

"Not at the same time," I yell while Paul starts laughing. When the laughter dies down, I spill another secret, "By the way, when I was back in Pine Ridge for Trina's wedding, I slept with Matt Neilson a few times."

Jenny giggles. "Small town—not a lot to choose from up there."

"You seemed to do all right back in the day," I joke.

"Shut up, Amanda. Go break Max's heart already."

* * *

When he picks up my call, Max asks, "Did you sleep all day?"

I'm glad he can't see me because I break out into a full on blush. "No."

"A weird thing happened today, Wildcat."

"What's that?"

"I came by your house to check in and help you clean up, and there was a squad car in the driveway."

My morals are beyond highly questionable. Even though I'm calling to break up because I cheated on him, I instantly respond with a lie. "I was robbed, Max. They were picking up an inventory sheet after I had a chance to go through everything."

"Well, that's a relief."

Isn't it? Because I don't want to tell you that I cheated. I can make this about two out of three and poor timing. Maybe we can part as friends.

His voice turns glacier. "I figured it must have been something like that so I ran some errands, met a buddy for lunch, and when I came back by your place a few hours later there was still a squad car in your driveway. Did it take *hours* to pick up an inventory list?"

After taking a deep breath, I throw away the possibility of any sort of friendship with Max. "Actually one of the responding officers last night was Shawn, and—"

"Don't tell me."

"Really?"

"No, you're going to tell me, Wildcat. I don't think I want to hear it."

"I... um. I... I'm going to get back together with him."

"I figured that's what you were doing with him all day today." His Sarcastic Scale is off the charts when he says, "But thanks for letting me know. Classy move breaking things off over the phone after all these years."

"I'm sorry," I reply quietly.

"We just said all that *I love you* crap. Did you make that up?"

"I meant what I said. I do love you. You're an incredible person."

"Apparently I'm not incredible enough."

"Turns out, I'm two out of three. I love that you love your job. You're a talented reporter, and what's that saying about *do what you love and you'll never have to work a day in your life?* You're lucky to have that, but I hate hockey season almost as much as I hate flying around the country firing people. It was only a matter of time before—"

"You fucked someone else."

Wincing because I hit Max where it hurts the most—in his dignity—I'm no different than all the women who came before me.

"Now that you've fucked the cop, you tell me that number three is our deal-breaker? Weak." *I'm an asshole, Max.* "Tell me one more thing."

"Okay."

"How many times have you fucked around on me?"

"Max."

"I need to know."

Tanner's words from so many years ago echo in my head. *"Fuck YES it matters, Amanda. Did you make a mistake one drunken, stoned night, or do you make fucking other men a habit? One guy? Two? Twenty? Fifty? ANSWER ME!" he bellowed.*

My eyes are full of *stupid tears* because we've had years to develop a solid friendship underneath the physical attraction, and I'm going to miss him. "I was faithful the entire time we were together—right up until this morning. I'm so sorry, Max. I hope that—"

"Save it, Wildcat."

* * *

I need more than luck, because while some things do change—Shawn loves me and wants to be in a committed relationship; some things don't change. He doesn't want to have even one tiny little baby with me. Now I have a decision to make. Is this still a deal breaker for me, or will my ovaries make the ultimate sacrifice so the rest of me can keep Shawn?

Maybe Jenny was right. Perhaps my ovaries should have asked that question before I jumped back into bed with him, exchanged *I love yous*, and broke up with Max.

Given Max's history with romantic relationships and my tendency to let my ovaries make decisions for me, I was bound to screw him over eventually. If I wanted to be a single mother, I could've done that by now. I suppose these are good things to learn about myself *before* I married a sports reporter or someone in the military or even a traveling salesman. Maybe my dad is right; I just haven't met *the right one* yet.

Shawn and I have numerous conversations about the status of our new relationship over the following weeks. I'm undecided if I can live with the no kids thing, but I'm also unwilling to kick him out of bed again. I start to ask questions about his children.

I'm surprised that he's now an open book and wants to tell me all about them. "Ashley is the oldest. Eighth grade, thirteen, almost fourteen. She's smart—used to play club volleyball, but her grades have dropped. She's... difficult lately. Emotional. Yells at her mom a lot and smarts-off to John."

"Who's John?"

"Debbie's husband. He has a couple of daughters himself, but they're older." *I know nothing.* "But Ash doesn't show that side to me. I just hear about it. My Natalie is eleven—sixth grade. She loves to read. She's still a little girl, but sometimes she acts twice her age, and that can change from minute to minute." He smiles. "I'll tell you, though, she and Ashley are close. I worry about her attitude taking a turn. And Trevor—he's in first grade. Smart, loves football, missing his two front teeth... Compared to daughters, he's a breeze, but he's only six."

"And time with them is hard to carve out?"

"Always, but it's not because of custody agreements or an unwillingness on Debbie's part. It's the damn night and weekend shifts, and maybe it's a mistake on my part. I have more than enough seniority to bid for a day shift and get it, but nighttime is when most decent people are home in bed. I like the excitement factor, and I still have the energy for it."

My lips form a smirk. "My superhero is an adrenaline junkie?"

"Maybe a little bit. But I don't take risks."

"Um... your entire career choice is one giant risk. I try not to think about that."

"That's why I don't talk much about it. I don't want to worry you or expose you to the elements out there. I make lots of tradeoffs, and I can't say they're always for the best. I do what I love and what I think is best for the community, but it means less time with my kids. If we were married, it'd be a different story. I could have them for longer periods of time, knowing you're here with them while I'm working."

"What would their mom think about that?"

"She'd love that. We've talked about it."

"You have?"

"Debbie wants me to be happy and have more time with the kids."

"Maybe she wants more breaks from Ashley's smart mouth," I joke.

He grins. "I'm sure it's both. We talk about the kids a lot and try to stay on the same page so they get a consistent message. Babe, you have to be sure that you want to move forward in this relationship before I bring you around them. They've never seen me with another woman. It's a big deal to me."

"I... um..." *I want one little tiny baby of my own.* "I understand. Let's see how it goes over the holidays, okay? Because..." *I want to breed with you.* "You're right—this is a big decision." *Isn't it? This is fucking colossal decision...*

CHAPTER 32

Territorial Cup—2000

THE MONDAY AFTER ASU CRUSHES us in a 30 to 17 victory, Max hits
me up on IM.

> Max: *Too bad we didn't place a wager on the game. I'd hold you
> to it.*
>
> Me: *You're talking to me?*
>
> Max: *Can't resist an opportunity to rub something in your face
> since I can't put my dick there anymore. Plus, I have a box of
> your stuff over here—girl stuff and some clothes. I can drop it at
> your office or on your doorstep. Lady's choice.*
>
> Me: *I like how you talk about rubbing your dick in my face AND
> refer to me as a lady all in the same paragraph.*
>
> Max: *Cheap shot. I'm sorry.*

Me: *My house behind the carport gate, please. When? I have some movies, CDs, and a few ASU t-shirts that I'm dying to use as toilet bowl brushes. I'll leave it out for you.*

Max: *Wednesday.*

Me: *Thank you.*

Max: *Any regrets?*

Me: *That I hurt you and lost your friendship in the process. I miss talking to you.*

Max: *It's a little fresh for the* let's be friends *speech.*

Me: *Maybe someday?*

Max: *We'll see. How many times did your quarterback get sacked?*

Me: *Seven.*

Max: *Spot on, Wildcat. I knew you'd have the answer. I was also keeping count. Then again, I like to keep count. Why did you go back to him?*

Me: *Timing is everything.*

Max: *I don't follow.*

Me: *There's no time for the real stuff together.*

Max: *Sounds like an ideal relationship.*

Me: *Except that you only saw the best of me. There's a whole train wreck going on behind the scenes. You have no idea, but I did you a favor.*

Max: *Inspiring.*

Me: *I find you inspiring.*

Max: *I could tell every time you screamed my name and raked your claws down my back.*

Me: *You've been my friend for years. I miss you.*

Max: *Let's keep it simple next year.*

Me: *?*

Max: *Next year, winner buys loser lunch.*

* * *

Even though my ovaries are on shaky ground, Shawn and I are solid through the holidays. I invite Mom and Dad to spend Christmas with me, and while they are surprised by the turn of events in my love life—yet again—they don't appear to have whiplash as a result. Shawn joins us for our *family by choice* day visit with Tanner and his family down in Tucson.

Tanner meets us on the front porch of the main house. He hugs my parents and thanks them loudly (while glaring at me) for visiting the twins over their birthday in July. My parents head inside to see the twins and meet their namesake—the strongest connection of my family to Tanner's—Michaela Claire Rawlings, born in August.

I only slightly enjoy the dude posturing when I introduce the two men on the front porch.

Okay, I absolutely enjoy it... Except...

Tanner stands as tall as he can, and, while he keeps in amazing shape, he's not quite as tall or broad, but, damn, these two men resemble one another—build, hair and eye color. Throw in the liberal utilization of *babe*, a compulsive need to be in control—all the time—both in professional and carnal positions of authority.

Stop. Wait a minute... Holy shit, Amanda. You're dating the hot cop version of Tanner Rawlings.

After trying to crush Shawn's hand, Tanner gives me a bear hug followed by an expected ration of shit. "Almost forgot what you look like, Panda. What's it been, two years?"

I retort, "Last time I checked, the I-10 runs east AND west, Tanner—even for pompous doctors."

"Yeah... been a little busy with Mikie and the twins who don't remember you—it's been so long."

"And I've been a little busy laying off two-thirds of CompuWorld. Jeez, Tanner, most people would say *it's wonderful to see you again* and *thank you for coming*."

"Speaking of coming, I haven't seen you since before Cherry got popped." He laughs in my face. "Man, I can't believe your Cherry is gone."

I glare. "Tanner... *Really*? Can't you at least behave yourself the first time you meet my boyfriend?" I look at Shawn who appears uneasy by our exchange. While I explained our history and I'm sure it helps that my parents are along for the visit, I can see how Shawn might find it confusing.

"Panda... *Really*? You think I'm ever gonna grow up around you?" He grins. I watch his eyes dance. Wincing, I brace for the throw down. "Besides, I'm not sure how to behave in front of your boyfriend. Haven't met one of those since I was one of those."

Grumbling, I push into him hard with my shoulder on the way inside—a common *fuck you* gesture back on the football field. "Get out of my way, you *little jerk*. I need to get my hands on those babies."

He calls from behind me, "Unless you count that nineteen-year-old. Should I count that kid as a boyfriend, Panda?"

* * *

I'm snuggling Mikie when she has a diaper *situation*. "Tanner, she's ripe," I announce.

"You ever change a diaper before?"

"I used to babysit *SIX* children, remember?"

"All right," he challenges. "Let's see if you have any skills."

"Oh no." Laughing, I shake my head. "I know what you're doing. You're trying to get out of this because Lorraine's in the kitchen."

He laughs in my face before plucking Mikie from my arms. "Caught me, Panda. Come with me, though. Let's talk."

Mom's reading to Abigail, and Shawn's outside with my dad and Andrew. I follow Tanner into one of the back rooms that serves as a nursery away from their actual nurseries. Lorraine spends a lot of time with her mom in the main house during the day.

Tanner changes a diaper faster than anyone I've ever seen. I sit in the rocker and he makes conversation. "Shawn... good guy? You look happy."

"He's a very good guy," I confirm. "But, um, there's a catch."

"Wanna explain?"

"Yes."

"You do?" His eyes are wide because, seriously, this guy has been pulling deep thoughts out of me for years, and now I want to offer them up without a fight. I nod in confirmation. He finishes up with Mikie and hands me a fresh baby. "Be right back—gotta wash my hands." When he returns, he takes a seat on the floor and waits for me to say something.

Looking down at Mikie with her soft dark curls and alert brown eyes, chubby cheeks, and the tiniest little feet in the world, I can't help it. S*tupid tears* roll down my face before I get a word out.

"Panda?" He smiles softly. "What's the catch with Shawn?"

"You have *everything*, Tanner," I sniffle while toying with Mikie's left foot.

Surmising correctly, he states, "And you want everything, too."

"There's no bench—it's just me and Shawn. Just talk to the guy, look at him. How the hell did I get a man like that to fall for me? I've loved him for years, Tanner, but the catch is... he has three kids from his first marriage. He's almost forty and he doesn't want more kids. I... I never envisioned not having children of my own."

Tanner asks me the question of a lifetime. "Can you live without baby Panda Bears?"

I take a hit from Mikie's head before looking back to him. "How can I give this up? I want at least one of my own—preferably two so they can conspire against me when I turn into my mother and start doling out old-school advice."

"You asking for my opinion?"

"Yes, please, although I'm shocked you didn't just give it to me. You're not big on manners today, Tanner." Our eyes meet as we smile at each other.

"If you want *everything*, a woman like you shouldn't settle for less."

* * *

I break up with Shawn before the New Year, and it's just as gut-wrenching the second time around. No, actually it's worse because I fell for him all over again, and, this time around, he loved me, too. Love isn't *everything*, though.

Shawn is pragmatic. As always when I laid it all out, he was kind and respectful, but he didn't change his mind because some things can't be changed. So that's it—again.

It's going to be difficult having kids when I'm totally, completely single. For the first time in a very long time, there's no one waiting on the sidelines to rotate in—a placeholder to distract me from my loneliness. I don't attempt to rebuild a bench. I nurse my broken-heart—again. I hit the bong a little too hard and continue to travel—laying people off and killing dreams.

I talk to Dr. Anderson once a week, but I don't tell her I'm smoking weed again. Instead, I tell her about what I want from my future. When she advises me to make a list of negotiables and non-negotiables in a life partner, I'm already two steps ahead of her. Whenever I'm tempted to pick up the phone and call Shawn, I refer to my list because lists are helpful.

When I'm in town and manage to scrape myself off the couch, I spend time with Jenny and her family. I reconnect with Katie, Nathan, and their son Nolan. I volunteer to babysit so they can enjoy time out, and I snuggle their babies and toddlers as if they were my own—but they're not. I read, journal, watch TV, and listen to country music.

After checking with my doctor, I start back in the gym at CompuWorld. My back and neck still aren't 100%, but I can't totally let myself go... Not if I still want to find *everything*.

Max and I talk over IM and share an occasional phone call. When I have thoughts of something more, I refer to my list. Lists are helpful, and mixed messages are not fair to Max who's dating someone new. And, yes, that burns, too, but I hope he finds *the one* for him.

April 2001

If coming to terms with my single self isn't enough, I lose a huge part of my identity when my career at CompuWorld comes to an end the first week in April.

We filed for Chapter 11 Bankruptcy back in February, and I knew the writing was on the wall at some point. I just didn't see it coming because the job was a huge distraction from my lack of *everything* else, and now... sigh, no more distractions. I receive a decent severance package, and I have savings—money from the accident settlement, and a healthy 401K balance.

Since I'm on the job hunt, after giving myself two weeks to mourn and smoke through my entire stash, I take a drastic step. No more. Wrapping up my two bongs and pipes and any related paraphernalia in a garbage bag, I dispose of them in the dumpster behind Target. Done. And, yes, that burns a lot, but it might be time to grow up.

I spend precious funds to join a women's only fitness center fifteen minutes from the house. Since my back is still a little sore, I try something new—water aerobics. That's right, it's not just for little old ladies, although the pool is full of them. I can kill half a day at the gym between light weights and a cardio workout in the pool. Swinging by Jenny's on the way home while Paul's still at work, she attempts to teach me how to prepare some basic meals. Mostly, I wind up playing with the girls. I need to keep busy, though. I feel antsy and nervous—like something bad is about to happen.

The country is falling into a post Y2K recession. It's not just the tech sector—there just isn't much out there. I use every business and MBA contact I have, which results in a few interviews but no job offers. Financially, I'm going to be fine through the end of the year—I think. But I have to start looking outside of the metro area. Arizona isn't a union-heavy state, and I'd rather focus on labor relations than employee relations, although, I'd take either at any point.

* * *

With plenty of time on my hands, I take my parents up on an offer to go with them to visit Brianna and her family in Germany as soon as Mom's school year is finished. I leave Squirt with Jenny and Paul, and I practically skip down the jetway with my folks in mid-June. My parents try to go every other year, but I'm shocked when I add up all the years gone by. I haven't seen Brianna and Marcus since I was an exchange student in 1990. I only know my nephews through pictures, email, and phone calls.

After two weeks, my parents fly to England, but I take a side trip to Bielefeld where I spent a year as an exchange student between high school and college. While I've exchanged occasional letters over the years with my host family, my communication dropped off during my darker days in college. Little Hannah grew up into a stunning young lady, and Lars married Sonja after the university and they have two children. My host mother Inge jokingly mandates German only in her house. I try, but I'm rusty after all this time. My dear friend Monika even comes to town so we can giggle like teenage girls in my old bedroom. As for Curt—the cherry-popping German—screw him. Alive or dead, I have no interest in laying eyes on him ever again.

CHAPTER 33

Age: Twenty-nine

WHEN I RETURN HOME IN July, I sift through emails and apply for more positions around the country. I have a phone interview with an auto parts manufacturer in Tennessee, but nothing comes of it. After I have a chance to catch up with the job search, I place a call to Tanner.

Lorraine picks up and I invite myself down for a few days over the twins' birthday. I offer to stay in a hotel, but she tells me not to be ridiculous. "There's plenty of space in the main house for you, Amanda. Don't spend the money. Just come and spend the time."

You'd think it would be weird, but it's not. I arrive on a Thursday afternoon, which means I spend an afternoon and full day with Lorraine, the kids, and her mom while Tanner is working. We converse like friends—which, I suppose, we are by now.

I brought a few of my old yearbooks and a box of old photos, which I pore through with Lorraine and Pam, filling them in on the life and times of a much younger Tanner Rawlings going all the way back to his Pop Warner days with my dad. We set aside a number of pictures so I can make copies for Lorraine to share with the kids one day. Oh, and their children with Tanner's dominant genes... I love them so much.

* * *

On Friday evening, Tanner and I meet Nicholas and Michele for dinner near campus. I'm astonished to discover that as close as I was to all of them in college, Tanner's never met them before. Following hugs and promises to see each other soon, I suggest a walk before heading back to his house. I haven't explored the campus of Arizona in years, and I have dinner and energy that I need to walk off.

We take a hot evening stroll across Park Avenue and enter campus off 2nd Street. Walking by Gila and then Yuma Hall, I stop and study the beautiful red brick building. "We moved in there ten years ago, Tanner. When did we get so old?"

"We're not old—just older. If those walls could talk what would they say?"

"That I was right—we should've moved in together," I tease and keep walking, turning right down a pathway toward Old Main and the Social Sciences building.

"Are you serious about that?" He grabs me by the elbow and stops me. "Because sometimes I wonder..."

"Wonder what?"

"I love my wife." His words are careful, "She's given me and the kids everything that's good inside of her, but... there's no...."

"No...?"

"No... thrill? Fire, maybe?" Poor Tanner; he looks so sad. "I wanna get in a heated argument sometimes—have her stand up to me. It's almost too easy."

"That's what you wanted."

"That's what I got."

I suggest, "Maybe you can find intensity in other ways—with other people."

He looks angry and rumbles, "Cheat on her?"

"I would *never* suggest that, and you don't have that in you." I pause to question him with my eyes. "You don't, do you?" To my relief, he immediately shakes his head no. I resume walking while explaining, "I meant that you can have colleagues and friendships that can give you those challenges instead. Like hire an office manager who tells you to shut the hell up when you're acting like a pompous little jerk. Plus, you have me—I'll always tell you when you're wrong and where to stick it. If you want to get in a good argument, just give me a call."

That cracks him up. "You're right. It's better to have peace at home than not. Lorraine is good for me."

"I agree."

"And you? Are you any closer to finding *everything*?"

"No." Pausing at the fountain in front of Old Main, I take a seat on the concrete bench around it. *Late one night Tanner and I had sex in pretty much this exact spot.* "I'm coming to terms with being totally alone, though. This time without a man or a bench—I think it's been good for me, actually."

"Do you remember that night I did you right here?"

I burst into laughter. "It's like you can read my dirty mind."

"Yeah," he grins. "I have one of those, too. And a lot of great memories with you."

"You're so important to me. You know that right? You, the kids, even Lorraine... I love your family, and I'm going to try to be a better friend—and aunt."

Sitting next to me, he slings an arm around my shoulders. "You're the best friend I'll ever have, and I'll always love you—no matter how busy we get or how much time passes."

"Same." And because this is starting to feel deep and heavy, I ask, "Did I ever tell you about my Sun Devil?"

"You had a Sun Devil?"

"Oh yeah." Jumping up, I head toward the Mall in front of the student union. As we walk the mostly deserted green space, I tell him about my maroon and gold orgasms and other exploits while he laughs at me. I have so much energy that I'm shaking it out through my fingertips as we finish our loop around the Mall and head back to Park Avenue.

"Your parents will be here tomorrow for the birthday party. Can't wait to see them."

"They wouldn't miss it."

At our parking spot, Tanner says, "I'm still waiting, Panda..."

"For?"

"To pay off my student loans so I can buy a fancy car and let

Michael take it out for a spin." Tanner's truck is a Chevy because some things never change, but this one is fairly new. You can take the boy out of Pine Ridge, but you can never take Pine Ridge out of the boy. He helps me into the passenger seat and pauses before closing the door. "Know what else I'm waiting for?"

"What?"

"For you to have *everything*, too."

September 11, 2001

The phone rings. Glaring at the bedside clock, as if the clock is to blame for the 5:58 a.m. call, I grab the handset and check caller ID.

"Did you forget there's a three-hour time difference?" I grumble.

Trina cries into the phone, "I can't find my mother."

"What?"

"My mom isn't answering the phone." I've never heard such desperation in her voice.

I'm not quite awake and definitely confused. Trina's parents still live in Pine Ridge. "What's going on?"

"Turn on your TV, Amanda. A plane crashed into Connor's building."

I bolt upright and throw off the covers. Racing to the living room to turn on NBC, I can't believe what I'm seeing. Falling back onto the sofa, I try to absorb the sight of the enormous plumes of smoke billowing from the North Tower of the World Trade Center in New York City.

Muting the volume so I can hear Trina, I ask, "Do you know what happened?"

"No. They're speculating. The plane just flew right into the building about ten minutes ago, and... I can't reach Connor. He's in there somewhere."

"And your mom?"

"I called her first. She didn't answer."

"I'll stay on the phone with you. What floor is Connor's office on?"

"Fifty-four." I can't tell from the images, and I'm no expert on the World Trade Center, but it looks like the plane hit much higher up.

"What happened when you tried to call him?"

"Straight to voicemail. No answer at his desk."

"I'm sure they're evacuating the building and you'll hear from him soon." I don't know shit, but I'll say anything to try and comfort her.

"What if he's dead?" she wails.

That's a valid question—one I can't possibly comprehend. "Where's Liam?" I ask to distract her.

"Morning nap."

"It's a little early to be napping already. How many naps does he take?" I don't care. I just want to keep her talking. I eke up the volume on the TV, trying to make some sense of this, and keep asking questions about Liam while I talk about Mikie, Sydney, and Nolan's nap schedules.

In the midst of talking about nothing, what happens next is something that we will never forget. It's 6:03 a.m. on the west coast, and on live television we watch a jetliner crash directly into the South Tower. It happens so fast, so violently... The jet disappears into the building leaving nothing but gaping metal and fire in its wake. Trina screams out. I'm shocked into silence. I sit and listen to her wail so loudly Liam wakes up and joins her.

"I have to get Liam," Trina says. "I'll call you back."

"I love you."

"I love you, too."

While I'm glued to the television, word comes in that a third plane crashed into the Pentagon, the FAA grounds all flights, and, if that's not horrific enough, on live television the South Tower collapses to the ground at 6:59 a.m. One hundred and ten stories come falling down with thousands of innocent people inside and on the ground below—including all those first responders.

And Connor? Where the hell is Connor? His building, the first to be hit, is reduced to twisted rubble at 7:20 a.m. Southern Manhattan looks like a nuclear bomb dropped. There's still a fourth plane out there somewhere. Where is that fourth plane?

"Anything?" I say into the phone when Trina calls back a few minutes after the North Tower collapse.

"No," she's sobbing—of course she is. "It's crazy here. A lot of the women from my Moms' Group have husbands down there. My phone won't stop ringing, but none of the calls are from Connor."

"Becky Haines with the hyphenated last name. What about her husband—that New York City lawyer guy? Where does he work?"

"Henry. Midtown."

"Have you talked to Becky?"

Trina sniffles. "She's on her way over right now. Henry's safe—out of harm's way. Unless... What if more shit goes down?"

"Let's not go there. What can I do for you until Becky gets to your house?" And whoever thought I'd be happy to hear that Becky

Haines-Whatever is able to comfort our dear friend in a time of crisis? Well, I am. Big time. Thank goodness for Becky.

"Talk to me. Pray with me. Don't hang up, Amanda."

* * *

Connor's boss immediately evacuated his employees—ripping phones out of peoples' hands and directing them to the nearest stairwell. He had no clue what had happened, but he didn't fuck around. As a result, every single person in Connor's company made it back home that day. I got the joyous call from Trina late in the afternoon. Sweating the news for eight hours is a small price to pay in comparison to the thousands of people who will never see their loved ones again.

In the days that follow, the images of the planes crashing into buildings, people jumping from the towers, stunned victims covered in blood and ashes, photo montages of entire fire battalions and police departments killed in the rubble, devastated family and friends... it's all too much. But, like everyone else, I can't look away, and I cling to the stories of heroism and acts of human kindness. Entire generations of people across the world will never forget or understand—how can we possibly?

Shaken by the fallen policemen and women, I'm compelled to call Shawn. I leave a message and hear back from him a few hours later.

"What going on? Are you all right, Amanda?"

"Yes. Aside from recent world events which made me think of you. Are you okay?"

"We're pulling extra shifts all over town. Not sure what will happen when they reopen Sky Harbor."

"All those first responders... So brave. Running into burning buildings when everyone else was trying to get out, and then... when those towers fell..." I sniffle. "It made me think of how you're always on the front lines, and I just needed to hear your voice. It sounds silly, maybe, but I needed to check on you."

"I understand. I'm tired—drained but fine. It's nice to know you still think of me."

"I do all the time, and I *wish*..." I stop speaking because there's nothing to be gained by continuing that thought.

"I'd love to see you, but I don't think that would be good for either one of us."

"No." Wistfully I release a sigh. I want nothing more than to be held in his strong arms, comforted, and taken in my bed. I hate feeling lonely—without comfort or companionship, but he's right. We can't get past our deal breaker—it says so right on my list. Lists are helpful. "Thanks for calling me back. Knowing that you're safe makes me feel better. I hope you get some rest soon."

"It's good to hear your voice, babe. If you need me, call again. Just because we're not together anymore doesn't mean I won't be there if you need me."

"Same. If you need to talk, I'm here."

"Thanks, Amanda."

"Please be safe out there."

"I always am."

I hang up—sad and weepy yet strangely comforted. I miss that hot cop. Deal breakers sting like a bitch, but I'm just going to have to face it because I can't numb it.

The next day, I force myself to turn off the TV and go to the gym. It feels like a selfish thing to do while the official death count is still rising. I have to do something, though, so I re-establish my daily routine and reserve my news consumption for the morning and evenings.

* * *

On another Tuesday—November 6th—the phone rings out in the early morning. I'm awake making oatmeal in the kitchen. Caller ID tells me it's one of my parents. Experience tells me that no call before 7 a.m. contains good news.

Heart sinking, I pick up the handset. "Hello?"

"Brown Eyes," Dad greets me. His voice is soft—too soft, too tender, and I *know* something is terribly wrong again because nothing is ever wonderfully wrong.

"Daddy? Is Mom all right...? Brianna?"

"There's no easy way to say this. It's Coach McLaughlin. I'm sorry, but he passed away yesterday."

Abandoning the oatmeal and coffee, I walk into the living room so my ass can find the nearest seat. Flopping back on the sofa, I choke out, "How? Was he sick?"

Was he sick? If he was, how could I not have known?

Because you never went to visit him again. You didn't even pick up the phone and call the man, Amanda.

"He had a heart attack while he was out on a morning jog. Bonnie found him halfway down the driveway when she left to go shopping." My eyes burn. Poor Mrs. Laughlin. "He was already gone. There was nothing she could do."

"Daddy..." I whisper his name as memories flood my mind.

The first day we met... His cheerful voice booming, "Who do we have here?"

It's not honey, it's Harrington.

Hit me, Harrington.

ASU has one of the best sports medicine programs.

I'll never smack you on the ass, but you're part of my team.

Don't lose control on my field. Lock it down, Team.

We'd love to see you.

You're welcome here anytime.

I always thought you'd make an excellent daughter-in-law.

I avoided him because his blue eyes were exactly like Braden's. I didn't deserve his unwavering praise and the light and love he shined down on me. I acted like a coward.

Coach is gone, Amanda. It's too late to tell him how much he means to you.

CHAPTER 34

WITH AN UNKNOWN JOB ON the line and potential drug test in my future, I fight my desire to make a phone call and get my hands on sweet relief... Kill the feelings and watch them drift away in a thick cloud of smoke. I can't do that. Instead, I call Tanner and we laugh about old times with Coach. I also curl up into a ball and try to face my feelings, but I wallow deep, long, and hard. There's a lot to feel sorry about.

The vigil is Friday evening at the high school auditorium. It's the only place big enough to hold a large crowd. Jenny offers to drive me to Pine Ridge, and I accept.

On the drive up, I share, "I feel sick inside. About Coach, of course, but I'm going to see Braden and his wife tonight aren't I?"

"Have you thought about what you're going to say to him?"

"Nothing profound comes to mind. And Coach... Jenny, I'm so

angry with myself. I *never* called him back after he told me that Braden was married. I haven't talked to that man in almost seven years. That's seven years of *Wisdom* I missed out on."

"I'm sure he understood that it was too difficult."

I release a nervous giggle before admitting, "After I told him that I love Braden, I ran out of his house like a lunatic. It's a huge lesson about not taking special people in your life for granted. I never thanked Coach for everything he taught me over the years."

"You thanked him by doing your job for the team and then some. He adored you."

"I wonder if he ever had another student trainer as cracked as me."

Jenny laughs. "Probably not. You were a little... serious about your job."

"Right?" Another thought hits me, "Oh no... Do you think Matt Neilson's going to be there? I never called him after Trina's wedding, and I was too busy firing people to hit the ten-year reunion. He probably thinks I'm easy."

"You haven't exactly been playing hard to get for the past ten years."

"Hey!" I glare, but she can't see me. "Look who's talking."

"I know." Her laughter is good-humored. "You were a late bloomer, though. He still lives in Pine Ridge. He married Kristen Beeler a while back. She was a few years behind us."

"Yeah, I kind of remember her. She was nice—I think. Do you keep in touch with him?"

"No. I just heard it through the rumor mill... from Janie maybe."

"Tanner couldn't make it all the way up here in time for the vigil. He feels really bad about that."

Jenny scoffs, "Poor Tanner."

"Come on, Jenny, you can't still hold a grudge, right? Coach was a huge influence on him."

"Oh, I can still hold a grudge, but I no longer wish him dead now that he's a father."

I groan. "That was a poor choice of words."

"Sorry—I wasn't thinking. What's your biggest fear about seeing Braden tonight?"

"Maybe he's holding a grudge and will be upset that I showed up. Like he'll think that I have no business being there."

"But you do. Tonight is about your relationship with Coach."

"I'm terrified that I'll feel *something* for him after all these years, and I have to see him with the woman who got *everything*. I never stopped thinking about him and wondering why he just cut me out of his life like that. I mean, these memories of him hit me out of nowhere... Good ones, bad ones... But mostly, I only had good with him—except when I told him about me and Tanner. He said, *I should've just gone ahead and fucked you when you spread your legs for me.*"

She gasps, and it takes a lot to shock Jenny. "Braden actually said that to you? You never told me that."

"Nothing but sweet from him for three years, and that's the last thing he said to me. It cut me so deep that I still haven't formed scar tissue. Eleven years ago, and it feels like yesterday. Why is that?"

"No one forgets their first love."

I ask, "It's Tanner for you, isn't it?"

She mutters, "Why do you think I hate him so much?"

"I'm sorry."

"I don't want to talk about him. So... Braden?"

Obviously, Jenny hasn't formed scar tissue either, but I let her redirect the conversation. "I know tonight is about Coach, but I don't want to see Braden with the pig farmer's daughter. I definitely don't want to have any feelings for him, because I might slap him—or fall at his feet."

"You're there for Coach, but maybe—married or not—you and Braden can find a little time to talk things out."

"To what end?"

"I didn't say anything about an end, Amanda."

* * *

After picking up my parents, the four of us trek over to Pine Ridge High School in Jenny's SUV. We're a somber group despite our clothing. Attendees were asked to dress in PRHS clothing and colors—green and white. Dad's wearing a dark suit with a green tie, and Mom and Jenny have on green sweaters.

I wore the oversized Pine Ridge football jersey Coach gave me at our junior season awards banquet. My face lit up when he presented it to me—my last name silk-screened across the back with the number 89 for my graduation year. I cinched it with a thick black belt and paired it with a black pencil skirt and heels. It seemed appropriate to dress it up a little bit.

The paved parking lot overflows with vehicles. We park in a dirt lot across the street. My heels slip on the gravel. I'm off balance in more ways than one. Dad steadies me with his arm while Mom comments, "I don't know why you insist on wearing those heels." I meet Jenny's eyes and roll mine. She returns the favor and we smile at our childish behavior because some things never change.

We fall in line with other mourners, and there are so many. As we wait to sign the guest book, Jenny and I step out of line frequently to greet and hug former classmates, friends, parents, and Matt Neilson and his wife, Mike Haines and his wife Chloe, his folks who've been close to the McLaughlins since college—but no Becky. Familiar face after familiar face are mixed in with people I've never seen before—the latest generation of Pine Ridge High School students.

They all look so young—crazy young. I never felt as young as they appear to be, but I was—just another girl like them with my fantasy diary world and all those intense feelings that I couldn't fully comprehend, much less handle. I want to impart *Wisdom* on the girls who aren't ready yet.

Develop a strong sense of yourself.

Your girlfriends are more important than any boy right now.

Don't be in such a hurry to grow up.

It's impossible to balance your hormones and heartstrings.

If you fall in love now, the memories of losing him will remain with you for the rest of your life.

But any wisdom I've gained won't matter to them. Some lessons can only be learned through trial and error, failure and regret, actions and consequences.

Mom signs the guestbook for Dad and her. Jenny and I follow suit, and I wonder if Braden will see my lonely signature on the page and remember me with any fondness at all. Logically I know he's here, but I swear I can feel him.

As we continue to file toward the main auditorium, I spot Luke Sanders, Braden's childhood friend from Phoenix. Speaking of guys from my list of *Men I've Screwed*, this former frat boy is eyeing me from a few feet away and makes an approach. He hasn't lost his arrogant swagger since I saw him last.

Luke's formerly unruly and tousled light brown hair is now cut short, and glasses make him look all the more grown up and handsome. He moves in for a chaste hug. "Mandy from Pine Ridge."

After accepting his hug, I step away quickly. "Luke from Sigma Chi. Please call me Amanda—everyone does."

"Um, okay."

It occurs to me how close Luke's family was to the McLaughlins—living just a few houses away for most of their childhoods in Phoenix. "How are you holding up?"

His broody sigh reminds me of Braden's—maybe Luke learned it from him when they were kids. "Not the best way to spend a Friday night. You talk to Braden yet?"

"No. You?"

"Mom and I drove up a few days ago. We're staying with the family."

"Oh." Of course, I know nothing about Braden's family and feel silly asking.

"When we lost my dad a few years back, Bonnie and Nick did a lot for us. My mom's helping with the services."

I never met Luke's dad, but I follow polite protocol regardless. "I'm sorry to hear about your father."

"Thank you. Are you sticking around this weekend? The funeral mass is tomorrow."

"No. I just came up for the night to pay my respects to Coach."

"I'm sure Braden will be happy to see you."

My stomach churns because I don't know. "So... you, um, what do you do with yourself these days?"

"I went into the family business—HVAC. Mostly commercial new business development."

"You'll never run out of work in this state. Are you in Phoenix or Tucson?"

"Why? You want to get together?"

My eyes fly to his. "*What*?"

"Easy, Amanda, I'm teasing." I release a quiet sigh of relief and he says, "I'm in east Phoenix—back in Arcadia. You?"

"Central Phoenix." This interaction with Luke makes me curious. "Did you ever tell Braden about... you know?"

Luke grins, fully knowing I'm asking about that ridiculous night we spent together back in college. He wants me to say it, but I won't. And I don't know why he's grinning—even drunk off my ass, I remember that he was selfish in bed. "Did you tell him?"

"No. Mainly because I don't like getting punched in the face. Look, I was a horny asshole back then. I'm sorry if I—"

Relieved that Braden doesn't know, which is all that matters, I interrupt, "Please, say no more. Intoxicated ancient history."

Luke's brown eyes dance with mischief. "You're single, right? Sure you don't want to meet up later?"

"Um…"

Nudging me with an elbow, he winks. "I'm messing with you again."

"Oh good, because I don't think God wants you to pick up chicks at a vigil."

"That probably only works at weddings, right?"

* * *

Rejoining my parents and Jenny, we enter the double doors to the main auditorium. It's a cavernous space with rows of seating already three-quarters full, and we're here fairly early. Coach's open casket rests in front of the stage with huge floral arrangements on either side. From the ceiling above hang the large green pennants usually adorning the walls in the gym from each football season he coached at Pine Ridge. I can hardly bear the thought of walking by his casket to see him lifeless and cold when he was anything but.

Like a magnet, my eyes instantly find *him* and fixate. I've never seen Braden dressed up—you know, because he didn't take me to prom junior *or* senior year. Positively handsome in his dark grey suit, crisp white dress shirt, and green tie, he's powerfully built. His eyes—*god those eyes*—still so blue and mesmerizing, albeit with much deeper crinkles at the corners when he smiles.

Surprisingly, he is smiling instead of brooding or appearing lost in grief. He greets each person with a gracious smile, a handshake, and a brief conversation—probably thanking them for coming, for their kind words, and putting them at ease during this most somber of occasions.

Still so *beautiful*. I'm compelled to study the boy who is all man now, and, *damn it*; the memories coursing through me are all the good ones. The flood of raw emotion sends tingles through my body. Every beat of my heart, every rise and fall of my chest releases a slow burn of visceral instinctual biochemical reactions.

After all this time, your heart only knows how to love Braden.

He's married.

Stop staring at him, Amanda.

I can't.

Where is his wife?

Maybe she's in the bathroom with one of the kids. Maybe they have so many kids that she stayed back in Iowa. Maybe there was a terrible accident on the pig farm and she's dead now.

Braden looks up. I'm caught in the act of examining him while imagining his wife being eaten alive by ravenous pigs.

I'm sorry, God. That was not very nice.

Our eyes lock.

Please, God—I didn't mean it. Okay, maybe just a little bit. I mean, You are God. You can probably read my mind. I shouldn't try to lie to You.

He holds my gaze.

Are you breathing, Amanda? Breathe, Amanda. Breathe.

I can't read his expression.

What is he thinking?

I have no idea, but I'm not the only one who can't stop staring.

If he keeps looking at me like that, I am going to fall at his feet.

When he finally acknowledges me with a lift of his chin, even from ten feet away, I see his eyes flicker with warmth before I'm offered *our* unmistakably unapologetic smile.

He directs his attention back to the person standing in front of him. Jenny gives me a gentle nudge from behind, and I notice the gap between my parents and us. In slow motion, while the distance between us narrows way too quickly, I hug Mrs. McLaughlin and Fiona, unable to focus on words coming out of their mouths or mine because...

Face-to-face for the first time in over eleven years. Braden and I continue staring before I hold out my sweaty right hand as a peace offering. While my eyes refuse to leave his face, he accepts my hand. With my heart skipping every other beat, I wonder when my legs will give out.

His fingertips skim over the top of my skin and one hand wraps around my wrist. *Goosebumps—everywhere.* Using my peace offering as leverage, he pulls me to him until I find myself pressed against him, fully engulfed in his muscular arms.

Instinct. My arms slip around his waist, cross behind his back under his suit jacket, and I press my palms into his starchy dress shirt. With a will of its own, my face nuzzles his neck to inhale *Essence of Braden.* My lips might have brushed against his skin but only for a second.

"Mandy." His whispered voice and hot breath fills my ear. Hearing that name from his lips after so many years causes my tears to spill involuntarily onto the shoulder of his suit. Braden is holding me again and it feels natural and true, but Coach is gone forever.

"I'm so, so sorry about your dad," I whisper in his ear.

"I really needed someone to *double so* me tonight. I'm glad you came through for me." His hand rubs my back while his voice tries to soothe me; yet I'm undeniably comforted that he remembers my double so. "*Shhh...* It's all right. We're going to celebrate his life to-night—remember the good times. Thank you *so, so* much for being here to do that with me."

Every vital organ, nerve, and cell is animated, thrumming. I allow myself a brief moment to hold onto *everything* that isn't mine. In his arms with our bodies pressed together, the scent of his skin, warmth of his breath, feeling his heart beat against mine...

You want him, crave him, ache for him.

This totally sucks.

Let him go, Amanda.

I want to keep him.

You can't have him.

Maybe just for—

No. Shut up, Amanda.

I will myself to release him and take a step back on trembling legs, but my eyes go straight to his because I can't stop staring at him. *Damn it.*

"Standing on the edge of time," he murmurs softly.

Standing on the edge of time? Is that what he said? *What. Does. That. Mean???*

This is not the time or place for a conversation. There are hundreds of people behind me in line.

Walk away, Amanda. It's time to say goodbye to Coach.

I turn my back on Braden and try to brace myself for another painful goodbye.

CHAPTER 35

DAD WAITS FOR ME AT the casket. He knows that I need him right now, and I fall into his side resting my head against his strong body. "I love you, Daddy."

"I love you, too, Brown Eyes."

I study Coach's face before I lean down and speak quietly to him. "You got us the last two years in a row, Coach, but we're taking that Territorial Cup back in a few weeks. You'll see." Tears streak down my face, and Dad passes me a handkerchief from his suit pocket. "It's okay, though. I'd rather you go out the winner."

"I'm sorry that I didn't come to see you again. I'd give anything to change that—to look you in the eyes and hear you bark out my last name from fifty yards away... to hear you say something, anything to me again. I respect everything you stand for, Coach. Thank you for taking a Wildcat like me under your wing."

I don't want to, but I can't help myself. Reaching out, I place my warm hand over Coach's cold ones folded across his body. As I take him in for the last time, I squeeze his hands and whisper, "I love you, Coach."

Turning away, I plant myself face first into Dad's warm chest.

We stay for the vigil. The Catholic pomp and circumstance, but more importantly, to hear the tributes from family, close friends, players. Coach's life and legacy shaped so many lives.

When Braden takes to the podium I freeze. He clears his throat and smiles into the darkened auditorium. His voice is strong when he says, "My dad loved God, Mom, family, friends, education, football, and Arizona State. He also loved the community of Pine Ridge."

He allows a small chuckle to escape before he admits, "I needed some convincing, but this week I fully appreciate why he moved our family here and never wanted to leave. Thank you for taking care of my mother. Every phone call, card, meal, prayer, and word of sympathy is valued. We are grateful and blessed."

One hand snakes around to the back of his neck and he bows his head. While he stares at the podium, I hold my breath and wait. When Braden looks back up, his watery eyes sweep the crowd again. My stomach flips, and I pray he can finish without breaking down.

"Dad was proud in the best ways. His joy came from watching others learn, grow, and overcome adversity. My entire life I felt loved, safe, and accepted. I couldn't have asked for a better father, and I think I'm going to miss his advice most of all. He was honest and straightforward, but never judgmental. He wanted..." Braden trails off and closes his eyes. I'm on the edge of my seat. "He wanted me to be happy. Such a simple wish from the greatest man I'll ever know."

Did you find happiness, Braden?

"I could tell you a thousand stories and keep you here for hours, but I won't." He looks to his far right—somewhere in the stage wing and nods. Words heavy with grief, he dispenses advice to the community of Pine Ridge, "Every conversation with your parents should end with *I love you*. You don't know if you'll have the chance to tell them again."

He inhales, gathers his composure, and smiles playfully at the crowd. "Father Francis, please forgive us. What's about to happen is a Pine Ridge High School tradition. Dad wanted it this way. Thank you for coming and good night."

As Braden walks off the stage and the music begins, I lose it completely. Dad's arm wraps around my shoulders as I'm thrown back to 1980-something; inundated by memories of Coach and pumped up football players singing along at the top of their lungs before taking the field.

KISS. *Heaven's on Fire*. Perfect.

Except... When I finally pull it together and my parents are ready to leave, Braden is surrounded by people—including Father Francis. I can't even catch his eye. I don't want to be presumptuous and interrupt his conversations. He probably has nothing left to say to me.

Goodbye, Braden.

* * *

In an attempt to avoid conversation on the drive back to Phoenix, I turn on Jenny's stereo and pop in a Brooks & Dunn CD. She reaches out and kills the music.

"Oh no, Amanda. You just saw *Braden* for the first time in forever, and we're going to talk about it."

"Okay. Let's talk about this. Where was his wife?"

"He wasn't wearing a ring."

"Are you sure?"

She spares me a smirk and a sideways glance. "I knew that would get your attention. No ring. I'm positive because I grabbed both of his hands and looked."

"Maybe he lost it on the pig farm," I grumble. "If you went through the effort to grab his hands, why didn't you ask him about his wife? Jeez, Jenny."

"Because you took up so much time clinging to each other. There were like a thousand people behind me. You should call him. He'll probably be in Pine Ridge for a while."

"I wouldn't know what to say."

"Hi, Braden. If you're not married, will you finally stick it in me? I've been single since January, and I'm about to explode."

"You're an asshole. That's so classy considering he's in town to bury his father."

"He might be home because of a tragedy, but that didn't stop him from looking like he wanted to eat you. I saw how he grabbed you and whispered in your ear. What did he say?"

"I'm not sure, but I think I kissed his neck."

* * *

Over the next week, I fire off at least twenty more resumes all over the country. I'll be lucky to hear back from one potential employer and might wind up in Arkansas or Georgia or some other state I've only visited to fire people.

My dwindling savings account tells me that if nothing pans out in the next forty to sixty days, I'll have to start selling off some designer handbags, or, if Walmart is hiring, I could end up stocking shelves for minimum wage after all.

I can't shake the darkness, the gloom and doom. My financial *situation*, Coach's death and all the years I wasted avoiding him, Connor and Trina's brush with disaster, the never-ending coverage of the souls lost on 9/11, and the country's new War on Terror which will lead to the loss of more lives.

I try to lose my dark thoughts in chores—cleaning, repotting plants, scrubbing tile grout, reorganizing things that are already organized. I listen to country music and try to lose myself in the lyrics, but they're all speaking directly to me, so I stop listening to country music. I log double time at the gym trying to lose my depression on a piece of equipment or the punching bag.

I spend more time at Jenny's trying to lose my loneliness in the noise and commotion of her family life, but she keeps imploring me to call Braden, convinced that some sort of deeper conversation is imperative to my mental health. Maybe it is, because I can't shake off my reaction to seeing or touching him again. The more I try to lose my troubles, the more lost I feel.

* * *

The Saturday after Coach's funeral is another beautiful day without a cloud in sight. I'm pretty pissed off about it. The weather in this overly abundant with sunshine desert never coincides with a crappy mood. After the gym, I shower and don Max's flannel ASU boxers that I forgot to return. I should be using them for a cleaning rag by now, but today they offer comfort and a tribute to Coach. Pulling a black tank top on over a sexy lace bra that no one but me will see, I run a comb through my long hair leaving it to air dry.

Needing to lose myself in something else, I close my curtains and pretend it's a dark and rainy day outside. Settling on the couch with a Diet Pepsi over shit tons of ice, a bag of microwave popcorn, and *Miss Congeniality,* I try to force Squirt into a snuggle position. He struggles for freedom and promptly abandons me and Sandra Bullock in favor of giving himself a bath. *Asshole Cat.*

Citizen, the domestic terrorist, is taken into custody and Eric calls off the mission. Gracie turns in her badge and gun but stays behind. She has women's intuition and knows that the danger isn't over.

As chaos unfolds on the pageant stage, the doorbell interrupts my movie. Pressing pause, I force myself off the couch and open the main door. I blink rapidly, attempting to acclimate my vision in the glaring sun.

I can't believe my eyes.

Once I unlock the deadbolt and swing out the security door, my hand flies to my mouth where I rub it hard over my lips and chin, staring at him. I *still* can't stop staring at him.

"Hi. Is this a good time?" His question violates my stupor, and I peek over his shoulder for the pig farmer's daughter. My dark house is flooded with sunshine and Braden McLaughlin. "Mandy?"

"Sorry." I shake my head, realizing that I was too busy staring at him to answer his question. "I'm... uh... um, sorry. No. It's not a bad time. Please come in. I mean, do you want to come inside?"

He smiles and my knees tremble. "That's why I rang your doorbell."

Stepping out of his way, I close up behind him.

He comments, "It's really dark in here."

"Yeah—um, hold on." I leave him in the entryway and open a few of the curtains in the living room.

When I return, he nods at Sandra Bullock frozen in the middle of some sort of *situation* and smirks. "You still have shit taste in movies."

"This is not a shitty movie, Braden. It's funny and it has a happy ending."

"If you say so."

"I do. I do say so, but I'm still kind of in shock and not at all prepared to argue its merits with you." When he laughs, it hits me just how long it's been since I've heard the sound of his laughter—and how very much I've missed it. I add, "But if you stick around long enough, I might rally, so you've been warned."

Looking around over my shoulder, he compliments, "Cute place—now that I can see it."

"Um, thanks. It's, uh, well, the neighborhood is kind of on the edge of might go historic one day or get taken over by gangs. It could, um, still go either way, but my money is on the latter so..."

His eyes widen as he takes in my attire. "Amanda Grace Harrington, are you wearing Arizona State shorts?"

"I was thinking about your dad."

"I can't believe my eyes."

"That's how much I loved him—enough to wear ASU gear, and look, my skin isn't on fire." I take a deep breath, "I'm so, so sorry, Braden. I don't know what else to say."

"That *double so*—always more meaningful than a single so."

"So you've told me." I give him a soft smile. We're quiet for a beat. Slightly buzzed with confusion and anticipation, hell no, I still can't stop staring at him. "Um... *how are you doing* is such a lame question considering why you had to come home. But how are you doing? What brings you by my house? How did you even know where I live?"

"You gave Fiona your address." He's right, and she's taken liberties with it. "Are we alone?"

"Alone?"

"Do you live here by yourself?"

"I know what *alone* means, Braden. Trust me. I'm not sure why you're asking."

"I dropped by without calling. I want to make sure I'm not interrupting anyone or anything."

"It's just us—except for Squirt over there. He's an asshole, but I'm stuck with him now."

"You."

"Me?"

"You brought me by." His brows nearly meet in the middle while he wraps one hand behind his neck and squeezes. Even though I can't stop staring at him, I notice for the first time the exhaustion and stress on his face. *Instinct* persuades me to comfort him, but *Wisdom* holds me back. "I didn't call first because I figured if I just showed up, the words would come to me. But... fuck—are you as uncomfortable as I am right now?"

Making an Uncomfortable Scale with my hand—which he may or may not remember—I change the measurements from small to large. "I'm not sure. How uncomfortable are you, Braden?"

He grabs my hand and *now* my skin is on fire. Electricity bolts through me as he adjusts the scale to medium. "Right about here."

While studying my Uncomfortable Scale inside his big hand, I resign myself to the fact that some things will never change. I feel like a fifteen-year-old girl with a hopeless crush on the cutest boy in school.

With my now considerable experience with boys and men and sports, I should know better than to take my eyes off the other player. Braden gently twists my Uncomfortable Scale behind my back. His free hand travels through my hair while his thumb slides down my temple, my cheek, before coming to rest at the back of my neck. Leaning in close, he presses his forehead against mine.

In absence of heels or any shoes at all, I'm both alarmed and exhilarated by how large his frame feels in comparison to mine. Speechless and completely turned on, all I can do is release a shaky sigh. Our faces are so close together that he can't help but draw my breath into his lungs.

Relinquishing my arm, he backs me into the front door with his body and his lips crash down on mine.

Instinct tells *Wisdom* to take a hike, and my spontaneous reflexes give him control of this *situation*. This kiss might feel like old times, but his hands—*god, his hands*—they travel with the confidence of a man—indecently, decadently—down my body, skimming over the sides of my breasts, thumbs intentionally brushing over my nipples, causing a moan to rise from the back of my throat and spill into his mouth.

While our mouths reunite with passion and vigor, he repeats this motion on my field several times, yielding the same reaction before his hands move down my waist, over my hips, my ass and back up underneath my tank top.

When his bare hands meet my skin, *Instinct* tells *Wisdom* to fuck off. My body reacts like a lightning strike to dry brush during peak fire season.

My fingers run roughly through his hair and scrape down the nape of his neck. Grabbing impatiently at his broad shoulders and backside, I try to pull him closer still. Catapulted back in time, we taste and explore like two hormonal teenagers with the house to themselves for a few hours.

Wisdom reminds me that this isn't August of 1990. In the present moment, I have nothing but questions and no answers. Removing his hands from my body, I step back and collapse against the door, struggling for composure, air, a rational thought.

Once again I've been felt down and up, branded—*kissed stupid*—by this beautiful man.

Braden, however, seems to have an explanation for this *situation* which he provides with playful eyes and a grin. "I wanted to do that the second you kissed my neck last Friday night."

I fumble my reply. "Um... Uh... I..." Sighing, I rub my hand across my forehead.

He loves this and laughs it up. "My Mandy at a loss for words. I'm going to mark this day down on my calendar."

"*What?*" I manage to breathe out an actual word. *His* Mandy?

His expression remains lighthearted. "I had a little talk with myself out in the car. Keep your hands off of her. Talk to her first."

"What happened to sticking with the plan?"

"I had to know how *that* would feel."

"And?"

"Fucking unbelievable."

Before I can stop myself, I whisper, "Oh my god."

Grinning, he drops a kiss on my cheek and keeps talking. "First— or is it firstly? Did you ever find out the answer to that one, Mandy?"

I snicker at his mention of yet another inside joke from our past. "No."

"First or firstly, I couldn't leave Arizona without seeing you. I was hoping we could talk."

Trying to shake the kissing stupor from my head, I state, "You blew right by first or firstly when you pushed me into the door and felt me up."

"I'm sorry." Except Braden is not one bit sorry because he's still smiling. "Can we sit down and have a conversation?"

"Of course. May I offer you something to drink before we do that?"

His blue eyes twinkle. "What are my *options*?"

Oh, Braden, you want to play this *game? Fine.*

Meeting his eyes, I boldly state, "You have three options. Option A is a flat water with shit tons of ice. Option B is Diet Pepsi but, too bad for you, no Dr. Pepper." I pause for dramatic effect. "Option C is alcohol—beer, cheap wine, or we can toss back a few shots of the hard stuff."

Rewarded with his laughter, I add, "All options are viable, Braden." I end with an unapologetic smile as I think about that conversation back in his family room when we were clueless teenagers.

"Option A: We didn't make out the other night. It never happened. With good faith, we re-establish our friendship as it was before. Which might not be possible—for me, at least. I mean, you did just spend the last several weeks ignoring me, and I'm not over it yet."

"Option B: Date and/or spend time together and see what develops. This option will not be discussed with any third parties without consent from both parties—you and me, and it will most likely include physical relations because you're a guy with hormones, but it may or may not result in a relationship or love or whatever you want to call it. I should also add—"

"Mandy, come on," he interjected.

"This is important." I silenced him with a glare and cleared my throat. "I should also add that Option B puts the future of our friendship in the most jeopardy. The variables are not defined, there is no control group, and we have no hypothesis. Or differing hypotheses, at this point in time. And we would need to discuss the ground rules, of course. And then there's Option C, the whole sex thing, which is not viable and therefore did not make the list. Is there anything you would like to add or remove? Maybe it would help you to read it yourself?" I tried to hand it over but he declined my list with a shake of his head. Whatever. *"I know which option I want."*

"Option C?"

"Not a viable option, Braden."

His smile melted me from the inside out when he reached for my hand and asked, "We're going to see how this plays out?"

"Yes."

"I get to kiss you stupid whenever I want?"

"Yes, but before we do anything really stupid, we need ground rules," I stated.

"You don't have those already jotted down on your little list there?"

"Not yet, but I will," I said, *tapping my pen on the paper.*

"'Course you will," he smirked.

He nods his head slowly in appreciation of my response and takes it one step further with that same smirk. "Option B was our go-to, but it's not very appealing if Dr. Pepper isn't on the table. You know I always thought Option C would be the best option for us, but, *for now,* I'll go with Option A."

CHAPTER 36

Braden follows me into kitchen while I get him a glass of flat water with shit tons of ice. He's immediately drawn to the Maytag, and I push my burning questions and fear of consequences aside, defaulting to talking about the history of my little tract home.

With flat water in hand, we return to the living room. Switching off the TV before sitting on the sofa, Braden takes the opposite end—a wise decision. We need to stay the hell away from each other until we talk.

I can't wait another second. "Are you married? Because I—"

"Divorced. No kids."

Looking down, I rub my temples and mutter, "Thank god I didn't make out with a married man, because I've never done that before." I look back up at him and confess, "I'm confused. I don't understand why you're here."

"I had to reconnect with you."

"Yeah—I think we just covered that part."

Braden laughs. "We did, and while I'd like nothing more than to reconnect all afternoon long, I came here to talk because I've never stopped wondering about you."

"Why don't you start?"

"I'd rather hear from you."

"I'm still a little lightheaded," I admit which makes him smile.

"I stayed in Iowa after college, got married right away. We didn't work out, but that's a whole story in itself. After the divorce a few years ago, I needed a change of scenery. I took a transfer with my company to Indianapolis. Great city—have you ever been?"

I haven't been there to fire anyone from CompuWorld or for any other reason, but I picture corn fields, basketball, and snow. Remaining silent, I shake my head no.

Braden shares, "I live downtown—thriving city center. Safe, walkable. Kind of small, but it has everything. It's like a little big city."

I've never given any thought to Indianapolis, but I am curious about his occupation. "What do you do for a living?"

"I work in outside sales—internet, broadband... tech stuff."

I raise my eyebrows. "Sales? Wow. So nothing that you went to college for after all? Not that I'm one to judge."

"I still love to write, but it's an interest now because it's difficult to make a living that way. As it turns out, I have an aptitude for building relationships, and I'm not easily discouraged."

Tilting my head to one side, I offer him an unapologetic smile before remarking, "Wouldn't have guessed that either."

He returns one in kind and acknowledges, "Nice one, love. I deserved that." Before I've fully digested—much less analyzed—his use of the *love* term of endearment, he moves on to a serious topic. "I had everything put back together in my life when 9/11 happened, and then Dad had his heart attack. These huge events got me thinking about all these moments in life—conversations, memories, people who've come and gone. Fuck, all those people on 9/11—gone in seconds without any warning. Dad is gone—no warning."

"It's beyond comprehension," I say quietly. "All of it."

He looks directly at me and nods. "It's life-changing, Mandy. After I got the call from Mom... I can't tell you how long I sat there trying to remember—and I still can't remember—the last thing I said to my dad." He closes his beautiful eyes on a long blink before turning them back on me and continuing, "I know we talked on the phone a lot, especially after 9/11, but I can't remember the day of the week or what I said before I hung up. I hope that I said *I love you*, but I don't know..." His voice trails off in regretful silence.

Wanting to comfort him, I decide to stay put. Comforting includes touching which will lead to more touching and then... Instead, I offer a verbal assist. "Even if you didn't say it, Braden, your dad knows how much you love him. Or maybe you can choose to remember the conversation ending that way."

"I remember the last words I said to you. Do you?"

The change in topic is abrupt. It throws me, and I answer, perhaps a bit too candidly considering his emotional state, "Those words are permanently seared in my soul."

He winces. "I was such a dick."

"You were."

"It was such a nasty thing to say to a girl like you. I'm not only sorry—I'm ashamed."

I let him off the hook. "I accept your apology. It was a long time ago."

"Too fucking long, Mandy. How did all these years go by without you in my life?"

I shrug. "Um, you're going to have to tell me that because..."

"You tried—repeatedly. Mandy, back then that phone call from you telling me that you and Rawlings were an item... it changed me. You crushed me."

Raising my eyebrows to convey uncertainty, I say, "I didn't know I could hurt you like that. You held back from me for years. It was always—*bye, Mandy... until we meet again. No promises until I'm ready to make promises.*"

"I couldn't make promises to you. What did I have to offer you? Instead I let that guy get into my head because he was so fucking sure about you."

"You just stepped aside for Tanner," I mutter. "It's fine. We made sense back then—had a good thing for a long time."

"How long?"

"Most of my undergrad."

"I can't believe you didn't marry him."

My laughter is caustic. "He's better off without me."

"Why would you say that?"

"The simple version is that we weren't meant to be."

"Rawlings is a doctor, right?"

"Pediatric medicine. He has three kids, and I'm sure another will be on the way soon. I adore them—beautiful, healthy children." I smile. "His twins call me Auntie Panda. So cute."

I watch his eyes narrow and hear his slight exhale before he asks, "You still see that guy?"

"Shared history is the most powerful common denominator. Tanner and I started off as friends, and that's what we came back to eventually. Everyone gets along in this weird way—like my family and his. It's fine now."

"No regrets?"

"A lot of years have gone by. We made our choices and there's no going back."

"Almost three years ago, I was in Pine Ridge over Christmas. Fiona couldn't wait to tell me that she ran into you at the store, Tanner had kids with his wife—and that wife was not you. It was my last Christmas with Jessica. We were set to file for the divorce when we got back to Iowa. Such a shit time, but my sister was all over my ass to pick up the phone and call you. I wasn't ready for you, though. I hoped that one day we'd see each other—never imagined it would be at Dad's vigil."

"God, Braden... I can't believe he's gone."

"I'd ask him about you. He said that you made yourself scarce."

My eyes burn with tears of regret. "When Coach told me that you were married, I... um, I never went back to see him again."

"Why?"

"Your eyes are exactly the same—did you know that?" Our eyes meet as we both smile softly. "I wasn't in a good place in my life when I found out that you married *her*, and seeing your dad was...

I wish I could get that time back, but you're too much like him. I couldn't deal."

"I'm sure you came to the vigil for my father. I had every intention of finding you after, but you were gone. I saw your mom at Mass the next day, but she slipped out at the end of the service before I could talk to her. You weren't there, were you?"

I shake my head. "No. You know, I'm not exactly a practicing Catholic. I wasn't sure if I'd be struck down trying to enter the church." Braden snickers, but I feel guilty regardless. Practicing or not, Catholic guilt lasts a lifetime. "I'm sorry I wasn't there. Mass is a religious thing, and, really, I just needed to hear the stories about him last Friday—not sit through formalities. Coach and I weren't big on formalities."

"You don't have to apologize for skipping Mass. You did that all through high school."

Yeah, that's funny enough for a smile to contradict the tears welling in my eyes for Coach. "I'm sorry for everything that you've had to go through and for what's ahead for you and your family without him. He was larger than life—certainly louder than life."

"Thank you." A soft smile continues to play on his lips. "Are we doing okay now? This isn't too uncomfortable anymore."

"I hesitate to show you my Uncomfortable Scale again because you might use it against me." Come on, that's funny and true. We both laugh before I tell him, "I'm glad you're here. Maybe we can put some things to rest. Closure and all... it's supposed to be good for the soul."

"I didn't come here for closure. Tell me about your life. Career choice?"

"Not a lawyer," I smile. "Human Resources—more specifically Labor Relations." At his puzzled expression, I add color commentary. "I specialize in creating and/or finding loopholes in Union contracts. If it's not explicitly stated in the collective bargaining agreement or the wording is left open for interpretation, I find the technicality to proceed in the company's favor. You might recall that I love technicalities."

He grins in understanding of why this career is perfect for me. My enthusiasm dies off when I share my unemployment *situation* and how long I've been looking for work.

"Are you worried?"

"Only if I have to stock shelves at Walmart—which is a real possibility, actually. Hopefully, something will work out. I have great experience with a Fortune 500 company—well, they were until the bankruptcy—and I finished my MBA a few years ago. I've been looking all over the country."

"You're open to relocating?"

"I have to be. I love the labor relations stuff, but there aren't many companies in Arizona with unions, at least none that are hiring right now. But, if I have to move, I'll be leaving everything I know behind."

"I still have my piece of the Berlin Wall," Braden shares unexpectedly. "It's had a place of honor wherever I lived. Do you have yours?"

"Of course I do. It's on the bookshelf in my room."

"Do you think our pieces will fit back together?"

"They should—as long as you didn't mutilate yours after I took up with Tanner."

"The thought crossed my mind, but there's not a nick or chip missing. I've been very careful with it. A huge reason why I'm here is to see if we still fit."

What are you suggesting, Braden? Anxiety rushes through me because there is so much he doesn't know about the forks in the road I've taken.

I warn, "I am not that eighteen-year-old girl you remember..."

"No. You're a woman now, but the core of you... it feels like I just saw you yesterday."

"Will you see me tomorrow?"

He shakes his head. "I'm taking the red-eye out tonight." I look down at the floor, positive I'm pouting. Braden adds, "I'll be back in another three weeks."

I look up and can't help smiling. "Oh?"

"Yeah. We have to help Mom sort through some of the legal and financial stuff. There are still a lot of decisions to make. If you have any interest in seeing me again beyond today, I'm coming back soon."

Do I have any interest in seeing Braden beyond today? Um, yeah... Like every single day, all day and night until I stop breathing. *Unless*... Braden has a past, too. There's a lot I don't know either. "Why did you and Jessica get a divorce?"

"I told you it's a long story."

"Red eye implies an evening flight. We have a few hours to kill, right?"

"I can think of better ways to kill time with you," Braden mutters.

"I really want to know."

Leaning back against the arm of the sofa, he closes his eyes while composing his words. "Ultimately, infertility and going against the Catholic Church. Failed in vitro attempts and everything related to that."

"Begotten not made."

"Exactly."

"Utter bullshit."

"Agreed. I told her it didn't make any difference to me if we had biological children or found some other way, but, going through something so devastating, she changed. We changed. It fell apart, and we still wound up going against the Church by divorcing. So..."

"I'm sorry." I keep my voice soft. As relieved as I am that Braden's not married, I'm also sad for him—and possibly *her*, too. If I had a man like Braden as my husband, I would never want to lose him.

"I'm okay with it now because—like you said with you and Rawlings—the short version is that it wasn't meant to be in the first place." He's quiet for a few beats then asks, "You're not married, but is there someone special in your life?"

As I decide how to answer this question because it makes me feel like a loser, Braden taps his hand on one leg—his nervous tell. Rubbing my forehead, I search for the right words.

"Listen," Braden says, "this is a cold call on my part. I knocked on your door not knowing what would be on the other side, so if you're happy with someone then—"

"I'm not happy. I'm exhausted."

"Why?"

"I keep making the wrong choices... Timing... timing is supposed to be everything and, well... apparently, my timing sucks."

He looks me in the eyes and smiles sweetly. "What do you want? If you could have anything."

"I want *everything*."

"*Everything*?"

CHAPTER 37

WHAT DO I HAVE TO lose by baring my soul to Braden? If he runs for the door, I'm no worse off than I was before he walked in.

"Everyone in my inner circle moved forward in the natural progression of life. I have a closet full of bridesmaid dresses that I'll never wear again to prove it. And my closets are really small."

He chortles and I continue speaking, "But not me. A few years ago my dad told me that when a man finds the right woman, he'll move heaven and earth to make her his." Shaking my head, I admit, "I don't think that's going to happen for me. Every time I got close, something was off. I thought we could overcome it. I tried or screwed it up somehow, and in the end... well, it just ended. I wasted more time. I haven't been out on a date in almost a year. God, does that sound pathetic? It does. When I say it out loud it sounds totally pathetic..."

"It doesn't sound pathetic to want someone who will move heaven and earth for you."

"How about not dating in a year?"

Braden's eyes gleam when he smiles. "Wish I could say that I'm disappointed for you, but that would be a lie."

"And it doesn't sound pathetic to settle for less than heaven and earth?"

His grin is lively. "All these years later and the girl who loved romantic movies and big gestures is *still* waiting for Jake Ryan to pull up in his red Trans Am."

"*Porsche*," I correct him immediately, and he busts out laughing.

"Right. How could I forget? You're waiting for your John Hughes happy ending."

"I'm not *waiting* for someone to show up and *rescue* me... exactly. I've been fine on my own, and the right person is hard to find. There are a lot of people out there in the world, Braden. The odds of finding *the one* seem astronomical at this point. And, really, any man who has to put up with me is going to have to love me deep—imperfections, neuroses, and all—to see him through the tough times."

Instead of running for the door, he ribs me a little. "Yeah, I can see where heavy doses of love and patience would be a requirement to handle a woman like you." I glare. He smiles without apology. "What? You said it. I'm just agreeing with you. *Everything* is a big word. What else does *everything* encompass beyond finding *the one*?"

"A husband, a career, and babies—dirty diapers, sticky floors, piles of laundry—and I want someone smart, funny, tall and built so I can wear my heels. I have some awesome shoes."

"I noticed those last Friday. Very nice." He smirks. "That all seems reasonable."

"There's more." Braden quirks his eyebrows as I continue. "He has to love football, and, of course, I'd rather he be an Arizona fan first and foremost, but that's a negotiable for the right guy as long as he isn't a Sun Devil."

"Says the woman in ASU shorts."

I pretend to glare. "Smart, funny, tall and built, will take me to football games and watch them on TV with me. Someone who wants a family and is loyal, handsome, and bossy in the bedroom, who wants to do everything with me—forever." I stop, *mortified*, because, "Did I just tell you that I like to be bossed around in the bedroom?"

He laughs at my candor. "Yup. No worries. I'm taking mental notes on *Adult Mandy* in case I need to refer to them later."

Goosebumps.

"Am I asking for too much?"

He responds wryly, "That's quite the list you have going there. Sure you didn't miss any bullet points?"

"Maybe, but I have them all written down. All the qualities and characteristics of *that* man, broken down by the negotiables and non-negotiables."

He tries and fails to suppress his laughter. Of course, I have a freaking list with bullets and sub-bullets. He has a good laugh, too. It comes from his belly and lights up his face. He laughs so hard he practically cries. When he finally locks it down, I stare at him because I don't find it funny. "*Jesus*, Mandy... I'm sorry. I'm not laughing *at* you—exactly."

"I'm not sure what He has to do with this conversation, but lists are really helpful," I defend myself. "That list keeps me from going back or getting into a *situation* that isn't right for me. I can't believe I didn't make a list like that years ago."

"It's just, fuck, the *inner workings* of your brain haven't changed all that much—if at all. I love learning that." He tilts his head to one side. "I don't have a list, but I know what I want."

"What do you want, Braden?"

"You."

My mouth drops open.

"Why do you look so surprised, love?"

"Braden, it's been *eleven years*."

"Yeah, so why waste any more time bullshitting and fumbling around? We're adults. Let's lay it all out and see if we have something."

"Jeez, one of us has totally changed."

"One of us is not going to make the same mistake again."

My skin tingles as I feel the heat of my blush spreading up my face. "I don't know what to say... We still live thousands of miles apart."

"You just rattled off an extensive must-have list of *everything*, and you're ready to settle down. We're both looking for *everything*. Not to sound arrogant, but I check all those little boxes of yours and some that you haven't thought of yet. I backed you into the door, we went at each other like we were famished, and that was fucking hot."

He pauses to offer me an unapologetic smile while I continue blushing because he is absolutely right. "I have a great job, you don't. I live in a union-heavy part of the country—you don't, but you specialize in labor relations. There's no need for a flow chart. Connect the dots, love. We could make all kinds of sense. Geography can be eliminated."

"Are you suggesting that I move to Indianapolis?"

"Yes."

"Move across the country and get involved with my high school... *boyfriend* isn't the right term since you never made it official... Just give this a go after eleven years?"

He uses my own words in his favor. "Shared history is a powerful common denominator, right? You think I don't know you anymore? You're overly opinionated about the strangest things, you rattle on and on when you're uncomfortable, and you have to make all these lists before you can make a simple decision. You're always trying to call me on a technicality, and I have to think in intellectual overdrive around you half the time."

"Wow. You just made me sound really annoying."

"All reasons why I fell in love with you in the first place."

"This isn't high school, Braden. In everyday life, those things might drive you crazy."

He shrugs. "We'll find that out when you move in with me."

"An hour ago I was sitting here with my asshole cat watching a movie. Now you're asking me to *live* with you?"

"Yes."

"That's beyond impulsive; it's completely ridiculous."

He makes his case. "It is not. Mandy, I'm not looking for a *girl-friend*. I want a wife and a family. Life is short, and if timing is everything, this seems like the perfect time for you and me to have our chance together."

"You're that sure about me?"

"Not entirely." My face falls but he explains quickly. "We need time together, but I don't want to *date* you. I want a future with you."

"This is out of nowhere... and after all this *time*," I mutter.

"I'm standing on the edge of time."

"Is *that* what you said to me at the vigil?"

"That's exactly what I said."

"What does that *mean*?"

"You don't know?"

"That's why I asked."

"I'm surprised you don't know."

"I don't."

"I play this one song so often that my next door neighbor probably dreams about breaking my boom box." He pauses. "You *honestly* have no idea where I'm going with this?"

"No."

"I can't believe you don't know where I'm going with this..."

"Braden," I snap.

"I'm kind of disappointed in you..."

"Braden!"

"Maybe you have changed more than I thought because you used to be really quick on the uptake..."

"Braden!!!"

"This song that I'm obsessed with is about a girl named Mandy. The song is actually called *Mandy*." He's clearly pleased but my return stare is blank. "There is no possible way you haven't heard that song. Barry Manilow? I'm a closet fan."

"I'm not a Barry Manilow fan—closet or otherwise. I've never heard the song."

"Impossible. The song is called *MANDY*."

"You keep *saying* that, but you're the only one who called me *Mandy,* until you stopped calling me at all," I don't know why I slid in that little dig, but I keep digging. "There is a song called *Amanda* by Boston. I know *that* song very well." I furrow my brow, "But I'm kind of burned out on it, so..." And then the anger hits me like a gut punch. I glare at him. "You know something, Braden?"

He looks a little worried and he should. "What?"

"You ruined a lot of great music for me."

His eyes narrow in confusion. "What are you talking about?"

"*We've Got Tonight, Never Tear Us Apart,* and don't even get me started on *Wasted Time*... Hey, remember that time you had to pull off the highway and I got sick, and then my dad asked if you knocked me up?"

He cringes at the memory. "I don't think I'll ever forget that particular conversation with your dad."

"Every song on that Over the Pond mix tape, every song we made out to—and we made out *A LOT*—those are *all* really good songs, Braden, but they all remind me of you. To this very day, all too painful to hear. That's a shit ton of good music that I can't listen to anymore—practically my entire high school life."

"Are you finished talking about how I ruined the eighties music experience for you? Because I'm trying to tell you something important."

"I'm not sure. And some of those songs were from the seventies. And, really, thank god you didn't like country music—although I never understood why because it's awesome. But you killed The Eagles. I love The Eagles." His body shakes with laughter while I ramble on and on. "I mean, every time I went to the lake we listened to The Eagles, and now they just make me think about puking my guts out on the side of a dark desert highway. But it's good to know you actually have a point," I smart off and take a deep breath because I'm running out of air. "I think I'm finished now."

He shakes his head at me. "Yeah, we'll see about that. Wait right there." He stands and picks up his keys. I hear him fumble with the deadbolts and leave. Braden's back in less than two minutes, doors banging shut. I hop up to secure the deadbolts because, no joke, I'm trained. He's holding a double CD—Barry Manilow's Greatest Hits. "Where's your stereo?"

I point to the entertainment center and remark, "That's a lot of Barry. You should come out of the closet already."

"It's the first song on the first CD—that's how *popular* the song is." He fumbles around in the entertainment center with different components and remotes before looking up at me. "Are you fucking serious? Do I need an MBA to run this thing?"

"There's a boom box in my bedroom."

"And a bed," he grins.

He heads into my room and queues up the track while I take a seat on said bed. "I know how hard it is for you to keep your mouth shut, but please listen to every word. By the way," he reaches for my jewel-toned blue silk nightie on the edge of the bed. Running it through his hands, he lifts it to his nose, inhales and smiles. "I *really* like your bedroom."

Oh my god.

Still whirling from that whole thing, music fills the space. When Barry sings about standing on the edge of time, I rest my head in my hands and close my eyes. I *feel* it, even if I'm not sure my jaded heart should *believe* it. My eyes flutter open when the music ends. It is the cheesiest and most beautiful song I've ever heard. I love it. Braden turns off the boom box and sits beside me.

His voice is soft and his eyes gentle. "You understand, Mandy?"

I murmur, "I can't be wrong this time. Not with you... I can't be wrong..."

Braden's arms wrap around me as he gently eases us back on the mattress. We turn toward each other. *Instinct...* Our bodies know exactly what to do. Limbs entangle while he brushes the hair from my face before our foreheads touch together.

"Yes, Mandy, we have some catching up to do, but it took me all of five seconds last Friday night to realize that I will always love you."

"*Oh my god.*"

"I'll move heaven and earth to make you mine." His pure blue eyes are full of honesty and hope. "All you have to do is love me back."

I direct my gaze to the ceiling and think this over. *He took a stand, made a declaration, and played you an epic love song on a boom box. How can you possibly say no to that, Amanda?*

I look into the eyes of this beautiful man and respond before he *kisses me stupid* again, "I love you back."

CHAPTER 38

Timing is everything.
When you know, you know.
Everything happens for a reason.
Love finds you when you least expect it.
Trust your gut.
Don't find someone you can live with, but
someone you can't live without.

WHILE BRADEN'S IN INDIANAPOLIS, WE use the time for marathon phone conversations, sharing many of the finer details from the last eleven years of our lives.

Despite the gap in time and the fact that some of these details are difficult to hear, we converse with ease—like old friends. Which, I suppose, we are. All of these life experiences have shaped us into the adults that we are today. No matter how painful, I want to know about him.

After I started my relationship with Tanner, the beautiful boy who wouldn't sleep with me started sleeping around until he decided to settle down. Jessica's infertility created intense feelings of guilt, and that brought on severe depression. As they tried to make it work, bitterness and anger became her go-to emotions. After counseling, a trial separation, and their last Christmas together, it was done. Braden moved to Indianapolis where his best friend from college, David Pratt, lives with his wife Cecilia—Jessica's best friend since childhood.

He went *through a phase* after his divorce. Fantastic, there are probably dozens of heartbroken woman walking the streets of Indianapolis who know what it's like to have sexual intercourse with Braden when I do not. That's still a very sore subject—at least for me.

Braden learns that I struggled to finish my undergrad, *experimented* with marijuana, and his reaction, although surprised given how adverse I was to drugs back in high school, is benign. He knows people who occasionally have fun with it and isn't opposed to it. He's even tried it himself a few times but didn't like how it made him feel.

I talk about cheating on Tanner and decide that he needs to know one of those mistakes was with Luke. Braden is furious because Luke lied to him—and not just by omission.

"I asked that fucker if he ever ran into you on campus. He said no, but Luke did a lot more than just run into you."

"It didn't mean anything. It was stupid."

"It matters to me."

"It shouldn't. And, honestly, it wasn't even good for me, so..." I try to laugh it off, but Braden's not happy with Luke.

"He's a fucking asshole."

"He's a nonissue. Please, don't let a drunken night impact your friendship with him. I only told you because if it came out later, it'd be worse, don't you think? Besides, that *situation* had nothing to do with Luke—he could've been anyone. It was about me drinking too much and feeling all twisted up inside about the fundamental differences between Tanner and me."

"Which were?"

"Tanner was on this trajectory, and I found myself lost. He didn't really want a woman like me anyway. Tanner needed someone more... compliant, easy-going. But the thing is, Braden, when I got really dark and at my lowest low, Tanner was there for me. He's always been such an incredible friend."

"What happened?"

"The last time I saw your dad, I was in Pine Ridge because I had to leave school for a while and get professional help. I take medication for depression. Does that scare you, given how depressed Jessica became?"

"Do you manage it?"

"Yes, with medication, supplements and sunshine, and exercise. Despite the whole unemployment *situation* and taking time out to be really, really single, I'm in a good place."

"Tell me about your last serious relationship."

"That's, um, complicated. I was sort of mostly involved with two men for the last few years. Both were older. Max was married to his career—such a cool job." I fill Braden in on his beat and travel schedule. "And Shawn was just too far ahead of me in life—divorced with three children, and he didn't want more kids, so we stopped seeing each other after Christmas last year, and Max and I ended a few months before that."

"Two guys at once?"

I tease, "I never had them in bed together at the same time. I haven't changed *that* much."

"Which one was bossy in bed?"

I decide to admit, "Both, but Shawn is a cop so he had handcuffs." Braden laughs, and I tell him, "I'm glad that we can be open about things."

"We need to know what we're getting into, Mandy, because..." We're about two weeks into these marathon conversations and Braden's next play is huge. "How soon can you move in with me?"

"If this doesn't work out, I'm screwed. I won't have a house or a job or friends out there."

"It's going to work out, and you'll have me. But we absolutely have to eliminate geography—as in yesterday, but I'll settle for tomorrow."

"Speaking of being screwed, or, in my case, not being screwed... I can't believe you threw the no fucking flag on me—again."

His deep voice and sexy words spike my heart rate. "You think after wanting you since the age of sixteen, I'd rush our *first time* together and leave you to get on a flight? Hell no. When I make love to you, I want all the time in the fucking world to savor the experience. I think it's so cool that we haven't gone there yet, and I can't wait. But first or firstly, I need you here with me. If I have to rent a red Porsche and drive you out here in it, I will. But I need an answer."

While I hesitate, he pushes me over the edge of reason. "I promise you, I love you. No holding back, no bullshit. We both go all in together expecting the best."

"Are we insane?"

"Is that a yes? You're going all in with me?"

"Yes," I agree.

"No, we're not insane. We're in love—which I suppose is pretty much the same thing."

* * *

Being in love is a lot like being insane, but, still, I refer to my *Ideal Husband* list over and over again. Dark hair and brown eyes are negotiables. I have no idea what Braden's like in bed, but I can make an educated assumption that we'll be compatible in that area.

I make two phone calls. Jenny can't stop screaming, so Paul takes over the call.

"Is she smiling or crying, Paul?"

"It's more like hysterical laughter, but the good kind. What's going on?" After I fill him in, Paul complains, "Great. Now I owe Jenny fifty bucks. She said the two of you were going to run away together."

Tanner asks, "Are you smoking shit again?"

And, really, that's a valid question. "I am not," I reply.

"You have to be."

"Pretend for a minute that my mind is perfectly sound right now... What's your first reaction?"

He responds immediately, "Panda, if I had any free time, I'd help you pack."

"Really?"

"You're serious, aren't you?"

"Yes, Tanner. I mean, I know it's happening fast, but everything inside of me is telling me to go. It's impulsive... But I think—"

"I don't know Dude at all anymore, but I know you. If you're telling me that there's not a catch, reservation, bullshit excuse, or missing bullet item on your list, then you have to trust your gut."

I can only hope that my parents will take the news half as well. Meanwhile, I make another list— a *To Do* list. I have a house to sell and a move to plan.

Territorial Cup—2001

I stay in Phoenix for Thanksgiving, and, I was right, Arizona took back the Territorial Cup with a 34 to 21 victory over Arizona State. Which reminds me, we haven't talked online in a few weeks, and Max owes me lunch.

We meet for lunch in Tempe on December 7th. Max still makes an impression on my senses, but over a year post breakup, our hug is fairly platonic and the sexual banter is toned way down—which is good because he's still in a serious relationship, and I have big news to share. News he thinks makes me clinically certifiable because he doesn't understand who Braden is to me.

He recaps, "Let me get this straight. You're moving across the country to live with a guy you haven't seen in *eleven years* after spending *one afternoon* with him? That must have been some afternoon, Wildcat." His look is all-knowing, but he doesn't know.

"I haven't sealed the deal with him."

"Have you lost your mind?"

"You're not the first man to ask me that. Thanks for your support." Casting my eyes down at my salad, it doesn't matter what Max thinks. Yet it does, because all of my other friends are being supportive.

"I may never see you again. The Cardinals and Colts haven't played each other since..." He searches his way back brain bank of stats and facts. "1996, I think. I'll have to look that one up. Indy doesn't have a professional hockey team. The closest we'll ever get are St. Louis or Chicago... both cool places but about three hours from Indy."

"Impressive stats, Max."

"I know."

"We don't see each other anyway. Besides, I don't think our significant others would appreciate in-person meetups like this one... although it's innocent."

"I wish you well, Wildcat. I do." His face softens before he shoots me a *devilish* grin. "But you should know that my thoughts of you are never innocent. My thoughts of you are very, very dirty, and you look amazing, by the way. I love the color red on you—which is ironic considering..."

"Right." My red sweater must have been a subliminal wardrobe choice, although it does match my favorite cowboy boots. "Max, you know that I value your friendship—I love that part of us. Plus, you taught me a lot about my body, and every time I have a multiple, I feel like I owe you a high-five."

His laughter is easy. "If that's what you take away from our relationship—friendship and multiples—I'm a proud man. Feel free to tell all your friends," he teases. "Are you sure this is the right thing for you, Wildcat? It's a lot of change in a millisecond."

"The sign went up in my yard two days ago. The house is on the market. So, yes, I'm sure. You'd like him for me."

"No, I wouldn't," he feigns disgust. "I hate him already. Did I mention how amazing you look?"

"Max..." I admonish, but the expression on his face tells me that he's playing. This is what we do.

"Hey, here's a fun fact—let's see if you know it, Wildcat. Which PAC-10 team has never been to the Rose Bowl?"

I grumble, "You never get tired pulling that one out of your ass every single time we beat you. Do you, Max?"

December 10, 2001

Braden and I are both in Pine Ridge, and we've synchronized the timing of the announcement of our plans to our respective families. I don't anticipate a nuclear reaction, but there might be a little friendly fire. It's sudden, and I know how Mom feels about cohabitation without a marriage license.

I break the news to them over the family dinner table. "I put my house on the market earlier this week."

They speak at the same time. Dad, "Why would you do that?" And Mom, "You're going to sell the house?"

I swallow hard and keep talking, "I'm going to use the profits to move—out of state—and look for a job."

Again with two different questions at the same time. Dad, "Where are you moving?" And Mom, "You're going to do what?"

"Please, one question and/or comment at a time. You're giving me a headache."

"Where are you moving?" Dad asks.

"Indianapolis."

You'd think I just announced my relocation to the moon. They are temporarily speechless. Dad's mad love for Larry Byrd aside, I doubt they've ever given a second thought to the Hoosier state because I sure hadn't.

"Why Indianapolis?" This question is also from Dad.

"That's where Braden lives."

Silverware clatters down on plates and mouths drop open in stunned silence. It's better than yelling, so I carry on. "Braden and I are together."

They revert to speaking at the same time. From Dad, "When did this happen?" And from a horrified Mom, "He's *married*. You're breaking up his marriage?"

"Relax, Mom. Please. Braden's marriage ended a few years ago."

Mom says, "This is fast."

I nod. "Yes. It is, but in my heart I know this is right."

"Your heart?" Dad digs in, "Is your head—your brain—involved in this decision of yours?"

"Yes, of course."

"Is he going to *marry* you?" Mom wants to know.

"We obviously need time together before taking that step. Since Coach passed away, we've had very long conversations getting to know each other again as adults, and we both want the same things with each other."

"You're going to pack up your entire life and follow this boy across the country and see what happens?" Mom asks, but it's not a question—it's a judgment.

"Yes. I am."

"And if it doesn't work out?"

"I wouldn't move across the country if I thought it wouldn't work out."

"Where are you going to live in this Indianapolis place?" Mom presses for more information.

Knowing this is the most controversial part of the discussion—which, really, it shouldn't be, I brace. "I'm going to move in with Braden."

"*What*!?!" Mom explodes.

"I'm a grown woman, Mom. I want to get married and give you grandchildren that you can actually visit. Braden and I have to make sure what we feel for each other translates into real life. I finally have a chance at *everything*. You want me to have that, right?"

Dad's in decision-making mode. "Of course we want those things for you. We're concerned because it's not the first time we've witnessed your interest in a man change on a coin toss—and flip back again and again."

"Because, Daddy, I wasn't with the right man. Please be concerned. You should be concerned. But I'm taking this fork in the road, and it would mean the world to me to have your support along the way."

"Where is Braden?"

"He's here in Pine Ridge. Probably having a similar conversation with his mom and sister right now. I wonder how that's going." I mumble, "Probably better than this one because his family was *always* nice to me."

Dad exhales. "Why didn't he do this with you?"

"This? This conversation right now?"

"Yes."

"Because you were hardly ever nice to him, Daddy. And we have too much respect for you to hit you from the blindside as a unified front. I needed to tell you in my own way, and ask for your... it's not a blessing that I'm after, it's your faith in me to do what I think is right. I need to know that you're on my side—and I prefer offense to defense, just so you know. But right now, I think I'm playing defense, and I'd like to go off sides. Without a penalty. Or just, you know, switch teams. Right now."

Dad chortles, always appreciative of my love for the game. "So I'm the quarterback?"

"Sure," I grin. "You're my quarterback, Daddy, and I want to play offense."

His eyes dance. "I can't believe I'm saying this, but you're right, Brown Eyes. It's your life. You need to do what's right for you."

"We're both playing offense?"

"Yes. You have my support—and my concern, but not my blessing. I expect that request to come from Braden when the time comes, am I clear?"

"Yes." I smile huge and turn to my mother. "Mom... offense or defense?"

She grumbles, "You know I don't understand these sports metaphors. They go right over my head, and I don't know why you two always do that to me..."

Her point is valid, so I rephrase the question, "Mom, do I have your support?"

"Do I have a choice?"

"Yes, but please choose me. You're an integral part of the offensive line."

CHAPTER 39

The Next Day

BRADEN AND DAD HAVE BEEN on the back deck together for the better part of an hour. I was finishing my makeup when Braden arrived, and, according to Mom, my dad led him through the house and straight outside again. Their backs are to the house facing the view. I can't see their expressions, but there's a lot of talking with hands.

"What is he doing out there, Mom?"

"Honey, he's trying to put his mind at ease. Braden's not here to take you out for pizza. You're moving 1,700 miles away with him, and your father doesn't know Braden very well. He acknowledges that he hasn't always been fair to the boy."

"And that's going to change today? I hope he's not threatening him," I grumble. "Or asking him if he knocked me up again. That was fun. Which, by the way, we still haven't had sex—you know, ever. So that's not possible."

"Good. That's one less question for you," Mom jokes, but I'm sure she's beyond relieved.

Finally, I see Dad's face. He's *smiling* as he shakes Braden's hand and clasps his shoulder before they come back inside.

"Hi, boys." I meet them in the living room. "Everything okay out there? It's a little cold for an outdoor interrogation—um, I mean, conversation."

Dad and Braden both look at me and smile. "Everything is just fine, Mandy." Braden stretches his arm out as I walk toward him. I duck under it and he drops a kiss on my forehead while I wrap my arms around his waist. "Always loved that color on you."

I wore pink for this déjà vu of occasions—except Mom's right; this isn't a Sunday evening pizza date and there's no curfew. This is *everything*.

"Drinks?" I offer. "Mom's got a veggie tray going and some chips and salsa."

"Jameson on the rocks," Dad says. He asks Braden, "Are you going to join me?"

"Sure, Michael. Why not."

Interesting... Mr. Harrington is now *call me Michael*...

"Two whiskeys," Dad says.

"Yeah, I'm going to make that three," I grin and head back into the kitchen.

When Mom and I come back with the drinks and snacks, the

sight of the two most important men in my life sitting together on the couch in my childhood living room is nothing short of magnificent. Dad isn't glaring; he's engaging Braden in friendly conversation.

They're in the middle of discussing my house. Yesterday, Dad wasn't happy to learn I'd listed it before talking to him, but it's my house and I went back to Patty. Dad's trying to predict how long it will take to sell. "I talked to her this morning, and Patty thinks it'll go quick if there aren't any issues with the inspection. The market is different down there, so I'll take her word for it."

"Quick would be ideal," Braden replies. "Maybe she'll get an offer before I have to head home."

"I hope I get an offer because I'm a few months away from not making the mortgage payment."

Dad's eyes narrow in on me. I shouldn't have said that. "Why didn't you tell me?"

"I'm a grownup. I mean, I wouldn't let the house go into foreclosure or anything, Dad, but my next options were making minimum wage at Walmart, selling off some of my handbags," I shudder, "or organ donation. I hear there's big money in that on the black market. I love my handbags, so I'd rather live without one kidney or part of my liver."

"How much money is in your savings account?" Dad asks me.

"That's a rude question. What's next? Are you going to ask me if I voted for Bush or Gore in the last election?" I pretend to be offended while taking a sip of my whiskey.

"Who did you vote for?" Braden changes the subject. "I mean, yes, that's a rude question, but I don't know if you're a Democrat or a Republican."

"I'm an Independent who would love to see the Libertarian party take off in this country." Three sets of eyes swing to me. "What?" I shrug. "Did I say something controversial here?"

Dad returns to my financial *situation*. "Do you need a loan?"

"No. I'm fine. Worst case, I have my 401K."

"You can't touch that," Dad warns.

"Then it's a good thing I'm selling my house."

Braden clears his throat. "I make more than enough to support Mandy." He looks at me, "You know you don't have to worry about that, right?"

"Um..." my face flushes because we haven't discussed this, and I take care of myself. "We can talk about that later."

Mom has a few questions of her own, and thankfully she changes the subject again. "Braden, how is Bonnie coping?"

"She's still in shock, I think. Dad took care of the finances and estate planning, and things keep coming up that she hasn't had to deal with before. It's difficult to watch her struggle without him, Mrs. Harrington."

"Please call me Claire. I imagine it'll be hard on you to go back to Indianapolis in a few weeks."

"Fiona's in-state, at least. I'm a phone call away, and she has a lot of support from Pine Ridge. But I don't like thinking about her in that big house by herself."

"How does Bonnie feel about Amanda moving in with you so quickly after all these years apart?"

Here we go, Mom. At least you didn't call it living in sin...

Braden curls his arm around my shoulder, and I snuggle into his side. He toys with a strand of my hair and replies, "My mom is thrilled. She said Dad's throwing a party in Heaven because he loved your daughter so much."

So sweet. Relaxing into him, I rest my head on his shoulder and close my eyes for a moment. I wish Coach was around to see us together as adults.

"Claire, I want you to know that I have nothing but honorable intentions where Amanda is concerned. I love her. Feels like I always have. There's no greater regret in my life than losing touch with her and wasting all the time we could've had together. As I told Michael outside, I'm not playing house or games with her heart. I intend to be with your daughter as long as she'll have me. I promise to take care of her—even when she doesn't want me to. Forever, I hope."

"Marriage?" Mom asks.

Blue eyes gleaming, Braden smiles at Mom. "Hopefully. And children in a house with a dog running around behind our white picket fence. One day. When the time is right."

Mom's posture relaxes as she sinks back into the sofa cushions. I think this is the end of it until she nails him with, "Did you feel that way going into your first marriage?"

"Mom!" I admonish.

Braden squeezes my shoulder. "It's okay, love. She has a right to ask."

"She does not," I counter.

"Yes, she does. It's relevant to my intentions and character." I sulk while Braden provides the condensed version of his failed marriage with Jessica and concludes with, "Amanda and I were raised with similar values. We both come from stable homes with parents who honor their commitment to each other. Ultimately, we want what you have."

I add, "But, you know, our own version of that."

A gentle smile warms Mom's face. I return it even though her nosy questions ticked me off. The nod of her head is subtle—and telling. She's definitely playing offense and Braden has a new fan.

The discussion shifts to logistics over the next few days, through the upcoming holiday season in Pine Ridge, and to Braden's return to Indianapolis thereafter. My move date is obviously up in the air until the house sells.

"I'll fly out and drive back with Mandy," Braden says to my parents. "She's going to have to sell a lot of stuff. My apartment is small—one bedroom with an office. I told her that it's already fully furnished with good stuff." He looks at me, "You heard that, right? Just bring you and your essentials. And your asshole cat. Which reminds me, I need to check on a pet deposit."

Dad interrupts my question about closet space and tells Braden, "I'll drive Amanda to Indianapolis. I've never been there. I want to see where she'll be living."

Braden acquiesces, "Fair enough, Michael, but, at some point, I owe her a ride in a red Porsche."

My parents look confused, but I start laughing.

"Ugh..." I flop back on his sofa—now our sofa—and drape a dramatic arm over my forehead.

"Tired?"

"Yes. And confused. How did this happen?" I have enough energy to gesture to the mountains of boxes and suitcases littering almost every surface of his loft.

"You have a lot of shit, Mandy. I told you to pare down."

"I did *pare* down." I narrow my eyes. "This is me, pared down."

"I told you that the loft is small."

"You should have elaborated or sent me a copy of the floor plan."

"We'll deal with your failure of paring down later. I'd rather have you bare down."

"Ha!" I raise my first in the air for a split second. It's all the energy I have left. "Your play on words is not lost on me—unless you meant B-E-A-R down. Then I misunderstood and no longer find it funny."

He laughs and crawls over my limp body forcing me to make room. Happy to share, we assume a familiar prone position—facing one another with complete entanglement of every limb. He inhales my wet hair. "Yum... sugar cookies and you in my arms. I can't think of anything I want more."

"Maybe some Option C?"

He responds with a kiss followed by a substantial grope and ends on a groan. "Yeah. About that..."

* * *

The house sold on day ten with a full-price offer that included most of the furnishings and a corresponding whirlwind of activities.

When Braden told me to pare down, I listened and left almost all of my furniture behind. Yes, I have shit tons of clothing and shoes and handbags and makeup—all of which are essential, so those came with. Along with my music and movie collections, Christmas ornaments, an antique maple gate leg table, favorite Tiffany lamp, electronics sans TV, and most of the contents of my kitchen.

Mom and I both cried buckets during our *until we meet again* moment, which won't be until this summer. She waved goodbye from the driveway of my empty house. She and Jenny made sure that the cleaning crew showed and the house was ready for its new owner—another single young woman who was a serious pain in my ass following the inspection. Since she'd made a full price offer, her realtor asked for every nitpicking detail on that report to be taken care of.

I almost told them to fuck off, but Dad participated in several conference calls with Patty and me, and he managed to keep my temper and expectations in check. Once we closed, I walked away with a nice bundle of cash to start my new life. Not a bad investment after all.

We managed to pack everything that I cared to still own in the Blazer, and Dad, Squirt, and I set off on a three-day cross-country drive. Oh, and Squirt... I made a rookie mistake with that asshole cat. We had to make an unscheduled stop in Holbrook to find a vet with tranquilizers.

I'm sure Dad regretted his decision to drive me somewhere in Oklahoma as he white-knuckled our way through some nasty weather. "What's wrong with moving in the springtime, huh, Amanda?" I assumed his question was rhetorical because—*duh*—I was starting a life with Braden. *Step on it, Dad.*

I called Braden when we approached Indianapolis. He wanted to meet us on the outskirts of the city to help navigate into the downtown area. I felt a little silly when I realized that I had to ask what kind of car he drove. There was so much we didn't know about each other that his black Lexus sedan was probably the least of our concerns.

I hopped into his car, and Dad followed us through the city to his brick industrial-looking building that sat near some sort of canal or river.

We found parking and commenced to unloading the Blazer. Braden's expression grew grimmer with the hauling of each subsequent box onto the freight elevator, up to the third floor, and into his unit. The loft seemed to fill up faster than the Blazer emptied, but I'm a woman and Braden was just beginning to witness the tip of the iceberg of my adult baggage.

When I started directing him to put the boxes marked "kitchen" into his actual tiny kitchen, his composure crumbled somewhere between box three and four. During box five, he let it fly in front of my father who stood on the sidelines enjoying the scene unfold.

"What is all this shit, Mandy?" he asked, and I didn't appreciate his tone.

"*Kitchen* shit, Braden," I bit back. "It even says *kitchen* right on the boxes."

"You don't cook."

"Yes, I do."

"You don't."

"I *do*."

"If you can *cook*, Mandy, why is it that the only meal you've ever prepared for me was mac and cheese—the *crappy* kind from the box—and hot dogs?"

"I cut up the hot dogs—they were *Kosher* by the way—and I *mixed* them in with the mac and cheese in that casserole dish, which is here somewhere, and I *covered* the dish with shredded parmesan, and then I *baked* it in the oven so the top was crunchy. So *technically*, I *baked* you a casserole, and did not *serve* you crappy mac and cheese."

Dad stifled a laugh and scratched the back of his head which swung to Braden awaiting his response.

"Same thing."

"Huge difference. I *baked* you a casserole. Were you not listening to me just now?"

"What's for dinner tomorrow night then?"

"I just got here and you want me to start cooking for you already?"

"You are going to *cook* for me eventually, right?" he mocked.

"Not if you're going to be ungrateful. I'm not a little housewife, and don't think that—"

"Kids," Dad interjected. "It's cold outside and there's still more stuff in the Blazer. If it helps, tomorrow night dinner is on me."

As quickly as the storm erupted, it rolled away. We finished moving in my baggage and Dad took his leave in my Blazer to check into a nearby hotel.

* * *

"Yeah. About that..."

"About Option C?" Fresh from the shower, I'm also freezing. Reaching for the throw blanket on the back of the sofa, I realize my little nighties aren't going to cut it. I need something full-coverage and made of flannel.

"Yeah," he leans in for another kiss. "The *first time* we have our *first time*, I don't want you exhausted. I have plans for you, and I need you in condition to fully appreciate it."

"Mmmm." Shivering, I go after his lips. Then I go after his jaw bone and the side of his neck.

It's possible that I dozed off somewhere halfway down his neck because I startle when he speaks. "We've waited a long time, and I'd feel more comfortable getting you settled in and your dad on a plane before we—"

"So you're telling me that you *still* won't sleep with me?"

"Mandy, I already promised you plenty of that, but first or firstly, I'm going to take my time and make love to every inch of you."

Sigh... That's the best idea he's had in his entire life. I snuggle closer and start to drift off when he jars me back with an open-palm slap on the ass. "We should make sure Squirt hasn't taken a crap anywhere and go to bed."

"Mmmm... okay. You check on Squirt. I'll go to bed."

CHAPTER 40

Two Nights Later

WE HAVE A DELICIOUS DINNER at a popular steakhouse called St. Elmo just off the Circle. Nervous with anticipation, I overdo it a smidge with the white zin, but it keeps my insides warm as we walk home hand-in-hand under a light dusting of snow.

Back in the apartment, he faces off with me and brands me with a kiss that I feel in my soul.

Before the *situation* escalates, he steps back holding my hand in his. "Wait here, love. Sit down and relax. I'll be right back... And no peeking."

Within a few minutes he returns and leads me into the bedroom—*our bedroom*. It dances with candlelight; rose petals spill across the white duvet. Music plays softly in the background, and it takes me a moment to catch on... *Never Tear Us Apart* by INXS.

"Is this the Over the Pond mix tape?"

I can tell he's proud when he replies, "It's my best re-creation. I want to give those songs back to you."

"God, Braden, you are so sweet."

"Well, I can't be responsible for ruining eighties music for the rest of your life—especially if that means you're going to keep playing that country crap you love so much." I narrow my eyes and try to force a glare, but he makes it impossible by kissing my cheek and turning me to face the main chest of drawers.

Sitting on top, nestled together inside of a shadow box are our pieces of the Berlin Wall.

"You are... that is... Braden... Our pieces of history are back together and they're a perfect fit." I laugh. "You know, that was probably the best metaphor of my entire life. Pure genius, and I love what this means. Thank you."

"Thank you for taking a chance on us."

"Thank you for rescuing me from my boring self."

His lips brush against mine before he charms me further with, "A woman like you could never be described as boring... You're one of a kind, love."

Braden's play is masterful, magical, and mine alone. There's only gratitude in my heart when he takes me in his arms and kisses me again. Softly, slowly—we have nothing but time. As he removes each piece of my clothing and lets it drop to the floor, he sweeps my bare skin with his lips and fingertips and his eyes—*god, those eyes*—the way he looks at me... He is *everything* I ever wanted.

During this tender act of stripping me bare, I vow to do whatever it takes to make him thankful for choosing me. Except every time I try to reciprocate, he gently redirects my arms back to my sides. Or, in other words, he throws the flag on my participation.

With my eyes I ask him *why*, and he gives me his heart in return.

"Mandy, I've been waiting to make this promise to you since I was sixteen years old." He runs his hands down my arms, captures my wrists, and gently holds them behind my back while his eyes look into mine. "Making love is a promise that we have a future together. For the first time in our lives, I can give that to you and mean it with everything that I am. I swear to God, making love to you—making you mine—has never meant more to me. Please, let me show you how much I love you."

I whisper, "That is the most beautiful thing I've ever heard."

"I might have rehearsed this moment in my head a few hundred times."

"Stellar execution, Braden. Really, I'm—"

"Shhh." He places his finger to my mouth. "We've done enough talking."

I stand in silence as he sheds his clothes. He backs me up against the mattress, and, with an unexpected move on the field, our mouths separate when he shoves me backwards onto our bed. I gape upward at his face and body looming over mine. He offers me an unapologetic smile before cracking, "I have it on good authority that *Adult Mandy* likes it bossy in the bedroom."

Adult Mandy breaks out into a huge smile and I nod enthusiastically. With one hand he pins my wrists above my head—*god, I love that move of his*—and uses the other to skim over the contours of my body. He peppers my skin with soft kisses from my temple to my navel.

His hands move all over my skin and come to my breasts. His touch is soft at first—palming, massaging, thumbs brushing over my nipples before his mouth takes over. I arch into his mouth and release a soft sigh. His thoughts are expressed in fragmented words as one hand trails down my skin, between my legs.

"So hot," he mutters when he reaches the very heart of me. "Heaven."

"Please," I moan and gyrate into his hand and fingers. "Oh god, Braden... I need you."

"Shhh..." he whispers. "Be patient, love."

"Ah... god, Braden," I arch my back off the bed again when he finds my favorite spot. "Right there." My eyes close and I surrender to his touch.

Our lips fuse and slowly separate to nibble and taunt.

Knowing full well his fingers are pure magic, he teases and asks, "Right there?"

"God, yes... So good, so close..." I mumble. "I love you so, so much."

"Mandy, look at me," he requests. I open my eyes and meet his... dark, hooded, happy... "I want to see your eyes when you come for me. Your eyes are so beautiful."

As his fingers and words and tender kisses bring me over the edge, he watches me unravel—his smile gentle, his touch perfection. When I still he says, "You are so worth the wait."

"*Technically*, we're still waiting..."

He laughs. "My girl loves her technicalities. Really, don't rush me. And keep your hands to yourself because if you try to make this happen any faster, it's going to be over really quick."

I burst into laughter but try to keep my hands to myself while he covers my body completely with his. His mouth plays with my neck and collarbone while he positions himself. I feel just the tip of him and smile when I think about graduation night in the back of my pickup truck.

He pauses and looks into my eyes while we breathe each other's breath. I focus on his scent and his beautiful blue eyes as I fight the urge to lift my hips up to meet him. "Mandy, I feel like I've never done this before."

"*We* haven't."

"I love you so much."

"I love you back," I breathe into his mouth and release a soft groan as he slowly sinks inside of me one centimeter at a time. As he fills me completely, tears spill from my eyes. There's no room left to keep my feelings inside because Braden is all-consuming. He kisses away the tears and smiles down at me because, of course, I'm crying.

He strokes my cheek with his finger. Rocking his hips slowly, brilliantly, he slides in and out of me. He has to control the pace, but I tilt my hips and wrap my legs around him. Each glide of him over my sensitized clit burns in the best possible way. His breathing quickens, and a bead of sweat breaks out on his brow, but he never takes his eyes off of me.

My beautiful man.

He might control the pace, but I can't control myself. I pull his lips to mine and cry into his mouth as I throb around him. "Oh my god... Braden..."

"*That* was beautiful. You're fucking incredible." Shaking his head, he breaks out into a beautiful smile. Shifting to his knees, he pushes further inside me, and stretches my right leg in the air. Turning his head, he administers kisses and soft bites from my ankle down the inside of my leg. When he can reach no further with his mouth, he hooks my leg over his shoulder; rooted so deep inside of me that a few thrusts later I detonate.

"Jesus, Mandy..." he groans, followed by an enormous grin. "I'm drenched."

I give him an unapologetic smile. "We might want to invest in a waterproof mattress cover. And, um, use lots of towels and blankets because I am not sleeping in that wet spot."

He continues to move slowly inside me. "I'll sleep in the wet spot."

"You say that *now*, but I'm not finished yet."

"No?" He arches an eyebrow.

I shake my head, "No."

He laughs and reaches for my left leg, trailing kisses down the inside until he hooks it over his other shoulder. Deeper still, he thrusts back inside and seconds later I ignite for him again.

His mouth is agape and his eyes are... *puzzled*?

"What?" I whisper.

"I'm so fucking turned on," he rasps.

"Yeah," I smile at him. "Me too. And if you keep doing that at this angle, I'll keep coming until I pass out."

Every fifth or six thrust, Braden stops because I fall apart around him.

I offer him some advice. "I know you want to be in charge here, but you aren't going to get there yourself if you keep stopping."

He laughs. "I don't care. Watching and feeling you come for me is better than coming myself."

I call for the blitz. "We can always do this again… and again… and again."

His eyes flash, and thank god I'm flexible because with my legs over his sweaty shoulders he leans into me to attach his mouth to my lips, and the blitz is on. He pounds into me and keeps going even as I cry out his name over and over, and possibly draw blood with my nails digging into the flesh of his skin. We're sticky and breathing hard, and even if I wanted to stop myself from coming for him over and over—and why in the hell would I want to—there is no possible way to stop. I have no control over myself or this *situation*. Every part of me belongs to Braden.

He comes hard and loud, and the words he says to me… I will never forget them. "I want you for the rest of my life. Only you, Mandy." He finally stills, kisses me deeply, and slides my knees off his shoulders before he collapses on me.

Braden is *mine*—still inside me and we're pulsing with aftershocks like live wires. We're out of breath and out of our minds, and our mouths aren't finished with each other yet. As we kiss, I laugh and cry at the same time. This is euphoria the likes of which I've never known.

I close my eyes and stretch before asking with shortness of

breath and a serious lack of oxygen, "What's better than absolute bliss? Ecstasy? Rapture?"

"I don't even know my name right now," he pants back and starts laughing.

"You should. I screamed it enough," I tease.

He continues laughing before slowly pulling out and rolling us to our sides. "You can never scream my name enough, Mandy... Jesus... Fuck..." He kisses me tenderly and then sucks my bottom lip into his mouth as his hand trails along my sweaty body. "I love you so much."

"I love you back."

* * *

His loft—our loft—is in a converted harness factory just south of the downtown's Circle Center. It is 956 square feet of immediate 2 bed/1 bath togetherness. We have soaring ceilings and exposed brick walls, pipes, and ductwork. Our living and sleeping spaces are long and narrow. The master closet can't begin to house my baggage. Our open concept kitchen is laughable. We have six upper cabinets, three lowers, four drawers, a breakfast bar, and absolutely no space for the full contents of one *kitchen* box—much less six *kitchen* boxes. Elevated over the kitchen is a tiny second room that functions as a home office.

Braden's company is headquartered three hours away in Chicago, and he's their only employee in Indianapolis. When he's not out in the field meeting with prospects and clients, he works from home. After I move in, he works from his home office/overflow storage room. Oh, and Squirt—that *asshole cat* LOVES Braden. He curls up on his desk as he works and crawls into his lap and onto his side of the bed for snuggles.

In retrospect, spring would have been a better time to move to the Midwest. It's almost spring. March 20th is right around the corner, and I can hardly wait. But Braden dashes my hopes for Spring Fever when he explains that it doesn't actually starting looking or feeling like spring until late April. *Um, what?* In his defense, he delivers the news with a beautiful smile and assuages my disappointment with multiple orgasms.

Indianapolis itself... well, it is a little big city. Everything we need is within walking distance, and it's actually quite charming with urban parks and a mixture of old and new architecture. The downtown bustles constantly with daytime professionals and stays lively well into the night with trendy restaurants and bars overflowing with people and noise.

Two months in, I still feel a bit like a tourist on an extended vacation in the arctic. Perhaps that's due to the system shock of abruptly trading in 75 degree and sunny desert winter days to this. Trees with leaves—naked. Grass—brown. Skies—gray. Rain—shit tons. Snow—occasional. Corn fields—dormant. Mountains—nope, hardly even a hill. The White River—everywhere. Every time you cross a bridge in Indy, you're crossing that river. Average daily temperatures—way too fucking cold.

I wear a shit ton of layers. I layer underneath the layers, but I'm constantly chilled to the bone, thus I sneak over to adjust the thermostat on a regular basis. Braden feels each degree of temperature times five upstairs in his home office/closet. We have the same version of this conversation.

From the top of the stairs, *"Mandy, did you crank up the heat?"*

"Define crank. I just bumped it a smidge."

"I'm sweating my ass off up here."

"Crack the window."

"I'm not going to crack the window. You don't run heat with open windows."

"Then take off your clothes."

"I will if you will."

"No, Braden, I'm cold."

"I'll keep you warm."

"Um... Just how busy are you right now?"

"I'm not that busy."

When he promised to fuck me a lot that was not a lie, and he is extraordinarily creative about it. Since Braden drops pretty much whatever he's doing at the slightest inclination of sex, there is shit tons of fucking. Sometimes it's fucking—other times it's making love. While he indulges my desire to be bossed around, he doesn't care when I want to take the lead. We are so sexually compatible, it isn't funny or the least bit fair to all the other couples out there.

When I'm not engaged in these delightfully sinful preoccupations, I pass the time looking for a job that doesn't exist yet, working out in the building's small gym, talking to my parents or girlfriends on the phone, bantering with Max over IM, running errands and/or exploring downtown while I freeze my ass off.

I keep in touch with Tanner and Lorraine, receiving updates on the kids and sharing news that Braden and I are ridiculously happy. I check out books from the public library and write in my journal. I also take over housekeeping and basement-level laundry duties.

It's the least I can do since Braden has a day job and he does all the cooking.

* * *

I try to pitch in on the apartment expenses and find myself shut down. "I would live here with or without you, Mandy." He winks. "Although it's way fucking better with you here."

I don't know how much money Braden earns. His car is really nice, but I think he makes payments on it. His apartment is cool, but it's not extravagant. His taste in furnishings and electronics are upscale. He favors mission/craftsman style furniture stained in dark oak, and the man has never met a gadget he didn't want to have. I've balanced out the exposed brick and dark oak with pops of color—my Tiffany lamp, colorful throw blankets, and artwork. Our personal styles mesh well, and he's not opposed to my feminine touch. He even likes going shopping with me.

"But I've never had someone pay my bills before, except, you know, my parents."

"Like I said, the bills would exist with or without you. You don't have a car payment and you have plenty of savings. Just hang onto it."

"Okay," I acquiesce. "But my personal expenses are mine. Stop offering to pay for the winter clothes I need. Like, I don't want to have that conversation with you ever again. And, for god's sake, please accept the fact that I've never been to a mall without finding a handbag or something I can't live without, so you're going to have to live with that."

"When we get a house, it better have huge closets."

I nod. "See, you totally get me. But after I find a job and whatever is left over, we should use that money for our someday house. What do you think?"

"I think that sounds like a plan."

"Still, this is weird. I feel like a moocher."

"If we were just dating, I don't split checks or let a woman pay. That's not how I was raised."

I'm used to most guys feeling that way—at least at first. But I'm also used to supporting myself. I guess this is another part of trying to adjust to being in a serious adult relationship. It's new for me.

CHAPTER 41

BRADEN IS NOT ONLY AN excellent tour guide in these early months, the instant togetherness mandates more crash courses in getting to know each other. While I'm still a cautious introvert with varying degrees of social anxiety depending on the *situation*, I discover that Braden has never met a stranger.

He's so different from that broody boy I met by the lockers my junior year of high school. Braden intuitively counteracts my unease around new people. He keeps me by his side, or at least within view, never wandering off unless he has an indication that I'm all right without him. I don't know how he knows that I need this reassurance—he just does.

He can and does engage anyone in charming conversation, and because people gravitate to his charisma, he has a circle of really nice friends. At the center of this circle are David and Cecilia Pratt, and the three of them are tight back to their freshman year at Iowa, got married within weeks of each other, and, of course, Cecilia has known the pig farmer's daughter since birth.

David works for a large pharmaceutical company headquartered in Indy. He's open and friendly, and loves to get us talking about our high school days. I think he and Braden are in love, but I'm not jealous.

Cecilia's a stay-at-home-mom, raising their son Jack and running their two-story, 4 bed/3 bath/fully finished basement home in the northern suburb of Carmel. (Not pronounced the same as the 'other' Carmel in California.) She's short and plumpish, and quite pretty with her brunette bob and assessing hazel eyes.

She is, however, not the president of my fan club. Clearly Cecilia wanted custody of Jessica in the divorce, but location and dude love dictated custody of Braden. Now Braden and I are a package deal, so she has to deal with me.

Incidentally, a fair amount of my *kitchen* and *other* boxes reside in their basement storage area until Braden and I are ready for a different living *situation*.

Cecilia tries to shake my confidence with her *remember when* stories of *happier times* with Braden and the pig farmer's daughter. Braden smiles and acknowledges the good time stories, usually ending his sentences with *but that was a long time ago*.

I know that establishing a friendship with Cecilia won't make or break my relationship with Braden, but it would be nice to get there with her. I'm new here, not working, and my entire life can't be about Braden—although it is right now.

April 2002

Signs of life return to the landscape late in the month. Trees bud, flowers bloom, and cold days turn into slightly less cold days. I take advantage and start to explore more of the city by foot or bike to get in some extra exercise, realizing that I took Arizona sunshine for granted.

I've been meeting with Dr. Anderson every other week by phone but might taper off the frequency soon because—honestly—I've never been happier in my entire life.

Bursting with life and energy and good feelings, even annoying things that pop up between us are funny. Braden and I top off every unpleasant *situation* with sex, which makes arguments totally worth having. When I explain this to Dr. Anderson, I find her response humorous.

"When a couple is falling in love, the brain releases neurotransmitters—adrenaline, dopamine, and serotonin."

"So I can stop taking my Prozac?" I joke.

"We could probably half your dose and you'd be fine for a while. But let's keep you where you are since you're sunshine deprived now."

"I would live in a cave as long as I could live with him."

"Yes, Amanda. You're in the *love is blind* stage... I think it's the only way men and women survive together in order to go on and reproduce and raise their young together. Initially, couples tend to idealize one another, magnify the virtues and ignore the flaws."

"Dr. Anderson, are you saying that I'm high, blind, and not thinking clearly, yet it's all completely legal?"

She laughs. "That's exactly what I'm saying. Enjoy it, but remember that this level of intensity fades over time. Things you might find endearing now, let's just say that while it's important that you're physically compatible, you need to be intellectually and emotionally compatible because the sex drive will fade and you'll be left with the reality of your relationship and true selves."

"All I know is I've never felt this way about anyone before. Never. I've always had questions about a relationship—there was always something missing, but now I feel complete—like I have all the pieces to complete the bigger picture. If I thought that I loved Braden as a teenager, those feelings are nothing compared to how I feel now."

"You've waited a long time to find the right man to share this level of intimacy with. Keep your eyes and ears open, and be honest with him. You're in a much different place in your life. I am rooting for you, and I encourage you to use your tools to stay emotionally and physically healthy as this relationship evolves. And, while I would never disclose that you are my patient, Amanda, I've known Braden's mother on a personal level for many years now. We're involved in the Pine Ridge Literacy Program together, and I consider her a close friend."

"Oh?" You have to love small towns. Nothing is sacred. "That's a little close for comfort."

"It is not a conflict of interest because everything you share with me is confidential. But I can share that Bonnie is delighted you and Braden found one another again. It brought her some peace following Nick's passing."

"I'm glad because her son has given me *everything*."

* * *

With spring turning into summer, my heart is still exploding with life and love while Mother Nature adorns the land with bright colors and warm temperatures. Having lived in a two-climate part of the country since the age of eighteen (Fucking Hot and Bearable), I develop a new appreciation for seasons.

During the week of July Fourth, my parents arrive to perfect weather for their visit. They're staying in a nearby hotel and rented a car because they plan to head south for a week and take a tour of the distilleries in Kentucky. When they knock on the door to the loft, I throw it open and greet them with huge hugs before they come inside.

Braden steps out of the upstairs office followed by Squirt, beams, and jogs down the stairs. "Welcome to Indy." He embraces Mom with a kiss on the cheek and shares a dude shake with Dad.

While happy to see both of my parents, I'm prepared for Mom's subtle digs and wordsmithing to passive-aggressively demonstrate her disapproval of our living arrangements. Instead, she tours the loft with a smile and uses words like *charming*, *wonderful use of space*, and *cozy*.

We decide to walk to the Circle and grab a bite to eat. Since it's nearing the lunch hour and it's a workday, Mom and I head over to the restaurant to grab a table while Dad and Braden take a small detour to walk around the monument in the middle of the Circle.

It's such a warm and sunny day that we select an outdoor table and order two glasses of wine while we wait on the men.

"You look happy, Amanda. You're radiant."

"Thanks, Mom. If I'm glowing, it's not because I'm pregnant." I laugh and finger the Celtic knot charm resting just below my collarbone. "It's because I'm living in the present and it's really beautiful." My eyes well with happy tears as I share, "I love him, Mom. Even Squirt loves him—*asshole traitor cat.* Braden is so good to me. I can't even explain it."

"You don't have to. Love is written all over your face."

"Did you have a partial lobotomy after I left?"

"Excuse me?" Mom's eyes widen in surprise.

"You haven't made a single remark about my living *situation* or anything."

Mom laughs. "What am I supposed to say, honey? You're almost thirty years old. My baby is almost thirty years old... My other daughter will never live in this country again, and I wonder if that's my fault."

"No, Mom." I shake my head. "Brianna's always been independent. She started looking for a way out of Pine Ridge the minute she hit town. You and Dad gave us a great childhood. I hope you know how lucky we both feel."

"Where did the time go?" Mom asks me.

A lot of it went up in smoke. "I don't know. Just, thank you for being here and supporting me and Braden. Because this is it. It has to be. I can't imagine spending my life with anyone else. He is *everything* that I've been waiting for—and to think I spent all this time looking for *the one* when I'd already met him."

She places her hand over mine, and I notice for the first time that her skin looks older—wrinkled, aging. If I'm approaching thirty, she's almost sixty. My mother's beauty is classic and elegant. While we share similar coloring, she is a good four inches shorter than both Brianna and me, and her figure is far from voluptuous. She's been a size ten for years with a trim waist and small chest. If I didn't inherit her coloring, nose, and thick hair, I'd wonder how we could possibly be related.

"You deserve to live in a beautiful present," Mom says as she rubs my hand. "Just hurry up and give me some grandchildren *in the future* before I'm too old to enjoy them."

I laugh. "I'm waiting for children until after marriage—whenever that might be."

SUMMER CAMP
Tuesday, July 17, 2012
Day Ten

My twenties—what a mixed bag of highs and lows. Somehow, I managed to become a productive member of society without straying too far from my bong. I concealed my double life from just about everyone who mattered to me—including my future husband. Too bad for him, he had no idea what lurked inside when he swept me off my feet.

I never intended to go down the *Stoned Off My Ass* fork in the road again. I didn't know that my drug use would escalate well beyond my first rock bottom back in college. I thought I could keep it in check—I honestly did, and I'm still struggling to figure out why I couldn't. I had *everything*.

Speaking of *everything*, I'm still avoiding my husband. I don't want to face him, and I've only talked to him twice since I got here; although I do call when he's at work and leave messages for our daughter Nicki. *Mommy loves you. Mommy misses you. Mommy saw a huge tarantula last night—it was so gross. You would've loved it.*

Tomorrow I'll start working on the next decade of my Timeline—my thirties—including the beginning of my supposed happily ever after. We made so many promises to each other out of love, hope, pure devotion, and ignorance. Promises I didn't break, exactly. But I sure did my best to test his love for me and push him away when I should've leaned on those sturdy shoulders he offered me time and time again.

When this is all over, I wonder what will be left of us and our *everything* together.

* * *

Today, I suck it up, make my way to the phone, and call him, but I nix yet another weekend visit. I can't face him yet.

My husband's disappointment carries through loud and clear over the phone line. "You don't want to see us this weekend either?"

"It's not that I don't want to see you. It's more that I can't handle it," I respond and turn my head to glare at Kelsey who's having a very loud argument with her boyfriend on the next phone over. Catching my evil eye, she lowers her voice.

"It's only Tuesday," he points out. "Visitation isn't until Sunday and you've already made up your mind about that?"

"I don't want Nicki to see me here. It's bad enough she has to see Pop Pop at—"

"I'll leave her with Jenny."

"No."

"Your fortieth birthday is on Sunday. Don't you want to spend it with me?"

How awesome am I? I spent my thirtieth birthday high on love and life, and I'll spend my fortieth in rehab—craving weed and withdrawing from Klonopin. My doses are getting smaller and smaller as they wean me off.

I tell him, "I'd rather pretend the eleventh anniversary of my twenty-ninth birthday is not happening."

His voice is soft as he unnecessarily reminds me, "It's the tenth anniversary of—"

"I bet you regret that decision," I interrupt.

"I don't." While he responds straightaway, I'm sure that he's just trying to be nice. Or perhaps he's lying to himself without realizing it.

"I'm a two-faced fraud—an imitation of who people think I am. I'm not a good person. You know that, right?"

He broody sighs into the phone. "You are a wonderful person. You just lost your way again."

Again? My stomach churns as I ask, "What do you mean by I lost my way *again*?"

"I called Rawlings."

Shit. Fuck. Seriously? Braden and Tanner are talking—*to each other*???

I hiss out, "*What*? How could you betray me like that and talk to him behind my back—especially after what he *didn't do* for my dad—for my family?" I start to sniffle and cry, and, *damn it*, there's no Kleenex nearby.

"You're not the only one going through some heavy shit. We've barely talked since I left you down there, and I had to make sure that place was right for you. Turns out, I should've talked to him about you a long time ago. That guy knows significant things about your past." He pauses and the words hang heavy in the air surrounding me. Braden's voice is loaded with accusation when he says, "If I'd known what happened to you back in college, I never would've let you touch that shit. I suppose that's why you never told me. Right, Mandy?"

Swallowing back my unjustified anger, I ask quietly, "What did he tell you?"

"You checked out of life—smoked weed for months on end until you were so depressed you wanted to kill yourself. He told me about the knife and bathtub full of water, that he kicked a crackhead out of your apartment and threw away your drugs before he took you home to Pine Ridge and your parents to get help."

"*Technically*, the crackhead had already vacated the premises, so Tanner just threw out his clothes and stuff, but, other than that, yes, that's fairly accurate."

"Rawlings is kicking himself for not telling Michael and Claire the whole story."

"He can go *fuck himself*." Yeah, I'm incensed, but I don't really mean it. Even my therapist thinks I should patch things up with Tanner. I'm furious, but loving that guy is still a spontaneous reflex—like breathing.

"With all of that media attention on your dad, he had to look out for his family and his medical practice."

My parents were *always* there for him—well before we got involved and long after. When my father needed him most—when we all needed him the most—after everything we'd been through, he turned his back on his *family by choice*. I respond with frustration, "We *were* Tanner's family."

"You know what I mean. He works with *children* and has a wife and six kids to support. They come first."

"I can't believe that you're defending him to me."

"Your dad told him to stand clear of this shit. Michael didn't want him involved. Did you know that?"

"No." My head is spinning with anger and regret. *Why didn't Dad or Tanner tell me?* Or maybe Tanner tried, but I stopped talking to him. I haven't spoken to him in well over a year. I've been a train wreck and so freaking stoned—struggling to keep up with my life of duplicity. Tanner's tried to put our relationship back together but I've refused him—just as I thought he'd refused my dad.

"If you won't see me on Sunday, will you see him? He's going to call in and get his name on the list. All you have to do is approve it."

"I'll think about it." And I will. I gave Tanner a piece of my heart, and I can't take it back or cut it out because it's interwoven in the fibers of his most vital organ. And the piece of his heart that belongs to me... it's decaying inside of me. I need our worlds to be right again—perhaps more than I need that with Braden. Which is weird, right?

"There's more stuff we need to talk about. I have some questions for you."

I warn, "I'm not ready to do the heavy stuff."

He stands his ground and asserts, "I need answers."

I barter, "I promise to answer your questions during Family Week. I'll be completely honest with you."

"While we're talking about *honesty* for a few minutes here, I've spent a lot of time on your Facebook app. Makes for some fascinating reading."

Shit. Fuck. Again—seriously? "I specifically asked you not to snoop around in my private accounts."

Braden matches my aggressive tone. "Yeah, well, I asked you about a hundred times to stop doing drugs."

Where did my husband the doormat go?

I snap, "Those conversations are private and none of your business."

"Bull-*fucking*-shit. You are *MY* wife. Unless you want to change that legally, you owe me some answers."

Who the hell is this guy?

"You want a divorce?" I challenge. "Just keep calling *my* ex-friends and looking through my private shit and see what happens." God, in this moment, in this *situation*, I wish he was standing in front of me so I could strangle him.

"Mandy, I don't want a divorce. I want you to get clean and come clean—about *everything*. You have a lot of explaining to do."

"I'm not ready."

"You can't hide behind that gate forever."

"I'm not hiding. I'm trying to get myself together."

"I'm so pissed off at you."

"I can't deal with that right now."

"Right." He bites out a chuckle. "Well, I suppose, as usual, it's all about you."

"Are you kidding me right now? I'm in *fucking* rehab," I snarl.

"Yeah, I'm well aware of that fact." His Sarcasm Scale is on the rise. "You're not the only one paying a price for your decisions."

"Whatever," I mutter.

He hits me directly. "When were you going to tell me about you and Max?"

Breathe, Amanda. Breathe.

When I don't respond, he barks, "Answer me!"

"It's not what you think."

"So it's not another betrayal from my wife? You expect me to buy that, *Wildcat*?"

Now you're snooping through my private messages AND using Max's nickname for me, Braden? This is bullshit. "Enough. I'm hanging up."

"Nicki's fine, thanks for asking. She misses you. And your mom—I helped her decide on a house. Wrote the offer Friday. It's about a mile down the street from us—adult community, nice gym, huge pool heated year-round. And Michael, I took Nicki to see him last Sunday. I'm taking care of *our* family while you *get yourself back together*. While you're at it, try asking yourself if you're even capable of being honest."

I remain silent, skin crawling, because I don't know if I am.

My husband—no longer a passive bystander in the shit show that is my life—has more to say. "You better let Rawlings through those gates this weekend. Now *I'm* hanging up." The line goes dead.

Who in the hell does Braden think he is?

To be continued...

For a sneak peek at book three in the Now & Then Series,
turn the page for the first chapter of A Wife Like You.

A WIFE LIKE YOU NOW & THEN SERIES

Friday, October 11, 2002

The Flamingo—Las Vegas, Nevada

"Here's the thing," I start in once I have Tanner, Jenny, and Braden seated around a low table in the bar with comfy seats. We have a round of fresh drinks, shit tons of tension, and, damn it, I forgot how much I hate casino sounds. "First—or is it firstly?" Normally I'd pause for comedic effect but I don't feel like laughing right now. "I know you have a pack of cigarettes in your purse, Jenny, and I'd like one right now, please."

She fishes them out while Braden stares at me. "What?" Lighting up, I shrug. I take a quick drag before explaining to him,

"Sometimes I enjoy a cigarette—especially when I drink and most definitely when I'm stressed out." Picking up my whiskey, I toss the entire drink back in one shot.

I add, "Just so you know, I'm totally stressed out and that waitress better get back over here because I need another drink." I inhale deep from my cigarette, letting it settle and burn in my lungs before releasing the smoke to the ceiling.

Tanner shakes his head and sneers. "That's disgusting, Panda. Shit's gonna kill you."

Jenny fires up her own cigarette only she exhales her first drag in Tanner's face. I've seen Tanner all variations of pissed off over the years—trust me—but for a brief second, I fear for her life.

"Give me that," Braden orders. I'm fully prepared to exercise Free Will when he grinds it out in the ashtray and light up another one. He won't stop me from smoking so I hand it over without argument. Braden takes a long drag and sits back in his seat with no intention of sharing.

I ask Braden, "Do I know you?"

"I like a smoke every once in a while. Now I don't have to sneak them behind your back."

My elbows hit the table and my face falls into my palms. Breathe, Amanda. Breathe. When I look up, Jenny has a fresh cigarette at the ready for me. She throws the pack on the table and tells Tanner to fuck off with her eyes.

I take another deep breath and dive back in, "The night Jenny married Paul, I was standing there listening to them exchange their vows and I had this weird flashback. I started thinking about that summer when I got back from Germany, and I gave each of you a piece of the Berlin Wall."

I cut off the questions proactively. "Yes, you each got a section, and, yes, each section matches up in some way to mine—like puzzle pieces—and, yes, I told you all the same exact thing. We all have pieces of history that fit together and even though we're living separate lives when we come back together, I hope that we will always fit, and blah blah blah. And there was some other stuff about no single bond making another any less meaningful—or maybe that last part was just something I said to myself because I love each one of you."

I pause to take in a gulp of air. "But before I get any deeper into this situation, I just need confirmation of one thing." I gesture between Jenny and Braden. "The two of you, like, never made out or slept together or anything, right?"

Braden opens his mouth to speak but Jenny beats him to it. "No way, Amanda." Smiling flirtatiously at Braden, she adds, "Not that I wouldn't have. I always thought you were cute, but Amanda called dibs first and there's a Girl Code..." she trails off until her accusatory brown eyes land on me. Jenny lets me have it after eleven years of keeping her true feelings about my relationship with Tanner bottled inside. "But not all girls follow the Girl Code, right Amanda?"

"Technically, Jenny, I made out with Tanner first. That makes him my leftovers not yours."

"Whoa—I'm nobody's leftovers." Tanner is clearly insulted.

Braden blows his smoke across the table in Tanner's direction. "There are two women sitting right here telling a different story, asshole."

"Asshole?" Tanner challenges, and, really, I should shut this down right now, but I'm enthralled. "I never did anything to you, dude."

"Senior prom night didn't suck and neither did all four years of Mandy's undergrad," Braden retorts.

"Took her five fucking years to graduate," Tanner fires back. "But you wouldn't know that because you cut her out of your life. Always too chicken shit to lock down what you want."

I sneak a glance at Jenny who looks positively giddy. I'm not the only one fascinated by the show.

"I'd say she's locked down, asshole. You're here for our wedding."

Tanner leans forward in his seat. "Dude, you call me that one more time, we're gonna have serious problems."

"I've waited years to punch your ugly face, but you wouldn't want to damage your instruments of healing now would you, asshole?"

My jaw drops open and my head swings to Tanner who's ready. "And what the fuck do you do with your hands all day, dude? Make phone calls and sign contracts?"

"I make Mandy come over and over while she screams my name."

I can't even believe Braden said that, although it's the truth. I'm about to interject when—

"That's not hard to do. Showed her the magic spot in our dorm on the first go, dude. She had no idea it was there before I had her. Shoulda seen her go off for me like a box of fucking fireworks."

Braden springs from his seat. I jump to head him off before he reaches Tanner. Trying to shove him backwards with two flat palms on his chest, I succeed in stopping the forward motion but wind up on Tanner's lap.

Braden grabs my wrist and pulls me to my feet. He growls in my face, "I'm going to kill that guy."

Tanner rises to his feet and I shout, "No!" I have a hand on each man's chest. "Stop it! Both of you!"

"But he—" Tanner starts.

I glare at him over my shoulder—more concerned with Braden's rage because I've never seen him like this. "Tanner, really? You went way too far." Trying to inject levity into this situation, I add, "Plus, Braden knows all about that spot now so it's all really good."

"I showed you the magic spot," Jenny sets the record straight on Tanner's female anatomy lesson. Braden's breathing heavy, but he cracks a small smile in her direction.

"Please sit down," I whisper to him.

He shakes his head. "Not until I teach him a—"

"Oh my god, Braden—Tanner loves his wife and family. He's digging at you because you called him an asshole." I swing my head from one to the other. "Both of you—stop it. Our wedding is tomorrow night, and I won't have black eyes or bloody lips ruining the damn pictures. Sit down. Right now."

The boys grumble; shooting dirty looks and mumbled fuck you's at one another, but eventually comply with my order. Jenny's declaration spared Tanner a broken nose and Braden an assault record. Plus, my pictures won't be ugly.

As I settle back in to my seat keeping a wary eye on Braden, I ask Jenny, "You showed Tanner the spot? No shit?"

"Yes, I did, and it took him weeks to get it right."

At this revelation, I'm struck by the layers of insanity and absurdity of our situation. I'm floored. I've seen and heard more than enough. Instead of getting angry or crying, I start to laugh. There's no stopping me now.

Tears roll down my face. I can barely speak. "Oh my god, Jenny. Thank you." I gasp between fits of laughter, "Thank you so much because..." I pause to catch my breath. It's hopeless so I wheeze out, "I. Really. Love. That. Spot."

With that, Jenny rides the crazy laughter train with me, although we stop for a high-five across the table. We laugh so hard I almost wet myself. "Who showed you?" I can barely get the question out.

"Matt Neilson."

I can't remember the last time that I laughed quite like this. My sides ache and I feel like I'm going to pass out. When I calm down enough to speak, I wink at Jenny and crack, "Oh, yeah—Matt—he was definitely not a waste of time."

Jenny and I go off again—never to return until Braden attempts to bring me back to the here and now with a tug at my elbow.

He rumbles when I turn to him, "Jesus, Mandy. You think this shit is funny?"

So much so that I can't even ask him what Jesus has to do with this conversation.

"I think this shit is funny," Tanner inserts with a huge grin on his face. But the grin disappears a second later. "Wait—you didn't fuck Matt while you were with me, did you?"

Given our history, that's a valid question. "No, Tanner. But thanks for teaching me about that spot. I passed it on to Noah—remember him?" I lose it again with Jenny, but this time Tanner joins in.

It feels so good to laugh like this, but when I turn to look at Braden he is so far from amused that my laughter begins to subside. I have to take into consideration that I've had years of friendship with Jenny and Tanner. Braden barely knows them anymore. I need to get a grip...

Rubbing my hand over his shoulder, I apologize to my fiancé. "I'm sorry. I should have stopped this shit five minutes ago, but it was so interesting." I scoot my cushy chair closer to his. "I'm really sorry. I forgot how much history I have with these two that doesn't include you, and this whole scene... It's my fault. I take full responsibility. Are we okay?"

"You and me? Yeah, Mandy. I'm sure I'll find the humor in it a lot later."

"It's funny, Braden, because it's so messed up, but we're all exactly where we're supposed to be right now." I include Tanner and Jenny in the conversation. "Which is where I was trying to lead this discussion earlier. Maybe I can finish my thought and we can all kiss and make up?"

Braden actually smiles at Tanner when he informs him, "If you kiss her, it's going to piss me off."

"Not as much as it would piss off my wife, dude."

Relaxing because they're both smiling now, I want to wrap this up and get back to our other guests after that scene in the lobby. "Before this situation escalated..." I have to stop because I'm overtaken by another fit of laughter, although this one is much smaller.

Wiping the tears from my eyes, I carry on. "I don't know why I still think it's so funny because it's totally fucked up—"

"That's why it's fucking funny," Jenny gives me an assist and a huge smile.

"Right. We've been through a lot together. I love each of you." I look at Jenny. "You're like a sister to me, and I wouldn't want anyone else standing by my side tomorrow night. I can always count on you to be brutally honest with me and make me laugh—often in the same sentence. I love you, Paul, and those beautiful nieces of mine. Even when I didn't always show it, I value our friendship so much. I almost lost you when..."

Turning my eyes to Tanner, I place a hand on Braden's knee. "You, Tanner Rawlings, are an amazing human being—loyal husband, incredible father, and you're living the dream you've had as far back as I can remember. That our friendship could not only survive but thrive after all these years... I'll never forget that during the darkest hour of my life, you literally picked me up off the floor and made decisions for me that changed my life for the better. I'm blessed that we are family by choice. I'd say you're like a brother, but that would just be gross. Still... I love you."

Thumping a fist on his heart, I know exactly what he means.

Pointing one finger between Tanner and Jenny, I say, "And hopefully you two will put your freak show of a juvenile relationship in perspective. You're so lucky that you didn't end up together."

Jenny glowers. "Yeah, apparently, since I've filled out so much I'm unrecognizable."

"Jenny, what should I have said to you in front of your husband?

Your haircut is sexy and your boobs look fucking amazing?" Tanner counters. "Because I was talking about your boobs—they're huge and they look amazing."

Jenny breaks into a smile because what woman doesn't love a boob compliment—even if it's from an ex-boyfriend she's hated for years.

I smile at both of them, although I'll admit that I don't enjoy Tanner's admiration of Jenny's boobs. Still, we're all getting somewhere so I tuck that aside. "Awe... See? Don't you both feel better now?"

Gazing into Braden's beautiful blue eyes, I reach for his hands and squeeze tight. "I saved the best for last. You remember what I was wearing when you first realized that you were in love with me. How many guys can do that?" I hold up a hand before Tanner can rise to that challenge. Tanner never forgets details. "I'm not going to lay it on thick with you right now. I have to save the good stuff for tomorrow night, but I've never been happier in my entire life. I can't wait to become your wife."

"I love you, Mandy."

With everything that I am, I reply, "I love you back. Forever."

Save for the annoying casino sounds, silence falls over the table. I request, "Can we put the past where it belongs? You're all part of my roots—the best friends anyone could ever ask for. I'm the luckiest woman in the world to have all of you in my life. It would mean so, so much to me if we could just move on and enjoy ourselves. Please. What do you say?"

My three best friends from high school are smiling and nodding in agreement, and this is such a beautiful moment until... Luke walks up with an attractive blonde on his arm and says, "Hey, guys. I hear we're all going to the Crazy Horse Too tonight."

My stupid, stupid past. Here we go again.

Also by Kate Ryan

NOW & THEN SERIES

***

A Girl Like You

A Woman Like You

***

Coming Soon:

A Wife Like You

A Family Like Yours

Everything to Me

Playlist for A Woman Like You

Alabama—Feels So Right

Barry Manilow—Mandy

Bill Ray Cyrus—Achy Breaky Heart

Bob Seger—We've Got Tonight

Boston—Amanda

Britney Spears—Baby One More Time

Brooks & Dunn—My Next Broken Heart

Chely Wright—Single White Female

Clint Black—Killing Time

Dan Seals—One Friend

Deana Carter—Strawberry Wine

Dixie Chicks—Wide Open Spaces

Eagles—Wasted Time

Faith Hill—This Kiss

Garth Brooks—What She's Doing Now

George Strait—Carried Away

INXS—Never Tear Us Apart

Jo Dee Messina—Burn

KISS—Heaven's on Fire

Lee Ann Womack—The Fool

Lonestar—Come Crying to Me

Marcy Playground—Sex and Candy

Nitty Gritty Dirt Band—Fishing in the Dark

Peter Gabriel—In Your Eyes

Rod Stewart—Fooled Around and Fell in Love

Shania Twain—You're Still the One

SHeDAISY—Little Goodbyes

Spice Girls—Wannabe

Terri Clark—Poor, Poor Pitiful Me

Trisha Yearwood—She's in Love with the Boy

About the Author

To receive notification of new releases, sign up for the Kate Ryan Newsletter
Bit.ly/KateRyanNewsletter
Twitter: @KateRyanBooks
Facebook: Facebook.com/KateRyanBooks

www.ingramcontent.com/pod-product-compliance
Lightning Source LLC
Chambersburg PA
CBHW052031260626
47163CB00005B/28